GIVING IN TO TEMPTATION

"No respectable woman behaves as you do."

"We both know I left respectable behind some time ago."

"Then you do this as a game or as punishment."

"You're mistaken if you believe this involves you alone," Ada said. "Perhaps I do this simply to see what *I'll* do next. I hardly know who I am anymore. It makes me wonder."

"Wonder what?"

"Am I the kind of woman to seduce you outright, or will I wait for you? Either way, you've become a most welcome distraction. You think you've cured me because I no longer shake or cry. But in that you're mistaken. The need is still here. Right here." She clenched one hand over the other and pressed it to the hollow between her breasts. "It's like thirst or hunger or lust. Can you understand that?"

Gavriel could only nod, and a weak one at that. A delicious and wanton angel stood before him, his own parable of temptation. But he wanted more. No matter his aims or his vows, he was a man who *needed* more.

"I can understand," he said.

"Then help me, Gavriel. Give me something new to crave . . ."

Books by Carrie Lofty

What a Scoundrel Wants

Scoundrel's Kiss

Published by Kensington Publishing Corporation

Scoundrel's Kiss

Carrie Lofty

ZEBRA BOOKS
KENSINGTON PUBLISHING CORP.
http://www.kensingtonbooks.com

ZEBRA BOOKS are published by

Kensington Publishing Corp.
119 West 40th Street
New York, NY 10018

All Kensington titles, imprints, and distributed lines are available at special quantity discounts for bulk purchases for sales
promotion, premiums, fund-raising, educational, or institu-
tional use.

Special book excerpts or customized printings can also be
created to fit specific needs. For details, write or phone the
office of the Kensington Special Sales Manager: Attn.: Special
Sales Department. Kensington Publishing Corp., 119 West
40th Street, New York, NY 10018. Phone: 1-800-221-2647.

Zebra and the Z logo Reg. U.S. Pat. & TM Off.

ISBN-13: 978-1-4201-0476-9
ISBN-10: 1-4201-0476-4

First Printing: January 2010
10 9 8 7 6 5 4 3 2 1

Printed in the United States of America

Acknowledgments

Thanks to my manuscript crew: Kelly Schaub, Lindsey Sodano, Cathleen DeLong, and the Circle Girls for their enthusiasm and sharp critiques, and to Lisa Yarde for her research assistance; to my head crew: Ann Aguirre, Liz Powell, Barbara Ferrer, Nancy Parra, and the generous women of Chicago North for keeping me sane and making me laugh; and to my heart crew: Jennifer Ritzema, Karen Martin, and my wonderful family for supporting me and loving me without end.

My special thanks to Hilary Sares and Caren Johnson for making this book possible.

Chapter 1

Toledo, Kingdom of Castile
Spring, 1201

Ada of Keyworth stared at the poppy pod, the one the apothecary rolled between his skeletal fingers. "What would you have me do for it?" she asked him in Arabic.

Seated, Hamid al-Balansi lolled the pod in his palm, around, around. A halo of sunlight from the doorway at his back left his aged, bearded face in shadow. But she could see his voracious eyes and the arch of his rank smile. "When was your last taste, *inglesa*?"

Englishwoman.

She licked chapped lips, darting a glance to his wide pupils. "Two evenings ago."

"Ah," Hamid said, his grin widening. "Without your ration, I do not envy your suffering come nightfall."

"Then don't make me suffer. Give me the tincture."

"The question is not what I would have you do for it." His sharp voice held none of the pity she sought. "Instead, I should ask what you are *willing* to do."

The cramped alcove at the rear of the apothecary's shop

pressed closer around her. Ada cringed, the tapestry-lined walls threatening like ominous sentinels. Angled rays of intense afternoon sunshine illuminated the ragged edges of the tapestry that covered the doorway, shining around it like a corona, polluting the air with the stench of heated wool. Seated on a scatter of worn brocade pillows, Ada hugged her knees and concentrated on the pale green seedpod.

"Please." The plaintive word grazed the parched tissue of her throat. "I have no money."

"Worse than that, pretty one. You have debts. Bad debts to unsavory men."

Panic caught fire in her chest, at war with the chills. "My debts are no concern of yours."

"Oh, but they are. If I give you the tincture for free, I keep you from asking for another loan." Hamid teased one of the pod's seams with a ragged thumbnail, releasing a drizzle of milky liquid. "Your creditors won't appreciate my taking business away from them."

"Do they have to know?" The grotesque little whisper hardly sounded like her.

"They always know. These people you owe, they are the eyes and ears of Toledo—not the high-minded courtiers you count among your patrons." He raised a bushy white eyebrow. "Why haven't you asked Doña Valdedrona for the money you need?"

"She is at the Alcázar in Segovia with King Alfonso, and most of the household with her," Ada said. "But even if she were here, I could never ask such a favor."

"And you have nothing else to sell?"

She thought of the scrolls, the ones she had pilfered from amongst the belongings of Daniel of Morley, her mentor. The English scholar had helped her and Jacob find patronage with the Condesa de Valdedrona, then spent the better part of a year tutoring Ada in the half dozen languages of Iberia. A ragged bit of her conscience had not let her bring the man's scrolls. They sat in a satchel in her room. Now she wished she had.

"No. I have nothing."

He laughed without mirth, the squawk of a crow. "More's the pity. We shall have to come to an agreement, you and me."

His fingers steady and sure despite his age, Hamid picked up a bowl from the squat table at his knee and placed the poppy inside. With a mortar, he crushed the fragile, unripe pod until nothing remained but moss-green filaments bathed in creamy resin. He added two more pods, pulverized them, and sluiced wine over the mash. Deep burgundy muted to a paler shade, swirling around the bowl. After draining the liquid to a flask, he added pinches of cardamom and cloves.

Ada absorbed the scene, taking in every familiar movement. She imagined tasting the foul, stinging tincture, feeling the blissful release of the opium. Relief washed over her. Soon. Soon, she would be free of the wicked torture of unending dreams, that terrible nightly spectacle.

The only remaining matter was what Hamid would ask of her. She closed her eyes. A distant part of her mind—the part that hovered above the pain and the insatiable cravings—recalled a very different life. Ada of Keyworth, the scholar. The translator. The woman from England who had once lived for reasons other than opium. But what had those reasons been? She could no longer recall, a failing that only added to her despair.

And what would Jacob do when he found out? He had asked her to make one promise, one ridiculously harmless promise for her own safety. And she could not keep it.

Hamid capped the flask. The liquid sloshed as he shook it vigorously, the fluff of his shabby white beard shivering with the movement. Watching, waiting, Ada faced an unassailable truth. She lived in that bottle. She would do anything to have it, devil take the consequences.

"And now the small matter of my fee," he said.

"Whatever you ask. I'll find a way to pay."

His rodent grin sent frissons of fear up her arms—or was that the sickness? Anything but the sickness of withdrawal.

If need be, she would stab the grizzled apothecary in the neck and steal his goods. She had killed once before, and memories of Sheriff Finch's bloody end revisited her nightly. Finch's ornamented dagger still dangled at her waist, the last item of value she possessed. But she could not part with the macabre souvenir, a talisman against those who would do her further harm.

Tension curled in her muscles. She clutched the hilt. Patterns of inlaid jewels and raised scrollwork gouged her damp palm. One quick strike and Hamid would fall dead. One quick strike and she would steal every poppy pod in his shop.

Movement at the curtained doorway caught her attention. Two giant men in black robes swished the tapestry aside, blinding her with a stab of bright sunshine. She released the dagger to shield her eyes. When they dropped the faded wool into place, the burly guards stood at either side of Hamid's bony limbs and parchment skin.

And the flask was gone.

"Where did it go? The flask? You said we could come to an agreement!"

"But our agreement had naught to do with murder," he said, the dark pools of his eyes alighting on her dagger. "I felt you were liable to become unreasonable."

Fingers, hands, arms—she could not stop shaking. "You know I need it."

Hamid pulled the flask from the folds of his white linen robe. He removed the cork and set it on the table at his knee. "Keep your peace, if you would. A hasty move might upset the table, and then your tincture will be no more."

"Please!"

Once she had been able to read people very well. Particularly men. She had read them like her beloved languages, knowing just what they needed to hear. But all she heard was a watery streak of hysteria in her own voice.

"Now here is my proposition," he said. "Will you hear it?"

Struggling for a breath, she looked up at the stern guards, their impassive faces and broad shoulders. One wore a massive mace at his hip. They made the tiny alcove even more confining. Backed against the rear wall, she would not be able to leave without their consent.

But she had no desire to escape, not without the tonic.

"Yes, I'll hear it," she said flatly. "Name your price."

For the first time, pity changed the old man's withered features. His toothy grin faded. With steady hands Ada envied, he gestured to the open flask. An invitation.

She snatched it from the table. Greedy swallows bathed her tongue in bitter, spiced wine, trailing a path of fire to her gut. The warm wash of opium soothed her tattered spirit and quelled the shakes. Warm. Floating and free. The price he would demand, how she would satisfy her next, inevitable appetite—none of it mattered.

As the tincture enveloped her senses, she smiled and retrieved the dagger from her belt. It was no use, holding onto that grim reminder. "For you. My payment."

"Keep your blade, *inglesa*," he said. "Where you're going, you will need it."

Hands clasped behind his back, Gavriel de Marqueda followed two other men from the Order of Santiago. They walked deep into Toledo's underbelly where the sun lost its way among dark holes and labyrinthine streets. He concentrated on the journey and eschewed the need to inquire after their destination. His novice master, Gonzalo Pacheco, revealed nothing before he was ready to do so, and novices who asked questions only raised his ire.

No, Gavriel would know soon enough. Working to dispel his unease, he breathed steadily through his nose despite the littered foulness of the alleyway. Returning to any city, especially one as large as Toledo, filled him with dread. An undercurrent of vice, sin, and violence spoke to him in a language he had struggled to forget.

He belonged to the Order now—at least, he would after completing Pacheco's final assignment.

Listening to footsteps in triplicate, he allowed the monotonous parade of sound to drown his misgivings. His place was one of submission now, and in submission, he would find peace.

Someday.

"I understand your gloom, brother," said Fernán Garza, a fellow aspirant. He eyed the dank alley with his usual mixture of disdain and amusement. "To return to life fettered by these robes—I cannot bear it, not when we're within reach of women and wine."

Gavriel pulled the white linen of his hood to one side, glaring at his companion. "You would rather partake in the sin than rise above it?"

"Yes. And I'll believe you a decidedly less interesting creature if you disagree with me."

"I disagree with you," Gavriel said.

"Ah, but what am I saying?" He rolled his eyes skyward and shook his head. "At Heaven's door or in a beautiful woman's arms, your foul temper would never abate. You're an example of all that is tedious about our, shall I say, profession."

Pacheco glanced back through the half-light of dusk, never breaking his powerful stride. "And you're an example of why noblemen should keep from having more than three sons."

"Master, my feet ache," Fernán said, his voice that of an ill-mannered child. "Shall we have a brief respite?"

Stopping at the top of a stairwell, Pacheco's white robes roiled around his legs. The red emblem of Santiago—a fleury cross tapering to the point of a sword—decorated the left side of his chest. He nodded toward an entrance at the foot of the stairs. "We shall take our rest down there. Inside."

Gavriel eyed the scarred wooden door as he would an armed combatant. Whatever lay beyond that portal would serve as his final trial. One more task and he would prove himself worthy of the Order. Failure would mean expulsion. Expulsion would mean a return to life with the de Silvas—or his revenge against them. He shuddered as sweat beaded at the base of his neck.

"Lead the way, Gavriel." Pacheco stared from beneath his white hood. "Unless you would rather forfeit your obligation."

Accept. Submit. God's will.

He nodded and descended the rough, crumbling steps. Splinters of shale slid beneath his boots, as did human refuse and slippery garbage. He scraped his palm along the stairwell to find his balance. Moist patches of rotting mortar gave way beneath his fingertips.

"Fitting you should lead us, as this place seems in keeping with your disposition," Fernán said. "Though when we've concluded our ministering, I should like to visit some happy place of love and verse—in keeping with *my* disposition."

Gavriel turned at the base of the steps and threw back his hood. Two days of Fernán's prattle on the road from Uclés would wear a hole in the patience of a saint, patience he worked hard to maintain. "Brother, I have taken a vow to abstain from violence—"

"Or else you'd likely cut out my tongue. I know. God grants small mercies."

Pacheco angled his head of cropped silver hair toward the door. "Proceed, both of you."

Fingers tensed on the rusted iron latch, Gavriel breathed deeply and prayed for fortitude. He knew this place. Rather, he knew places like this. Hidden from sight. Shrouded in lies and crime and hopelessness. Rife with temptation.

He pushed open the heavy door, and the brothel inside confirmed his darkest fears.

"Well, well," said Fernán, peering over his shoulder. "Perhaps this is my sort of destination after all."

Illuminated by meager torchlight, a score of women in varied states of undress lounged on pillows and sloping chairs. Men lingered with the harlots, ducking beneath low, irregularly spaced beams. The shadowed mess of garish colors contrasted with the dark streets outside, but finery and incense could not mask the underlying stink of unwashed bodies and sex.

At the far end of the wide, windowless room, a man stooped on a raised platform. An olive-skinned girl wearing only a kirtle stood at his side. The man spoke in a clipped mash of languages—Castilian and Mozarabic, the vernacular of the underworld—and espoused the girl's virtues. She had no family, no disease, no debts. Neither did she have her virginity, the man disclosed, but patrons lined the platform anyway, gold and morabetins in hand. Eyes closed, the girl swayed on the verge of collapse.

Merciful Lord. An auction.

Six brawny guards surrounded Gavriel and his companions, an offensive maneuver for close-quarter combat. He watched for weaknesses but found none in their formation. With the exit at his back, he felt confident in his ability to make a hasty escape—except for Fernán pressing close and whimpering.

The largest of the six men drew a lustrous, engraved sword

of Berber origin, barring their entrance. "What business have you here, Jacobeans?"

The blade glinted beneath the torchlight. What Gavriel would have given to grip that sword. But his hands were empty and his vows heavy. He was an aspirant to a sacred order, an obstinate fact that had been much easier to remember while secluded in Uclés. Before any manner of belligerence, he was defenseless.

Pacheco pushed forward and addressed the lead guard. "Salamo Fayat is expecting us."

The words were a key to unlock the human gauntlet. Five of the armed men dispersed, blending with the shadows, tapestries, and patrons. The lead man sheathed his sword and offered Pacheco a curt bow. "This way, honored guests."

Gavriel exchanged a quizzical glance with his fellow novice. Fernán smiled and said, "This is a greeting more befitting the Order, don't you agree?"

"At a brothel?"

"Pacheco has influence enough, and the Order has gold enough, to ensure everyone finds a happier afterlife. No wonder they welcome him."

"I am curious," Gavriel said with a heavy sigh. "Why would the owners of such a place want their clientele redeemed?"

"What would it matter to them? Sinners are easy to come by. Tomorrow there will be just as many eager to gain entrance." Fernán grinned, his pale skin shining with sweat and oil and his eyes wide to the room's delights. "Oh, that I could be one."

Weaving a narrow and careful path between the harlots and their patrons, edging nearer the auction platform, Gavriel followed the burly guard. He wished he had kept his hood in place, for he felt curious eyes walking over his face, his neck and hair, while his own curiosity swelled like a gorging tick. Waiting. Waiting for Pacheco's decree. The brothel's ominous temptations and his worries about the upcoming test crushed against his breastbone. The air vibrated with currents of lust and greed, the laughter of the damned.

"Stay near the platform," Pacheco said before slipping into the crowd.

Gavriel lost sight of the slender man's silver hair near a rear alcove. Minutes passed, leaving him no choice but to confront the auction proceedings. The girl in the linen kirtle had been replaced by a young Moorish boy with skin like oiled wood, dark and smooth. He wore wrapped breeches and a neck manacle, his skittish eyes the size of eggs. A handful of murmured bids later and the boy was sold.

The hands Gavriel clasped at his back tensed and released, almost of their own accord. He stilled the anxious rhythm and fought a quick surge of nausea. Sweat slid between his shoulder blades, pressed on all sides by the heat of torches and bodies and wild memories. The urge to flee was nearly as strong as the urge to fight.

"You are to choose one," Pacheco said upon his return. "Each of you."

Gavriel turned to him. Questions stuck in his mouth. But Fernán found no difficulty bridging the silence. "I have dearly missed the luxury of personal slaves since leaving my parents' estate. Very thoughtful, Master."

"This is your trial, Fernán, just as you are mine." Pacheco's black eyes narrowed and swiveled between his aspirants. "These souls are in desperate need of redemption. You will work with one to provide spiritual guidance. Turn them toward the Church. Help redeem them of their wicked ways and you will pass your final test."

A year spent within the confines of the Order and living by its doctrines had taught Gavriel not to disagree with Pacheco's commands. His word determined if and when men passed their novitiates, the period of penance and trials before being accepted into the brotherhood.

But how Gavriel wanted to disagree.

The lines on either side of Pacheco's mouth deepened into trenches. "You fear this challenge, Gavriel. Why?"

Because I am not ready.

For once, he wished Fernán would intervene with some inane drivel, but the man was busy assessing the next slave standing at auction. Gavriel exhaled through his nose and forced tense muscles to relax. He toughened his lies until they became the truth.

"I have no fear, Master."

"Then choose one," Pacheco said quietly. "It's quite intimidating, I know, to look upon a sea of depraved faces and know that you can give such a gift to only one. How do you choose?"

Fernán rocked back on his heels, that idiot grin stretching his lips. "I, for one, will choose some terrible good-for-nothing. No sense busting my hopes on a near miss."

Pacheco scowled. "You will regard this challenge with great sincerity, or you will not be returning to Uclés."

"And how is this a threat?"

"Your father has indicated that you are no longer welcome at your family estate. As of last week, the retreat at Uclés is your one and only home. Treat it with the respect it deserves."

Fernán's features drained of their scant color. He used a wide sleeve to mop the sheen of sweat from his forehead. "Well, then, that changes my standards considerably." He turned toward the bulk of the room and addressed its seedy occupants. "Are there any virgins here? Virgins with an inclination toward study and prayer? And perhaps rudimentary husbandry skills?"

Gavriel tugged on Fernán's arm. "Stop it, you fool."

"This isn't working. Should I try speaking in Mozarabic?"

"You should try behaving as if you wear the Cross of St. James," Pacheco said with unmistakable menace.

"Master," Gavriel said. "What if the one I choose does not wish to accompany us?"

"This is a slave auction. What choice will they have?"

"You intend that the Order will own them?"

"Of course," Pacheco said with a shrug. "Gavriel, you of all people should know this is no ordinary brothel. Make your selection and let us have done with this place. Now that our business in Toledo is concluded, we will return to Uclés tomorrow."

Fernán nodded toward another Moor on the platform. "I'll take him then. One's as useless as another."

Pacheco placed the appropriate bids and purchased the slave. The stooping auctioneer led his most recent sale down the steps. Fernán looked the young man up and down, his expression twisted in a distasteful sneer. "I wonder if he even speaks Castilian."

"You could ask him," Pacheco said.

"Oh, the hassle this will be."

A woman with fair skin followed the auctioneer to the center of the platform—a woman to stop the breath in Gavriel's lungs. The muddied sounds of the brothel faded. Fashionably dressed in a deep blue linen gown decorated with fine embroidery, she surveyed the crowd of buyers with a placid look. No fear tainted her shadowed eyes. No tension contorted the muscles of her body. No bitterness ruined the smile on her mouth. For all the world, she embodied the peace Gavriel had yet to find, this woman on the verge of bondage.

She rolled her eyes shut and licked her lips, head falling back. Unbound hair the same red-brown of ripened dates stretched to the shapely curve of her waist. Gavriel imagined digging his hands into those silky strands, bending her body to his, tasting her white flesh. Mouth dry, he choked on the image of transforming her look of peace into one of desire. Desire for him.

A quick glance revealed that animal hunger mirrored

across dozens of faces. Fernán bathed her with a look of abject lust. "Can I change my mind?" he asked.

The muscles in Gavriel's arms and torso tensed. The nameless woman inspired more thoughts of sin than he had suffered in a month. Lust. Envy. Wrath. He closed his eyes, breathless, but dark imaginings would not leave him be. Squeezing his fists until he thought his fingers would break, he prayed for strength—strength enough to hold his temper until she was gone, until temptation passed.

A loud commotion of shouts and drawn swords clamored from the entrance. Heads turned. The same six guards materialized out of the shadows, barring entrance to a young man with black, curling hair. Patrons around the auction platform backed away from the disorder, cramming bodies against bodies. One man elbowed Gavriel in the stomach. A woman screamed.

And so did the man at the door.

"Ada!"

Chapter 2

The intruder, nothing more than a half-grown boy, dodged swinging swords—jumping first, then rolling clear. He scrambled between two guards and slipped like a fish from their grasp. Spinning once, he drew a pair of exotic, curved blades from their sheaths. Metal met metal as he defended against another guard, a man twice as wide and twice as slow. The boy caught his opponent's sword between the curved blades and twisted, sending the much heavier weapon to the ground.

Gavriel watched the display with curiosity, admiration, and envy. Saints save him, mostly envy. He had not seen fighting skills of such refinement and natural grace in years, not since he last held a weapon. Young and agile and calculating, the intruder fairly danced through his attackers, disarming them when possible, incapacitating them as a last resort.

Well, that was one difference. Gavriel had never hesitated to kill.

The brothel's patrons bunched and shrank like sheep in a pen. Women screamed and covered their exposed bodies; only now, with the threat of violence, did they find their modesty. The musicians tucked close to the rear alcove continued to play, oblivious to the threat, or perhaps accustomed to a steady diet of violence and nightly disruptions.

"This way," Pacheco said, grabbing Fernán's slave by the arm. "Toward the alcove. There's a back door."

Hood in place, mouth agape but blessedly silent, Fernán followed their master's urging. Tugging his slave's arm, he turned toward the task of navigating a safe escape. But Gavriel did not move.

Another handful of guards emerged from secret places. Roused from sleep or maybe from a harlot's bed, one had forgotten his tunic but not his sword. Another strapping man picked up a piece of wood from a broken table and used it as an impromptu shield. The boy was outnumbered, and for what? Why? The slave girl?

Gavriel found the woman rooted to the same spot on the platform. The boy's desperate shout, the rolling waves of violence and fear—none of it had changed her placid expression. She idly reached a hand to the low beam ceiling, the stretch pulling her fitted bodice taut over her breasts. A private smile turned the corners of her lips as she teased loose a bit of crumbling plaster.

"Gavriel, we must leave. This is my command." Pacheco's thundercloud expression left no room for argument, but Gavriel offered one anyway.

"That boy stands eight to one."

"Do not think of going to his aid." Pacheco squinted, reddening with anger. "Now do as you're told, novice."

Gavriel retrieved a fallen sword and stood ready to aid the boy, to defy his master. He tightened his fingers around the hilt and sank into a relaxed stance. The heft and weight of the weapon was a homecoming, more familiar than the billowing robes he wore. But the contrast gave him pause, that place where the white linen at his wrists draped over gleaming steel.

"You have responsibilities," Pacheco said, his voice devoid

of the previous flash of anger. Cold now. Threatening. "You made a vow—not to me, but to God."

Yes. One of three. He would abstain from violence.

The second vow, obedience, pressed down on the backs of his hands. The sword grew twice as heavy, then heavier still, until it dropped from numb fingers. The muffled clang of metal against the swept earth floor rattled into his bones.

"Come away now." Pacheco tugged his sleeve.

Atop the auction platform, the strange slave girl yelped. Surprise marred her peaceful features as a man grabbed her around the waist. Gavriel recognized him as one of the patrons who had been prepared to bid for her. The sleepy-eyed slave laughed, but when her captor did not relent, she struggled to escape his clutching arms.

"Ada!" The boy intruder fought past one more guard to within a body's length of the platform. Blood stained his tunic. "Stop him!"

Gavriel jumped onto the platform without thought and thrust out his leg.

The abductor and his comely treasure took a tumble, rolling down a trio of steps near the rear alcove. Startled musicians stopped short with a screech of dissonant instruments. Her arms and legs flailing beneath the man's weight, the woman fought with unexpected zeal. She shrieked in an unfamiliar language and kicked free of entangling skirts, hooking a boot heel into his calf. He slapped her cheek with the back of his hand.

But she would not be contained.

She slammed a knee between his legs and thrust the howling man aside. On all fours, she scampered past fleeing patrons and screaming harlots to find the sword Gavriel had dropped. She stood, wiped a mess of tangled hair from her forehead, and raised the weapon in a convincing stance. Someone had taught her how to hold a blade.

Perhaps the boy warrior who fought to reach her side.

She began to laugh again and swayed to a rhythm the frightened musicians had stopped playing. Her purloined sword dipped. Gavriel hopped off the platform, intent on pulling her from danger.

"Down!" the boy shouted.

Gavriel dropped to the floor and dragged the woman with him, flinging aside her weapon. A squeal of metal sounded above their heads where the boy used his curving blades to deflect a dagger—a dagger aimed at Gavriel's neck. The thwarted abductor wanted his prize back. Two parries later and the man dropped dead beside Gavriel and the slave he still held.

She smiled up at their champion. "Jacob!"

The boy named Jacob panted. A riot of sweaty black hair curled across his brows. He caught Gavriel's eye. "Can you take her out the back?" he asked in Castilian, his accent thick and unfamiliar.

"Can you fight free on your own?"

Jacob only nodded, turning to defend against another guard.

Gavriel hauled the woman to her feet and hoisted her over one shoulder. She fought him just as she had fought the eager patron. Wild limbs struck his back and kicked the air in front of his face. He squeezed tighter. Some detached part of his brain recognized the curve of her backside and the deep satisfaction of using his muscles to keep her close.

Woman and man.

He flinched at the thought, but not at the chair flying past his head. It crashed into the nearest wall and splintered. Spongy pillows gave way beneath his feet as he picked through the messy brawl toward the alcove. Although he wondered about the boy's success against the armed hordes, he dared not look back. The temptation to exchange a flailing female for the cool power of a blade might be too great.

Pacheco and Fernán awaited him in the alley behind the brothel. The stench of fetid but temperate night air was a welcome change to the heated poison of smoke and perfume. Gavriel's infuriated burden used the change of scene to renew her efforts. She pounded his back and scratched his neck with long nails. He cursed, pulling her from his shoulder.

The woman landed with a hard thump on filthy cobble-stones. She wheezed, her breath gone. Gavriel knelt and pressed his thumbs against two points at her throat, applying pressure until she collapsed.

"You killed her!" Fernán gasped.

"I did nothing of the sort. Now she rests." He unfolded his long limbs and stood tall. "What happened to your slave?"

"He escaped," Fernán said, beaming. "Can you believe my luck? I think it means God has freed me from my obligation."

"Hardly. We'll discuss that later." Pacheco stared at the motionless woman, eyebrows bunched together. "Who is she, Gavriel? And what are you doing with her?"

Jacob burst through the alcove door with a shout. He and Gavriel pushed the door closed and wedged it shut. Pounding fists echoed into the alley like a war cry.

Picking up the woman in the midst of chaos had been one thing. Touching her again gave Gavriel pause. But the pounding fists did not relent. He steeled himself and lifted her limp body.

"What is this about, *niño?*" he asked.

"No time," Jacob said, breathless. "Run."

Through Toledo's winding cobblestone streets, where every surface was bathed in shadow, Jacob ben Asher split his attention between his unexpected companions. The silver-haired man led their ragged group, while the thin one stumbled behind him, his face a waxen gray color. The tallest of the three—the one who had tripped Ada's captor and hauled her from that disgusting place—carried her over his shoulder.

Jacob would have rather taken Ada back to the condesa's

palace, but he could not risk being caught. Not by the guards at the brothel. Not by *los pedones*, the city infantry. Upon finding a Jew alone with a dazed Christian woman after dark, they would not ask questions before detaining him. Or worse.

And as blood flowed from his collarbone, seeping under his tunic and down his chest, Jacob could not be certain of making it to the palace himself, let alone with Ada in tow. Pain gathered in a dull pulse, refusing to be ignored.

He tensed his fingers around the hilt of his knives. The silver-haired man led them deeper into a part of the city Jacob had never explored. Worry escalated with every fatigued step. These men were members of a religious order. Their white robes emblazoned with red crosses and their closely cropped hair said as much. Whether knights or clergymen, he no more relished being subjected to their varied sense of justice and inherent prejudices than he did seeing Ada on that auction block. Bitterness welled beneath his ribs, making it hard to breathe.

Foolish woman.

They stopped before a large building, some blend of residence and place of worship. The exterior, although austere, was graceful and attractive. Brick and stone alternated up the high, sheer walls, their creamy color glowing faintly in the deepening darkness. A defensive wall ran around the second story, and wooden balconies scattered across the patchwork of windows and arched brick doorways.

"This is one of our properties," the silver-haired man said in Castilian, his black eyes intent on Jacob. "You and the girl are welcome to stay with us tonight."

The design was Mudéjar—Moorish people who had long lived within Christian communities—and Jacob wondered how these men had come to own a property they obviously had no hand in designing. Except, perhaps, for the bell tower. Christians added bell towers, and Moors added minarets. Like stamps of ownership.

"Who are you?" he asked, working his tongue around their words. Even after more than a year in Toledo, he claimed no genuine fluency.

"I am Gonzalo Pacheco. This is Fernán Garza and Gavriel de Marqueda, two of my novices from the Order of Santiago. We are *freyles clérgicos*."

"Clergymen?" He glanced at the one called Gavriel whose height and strength hinted at a capacity for combat, not prayer and sacrifice. "You are not *caballeros?*"

"I understand your hesitancy," Pacheco said, smiling. But whether because of circumstances or night shadows, the smile did nothing to reassure Jacob. "We have no intention of trying to convert you this evening—merely in tending the girl and your wounds."

Jacob flicked his eyes to armed men walking along the defensive wall. "I worry nothing of conversion."

Gavriel hiked Ada on his shoulder, her long hair trailing down his back. "We've had enough violence for one night, *niño*."

Boy.

Jacob rubbed his tongue along the roof of his mouth. Once he had stood alongside Robin Hood and Will Scarlet—those legendary heroes of England. They had worked to bring low the villains who had imprisoned Ada and threatened the whole of Nottinghamshire. Jacob was a clever and worthy fighter, respected by those who knew him.

With that litany running through his mind, he said, "I am called Jacob ben Asher, and I appreciate your generosity."

A maze of corridors and a dozen inquisitive faces later, Jacob sat bare-chested on the floor of a private room, the austere space in keeping with the dictates of their order. Pacheco sat at his side bearing a tray of clean linen strips and a bowl of runny, milky salve.

"I'm surprised you did not suffer worse," he said, examining Jacob's wounds.

"Master, why tend this Jew?" asked Fernán. The thin, sallow novice stood in the doorway to an adjoining room. His frightened expression had been replaced with contempt.

"Although I disagree with his faith, he saved Gavriel's life," Pacheco said. "He deserves medical attention at the very least."

"*Gracias*," Jacob said quietly. He had known too many eager zealots who would have left him for dead in an alley. The aging Jacobean's generosity eased his apprehension.

When the salve bit into the nasty slice on his upper arm, he clamped his lips together. The other, deeper gash just below his collarbone awaited treatment, but he would not give Fernán the satisfaction of seeing him cringe.

The tall one, Gavriel, patted a strip of cotton to the back of his own neck. Dark dots of blood colored the strip and stained his draping white hood. Jacob looked to where Ada lay prostrate on a simple cot and wondered how much of the man's flesh was embedded under her fingernails.

"Now explain yourself," Gavriel said. "You took an unforgivable risk to your person, charging in as you did."

"That is none of our business," Pacheco said.

Jacob worked to keep pace with their conversation, their words a jumble in his brain. Ada was better versed in the Castilian language. No, she was a master. Truly gifted.

Gavriel loomed above where he and Pacheco sat, appearing more formidable than pious. "Master, his actions put us in danger. I for one would like to know why."

"Mind your tone, novice."

Gavriel dropped his gaze and muttered a thick-voiced apology. He turned to the room's single window, hands clasped at his back. The thick stained glass was nearly opaque, but light from the room's two torches reflected patterns of color across his face.

Pacheco exhaled a weary sigh and returned to Jacob's wounds. "This one at your collarbone may require sutures. Do you have a physician who can attend you?"

"One of your own kind, no doubt," said Fernán.

Jacob shook his head and ran an unsteady hand through his hair. Sweat had dried, curling the ends to the texture of straw. "Her Excellency's physician is Christian."

Pacheco raised an eyebrow. "Who?"

"The Condesa de Valdedrona. I was sent afield with her men and returned only this afternoon." He glanced at Ada again, her skin pale like the brothers' robes. An impotent feeling of anger and sadness settled in his stomach. "I searched the palace but Ada was missing again."

"Missing?" Half of Gavriel's face caught the torchlight, the other half hiding in night shadows. "She'd been abducted?"

Jacob hissed as Pacheco probed the wound at his collarbone. He could endure pain of the flesh, but the pain Ada had caused burrowed deeper, proving far more destructive. Life in Castile had aged him more than he cared to contemplate.

"No. *Creo que . . .*" He exhaled heavily, searching for the words. "I believe she was there by choice."

Gavriel frowned. "Why?"

Meeting the man's fathomless eyes was a challenge. Admitting the truth was almost impossible, a failure unlike any he had known. "She has a taste for opium."

The three Jacobeans stilled. They exchanged soundless looks until, inevitably, they turned to Ada. She always seemed so peaceful when she slept, cradled by the drug—perhaps in compensation for the terror of her waking life.

"And she was willing to sell herself to slavery?" Gavriel's expression held none of the sympathy Jacob would have hoped for from a man of God.

"Perhaps her debts are too many." Months of unshed tears clotted in Jacob's throat. He wanted to sleep, sleep without burdens. This devotion did neither one of them any good. "I could not leave her in that place, a terrible fate. She would never break her promise, not when well. Her choices are not her own."

Pacheco tied the last of the dressings. "And what is your connection to her?"

"We have both come from England and serve Doña Valdedrona. I am . . . her friend."

"And more if you'd have your way, *judío?*" Fernán asked. "But she wouldn't have you, would she?"

"Fernán." Pacheco's warning tone silenced him, but Fernán's smile remained fixed and taunting—reminding Jacob that he had shed his weapons upon entering the Jacobeans' house. Probably for the best. "We'll offer what assistance we can and deliver you both to Doña Valdedrona's residence here in Toledo."

"No, no—please," Jacob said.

"Your pardon?"

Jacob stood and pulled on his tunic and mail, his mind turning. He pressed the heels of his hands into his eye sockets, feeling the ragged scratch of fatigue and grief pressing back. He was far too tired to take care of her any longer.

The solution was a good one. She would never forgive him, but perhaps she would live and grow strong and escape this terrible half-life.

"I beg you," he said quietly. "Take her with you."

Gavriel had been studying Ada's peaceful face, revisiting the violence he had felt in the brothel—that black and deadly surge. He had not held a sword in a year. He missed it, just as he lamented the loss of power, status, and authority that had been his.

But young Jacob's request snatched him from that picture of false peace. "What?"

"You are brothers of the Order of Santiago." Jacob met each man's gaze in turn. "And your monastery is to the east, in Uclés, *sí?*"

Pacheco nodded. "That is correct."

"Please, take her with you."

Old fears slithered over Gavriel's skin. The girl was dangerous. "Absolutely not."

Jacob drew back his shoulders, a motion that must have aggravated the wound at his collarbone. But he stood straight to look Gavriel in the eye. "You owe me a debt of life."

"Your actions put us in danger in the first place."

"I saved you," Jacob said. "Pay me in return by saving her."

"You're not able?"

Those same proud shoulders slumped forward. "I . . . I try. All that I can think and do—it falls short." The boy no longer aimed his pleading gaze at Pacheco or Fernán. Only at Gavriel. "I ask for her sake."

"No."

Jacob curled his hands into fists. "You turn on a soul in need? What manner of man are you? What manner of Christian servant are you?"

Fernán snorted. "More than you can claim, *judío.*"

The boy leapt. Colliding with Fernán and falling to the ground, the weight of their bodies broke a chair into a heap of splintered timber. Jacob grunted and landed a solid punch before Gavriel and Pacheco hauled him up.

Jacob sputtered and kicked, planting his boot in Fernán's side. "I will kill him!"

Gavriel squeezed the back of Jacob's neck until he calmed. "And I'll pretend I didn't hear you say that. The magistrate would not take kindly to a Jew making such a threat."

Struggling to his feet, Fernán wiped blood from his mouth. "I want him jailed."

Pacheco raised a restraining hand. "Enough, Fernán. The boy is distressed, and you test the steadiest souls."

Fernán spit and dabbed his lips with shaking fingers, looking around to wipe them on something other than his robes. "Oh, go ahead and take her, Gavriel. What's the worst that could happen? She's a senseless, voluptuous, completely vulnerable woman who'll depend on your care for all the hours of the day and night." He snickered, but his body was still cowed. "That's hardly any challenge at all."

"I can let him finish what he started," Gavriel said. "I doubt the outcome would be in your favor."

Pacheco stepped between them. His age, authority and a single cautionary look quelled the fight. "You behave like squabbling children, not Jacobeans." He pointed to the adjoining room. "Fernán, leave us."

Gavriel released Jacob and bowed his head. The brief violence had only delayed their master's decision.

"I ask that you return to Doña Valdedrona's estate," Pacheco said to Jacob. "I'll arrange an escort of knights for you. Return with the girl's personal effects and we will discuss her care in the morning, when tempers have cooled."

Jacob nodded, still flushed, his eyes keen. He pulled on his boots and strapped a belt around his waist. He left the room after one last glance toward the woman on the cot.

"Master." Head still bowed, Gavriel struggled for calm. "Master, tell me what to do."

"She will be your responsibility now."

A judgment. A sentence. Not for the first time, he thought that exile would have been the wiser choice. This life of sacrifice and restraint was far too grueling.

"And if I cannot?"

"You will," Pacheco said firmly. "And we both know the consequences if you do not."

Chapter 3

Ada awoke in the back of a cart. Her head rattled as fiercely as the rickety wheels. Her stomach tightened, that place where hunger met nausea, but she thought she would never be able to use her sticky, swollen tongue again. The side of her face ached with a bruise the size of a fat, ripe olive.

She sat up, her joints and muscles stiff. Squinting against the sun, she saw a gray donkey pulling the cart. Two men riding ahead on horseback wore white robes. The one holding the donkey's tether might not have needed reins; he rode his animal with graceful ease. His tall, lean body absorbed every movement of the horse's plodding steps. The other man, however, fought his mount with stiff and jerking movements.

Toledo was nowhere to be seen. The jagged mountains that bounded the city looked like pale blue teeth, far behind her on the horizon. Limitless grasslands stretched wide, broken only by dots of windmills, the occasional cluster of distant sheep, and the banks of the Tagus River. Its waters ran quietly beneath the bright spring sun.

But where was Jacob? The previous night's events were a blur of colors and melodies punctuated with bright moments of fear and anger. More nightmares. They seeped into every breath, even when she abandoned herself to the throes of the tincture. She would never escape if they followed even to that otherworldly place.

But she distinctly remembered Jacob. He would help her banish the headache that throbbed like goblet drums.

"Jacob?" His name stuck on her tongue. She cleared her throat. "Jacob, where are you?"

Overly loud, her rusty voice croaked across the wind-stirred mesa. The horse carrying the awkward man shied and reared, casually tossing its rider.

"Fernán," said a third man, also on horseback at the rear of the cart. "Other horses would ride your mount better than you do."

Tired and disoriented, Ada worked to keep up with his use of the Romance language. A Castilian dialect. Well educated.

"But he's a gelding, Master," said the man called Fernán. "The beast should enjoy my slight imposition a great deal more than that of a randy stud." He stood and dusted half the road from his robes. With a hand pressed to his lower back, he walked toward the spooked horse. It skittered a few steps clear. "Could you assist me, please?"

The tall man, surely a knight, pulled on the reins, bringing his horse and the donkey to a halt. He swung gracefully to the ground. The flat, endless expanse of the Mesa de Ocaña made whole towns appear small and insignificant, but even against that inhospitable landscape, he looked intimidating. White robes did nothing to soften the hard lines of his face. Closely cropped hair as dark as kohl shone with highlights of red and amber, burnished by the rising sun.

"You've been thrown three times now," he said without sympathy. "Why don't you ride with the woman?"

"In a cart? Pulled by a donkey?" Fernán straightened his body with a jester's false dignity. "I'm still a man."

"Then sit a horse like one."

"Spoken with the patience and charity of a true man of God, Gavriel."

Gavriel. That man.

"Hello? Pardon me, but where is Jacob?"

All three men turned quizzical looks her way. She had used English. Few people on the Peninsula spoke English, and these holy men showed no signs of comprehension. She tried the question again in Romance, using their Castilian dialect. "*Dónde está* Jacob?"

Gavriel boosted Fernán back onto the horse and tugged the reins, looping them around his own saddle's pommel. One burden discharged—for that was how he stalked about, a man burdened by a great weight—he turned to Ada. "Your friend Jacob is on his way to the capital."

To make sense of the words, she pushed aside the details of his body: the breadth of his muscled shoulders, the intensity of his dark brown eyes, and the unexpected glint of anger she found there. "To Segovia?" she asked.

"Doña Valdedrona is at court with King Alfonso, and Jacob went there to meet her."

Betrayal like a shard of glass sliced into her heart. Loyal, steadfast, and adoring, Jacob had been her only true friend in Toledo. Most were suspicious of her education and talent for languages, while others thought to use her for their ends. She had balanced them all to gain favor with the widowed condesa, relying on Jacob as her trustworthy confidant.

And when the thirst for another sip of the tincture got the better of her, she could rely on his caring and discretion.

That he could abandon her for the beautiful young noblewoman, leaving Ada to these men, smacked of the treason her sister had committed—Meg, who had chosen Will Scarlet over her own flesh and blood.

But if Jacob thought to treat her so cruelly, she would

leave him behind as easily as they had England. She owed him nothing.

"Now I know where Jacob is," she said tightly. "But where are we? And who are you?"

"We're clergy from the Order of Santiago, on the road to Uclés," Gavriel said. "To your new home."

"Are you mad?"

"Keep your voice down, *mujer*."

The warm spring wind tossed hair in front of her eyes. She swiped it back, her fingers catching in tangles and snarls. "My home is at Her Excellency's residence in Toledo. My belongings are there, and I demand to be returned at once."

"Your belongings are with you in the cart," he said. "And we're not returning to Toledo."

"This is an outrage!"

He lifted a black brow. Some men would have accompanied the move with a smile or smirk. But his face hardly shifted, pinning her with a steady stare. "I wonder, where would 'home' be today had Jacob not saved you from the auction?"

The auction. Memories and fears and wants crowded back like a flood. Humiliation chilled her skin but ran hot through her blood.

"Have none of you a shred of kindness?"

Gavriel regarded her as would a statue. The elderly man shook his head, a mask of pity shrouding his aging features. "This is for your own good, child," he said.

"More like, she brought this on herself." Gavriel stepped closer to the cart, his white robes snapping like an unfurled sail. "Before the week is out, you'll bear much worse."

"What do you mean?"

"Your boy Jacob will come for you in a month. My task is to ensure that you are safe and free of the opium by the time he returns."

No opium. No release. Only the terrible pains of withdrawal

and the desolation of failure when she succumbed again. Always succumbing, because the alternative was simply too terrible.

More nightmares.

"You cannot do this!"

"I intend to," Gavriel said, "with or without your cooperation."

"You would keep me captive?"

"I'll be a kinder master than any who would've had you last night."

She shot to her feet in the cart, but two hands as hard as iron clamped her shoulders. For the span of a lightening flash, they were face to face. Like his hair, his eyes contained flecks of other colors—colors of sunset and the high plateau. In those eyes, she saw no glint of sympathy or kindness. Only more anger.

A looking glass. The reflection of a rage as deep as her own.

She smoothed her expression to match his and glanced to where fluttering white linen met the tanned skin of his neck. She licked her lips.

And then she was back in the cart, thrust down by powerful arms. Her backside met wood. She grimaced, but a grin snuck over her mouth. He was not so impassive after all.

"We should arrive at Yepes by nightfall, halfway to Uclés. Sit in silence or be bound and gagged." Gavriel stepped back and sketched a mocking bow, one at odds with his stoic face. "Those are your choices."

Ada glared at each man in turn, resting her scowl on the back of Gavriel's shorn head. He urged the horses to continue an eastward trudge, and she gripped the hilt of her dagger.

He rode ahead of the others, back straight and eyes on the endless horizon. His agitated mind, however, returned to Ada like a thirsty animal to a stream. Queens regarded their subjects with less hauteur than she did. But unlike a subject, Gavriel was not obliged to lower his gaze or obey her dictates.

Resentment boiled in his body, every piece of him rebelling against the task Pacheco had assigned. He would have to live with the burden or risk being cast back into the world where his need for revenge would reign unchecked. The Order stood between Gavriel and doing murder.

His vows had been much easier to keep at Uclés. Except *she* would be there too, bringing with her all of the temptations life had to offer.

No. The drowned rat of a woman was just short of a harlot, no matter her fine clothes and patrons. Scrubbed of the opiate, her blue eyes held none of the intoxicating peace he had envied. It had been a lie. She was a woman torn by vice, and the spell she had woven around him at the brothel was thankfully broken.

He inhaled deeply. He would obey his master and do right by Ada—no matter her reluctance—and take his place as a Jacobean.

With Fernán marginally in control of his mount and Ada momentarily accepting her confinement, the small party resumed its journey. The plateau stretched east ahead of them, bleached of every color except parched brown earth and pale green wheat and scrub grass.

How different from where Gavriel was raised in Marqueda, a small city in León, the kingdom just west of Castile. Temperate and green, Marqueda supported lush vineyards and citrus and olive orchards. Sitting high on his mount, dwarfed by an endless sky and flat land, he felt exposed, restless.

He topped a slight rise and gazed on the shallow valley below. In the far distance, a caravan of merchants plodded eastward. Men on horseback flanked three ponderous wagons, their drivers and horses. Sunlight twinkled off weapons and helmets. A flock of sheep milled in front of the lead horses, spanning the road and ambling toward the Tagus River, just to the north. The calls of the wagon masters echoed dully over the grasslands. The lead wagon driver and one of the shepherds exchanged angry gestures, their body language conveying more than Gavriel could hear of their exchange.

Fernán nickered to his skittish mount. Gavriel shot him a dark look. "What?" the other man asked. "This horse is the terror!"

Pacheco rode alongside him. "What goes?"

"Seems harmless enough," Gavriel said. "There, the armed men are helping to push through the sheep. Watch the woman while I ride ahead. I wouldn't put it past her to—"

"To try and make an escape?" She had climbed out of the cart and stood just to the rear of the horses, smiling like an angel. The rough leather satchel she wore looked at home draped across her spoiled garments. She shook her head, sending shivers through unkempt hair. "What would give you that notion?"

He tugged the reins and swiveled his mount to face her. "Get back in the cart."

"No. What are you called?"

"Gavriel de Marqueda. Now back in that cart before I drag you there myself."

"We might enjoy that." Full lips curled into a wider smile. She spoke flawless Castilian, but her unusual accent fashioned familiar words anew.

She eased nearer with the grace of a cat. He leaned over on the horse, bringing his face to hers. "You'd say that to any man who has what you want," he said.

"*Sí.*"

"You forget, I'm not a man," he whispered. "I'm a servant of God."

"And my captor."

He nodded. "For now."

"And for my own good, I suppose?"

"To be certain."

She looked to his groin. Her parted lips invited every sin he could imagine, and no amount of prayer or penance could blunt the vividness of his imagination. "For my own good or for yours?" she asked.

Fernán slid off his mount at the top of the rise, but he had eyes for only Ada and Gavriel. "No one told me there would be merrymaking on this expedition."

"Keep quiet, Fernán, and take the donkey's leads," said Pacheco. "We must circle this impasse if we're to make Yepes by nightfall."

"Or we could be attacked by bandits." Fernán pointed behind them. His idiot grin dissolved. "Those ones, perhaps."

Gavriel jerked around. Nine roughly armored men rode light chargers from the southwest. Their flanking position was loose and undisciplined but retained the hallmarks of their military style. Almohad raiders. Thieves bent on finding human fodder to exchange for ransom.

To her credit, Ada did not flinch or scream. She propelled herself onto Fernán's horse. Yanking the reins, she swiveled it around with an expert hand, belying Fernán's claim that the animal had been the source of his trouble.

"We cannot outrun them," Pacheco said. "Nor can we fight them."

"No, but *they* can—the guards who ride with the caravan." Gavriel hoisted Fernán up to share his saddle. He circled and wedged a bar across the wheels of the cart to keep it still. "Last chance to behave yourself, *inglesa*. Or should I waste time tying you to your horse?"

He could have saved his breath, for she held a jeweled dagger in her hands. A determined expression hardened her features.

"I'd have cut you if you tried." She looked him up and

down with an appreciation only a corpse would miss. "And that would've been a shame."

Her bottom still smarted from when Gavriel had shoved her into the cart, but Ada rode hard into the shallow valley. Spring winds became a torrent at that speed, flinging her hair and skirts behind her like an army banner. Her colors. She squinted against the full, bright glare of the sun on the pale grasses. The mass of wagons and sheep became clear, closer.

Gavriel's horse ran alongside hers. Fernán clung to the taller man, his eyes pinched shut. Gavriel urged the animal to a faster pace, hunched low, a warrior's steady resolve on his face.

Ada squeezed her thighs to propel her horse over a shallow ditch, landing with an easy thud. Already the men of the caravan had circled a trio of wagons in preparation for the bandits' onslaught. Six armed guards took position and brandished long blades of steel. She sucked in a mouthful of fear and scorching air, aiming for the safety of those drawn swords.

Panicked sheep bleated and scattered. Gavriel pulled his animal to a stop, dust tinting the wind a sandy brown. "Almohad raiders," he said. "Fast approaching."

"How many?" asked a guard with a jagged scar down his cheek.

"Nine."

"We are clergy of the Order of Santiago," Pacheco said. "May we depend upon your protection?"

"You'd be better to take up a spare sword and help defend," the scarred man said.

Ada wiped sweat from her forehead and looked to the south. The bandits closed in like a deadly swarm. "Give me a sword." She must have looked determined enough—or wild enough— because the guard reached for a second blade at his hip.

"Don't be absurd," Gavriel said. He dumped Fernán on the

packed road and grabbed the huge sword from the bald man.
"Take him and the girl to safety."

She tightened damp palms on the reins. "I'm not getting
off his horse."

"That dagger of yours will do nothing to protect you."

"True. I would've had a sword, but someone just kept it
from me."

He glared at her, temper fraying behind his eyes. "I can't
save a woman intent on meeting her death. Find her something lighter. Smaller."

A squat merchant wearing a white cap hurried from the
nearest wagon and handed her a short sword, its blade gleaming. Ada smiled.

"*Diós* keep you safe," Gavriel muttered, brandishing his
own weapon.

"Gavriel, you cannot," Pacheco said. "Put that away!"

"As a last resort, Master. I swear it."

Ada flashed her eyes between them. "How do you mean,
'as a last resort'? You're a *caballero*, surely!"

"I've taken a vow to abstain from violence."

She looked him up and down. From the width of his shoulders and the tight set of his jaw to the tall, assured way he sat
a horse, he cut the very figure of a man meant for warfare.
"You jest."

Gavriel did not answer. He turned his mount and ran a
quick circle around the wagons, proving right Ada's initial as-
sessment: he could ride without use of the reins. His robes
bunched at his waist and furled in his wake, revealing muscled legs wrapped in close-fitting breeches. Every flex and
move of his thighs directed the animal, leaving hands free to
hold the massive sword and direct the guards.

"You there, close that gap. They'll try to pin us against the
river. Steady!"

She stared in amazement. The guards listened, as did their scarred and hardened leader.

The raiders closed in on the merchant caravan. Tunics dyed to match the browns of La Mancha covered them from head to mid-calf, hoods draping down over close-fitting metal helmets. Some wore quilted armor over their tunics, and full beards covered most of their sun-darkened faces. Their horses trailed the colors of the rainbow from trim, functional saddles. And weapons. So many weapons. The hilts of short knives glittered at waist scabbards. Cavalry axes and swords were drawn and ready.

A heavy pulse clogged Ada's ears. No one in Castile was ignorant of renegade horsemen who lived on the frontier; kidnapping was their sole occupation. They valued Christian women of good breeding, especially, because of the reliable ransoms paid for their safe return. But parties to negotiate ransoms with the outlaws could take months to organize. With Jacob and the condesa in Segovia, no one would realize Ada's absence. She would be a prisoner again. No rescue in sight.

But the sword, the dagger, even the bodies of these men—all would protect her. She would not be taken. She would not be held.

The pounding of the horses' hooves rolled like thunder, ever closer. The raiders attacked with the ferocity of seasoned combatants, their war cries splitting the searing midday air. Fanning out across the plain of battle, the cadre cut down stray sheep and hacked toward the wagons. Steel danced in the sunlight and connected with shields in a thick, irregular cadence. The guards held their ground. Horses screamed. Hooves kicked the sky as their riders dueled.

Master Pacheco huddled with Fernán in one of the wagons. Ada dismounted and tied the reins to a lateral wagon slat. She edged closer to the holy men. Her thighs trembled from wild streaks of fear. A raider sped toward her, blocking her path.

She dropped to her knees and rolled beneath the wagon. Metal cracked above her head and shavings of wood rained down.

Crouched behind the spokes of waist-high wheel, halfway between her horse and the Jacobeans huddling one wagon over, she looked up. A pair of shepherds snuck behind the lone rear guard and pounced, dragging him from his horse. Dark blood sprayed from the guard's neck. His body jerked to sudden stillness.

Ada fought a gorge of rising bile. She had been determined before—*she would not be taken*—but that determination splintered, broken by fear. She had not seen a man killed since she had taken the Sheriff of Nottingham's life. Old memories mingled with that nightmare scene, stealing the strength in her hands. She looked down and saw the sword, gripped tight in her palm, but she could no longer feel her fingers.

She searched the noisy, furious scene for a tall man in white robes. Gavriel circled his horse, waiting, not attacking, his face a twisted mask of conflicted emotions. He held to his vow, yes, but the effort was written like words across his pinched lips and narrowed eyes.

"Gavriel!"

He whipped his head toward her and raised his sword.

She peaked out from beneath the wagons. "The shepherds! It's a trap!"

Chapter 4

The vicious brawl faded, slowed, as Gavriel watched an Almohad raider pull Ada from beneath the wagon.

His arm beneath hers, clamped around her chest, the bandit dragged her onto his horse and stripped her of the short sword. She thrashed and kicked, but he held fast until she sat on his lap. His free hand wove into her long tangles and yanked back, baring her neck. He pressed a knife there, the horse's dancing steps shifting the blade, tempting disaster.

Gavriel jerked hard on the reins and turned his mount toward the fray. Everywhere guards fought bandits, thrusting and shouting desperate orders to one another. He wove through the confusion, past the laden wagons and the cowering, ashen-faced merchants. His eyes never left the knife at Ada's throat.

That is, until another glint of metal sliced across his view.

Her flailing hands had not been searching for balance but for her jeweled dagger. She knocked her head back, connecting with the raider's nose just as she jammed the dagger into his thigh. The man shrieked. She used the moment when his hands went slack to snake free.

She jumped without grace to the ground, rolling in a tangle

of skirts, rolling again, getting clear. Gavriel lifted his sword. Once, he would have decapitated the man. He would have enjoyed watching the villain drop, headless and bloody— a threat dispatched.

But he had vows to keep.

The bandit blanched at the sight of Gavriel bearing down on him and put up his hands. Ada grabbed his leather belt and yanked him to his knees with one fierce pull. She retrieved her dagger from the fallen man's leg and ended his life.

Gavriel could only stare, mouth agape.

She stood and wiped the blade along her skirts, then turned to him. Eyes that had once tempted him with a false peace raged with wild madness. Her voice was lower as she asked, "What stayed your hand?"

"My vows."

"I have vows of my own," she said. "I'll never be held captive again."

The pair of shepherds jumped between them. Gavriel kicked one man in the head, sending him in a twirling flight to the dirt. The second lunged and caught Ada's gown, ripping the linen down her back. She spun in an erratic dance and caught the man's hand, biting down hard. He screamed, then elbowed her hard in the chest. She collapsed and gasped.

Gavriel spurred his horse. Leaning low, he looped his arm around the shepherd's neck and squeezed, dragging him off the ground. The muscles of his right arm protested. His writhing prisoner kicked and gagged, his face darkening to a sickly purple. The horse carried them into to the rushing current of the Tagus. Gavriel shrugged free of the scraping, sputtering man, and watched him flail in the waist-high water.

He veered back to the skirmish. Only three guards remained and as many bandits.

And Ada—Ada had climbed atop Fernán's horse once again, riding hard to the west.

* * *

With the furious howl of air rushing past her ears, Ada could hear nothing else. Crouching low, urging more speed from her tiring mount, she chanced a look behind her. She had hoped to reach a village or perhaps another caravan, but Gavriel dogged her every cut and jump. His horse gained, charging as if it did not carry a muscled male rider and his hefty sword.

She had killed a man. Her second. The fresh image of blood and the glint of jewels merged with old nightmares and gave them new life. How often had she tried to force those gruesome pictures into a box in her mind, memories of what Finch had done to her?

Although she wanted to close her eyes against the terror, her safety atop the sprinting horse claimed her attention. The terror would wait, as it always did.

The thunder of her mount's hooves gained strength. No, a harmony. Gavriel had bridged the entire distance. Ada veered her horse toward an irrigation ditch and cut hard to the left. Propelled by momentum, Gavriel had no choice but to make the jump over the channel. She pushed several hundred lengths between them by the time he slowed, circled, and followed in pursuit.

She rode without destination. The plateau stretched in all directions, a flat and endless prison. No village. No caravan. Never had she experienced a moment so wide and open. It should have made her brave, set her free, but she recognized the inevitable. Her horse would tire. She would be left to the whims of the harsh mesa—its foul weather and bandits—with nothing but a dagger and an exhausted animal.

She straightened and pulled the reins. The horse slowed beneath her, its flanks lathered and chest heaving. The wind tugged at her ruined gown where it flapped open across her back, offering relief from the heat. Her hands were sticky, and a taste like the bitter rind of a lime coated her tongue.

Gavriel caught up with her even before she could crawl out of the saddle and crumple into the tall, wild grasses.

"Why did you flee?"

Gavriel's nostrils flared with every harsh inhale. When he went to dismount, his robes caught on the pommel. He whipped the abused linen over his head and tossed it into the grass. Dark woolen breeches clung to lean legs. A tunic, dyed blue like the color of a midnight sky, stretched across his wide chest and draped past his hips. The ties at his throat dangled open, revealing a glimpse of his chest—paler skin and dark hair.

"I knew you were a man beneath those robes. Care to remove any more?"

He grabbed her upper arms and pulled her to unsteady feet. Her pulse throbbed in the soles of her feet, a ghostly pain.

"I asked you a question," he said.

"I was breathless with fright."

Dark eyes scrutinized her. Cheeks, mouth, forehead, and back again. "You're mocking me."

"Of course. I was running from you and you know it."

"You killed that man."

Blood and shining jewels. Death throes. Weeks of isolation ending in fire. She pushed those memories aside and focused on her mysterious menace. Gavriel. Playing with him was more entertaining. And if she had any chance of returning to Toledo, she needed to learn more about him.

"Me? Kill a man? Are you sure you didn't mistake me for someone else?"

He scowled, pointing to the scene of the attack. "I saw you!"

"But it couldn't have been me, *señor*. My dagger is of no use. You said as much. And I'm but a woman."

He stood there, his face a mask and his finger still pointing in mid-air. Only when she smiled did he react—not with violence or more irate words. He simply stepped away, crossed himself, and knelt. He lowered his head. She could not make out every word he mumbled, but the meaning was clear.

For the span of a breath, surrounded by endless crops and grasses, covered from neck to knees with a dead man's drying blood, she wanted to tap him on the shoulder and beg a favor.

Pray for me, too.

Ridiculous.

She searched Fernán's saddlebags and found a half-filled flask of young ale. She drank with greedy gulps, then poured some on her hands to wash away what she had done. To no avail. Fingers, palms, forearms—all remained inked in sticky red.

"Would you like to make confession?"

She yelped. "Do you sneak up on people at the monastery? Or are you too busy maintaining vows of silence?"

"I'm under no such obligation."

"Are there other vows I should know about?"

"Chastity," he said, his voice thick. "I've sworn chastity as well."

"I'm not surprised."

A tremor of cold shook through her limbs, suddenly stealing her attention. A quick glance at the sky revealed no change in the weather. Only more sun, more wind. The shiver had been on the inside. And again. Her hands jerked and the flask landed on the ground, spilling the ale.

Oh, please. No.

Gavriel held fast to his patience. Barely. The moment of prayer had done wonders while he was still kneeling. But standing before her undid all of his calm, especially because her gown hung loosely around her shoulders, open at the back. He had resolved to be strong and of use to his new charge, this peevish woman, but her every gesture was a threat: You'll break your vows.

Unacceptable.

He retrieved another flask from his own saddle. "Put out your hands. Let me help."

"Gramercy, I'll do it myself."

"Do you think because I've taken vows to obey and abstain from violence that I cannot be strong?"

A smile pulled the corners of her lips, dimpling one cheek. The left one. "You cannot fight or lose your temper or lie with a woman? However do you find a release?"

"Prayer and contemplation."

She reached between their bodies and touched his forearm. Her fingers became snakes slithering up to his bicep. "Does that work?"

"Better than opium."

Her twisted smile widened. "Have you tried it?"

"No," he said, shrugging free of her distracting touch. "But I can see that it brings you only a false peace."

"It's not false. Not if I . . ." She shivered once and dropped her head.

"What?"

She inhaled, the breath hunching her shoulders. "'Tis not false as long as I have more."

Gavriel tipped up her chin. "That took quite some courage to admit."

She jerked away. "That was no admission, you simpleton— merely the truth. If you men of merit wouldn't keep it from me, I would feel better. I would *be* better."

She balled the cloth in her trembling hands. Ball, clench, release. Ever more trembling. Her eyes had clouded. They rolled and jumped, skittering.

"*Inglesa,* are you well?"

"Of course not! This is your fault. You and your mission, dragging me away from the world!"

"Away from the nearest apothecary, you mean."

"Yes! You could've left me be. I would've been fine." She sneered and spat at his feet. "Better than being here with you."

Energy pulsed from her body in steady waves. Her eyes moved in ever-faster skips and jumps, refusing to rest. The long night, during which he would have to keep her from harming herself or anyone else, stretched ahead like a never-ending journey.

"We should ride back to the others," he said quietly. "We'll go to the archbishop's villa in Yepes. You can change clothes."

"I want to go home."

"Home is Uclés—for one month. I've told you that."

"Madness. You're a fool and a hypocrite and a bore and—"

"I thought I might be of assistance to you, but I was wrong. I cannot even get you to wash your hands!" He dropped the corked flask to her feet. "Godspeed, *inglesa*."

"No! Don't leave. I'll do whatever you want."

"And what would you do?"

Ada threaded her fingers into her hair, down to the scalp. When she raised her eyes, she flung her hands away and laughed, her mood a shifting wind.

"I'll do anything," she said, a stranger's smile warping her mouth. "Name your price, novice. Out this far from the others, we could do a great deal."

Gavriel scowled first, glad to know his initial reaction to such a brazen proposal was outrage. But the fear and the shock of desire followed closely behind. He wrestled both into submission. "I want nothing of your bawdy offers, *mujer*."

"So pious."

"I'm trying, yes."

"No, you're lying to yourself."

He tethered his hands to the reins. "'Tis no concern of yours."

"Forgive me," she said with a sneer. "I'm more accustomed to dealing with *men*, not servants of God."

"You're accustomed to dealing with a lovesick boy who could not refuse you. I'm no such boy, and I want you to use your manners."

"Manners?"

"Yes. When you ask my help, you'll say 'please'."

Her eyes lost their brightness. Every drop of blue melted into an overcast gray. "Never."

"I won't offer my assistance again," he said. "Do this willingly, or you'll spite yourself much worse than I ever could."

"And that will cure me?"

"Eventually."

"I'd kill you first," she said.

"But I want you cured more than you want your poison."

"I very much doubt that."

"And when the next band of renegades comes this way, they'll number too many for you to defend against."

A quiet voice, one unlike any he had ever heard, crept across the mesa. "But then I might have an end to all this."

An unwanted flicker of sympathy and a stronger, more nourishing anger propelled his words. "Do you seek death, *inglesa*? Is that what you crave?"

She retreated one step, then two. "You know what I need. The alternative is going without, and that I cannot do. Not again."

"You're a coward."

"And what would you know of bravery, hiding away from the world?"

The image of a battlefield dotted with corpses and fallen horses appeared in his mind's eye. Alarcos. That heady victory. He had been as brave as ten men on that long day, slaying enemies with glee and impunity. His bravery had bordered on bloodlust, devoid of thought or humanity. But to what end? He had been on the winning side, but those who had fallen under his sword had been Castilians.

He was a better man now, denying that barbaric part of him.

"I'm a student, learning to submit. As must you."

"I will not—"

Before Ada had a chance to finish, he grabbed her forearm and spun her. Their bodies came together, her bare back against his chest.

"I asked you before," he rasped. "Now I'll have that answer. Do you want to die?"

"Release me!"

"Submit, *inglesa*." Closer now, he pulled up on her arm. She winced.

"I will not."

Her dagger flashed in the sunlight and sliced through his sleeve and skin. Blood welled red and fast. Tensing against the pain, he snatched the blade and slung it to the ground.

The memory of her agonized voice punched into his mind, through the pain and past his frustrations. *I will not be held captive again.*

Gavriel had known captivity, and the very idea of returning to the service of his former master chilled him. He would rather die. Whatever this woman had suffered backed her toward the same conclusion. Death was better than captivity. And while Gavriel tried to find comfort in submission, she only saw it as weakness. Another trap.

"You don't want to die, but you cannot live with the fear." He turned her to face him. Their eyes met across an ocean of anger. "That's why you fight, isn't it? Likely, it's how you've learned what you know of combat."

She nodded, just barely.

"Then let me help you."

Chapter 5

Help. This was his idea of help?

Ada glared at the back of Gavriel's head. He rode high on his steed, keeping company with his morals, while she walked behind the horses, tethered like a criminal. The harder she fought against the ropes binding her wrists, the tighter the knots became. A second, shorter piece of rope laced the back of her gown shut. She would have sworn his hands shook as he had worked in quiet diligence to make her decent.

The caravan merchants had crawled from beneath their wagon hiding places to assess the damage. Two of the guards still lived, as did Pacheco and Fernán. The latter appeared an unbecoming shade of green. Streaks of vomit sullied his white robes.

Down from his horse, Gavriel stalked from wagon to wagon and appraised the scene with a quick, intense gaze. She watched as he checked each corpse. He moved as if he had often patrolled the aftermath of a battle, wary of continued threats.

"This one yet lives," he said to a guard.

"For but a moment longer." The guard performed his duty with an unsteady hand.

"What happened to the others?" Gavriel asked, his face grim but composed. "There are only seven dead here."

The guard pointed to the south. "They fled."

Their conversation faded for Ada as she suffered another bout of trembling. Limbs and bone became a quivering mass. The ground did not feel as hard as it should when she melted into the thorny grass: Cold. Thirst. Violent dizziness. She shivered, the sky moving in sickening circles.

"What ails her?" asked the guard.

"She's unwell. Nothing more."

Pacheco hovered nearby. "What happened? Why is she bound?"

Gavriel hesitated. She watched with detached amusement as he grappled for a response. But the mocking laughter in her head found no voice.

"For her own good, Master." Gavriel knelt beside her and pushed the hair from her face. With a quick move, he untied the knots at her wrists. "Get her a blanket, Fernán."

"I don't want your blanket," she said past chattering teeth.

He exhaled, looking more than a little lost. "Will you walk to Yepes?"

"I cannot."

"You will, if you do not relent. And you'll say 'please'."

"I'll not beg."

"Then you have a long road ahead of you." He accepted the blanket from Fernán and held it out to her. "What say you, *inglesa?*"

She slumped back and dug her fingers into the dirt and grass. "Fiend."

He stood, his face carved of stone. She closed her eyes and remembered lying on the pallet she had once shared with Meg, at home in England. Ada had dried wildflowers in colorful bunches and hung them from the ceiling beams. As night fell, she would watch the shadows they cast in the flickering firelight. When daylight returned, their muted, subtle colors offered places of brightness in the forest and in the life she had resented.

But what she would give to have that life returned to her. And rain. She missed the rain.

She had not been home for more than a year, having burned bridges with terrible and bitter efficiency. And now Jacob was gone too. She had no one and nothing, plagued by a bizarre novice and his strange determination to see her cured.

Part of her wanted to relent. He would help her through the worst of the withdrawal. Despite his temper, he was motivated by an unknown need to win their battle of wills, not by an impulse to do her harm.

But the part of her that wanted help was not as noisy or brutal as her craving. If Gavriel stood between her and the opium she needed, he was her enemy. He was her captor. The monastery at Uclés could be like heaven on earth and she would still regard it as a prison.

"Gavriel, help her." Pacheco was not so tall, and despite his age and position of authority, he seemed to be asking the novice to comply.

Tell him. Make *him help me.*

Gavriel seemed to have heard her silent demand. He forced her uncooperative limbs to work, to stand. Strong arms offered support, banding her lower back and pulling her close. Heat from his body soothed her chills. She ached to push closer, hold tighter—any relief from the gathering storm inside her.

"Come now." The deep, quiet timbre of his voice, so near to kindness, threatened to start her crying. "Stand for me. Good. Now keep your feet." He forced a scant distance between their bodies and met her unfocused gaze. "You'll need to be strong. Yepes is quite a distance to walk."

She stumbled. "You're a monster!"

"I'm helping you, whether you see that or not."

"How? By making a sick woman walk?"

"By curing the sickness you've brought on yourself." His wide and muscular chest blocked the sun, blocked thought. "I told you, in this I will not be deterred."

Reflexively, she touched the petite sheath at her hip. She needed to feel the reassurance of its cold metal. Safety. But it was empty.

"Where's my dagger?"

"I have it."

"You cannot keep it!"

"I won't let you cut me again." He lifted his forearm and pinned her with an excruciating glare.

Ada blanched at the damage she had done. A clean slice scored half the length of his forearm, crusted with drying blood. She touched it with wobbling fingers, gently. He hissed but did not flinch. Tendons flexed on the inside of his wrist.

He deserved what she had done, or so she tried to believe. But all hard flesh and power, doing him harm seemed an affront to nature.

"I've yet to hear an apology."

Ada swallowed. "You never will."

"We must continue," said Pacheco. "Nightfall approaches."

Gavriel nodded. "Master, has anyone retrieved the cart?"

"It was burned and the donkey taken." He handed Gavriel a canvas sack and Ada's satchel. "But we've protected most of our belongings."

Fernán, pale except for the dark circles below his eyes, raised his brows. "And where will she ride? Perhaps I could make room on my saddle."

"She'll walk. Seems the lady prefers it that way." Gavriel stalked to his horse and climbed up. He stared at her, unrelenting and cold. "And if you refuse, I'll not hesitate to bind your wrists again."

Pacheco shook his head. "Gavriel, you—"

"Master, please. If this is my obligation, allow me to proceed as I see fit—as long as I act within the bounds of the Order. Trust that I can do this." He waited. They waited. Even the merchants and the remaining guards watched the contest. "Do I have your permission to proceed, Master?"

"Yes, Gavriel. Do as you see fit."

Gavriel turned to Ada, his face without emotion. "Will you come to Yepes or stay here with the caravan?"

The beast had the nerve to abduct her under the guise of a clergyman's goodwill, wrenching her from of the pleasures she had enjoyed. So be it. He would offer diversion until she was free to return to Toledo. Then she would wring Jacob's idealistic neck.

"Yepes it is," she said, smiling sweetly. The flicker of panic on his face assuaged her ragged pride. "Lead the way, novice."

Yes, she would enjoy pulling him down to the ground. He was not who he longed to be, and she would prove it. She would make Gavriel de Marqueda break each of his precious vows.

They came to Yepes an hour before nightfall. Long shadows stretched behind each squat building, the western faces burnished by fading gold. Never had Gavriel been so relieved to see a day come to an end. Any more surprises and he would lose his footing completely.

He glanced back, a gesture he had repeated often enough to cramp the right side of his neck. Ada still followed. Head bowed, her hair like a curtain over her pale face, she trudged with the resignation of an animal to slaughter. The fact she walked at all was proof of her continued defiance. Her feet dropped heavily with each step, her arms dangling uselessly at her sides. Perhaps she would collapse into sleep without another confrontation.

He should be so lucky.

But the question of *where* she would sleep had nettled him for three hours. Sleeping alone was not an option for the unpredictable trickster. No, she was predictable. She would try to escape.

"Gavriel!"

He turned. Pacheco and Fernán both looked back to where Ada lay crumpled on the road. Gavriel jumped from the horse and chewed the scant distance between them, anger adding speed to his long strides. Another trick. Her insufferable antics tested his patience nearly as much as her—well, all of her. Almost.

But it was no trick. Cold and pale, her skin shimmered with sweat. Irregular breaths jerked her chest. Her whole body shook. Fine tremors, full shudders—even this black sleep could not keep her still. A trickle of blood oozed from the base of her skull. She must have hit her head when she collapsed.

Gavriel choked on a mouthful of bitter guilt. He had been certain of his course. But what did he know of opium or of women? As for medicine, he had only ever tended war wounded, patching holes and gashes, not invisible hurts. She brought out the stubborn worst in him, leading him to think in terms of combat, not compassion. An enemy. Someone keeping him from his objective. How could he save her, thinking that way?

The thought of touching her was no less worrying. Having been raised knowing only fists and swords, the shock of touch—his skin against the skin of another—still had the power to shake him to the core. He missed his isolation. The certainty of it.

But she needed someone.

Cradling Ada's head, he lifted her trembling body and fought the tremor of disquiet at holding her. He returned to the horse and shoved their satchels out of the way. Pacheco assisted in settling them both onto the saddle. Her body pulsed with an unnatural heat and her head flopped back. She cried out as the muscles in her belly convulsed. Gavriel pulled her closer to his chest and began to pray, not for himself but for this woman who had strayed so far.

Upon reaching the walls surrounding the small city of Yepes, Pacheco consulted with the guards and secured their entry. They proceeded through the darkening streets. Merchants concluded their business for the day, packing their stands and closing modest shops. As with most towns on the plateau, once governed by the Moorish regimes of the south, its citizens comprised an uneasy mix of cultures. *Convivencia,* the subtle art of living and prospering among diverse peoples. On that evening, beneath a clear, cool sky, it seemed both easy and right.

Pacheco led the way to the villa owned by the Archbishop of Toledo. Constructed in the style of the Mudéjar, a square tower decorated with intricate brickwork and glazed ceramics looked over the wide residence. Beyond its walls, fields of wine grapes were just beginning to bear fruit. They passed through a series of arched entrances to where a dozen attendants waited.

"Greetings, Brother Pacheco." Short and round, the archbishop's majordomo, Miguel Latorre, wore dark, billowing robes trimmed in red. He compulsively stroked a full and well-groomed beard. A reading stone dangled from a gold chain at his waist. "The archbishop is not in residence this evening, but permit me to offer our hospitality on his behalf."

Pacheco smiled and bowed as groomsmen led the horses to adjoining stables. "We seek another night's shelter on our return to the monastery."

"Of course."

Although he spoke to Pacheco, Latorre's deeply set eyes flicked to where Ada draped in Gavriel's arms. Gavriel had never liked the officious little toad, a sentiment that did not alter as he stood there, desiring only a place to ease Ada through the night.

Pacheco noticed the man's curiosity. "Ah, yes. This is our new slave. She is unwell, and we should like a private room for her."

Latorre covered his mouth and nose and peered closer. "Unwell? Is it catching?"

"No, we would not dream of bringing a contagion into your midst," Pacheco said, his voice nearly bare of politeness. "But we should like to get her settled."

Latorre turned his small black eyes to Gavriel, assessing him as he would a horse for sale. "Has she a chaperone?"

Pacheco colored red. Gavriel held Ada as his shield against mounting frustrations. Fernán pressed his back to the nearest wall, his eyes lifted to the high woodwork and painted plaster ceiling. A smile graced his thin face, the first he had worn since the Almohad raid.

"No," said Pacheco with a sigh. "She has no chaperone."

"On the road from Toledo, we were attacked by those intent on kidnapping. Local shepherds aided them in setting the trap." Gavriel shot his novice master a dark look, willing him to keep quiet. "Her chaperone . . . well, you understand."

"I see. Pardon my disrespect." Latorre cleared his throat. "But you are a novice, are you not? Where are your robes?"

Arms aching, he glared at the squat man. "I believe I mentioned we were attacked. If you should like to see the injury on my arm, I'll be glad to offer proof."

The majordomo paled but did not put his fussy manners aside. "All for the sake of propriety, I assure you. I shall have our personal physic see to her, just to be certain."

"She needs no doctor, only rest," Gavriel said.

Ada moaned. Latorre skittered back. "You'll forgive me if I don't believe you," he said.

"'Tis not my place to forgive you."

Pacheco stepped between them, a look of warning on his aged face. "We appreciate your kindness. Please, send for your doctor and have your people show us to our rooms."

Latorre bowed and departed through a nearby archway, his gaggle of attendants close behind. Pacheco said under his breath, "You lied to him."

"No. I said, we were attacked. He made his own assumptions."

"This isn't right, Gavriel."

Fernán, always climbing out of the shadows when the confrontation had passed, stepped away from the wall. "Let him say what he will, Master. 'Tis that or sleep in the stables. I prefer a pallet to hay myself, but I cannot speak for everyone. What say you, Gavriel?"

"I say you talk too much."

Pacheco held up a hand to silence them both. "Latorre is right to wonder where she will sleep. None of us can stay with her."

Gavriel knelt and gently stretched Ada along the polished marble floor. His arms shook from the exertion. But his trembling was nothing to hers.

"She is a danger to herself," Gavriel said. "Would you rather have her sick, on her own? Or have her recover before dawn and try to escape again?"

"What would you suggest?" Pacheco asked.

"Perhaps this physician might recommend a woman who can stay with her."

Pacheco nodded and exhaled. "Good."

Rolling his shoulders, Gavriel caught sight of the bloody gash on his forearm. It burned with a slow and persistent ache. "What did you expect, Master? That I would stay with her myself?"

Fernán grinned. "I was about to offer my services, actually. I'm a renowned nursemaid."

"Cavorting with nursemaids doesn't qualify you as one," Gavriel said.

"You know nothing of the mystic arts of healing."

Pacheco looked heavenward and mumbled quick prayer. "I'm going to find whatever slothful attendant is to show us to our rooms."

He turned and strode along the wide corridor. Fernán knelt next to Ada, his face momentarily composed and somber. "She's in a terrible way. Can you do this, man?"

Ada thrashed once and moaned again. She needed cool water and a soft place to rest, not delays and intrusive questions. Gavriel looked at Fernán, almost wishing for the return of his wretched sense of humor. At least that would be normal. And he desperately craved normal.

"I must, Fernán. This is my duty."

God help me.

Chapter 6

Fernán Garza stretched on his pallet. The sight of those bloody and limp corpses on the roadside danced in his brain, no matter how many times he rubbed his eyes. He should have fainted.

Pacheco, however, seemed untroubled by the surprising bout of violence. The novice master smoothed his robes, checking here and there, picking lint from one sleeve before sitting on his pallet. No concern marred his wrinkled skin and neutral expression. Fernán continued to watch his easy demeanor, all the while staunching the need to vomit again.

"Sleep now, Fernán. All will be well come morning."

Fernán thought maybe, perhaps, on some deep level, he should take offense that a man of advanced years such as Pacheco would feel the need to coddle him. But no, the offense never came. Being coddled was far preferable to the time-honored notions of strength, nobility—or God forbid—making one's own way.

And besides, Pacheco knew his secrets. No sense in resisting.

Sinking into the stiff straw of his pallet, Fernán glanced one more time at the door. "Master, you cannot truly expect Gavriel to look after that woman."

"And why not?"

"The trial is unjust. Cruel, even."

Deeply damaged and unpredictable, the Englishwoman possessed the face of an angel and the body of the most sumptuous harlot. The idea of spending time in her company without taking advantage of those rare female attributes was too severe to contemplate—even for Fernán, who had one beautiful, compelling reason to confine his desire to bawdy jests.

"She's quite a woman, Master," he said. "Even you must see that. I cannot think any of our lot could gird himself against one such as her."

Pacheco leveled cold black eyes, eyes that made for an eerie contrast with his curtailed silver hair. "Nor do I expect Gavriel to."

"You—?" Fernán lost track of his customary glibness, at a loss for words. Uncomfortably so. Ignoring the trickle of sweat along his spine, he tried not to cower. "You want him to fail? It would be a waste of my breath to ask why, I suppose?"

"Quite."

He grinned. "But Master, why not give her to me? If failure is imminent, I would enjoy the fall far more than Gavriel."

"We both know that's a lie," Pacheco said, rising from his pallet. "I want you to keep your mouth shut. No, let me correct that: Prattle on as you always do. No one listens to your nonsense."

"Surely, and of course."

"But I expect discretion." He took Fernán's chin in one hand, twisting slightly, pulling his gaze up. "All you have to do is consider the alternative."

Fernán tried to smile again, anything to crawl from under Pacheco's condemning stare, but the smile he managed felt warped and melted.

Pacheco finally let him loose. He turned to a squat table

and poured a mug of wine. While the novice master drank deeply, Fernán rubbed the bruised skin along his jaw.

"Gavriel is a grim sod, but I pity him."

"Do not," Pacheco said. "He's bound for greater purposes."

"You speak in puzzles, for certain. What would the Grand Master think if he heard you say such things?"

Pacheco's eyes narrowed. Every breath flared his nostrils like an angered bull. Aging hands that bore no calluses, only pale blue lines beneath leathery skin, clenched into fists. Fernán had thought the man incapable of committing the same violence they had witnessed on the roadside, but he altered that opinion.

"Remember your tongue and where your loyalties lie," Pacheco said, his voice unyielding. "Not with the Order. Not with the Grand Master. With me. I determine your future. That is, unless you'd rather I reveal to your father the location of your Moorish bastard."

Najih. His son.

"Ah," Fernán said unsteadily, bringing shaky fingers to his throat. "I'm hearing threats. At least, I believe them to be threats. Alas, I am as dumb a fool as ever you saw."

Pacheco grinned, a predator toying with its next meal. "And I have never expected more from you."

Gavriel laid Ada on a fresh pallet, her room across a corridor from the one Pacheco and Fernán shared. He dropped their satchels. Compared to the modest accommodations of the Jacobean house in Toledo, this room was sumptuous and smelled of sweet straw, incense, and herbs dusted among the floor rushes. Dark murals adorned the smooth plaster walls; it was a cool and private retreat illuminated by a pair of oil lamps.

His burden discharged, Gavriel should have turned and

walked away. Weariness and his inner turmoil demanded rest. But he could not leave, not until she was cared for.

Ada's shivering would not abate. Looking around the room, he found a thick sheepskin throw. He draped the heavy mantle over her and knelt to touch her forehead. Cold skin, still, but slicked with foul sweat. A most abnormal fever.

He set about attending the wound at the base of her skull. Her scalp bled considerably, binding the hairs at her nape in a sticky mass, but the cut was shallow and no longer than one of his fingernails. He washed the area with cool water and a strip of linen until he was satisfied the bleeding had stopped.

She gasped. Pale lids opened wide to reveal panicked blue eyes, her pupils shrunken to tiny points. Her hands flailed wildly as she struggled to sit up. "No! Don't cut me again!"

Gavriel dropped the cloth and held her wrists. The sudden gentleness he found within himself came as a surprise. She was sick and lost—and he could understand being lost.

"*Inglesa. Inglesa,* settle yourself."

She fought him, albeit with less strength. "You'll let him cut me. Don't! I haven't done anything wrong!"

"Ada," he said, her name feeling heavy and unfamiliar on his tongue. "Calm yourself. I'm here to offer aid."

Her struggles eased, those blue eyes still wide and shimmering with tears. "You won't let him?"

"Let him what? Who? Who cut you?" He glanced around the room. "See, no one else is here. Do you remember who I am?"

She sank into the pallet, overcome by ceaseless tremors, but she studied his face with something akin to her previous, sharp-minded thinking. She was in there, whoever she was. And she was suffering.

"You are Gavriel."

The words rattled past her chattering teeth, a surprise. But more surprising was his reaction to hearing his name from the disturbed woman. A warmth like anticipation spread across his chest. Whether he awaited danger or pleasure he could not know.

"Yes," he said.

"Gavriel, my captor." Her unfocused eyes veered to the ceiling. "My feet ache. Will you remove my boots?"

He rubbed his eyes, clinging to his dwindling patience.

"Need a moment to pray?" She stretched on the pallet, arms above her head. "Although I can't imagine why you might ask for divine intervention. They're only boots. And you're only offering aid."

"You enjoy baiting me. Why?"

"A man who sets himself apart as purer than anyone else is asking to be brought low."

He stood, jaw aching. "You intend to bring me low?"

"If I must. All I want is to be free of here and to make my own choices."

"So you can choose more opium? That's not freedom."

"You righteous—"

"Stop." He stalked to the end of the pallet and began to unlace her boots. "I'll feel more inclined to help if you cease the name-calling."

"I've said I don't want your help."

He opened his hands. Her foot dropped to the bed. "Then take off your own boots."

Ada raised her upper lip in a snarl and threw back the mantle. She swung her feet to the floor, hiked her skirts to the knee, and knelt over the complicated leather laces. Her fingers grasped and fumbled, too impaired to unravel the mystery of those knots. She yanked hard, whimpering. The shaking increased until she could hardly stay seated on the edge of the pallet. Her foul cry split the air.

Gavriel knelt and caught her shoulders, steadying her. He said nothing, only met her eyes and slowly shook his head. She looked away, a silent acquiescence. He lifted her foot to rest on his thighs, making short work of the puzzle that had thwarted her so completely. He urged her to lie back, her feet bare. Only when he went to replace the sheepskin mantle over her lower body did he notice the long, matching scars on her soles.

A vice pinched his chest. She flinched when he traced one silvery scar, heel to toe. He needed to swallow twice before finding his voice, an unsteady one at that. "*Inglesa,* what happened to your feet?"

"He cut me," she said, her voice faraway.

"The man who held you captive?"

She sighed. "Yes. And now he's dead."

"Who was he?"

The door to her room clanked opened to reveal a slim man and a stout, whey-faced nun. The man held more in common with a bird than a person, all sharp angles and quick movements. A hummingbird, perhaps. Agitated. And all without an introduction.

"What seems to be the concern, *señorita?*" he asked.

Ada burrowed deeper within the shelter of the sheepskin. "What do they want?"

Gavriel glared when the man pushed him aside, the nun bumping into place beside him. "This is the physician, I assume. Here to help."

Apparently.

Ada would not look at the newcomers. She worried her chapped lower lip and pinned Gavriel with a look of wild fear. "I hardly want *you* here, let alone strangers."

The bird puffed up the feathers of his dark robes. "I'm no stranger," he said. "I'm a physician, a servant of God sent to tend your sickness."

"I've been hearing that entirely too often," she said.

When the physician put a hand to her forehead, she drew back with a hiss. Gavriel watched with growing irritation as the man treated her with less consideration than would a shepherd inspecting his livestock. Ada withstood the curt appraisal longer than he would have imagined—that is, longer than a breath or two.

"Stop touching me!"

The physician blanched at her ear-splitting command and jerked his hand away. "She is clearly disturbed and suffering from a fever. Her humors are out of balance and must be corrected."

Gavriel curled a fist to his mouth. "Corrected how?"

"We would make an incision—"

"Cut me?" Ada's face turned the color of ash.

"No, no, no. Nonsense." The physician waved his arms to placate her distress, flapping the wings of his waist-long sleeves. "A bloodletting is healthful and restorative, not at all to be feared."

"No!" Ada tried to jump clear, but with the stout build of a peasant farmhand, the nun seized her shoulders and pinned her to the pallet. "Let go of me! You can't do this!"

The nun glanced over to Gavriel, her veiled headdress set askew by Ada's violent struggles. "I'll need your help to hold her steady."

He shook his head tightly, his gut in a knot. "*Por favor*, wait a moment—"

"Young man," the doctor said, his voice reeking of condescension. "No matter the origin of her illness, she is not at all like herself. Do not expect her to react sensibly to proven techniques."

Frowning, Gavriel tossed his gaze between Ada's wild panic and the dispassionate duo. "Why shouldn't the origin of her illness matter?"

"I am the physician to the Archbishop of Toledo, and I do not appreciate—"

"Gavriel!"

Ada cuffed her female foe and stumbled from the bed,

pushing past the startled physician. The nun lunged after her, fleeter of foot than Gavriel would have guessed, but she landed on her side, arms empty. He caught Ada and twirled her down to the floor. She hugged closer, a mass of shaking limbs and sobs.

"Give her to me," the nun said, standing and rubbing her hip. "Or I shall call in the guards."

Gavriel denied her demand with a dark glare. "Wait. Both of you."

"Don't let them," Ada whispered. He had a difficult time understanding her, between the shivering and her unusual accent, but her fear was tangible. The sweat on her skin even smelled different—potent, almost corrosive. "I would rather die tonight than bear his cure."

"*Inglesa,* if it's for the best."

Feverish eyes met his. She panted, briefly managing to quell the tremors. "Have I begged anything of you? I'm begging now. *Please.*"

He closed an arm around her shoulders, angling his body between her and the red-faced physician. The nun stood as tall as she could muster and looked ready to pounce. Whatever frustration or confusion he had felt only moments before was replaced by a single, instinctual demand: protect.

"I want you out of this room," he said quietly.

"You cannot be in earnest," the physic said. "This woman's humors must be balanced or she will suffer the consequences. They are a threat to her health."

"And to the health of others." The nun's face had squished into a mask of displeasure beneath her crooked headdress.

Gavriel glanced down at Ada. She had curled into herself, clinging to his arm as if to a branch in a raging stream. "Can that be done without the bloodletting?" he asked.

"Bloodletting is the most effective—"

"Out," Gavriel said. "Now. Before I assist you."

"You cannot—"

"Cutting her is unacceptable. I asked for alternatives, and you provided none."

The physician sputtered, his eyebrows twitching like dun-colored caterpillars. But the nun found voice enough to speak for both of them. "We will inform Señor Latorre about this, as well as your novice master. This disrespect will not be tolerated."

"I will not be intimidated by your threats. Now get out."

The door closed behind them with a force just short of slamming. The nun's chattering indignation echoed behind the heavy oak partition and down the corridor, blending with the slashing tempest of noise in Ada's head. The screams of goblins, the cries of babies—they demanded the same thing. More. More opium. Anything to silence the noise, end the pain, banish the nightmares.

She huddled closer to Gavriel, if such a thing were possible. She wore him, a second skin. Sweat covered her like drenching rain but not nearly so clean or refreshing. And still she felt cold, ever more cold—the kind that gnaws on bones and invades even the most restful sleep. He was her tormentor and her captor, yet he offered the warmth of his body and stood against those who would do her harm.

Could it get any worse?

Yes, when she did the worst to herself.

"Why did you do it?"

Gavriel shook his head and met her gaze with a frown. English again. She had never experienced such trouble with her translations. Keeping thoughts straight and in the proper dialect burdened her, just like the bootlaces—simple things she knew like breathing. But even breathing had become a challenge.

I do this to myself.

She sidestepped the thought and saw the face of Sheriff

Finch. *He* had done this to her. And all the while, people like Gavriel judged what she did out of fear and desperation—holy men with more answers than compassion.

Pain burst in her stomach. She cried out and dug fingernails into flesh. His flesh. A corner of her mind recognized his sharp intake of air, but another cramp shoved away every concern. She struggled for a breath that did not pierce and gouge. Colors responded in frantic patterns, crossing but never blending, shooting into her eyes even when she pinched them shut.

Patient hands stroked her hair just as soft words eased past the brunt of her agony. She felt calmer, more in control with that soothing presence. Peering past the mélange of colors, she tried to see if a kindly nurse had entered the room.

But there was only Gavriel. His touch. His words. Him.

Stubborn fool.

She raised a hand above her face, watching it quiver like a flower trembling on its stem. Castilian this time. "Why? Why did you do it?"

"Too many reasons."

"I have nowhere to be." She watched as her feet danced a nervous pattern beyond the hem of her kirtle. Someone else's feet, certainly, except the scars were hers. She felt them still, the burning. A shiver slid under her skin.

Gavriel pulled her upright. His firm grip on her forearms permitted no refusal. "I've learned to obey my superiors in the Order, but no one else. Apparently."

"That's why you saved me? You were stubborn?"

He caught her gaze, looking deep, banishing the garish streaks of color with his dark and steady eyes. "And you said 'please'."

"You require no more?"

He shrugged. "It worked this evening. Perhaps you should keep that in mind for the future."

He stood and scooped her into powerful arms, carrying her as warily as he would a burning log. Another cramp coiled her belly into searing knots. She bent in half and cried out. Gavriel held fast until the pain subsided, his arms as firm as hers were trembling. She sagged against that effortless strength, wishing to siphon it from him and fill her veins.

He laid her gently on the pallet and returned with fresh water from the washbasin. "You'll find another reason less agreeable," he said.

Words spun through her mind in English and Castilian, a mash of language. She grabbed the correct ones and forced her tongue to move. "You know me so well already?"

"I thought you would be able to manipulate the physician into giving you more opium."

She laughed. The unexpected sound fairly jumped from her mouth. Gavriel tensed. But that was not the sound of Ada, a girl from Keyworth; that was an unhinged jester. "I'm not thinking clearly, for I hadn't considered that."

His mouth flattened into a grim line. Even as he sponged the cloth over her forehead, his expression never altered. Did he even know how to smile?

Light stabbed her eyes and pain spiked like an ax at the base of her skull. She flung her arms as if defending against a blow to the face. An earthenware bowl dropped to the ground and shattered. But no maneuver shielded her against the torture of those seizures. She had never come so far before. Never. Jacob had given her what she needed to keep her well. This fiend, this holy hypocrite wanted her to suffer.

"Do you believe this benefits me?"

Gavriel pulled the fists from her eyes. "I look at you, and I wonder who you were."

The openness that softened his expression invited intimacy. In that moment, she trusted him—trusted him with her deepest desire. "May I have opium? Please?"

"No, *inglesa.* I'll refuse you until you can do the same for yourself."

She twisted her neck, left to right to left again. The noise had returned, and she wanted to shake it from her ears. "I'll hate both of us."

"You don't already?"

"It hurts so badly." Arms—hers, it seemed—clenched her middle and tightened. A wolf writhed inside her, snapping its dagger teeth and slashing without mercy. Tears wet her cheeks and hair, mingling with sweat, but her mouth was a dry wasteland. "How did I get this far?"

Gavriel reached an arm around her trembling body, and she sank, sank into that bastion of comfort. Anything to keep from doing this alone. He leaned close, the warm breath of his words skimming over the path made by her tears. "Life takes us to dark places," he said. "We can either stay there until we die, or we can fight free."

"And how did you fight free?"

All tenderness drained from his eyes, like a flask turned upside down and emptied. His arm remained in place and gave her his heat, but there was no mercy to be found in his body of stone and steel. None for her. None for himself.

"Who says I have?"

Gavriel picked up the last shards of the earthenware basin Ada had destroyed. He kept one eye on her still body, watching for her unpredictable return to the world. Her howling pain combined the violence of high tide and thunder and angered demons, all whirling forth from one mindless woman. She had lost track of her tongue an hour before, shouting incoherent phrases in her native language, resorting to shrieks, moans, and wordless pleas.

He slumped to the floor, his back against the oaken door.

His eyelids rolled closed, pulled by the weight of his burdens. He edged toward slumber like a man approaching the lip of a high cliff, walking along, looking over, but never quite stepping into the abyss.

He needed to sleep. But what did she need?

To start, she needed a room made entirely of linen and straw. No sharp edges.

She wanted no one's help, and Gavriel had run clean of options. Short of locking her in a windowless room for weeks, he had no notion of what her care would require. The idea of having to tend to her needs, to break her of the opium sickness clinging to her like death—he could not have chosen a more fearsome task.

The door rattled at his back. "Open up! We demand entry."

Old habits refused to die. No matter how long he had lived in the safety of the monastery, the sudden clamor in the corridor set him in search of a weapon. He had scrambled away and grabbed a sizable shard of earthenware before thought caught up to instinct.

He unlocked the door and stood between Ada and the men who entered: Pacheco, Latorre, the physician, and three armed guards.

He glared at each in turn before settling on Pacheco. The shard pinched the inside of his palm as he squeezed. "She rests for the first time in an hour and you choose now to intrude?"

Pacheco glanced at Ada, then pinned his black glass eyes on Gavriel. "What is this I hear from the physician?"

The bird man puffed out his chest. Gavriel looked him up and down, once, before asking, "Does he even have a name?"

"I am called Mendes, novice, and—"

"He didn't have the courtesy to introduce himself." Gavriel rubbed the back of his neck but found no relief from the festering tension. "And he insisted on performing a bloodletting."

Pacheco's eloquent shrug cast doubt on actions that had

been so clear. "And? If her humors are out of balance, it may be necessary."

"It *is* necessary," Mendes said, his narrow face darkening to the color of thinned wine. "She is clearly disturbed and a threat to everyone here."

Gavriel inhaled. The more he thought about what he had seen and heard and—saints save him—*felt* in her company, the more pressing became the need to escape. But then Mendes made ridiculous comments and his every protective impulse raged to life.

Rage. Yes. He breathed it in, welcoming an old friend.

"Look at her," he said, pointing with the shard. "That sleeping woman is a threat to you?"

"For certain!"

Gavriel stepped closer, bearing down on the scrawny physician with all the force he could reasonably contain. "Then what does that make me?"

The guards drew their weapons.

"Gavriel!" Pacheco's expression remained mild despite the sting of his voice. "You cannot threaten these people! We are guests in this place."

"But perhaps not for long," said Latorre. "This novice deserves discipline for such behavior, Brother Pacheco."

Gavriel tossed the shard to one side, secretly enjoying how each of the three guards flinched behind their weapons. But not only would a disciplinary action mean confinement or fasting—never an inviting prospect—he would be separated from Ada, his trial a disastrous failure. For both their stakes, he banked the rage that had been such a brief indulgence.

He appealed to Pacheco, the only man of the six who might yet be a friend to her cause. "Master, she is . . . she is afraid of being cut."

"'Tis the opium," Pacheco said. "You're letting her speak her mind when she has no mind of her own."

Gavriel flinched, suddenly ashamed for having Ada's ailment spoken aloud. Latorre and Mendes no longer regarded her as a witch or a contagion, but as a creature to be pitied. For Ada's sake, he wanted none of their shame.

He awaited only Pacheco's decision, but he did not know what he wanted to hear. An unwilling part of him was invested in her well-being now, if only to win against a very determined opponent. Gavriel had not had the opportunity to compete—to truly test himself against another person—in years. If he could not do it with swords and tactics, he would do so with strength and skill of another kind.

"What happened to allowing me to proceed as I saw fit?" he asked.

"Your judgment is in question," said Pacheco.

"But I know the difference between when the opium speaks for her and abject terror."

Latorre raised his eyebrows and leered. "You know her so well, novice?"

Gavriel turned and removed the sheepskin mantle. "Look for yourself. She has scars on the soles of her feet. Someone deliberately tortured her."

Pacheco stared at him. Ants crawling over his skin would have been more pleasant. "You're tired, Gavriel," he said.

"You cannot possibly understand her fear. She was frightened, and this arrogant swine treated her like the lowest animal."

Mendes sputtered again. His eyes bounced between Pacheco and Latorre, perhaps looking for someone to voice the indignation he could not.

But Latorre only gaped at Ada's bared feet and calves. "You removed her boots? Without a chaperone?"

Gavriel yanked the mantle into place. "She has a fever and was unable to remove them. What was I supposed to do?"

"Send for a maid or a nun," said Latorre.

"Like the one who held her down?" The sharp spike of his voice bounded around the room's low stone walls.

"She did so that I might perform bloodletting," said Mendes. "This woman would be recovered by now had you not interfered."

"You did not even inquire as to her illness," said Gavriel. "Opium, plague, dropsy—the remedy is all the same to you."

Mendes pointed with his flapping sleeve. "This is intolerable. I want him disciplined!"

Latorre nodded, turning his doughy face to Pacheco. "I agree with Señor Mendes. This boy must be reprimanded."

Gavriel clenched his fists. "I'm no boy, you—"

"I'll not be told how to oversee my own novice." Never raising his voice to the others' distress, Pacheco's black eyes held each man enthralled. "Do you understand my meaning?"

"I understand," said Latorre. "But I also understand that my place as the archbishop's majordomo entitles me to permit you refuge. Or to deny it."

"Brother Latorre, are you threatening me?"

"No, only this novice of yours." Latorre glanced at Ada. "Him and the madwoman you've brought into our midst. I want them both out. Tonight."

Chapter 7

"They made us leave? Because of me?"

Gavriel said nothing, only supported her weight against his shoulder. Their possessions, hastily gathered, thumped against their backs with each shuffling step. Ada's knees and ankles had turned to water. The springtime chill wrapped around her and filled every pore. She nestled deeper into Gavriel's arms for both steadiness and warmth. She hoped that, in her moment of desperation, she would have held to any man with as much fervor.

When she lifted her head, she saw two parallel lines of houses stretching before them. An interminable length. Nausea blossomed at the prospect of walking such a distance—or being dragged, more like.

"Hardly seems fair to you," she said, choking back the taste of bile. "Cast out with me."

His voice rumbled near her ear, a quiet thunder. "Is that an apology?"

"I don't believe so. You brought this on yourself."

"Keep saying that, *inglesa*." He stopped and hiked her up as she slumped. "Then you won't share the responsibility."

She licked her lips, thirstier than she could ever remember. "You're not my master."

"Nor do I want to be."

"Then why do you do this?"

"I am bound to," he said quickly. "All I want is your cooperation."

She stumbled, but he did not let her fall. Anger and the familiar whiplash of betrayal struck against her breastbone. "This is Jacob's fault, isn't it?"

"Not entirely. You are my . . ."

"What?"

He stopped before the wide arches and painted brick of a former mosque, now a renovated cathedral, and scowled down at her. But the hesitance in his voice spoke of doubt. "You are my final test before joining the Order. I must get you well or risk failing my novitiate."

Every sensation of safety and unexpected comfort fled. He had defended her against the physician, keeping her warm, all to fulfill an obligation. "You treat me as a game you must win."

"And I will win, for your sake and for mine."

"Do what you must. I haven't the energy to fight you. Not tonight." The dim, narrow street threatened to tip upside-down. Her pulse thrummed at the pace of a galloping steed. She swallowed like trying to gorge on her own tongue—anything, *anything* to keep from vomiting in his presence. "Where are we going?"

"You shouldn't talk," he said.

"Ask questions, more like. Because you don't know yourself?"

"I seek a place that has neither a mewling physician nor delicate furnishings. With you, sturdiness takes precedent over all."

He nodded to an *adarve*, a dead-end courtyard opposite the cathedral. They hobbled across the narrow street to one of the meager dwellings that abutted the courtyard's far side. Although deserted, the poorly lit stretch of crude brick hovels fairly hummed with unseen activities. Night places.

"Jacob rescues me from a brothel, you hobble us both with the need to keep me from harming myself, and then you bring me here? Odds on my finding opium are high."

"I have no intention of letting you try," he said. "Master Pacheco gave me the name of a woman who might take us in."

Ada stared at him, trying to interpret the strange catch in his voice. The pale moon and sprinkled stars did not provide light enough to read him—but then, neither would full sunlight. But he was uncomfortable. The arm he wrapped beneath hers had tensed, as had the rippling strength of his abdomen.

"Tell me."

Gavriel frowned and shook his head. "She . . . the woman. She's a *covigera*."

Laughter pushed into her throat where bile had been. She savored that brief moment of levity, watching his embarrassment. "I have nothing to tempt a *covigera*."

Eyes made black by shadows probed hers and skittered over her features, cataloguing each expanse of skin. Ada felt a blush crawl over her cheeks, following the path of his eyes—a heat altogether different from her fever.

His arm still banded her middle, pulling her closer than she had been. With a voice almost too low to be heard, he whispered, "You . . ."

"I *what?*"

"You tempt me."

She breathed. Only just. The harsh honesty of those three words peeled past her pain and anger, just for a moment, and revealed a much deeper need for hard muscle and warm skin. But to acknowledge that need—*no*. She had no desire to surrender to the man who insisted on keeping her prisoner. One foolish craving was already more than she could bear.

"But you're not in the business of arranging illicit affairs with married women," she said, trying to revive her fleeting laughter. "One such as me would not be worth her notice."

He pulled his spine straight and withdrew to a place of safety within himself, like donning armor before battle. As he knocked on the *covigera*'s door, his eyes blank and his face impassive, he concealed that spark of honest lust. He hid it so thoroughly as to make Ada doubt its existence. The tingling along the backs of her thighs could have been fever, not the effect of his heated stare. And those throaty words could have been a whimsy created by her addled brain.

Caught by sickness, her body and her mind could not be trusted.

Yes. That was it.

"She's a mess," said the grizzled woman, her wispy gray hair like a halo. Pacheco had referred to her as simply La Señora.

A constellation of brown spots colored her papery skin. Watery eyes, one of them pure white, roved over Ada where she had slumped against the wall, awake but quiet and still. "You looking to sell her?" she asked.

Gavriel pushed his lips together and worked to keep his temper in check, an increasingly difficult task as fatigue ate his patience. "No. I need a place to stay with her, unnoticed. Most likely for a few days."

"Ah, keep her for yourself. *Comprendo.*" The crone hobbled to Ada and bent low, taking her chin between gnarled fingers. Ada did not resist, but neither did she meet La Señora's eyes. Her listlessness and pallor could only mean her fever had returned, shoving her personality into a distant corner. "Could be pretty when she's clean."

He pulled a bag of morabetins from his satchel and rattled the heavy gold coins. "Do you have water? And a room?"

La Señora stood and looked him full in the face. "You a *caballero?* Here to mess my business?"

"The girl is my only concern."

A bright cackle sprang from her mouth, revealing crusted yellow teeth spaced with gaping holes. He stifled the need to shield his nose from her foul breath. "Girl is your only concern. Ha! I like your mind." She pointed a knobby forefinger to his chest, then snatched the bag of coins. "But mess my business and you leave. Wives want no witnesses, hear? None. Lovesick boys don't want no wives scared off. And me, I don't want the pyre."

He bowed his head, just slightly. "As you say."

"This way."

Gavriel tried to bury his distaste for both his hostess and her residence. The purpose of a *covigera* was to arrange affairs between married, highborn women and clandestine suitors. Their disruptive presence in the community—subverting marriage vows and tempting respectable women to fall— meant harsh sentences if convicted. Gavriel no more wanted to finance such a woman than he wanted to be trapped in her peculiar little residence. With Ada.

But the situation had become desperate. Pacheco had ordered him to stay in Yepes for as long as he needed to insure Ada's initial recovery. Then they could travel the remaining distance to the monastery.

At least the tiny old woman would be discreet. Her business demanded it.

"In here," she said.

He shifted Ada's limp weight and angled her through the narrow entryway to a private, windowless room. A single pallet was its only furnishing. He laid her down and returned to the hallway for their satchels. The crone stood in the doorway, watching Ada.

"She sick?"

"Yes."

"Don't like none of that poison. Not in here. You keep her clear of it or you can go. Don't care the gold."

Gavriel studied her lined face and nodded. "Good. Bring the water, please."

La Señora shuffled down the hallway and out of sight, returning moments later with a simple clay pot and scraps of linen. "Need *una herbolera?* Make you potions? My niece does good potions. She make your girl strong and make you—" She glanced down to his groin, that sickly smile returning. "She'll make you stronger."

"No." He ground his molars together. "Water is all we need."

He closed the door and locked it, taking the pot of water and the linen to where Ada lay. The cool water felt good—refreshing him, grounding him—and he splashed some on his hair, face, and neck before wringing a cloth.

Ada opened her eyes and met his with a look of panic.

"Are you going to fight me again?" he asked.

"What do you know of tending people?" Her eyes narrowed and probed around, deep in his soul, chilling him from the inside out. She was right to ask. What did he know of caring for others? He had only known hardness and cruelty. The instinct to protect and care for her was as foreign as her native language. Doubt threatened to rust his good intentions.

No, not good intentions. Not really. Merely selfish. Her well-being would determine his future. No sense covering his deeds in a cloak of charity.

"I'll be honest with you, as I'm sure you appreciate honesty more than being played for a fool."

She shivered. "Very considerate."

"I've no experience tending the needs of another person." He smoothed the hair from her face and brought the dampened cloth to her forehead. Had he not been kneeling already, the heavy, contented sigh that escaped her lips would have brought him to the floor. "But I'm trying. What more can I do?"

"More of that." She nuzzled against the cloth, arching her neck. "Feels good."

"Not too cold?"

"Just right."

He returned to the basin to refresh the cloth, each time pausing to summon from his depleted stores of strength.

"Thirsty," she said weakly.

Gavriel looked around but could find no cup. He dipped a new cloth, not bothering to wring out the excess. He supported the back of her head and brought the cloth to her mouth. She sucked greedily, eyes drifting shut. He did the same, closing his eyes against that erotic and vulnerable act.

When he opened them again, he found her watching him with the smallest smirk, their faces nearly touching. She blinked, parted her lips. "More."

"Please."

She looked away. "More, please."

Nodding once, he dipped the cloth again. He felt like celebrating a tiny victory, but any victory was tainted. He used the same techniques against Ada that had been used against him in his youth, forcing obedience. The realization sat heavily on his upper back, pressing on his conscience. But he did it for her own good, not to turn her into a broken and compliant slave.

He touched the water-laden cloth to her lips and she sucked again, covering his hand with one of hers. She twined their fingers and held fast. The air thickened between them like a hot, sticky summer fog. All he could think was that, without the cloth, she would be pressing her lips to his palm. His skin. Suckling and teasing him, flesh to flesh.

He unwound their fingers and eased her back into the pallet's softness. A cat's grin shaped her mouth.

"The boy, Jacob," he said. "He mentioned a promise you'd

made and broken. What was it? Did you promise him not to use the tincture again?"

"No, nothing so grand." She licked her lips, eyes closed. "I—I promised that I would refrain when he was not there to care for me."

The tension in his shoulders doubled until the muscles felt hewn of rock. "He gave you permission?"

"No, no." Ada reached for the linen, dipping it and sucking her fill. "Do not disparage Jacob or his efforts, please. I've done too much of both. He does not deserve it."

"He could not stand up to you."

She nodded slightly. "I know."

"Yet you pressed the advantage?"

"I worked at Doña Valdedrona's palace where he could watch over me. He made sure I never consumed to excess. He kept me safe from people who would harm me." She slumped back onto the pallet, her chin wet. "Perhaps that's why I thought myself more in control than I am. He protected me."

Gavriel pressed the heels of his palms together, wringing his fingers until his mind registered pain. "Did he buy it for you? Did he hand you the bottle?"

That little nod. "On occasion."

"Merciful God," he said on a quiet exhale. "He was in love with you."

"Yes. Has been for years." Tears gathered at the corners of her blue eyes. She looked away from him, a blush darkening cheeks already beset by fever. Her full lower lip trembled, whether from the withdrawal or emotion he could not be sure. "I took advantage of his affection to get what I wanted."

"And with this tearful confession, you think to manipulate me as well."

"No. I'm being truthful. I'm simply . . . tired."

"I don't believe you." He stood and ran his hand over his good forearm, unable to banish the strain of being in the same room with her. She wove under his skin like a needle and thread. Every joint stiffened against the need to leave her, to abandon his responsibilities. "You must trust someone to believe them, *inglesa*. And I don't know you. I don't trust you."

She doubled over suddenly. Anguish blended guttural cries with her native English and its clipped sounds. Unable to stay away in the face of that pain, Gavriel knelt beside her. Her neck was slick with sweat, and he bathed that fiery skin with the damp cloth. She groaned, a low and wrenching torture.

"Should I stop?"

"No," she said.

He continued to bathe her heated body until the pain relented. She lay on the bed like a crushed flower, her red-rimmed eyes unfocused and staring at the low, cobwebbed ceiling. Her voice, when it returned, was like that of a woman twice her age, all misery and resignation. "All of two evenings and you expect to know me?"

"You could be in my company a year with no alteration— as long as the opium yet claims you. No amount of time would make a difference. It will always speak for you."

He laid a hand on her forehead, smoothing, trying to say with his touch what sounded so awkward from his tongue. She met his eyes with a directness that stalled the breath in his chest. For a moment, he glimpsed who she must have been. Stubbornness shone like a hot blaze, but a deep intelligence tempered it and gave it strength.

The compulsion to make her well filed through his veins. Cured, this formidable woman would put his untoward impulses in their place. She would stare his unnatural lust in the face and reject him. Deservedly. And he would welcome the rejection as a return to his chosen life.

"I wonder if you even realize that you've given it your voice," he whispered. "All your power."

She shook her head to dislodge his hand. "I'm beginning

to mislike when you minister me. You stand on your pedestal and look down on my mistakes."

Gavriel moved the jug away and stretched on the floor between her and the door. "I'm not looking down on you, *inglesa*. I'm trying to do more good than young Jacob did."

"Trust goes both ways," she said. "I don't trust you because I don't know you. You watch me sideways, waiting for me to make a mistake."

"How else should I approach this situation? You're an untrustworthy person. Whether or not that is due to the opium, I cannot know."

A hearty shrug rumpled her coverlet. She hauled it back into place. "You may as well tie me up for the month and have done with it. But that would be too difficult for you, wouldn't it? Tying me up?"

A tingle of lust shot through from head to feet, gathering halfway between. "I've no notion of what you mean."

"For at least one year you've been without a woman in your bed. And the notion of tying me up, having complete say over what I do or think or feel isn't attractive to you?"

"You think me so cruel?"

"No, I think you so wretched." Her eyes drifted shut and her throaty voice slowed. "Your robes fool no one, Gavriel."

Chapter 8

If he stayed in the world for too long, someone would recognize him.

Lying on the floor, fitfully striving for sleep for the third night straight, Gavriel faced the unavoidable truth. Until he returned to Uclés and donned those protective white robes once again, he would be vulnerable to his father's searching henchmen, to punishment for his part at Alarcos, to temptation. But with the Englishwoman in tow, he would remain so. She threatened to tear down the very shelter he had worked to create. A new life. A new purpose. A means of dispelling the murderous need for revenge that burned under his skin.

He closed his eyes. Joaquin de Silva's image appeared out of the blackness. His father's eyes were ice blue, but they shared the same hooded expression and grim mouth. Gavriel's dark coloring, from his hair to his skin and eyes, came from the Berber woman who had never lived to see his first birthday. A slave raped by her master, she had been left to die after childbirth so that her son might be stolen, conditioned, and raised to become the family's deadliest defender. As a slave, he had been denied an education beyond what could be learned with fists and swords and horses.

He had been little more than an animal.

But he had escaped that spiral of death, confronting his barbarism and trying to become a better man.

He raised a hand to his eyes and pushed against closed lids, rubbing until bright blue blemishes floated there. Breathing slowly, he struggled for calm. Calm heart, calm mind. He was not an animal but a servant of God. And even more than the need to take revenge on his father, he feared returning to that violent, mindless way of life. It called to him, so much easier than the struggle to be virtuous.

Better he should recall the horrors of two days spent confined with Ada, the screams and keening and mindless violence. He wore scratches after having removed her torn blue gown, and was covered in bruises after struggling to dress her in a dark red one—proof that a woman caught in the throes of such desperation could do untold damage.

Her distress did not prevent Gavriel from noticing the ivory luster of her skin and the smooth flex and pull of muscles beneath it. Lithe and firm, her flesh awakened a deep and needy part of him. But indulging those enticing memories and temptations would do him no good.

She cried out in her sleep, thrashing again. Another nightmare—a small and deadly beast scratching its way out of her brain. They occurred as regularly as a muezzin's call to prayer, laying waste to whatever strength and peace she managed to gather. If they continued, the dreams would tempt her back to the drug she battled.

With a heavy sigh and a quick prayer, he crawled the miserable distance between his place on the floor and her shivering body. Touching her was not as difficult now. He even anticipated the feel of her skin, a fact that teased him in his own troubled sleep. How much more could they endure of this torment?

But when he circled her in his arms, he banished the despicable thought. She bore the brunt of the torment. All he had to do was get a ragged and defenseless woman safely through to morning.

"I'm trying, Ada," he whispered.

"I'm not as afraid of the dark, not with you." She sniffed and wiped a few stray tears as her nightmare receded and the sobs calmed. "You think I don't know what is happening here—"

"*Inglesa,* don't—"

"—but I do. No matter your motives with the Order, you've stayed with me." The golden glow of the lone oil wick caught the tears in her eyes. Gavriel saw no pretense or manipulation, only the potent emotion of a humbled young woman. "For that, I thank you."

"Does that mean you'll refrain from taunting me?"

A weak smile turned up the corners of her full lips. "Afraid of a little teasing?"

"Not at all."

"Good," she said, folding into his body. "And you should be careful, Gavriel. That was nearly a jest."

Ada awoke to find Gavriel sleeping. He sat upright, legs outstretched, his back pressed against their small room's only door. The oil lamp at his side burned low. His features were a study in firm, strong edges: the rugged cut of his jaw, the straight slope of his nose, and the black slash of his brows. But even sleep did not loosen the rigid line of his lips, pulled taut, and the tension stretching across his broad, muscular shoulders.

Did he dream, too? Did he know about the cloying darkness?

Was that why she trusted him?

For no matter how much she resented his high-minded interference, she had never been afraid of him. He was achingly, frustratingly courteous. Had he been any baser sort of man, his body would have betrayed him by now. She might have traded a quick romp for another dose, or for her freedom.

The nausea that swirled in her stomach had naught to do with her keening need. Mother Mary, she had become the lowest sort of wretch. That she even contemplated such a thing . . .

What have I become?

She pulled upright on her narrow pallet. The base of her head ached where she had fallen. The lump on her cheek had receded but still throbbed if she spoke. On top of those injuries, every part of her body ached—bruised and swollen and hurting from the inside out. Dizziness clouded her vision with a field of little white spots.

Although Ada expected him to stir at any moment, Gavriel remained asleep. Deep circles beneath his eyes spoke of their endless, sleepless nights confined together. A shiver of tenderness toward the man, a thankfulness for his tenacity and grudging care, threatened her with tears. Instead, she found a pitcher and used shaky hands devoid of strength to carefully pour water into a fired clay mug. When greedy swallows would not allay her thirst, she poured another and returned to her pallet.

With no notion of whether it was night or day, and with her capacity for sleep momentarily depleted, she searched the room—whether for entertainment or escape she could not say. She found her satchel of soft, worn Cordovan leather. Only now, days later, did she even think to rummage through and discover what Jacob had packed for her. Clothing took up much of the space: two plain kirtles, a deep green gown, and a black woolen cloak.

Past the garments, she found her late mother's tortoiseshell comb, one of the few possessions she had brought with her from England. With time and patience, she used the small comb to work through every snarl and tangle. The task did nothing to clean her hair, but at least she could get the long, dark strands off her neck and into a half-hearted plait.

Returning to the satchel, she dug into its contents and caught her breath. The scrolls. The ones she had pilfered from Daniel of Morley's possessions. Jacob must have simply grabbed her bag and stowed it with a few sundry necessities. The fine vellum parchment could be gently scraped of its ink, washed clean for another use. If she managed to escape from Gavriel's care, she would have a means of bartering her way back to Toledo.

She smiled. Maybe they would fetch morabetins enough to buy another dose. Now that Gavriel had helped her endure the worst of her sickness, she would know better how to moderate her craving. This time, she would be able to control herself.

One kirtle swathed a small hard box. She unwrapped the linen and found her chess set. Her heart pinched. Jacob. Silly, foolish, thoughtful Jacob.

She opened the polished wooden case, no bigger than the width of her knees pressed together, and pulled out one of the carved waxed pieces.

"Ada, what do you have?"

She jerked. The box snapped shut between her knees and fell to the floor. Gavriel was on his feet and across their small room before she could slide the box out of sight.

His expression contorted with anger yet blurred by sleep, he grabbed her wrist. "Let me see!"

"'Tis a queen, from chess," she said, yanking free. "A chess set, Gavriel."

She opened her fingers to reveal the small figurine. When Gavriel took it, she retrieved the fallen box and offered it for his inspection.

"Chess?" His expression faded into confusion as he touched one piece, then another. "I thought you had—"

"You thought I hid opium in my satchel?"

He nodded.

The scrolls might eventually buy her as much, but Ada

preferred to set that knowledge aside. Seeing Gavriel contrite was a happy treat. She had to keep the scrolls away from him, lest he discover their value and strip away her last means of freedom.

"I adore chess," she said. "And behind this sham of playing at a holy man, I believe you have the mind of a tactician."

"I'm no sham, *inglesa*. And I have nothing so devious as a tactical mind."

"I've seen how you move, how you watch." She opened the board and began to arrange the remaining pieces along the tiny, checkered field of battle. "Men who live their entire lives in cloisters and libraries and churches do not watch the horizon as you do. They look only as far as the nearest bookshelf."

She stared at him, flaying the layers of his skin, his muscles, his bones, until Gavriel felt exposed to his very soul—if he had one. The feeling that she could see that deeply unnerved him. His heart still hammered at having awakened to find her crouched low over some mysterious possession. Thoughtless man, he should have checked her satchel. But he had compromised so much of her privacy already.

"And those are the men you know?" he asked. "Academics and theologians?"

The last he had seen of her, just before he slept, she had been a witch made real, wild and disheveled. Now her hair, woven into a makeshift plait, hung heavily across one shoulder. The deep red dress made for a striking contrast to her pale skin. And her expression was entirely lucid. Frighteningly so. Blue eyes the color of the sky at midday continued to scrutinize him without shyness or fear, as if seeing him for the first time.

"My father was an alchemist," she said, her voice steady and measured. "He learned from his great uncle, Adelard of Bath, who had traveled to Toledo in his youth to study philosophy and languages. What he learned here in the Peninsula was passed down to my sister and me."

"Is that how you can speak Romance so well?"

She waved a hand. "Romance is no trouble. Portuguese, Catalan, Castilian—not much more than dialects of Latin. Mozarabic, however . . ." She squished her features into an expression of distaste. "That took a few months."

He frowned, wondering at the woman sitting before him. "Months?"

"Daniel of Morley is an Englishman who works as Doña Valdedrona's translator and resident scholar. He helped me learn."

"How many languages do you know?"

"I've lost count. I was training to take Daniel's place within Her Excellency's household." She paused, shadows at work behind her eyes—an echo of the lost girl he had so recently known. "Maybe. Maybe one day."

"Why hide it?"

"People find my education intimidating," she said, setting her last piece into place on the checkered board. He still held the one he had taken from her hands. "They might not appreciate my understanding of a game of war. Fancy a round?"

Shame mingled with frustrated rage, that old insufficiency, until red dotted his vision. He could not read, he could not write, and he certainly could not play courtly games.

"I know not how," he said tightly.

All guile lifted from her expression. "Then I shall teach you. I'll be grateful for an occupation, now that I've come free of my other . . . pursuits."

"Is that what you call it? Like recreation?"

An invisible pressure bowed her shoulders, the posture of defeat and submission. She closed her eyes and let her chin drop to her chest. "It was medicinal, initially."

"Your feet."

She blanched. "I forgot you knew. These few days—forgive me if I cannot remember much beyond disliking you."

"Tell me."

He thought she would deny him. A flicker of that reflexive defiance tightened around her mouth. Then she sighed. "I was detained for a minor crime. Because he thought I could fabricate emeralds and gold, the sheriff tortured me."

Her voice caught.

Gavriel curled his fingers into fists. "But why? What he asked of you is impossible."

"Not for my sister." A wan smile tugged at her lips, and quiet pride shaded her words.

"Una bruja?"

"A witch? No. Merely an alchemist, like my father was." All emotion disappeared. She narrated events as if they inhabited someone else's past. "It was a case of mistaken identity, I'm afraid. The sheriff enjoyed the sport of hurting me. Afterward, my feet became putrid and I turned to opium to ease the pain. I've not had idle time without it in . . . in more than a year."

"Has it been so long since your life was different?"

"And let that be a lesson to me, I suppose?"

Rubbing a hand over the back of his skull, he concentrated on the spiky bristles of his cropped hair. "I said no such thing."

Ada pushed the fat plait over her shoulder and looked around the room. "How long have we been here?"

"Five days, in total," he said, although that seemed paltry. A year would have done justice to the fatigue he felt.

"And how long will we stay?"

"Until you're well enough to travel. Perhaps on the morrow."

She nodded to the board and its opposing wooden armies. "Then let me teach you chess."

"I should not."

The days-long temptation of Ada—knowing her, being with her—returned with more force than before. She was no needful harlot, just another wounded soul. But smart, too. Her intelligence made him all the more aware of his own barbarous upbringing.

"What's the harm, Gavriel?" Her smile returned, revealing the dimple on her left cheek. "You've sworn not to use your skill or your sword. Use your mind instead."

He wanted to argue, that old response. No mind. No soul. Only a conscience so very aware of his deficiencies. But they had ages until dawn, and he was suddenly curious. Anything to withstand another handful of hours trapped with Ada and her clear, keen eyes.

The protests faded as he examined the piece he held. "She is the queen?"

"Yes," she said, setting the queen alongside her dark countrymen. "One of the least powerful pieces on the board."

He raised his brows. "Least powerful? Whoever invented this game had no notion of women."

"Perhaps that will change one day," she said with a laugh. The light, carefree sound and that frustrating little dimple had him thinking of far more than chess. Dark and dangerous urges, willing him to be reckless. But he shut out the sound, the thought, the temptation, and focused on where her finger pointed next. "Now, this is the king . . ."

Ada chewed a fingernail as Gavriel moved his rook. She had seen her fate coming for three moves, but he must have been planning this final blow well before that.

"Check mate," he said.

"And you're being honest with me?" She tipped over her king, resigning the round. "You've never played before?"

The severity of his taut lips softened—not a smile, but something akin to it. "Not once."

"I suspected you had a mind for strategy, but this . . . this is astonishing."

He seemed embarrassed, twirling one of Ada's slaughtered pawns idly between his fingers. "A lucky beginning, nothing more."

"Luck has naught to do with this. I claim one victory, then you win five straight games."

"You're only upset I beat you."

"Not a bit. I never stood a chance."

"Ah," he said quietly. "Then you let me win."

"Do I seem like the kind who enjoys losing?" She leaned across the chessboard, one still replete with his tiny pale army. He held all of her pieces but, at her approach, his expression shied toward panic. She smiled, needing to restore the balance of power between them, to offset her growing fascination. "Who are you, exactly?"

"A novice to the Order of Santiago."

"So I've heard." Looking at his lips made her lick her own, wondering at the feel of him, this strange riddle of a man. "Keep your secrets," she whispered. "For now."

His dark, bottomless eyes widened. "You don't frighten me."

"Oh, but I do."

The door to their room careened open. Scattered rushes did little to cushion where her elbows met marble, startled backward. Gavriel rolled to put his body between her and the door.

"Come with me. Quickly!"

The unfamiliar female voice in the doorway did nothing to dispel her confusion. Ada blinked against the harsh light, unable to discern the face behind a lit torch held aloft.

"Come away now or find yourselves before the magistrate," the woman said. "They are raiding La Señora's home. Hurry!'"

Chapter 9

Beyond the doorway, shouts and the splintering of furniture broke the night silence. Gavriel jumped to his feet. Ada tossed the chess set in her satchel. Her knees gave way as she stood, but he caught her beneath her arms. "Can you walk?" he asked.

"I will." She furrowed her brows and managed to stay upright, leaning heavily against his side.

With both bags over his shoulder and Ada's dagger tucked in the tie of his breeches, he nodded to the faceless woman and followed her into a narrow corridor. The flickering play of light and shadow guided their way to the rear of the dwelling. He no more trusted their unknown guide than he would trust Ada—or himself—but he followed for lack of an alternative. The shouting and violence was to their rear, which helped put one foot in front of the other.

"Keep with me, *inglesa,*" he said, half hauling her along the narrow corridor. "We've outstayed another welcome."

"I sense a pattern. We should notify wise men and report our discoveries."

He frowned at her, the only alternative to laughter. "I know only clergymen and knights."

"No learned men there. And I see you trying to remain

grim. Does that effort grow tiresome?" She sighed. "Forget I said a thing. You won't answer."

Gavriel fled from mysterious villagers and followed an equally mysterious guide, while Ada settled into his body with neither worry nor malice. And the minx was teasing him. He did answer then, perhaps because his tired mind and restless, traitorous body had loosened the frantic grip on his emotions. "Yes, *inglesa*. It grows tiresome."

The sharp blast of night air hit her face with force enough to rouse Ada completely. She had been happy to take shelter against Gavriel, almost free from the terror and pain. Only for a moment. Neither distant nor scornful, he had seemed caring—a person, freed from his stoic nature. She had seen a glimpse of that man as they sparred over the chessboard. He was competitive, yes. A natural strategist. He was also strangely reassuring company, quiet, with the driest sense of humor. She could have hidden in that room forever, working into his mind just as his chess pieces slid past her defenses.

But the warmth and comfort had disappeared. They faced exile again, her sickness driving him from even the negligible refuge of that tiny room.

The woman who guided their flight pushed the head of torch into the damp dirt outside the dwelling's rear door. Darkness enveloped them in an instant.

Ada blinked into the night, her eyes slowly adjusting. The impairment sent her mind back through time and distance, across water and land to England, to Meg, her blind sister—the sister she missed at that moment more than she could bear.

Contemplating how low she had fallen and how far she had traveled could consume the remaining days of Ada's life. But the immediacy of their new peril pushed maudlin thoughts away. For that, at least, she welcomed the unexpected danger.

"This way," said their guide.

"Who are you?" Gavriel asked. He took Ada's hand as they followed the woman to the north, through the courtyard.

"My name is Blanca. La Señora is my great-aunt."

"You're the herbalist she mentioned?"

Blanca tossed a sour look over her shoulder, her round face like the moon hanging overhead. "She mentioned that? La Señora only refers to people by what they might offer her. She didn't take you in for charity's sake. The old man from your order—what was his name?"

"Pacheco?"

"Yes. He gave her money."

"We did, too," he said.

Blanca laughed quietly. "Then she did well for herself. Perhaps if she's lucky she can buy her way out of trouble."

They turned the corner around the converted cathedral, but when they did not stop to take shelter there, Ada and Gavriel exchanged questioning looks.

"Where are we going?" Ada asked, her mind beginning to work and see and breathe once again. Yes, like breathing after a year below water. She had never stopped to realize how demanding her cravings had become. The damage that could have been done, if she had been sold into slavery—she shivered and swallowed a bitter copper taste.

"Out of sight," Gavriel said, tugging Ada into a brick alcove between buildings. "They're in pursuit."

Blanca squeezed into the shadows with them, the fine sheen of sweat on her forehead dampening the band of her dark cowl. Her skin smooth and firm, she appeared no older than a girl. The flat bodice of her modest wool gown, some color between blue and black, raised and lowered with each quick breath. The whites of her eyes fairly glowed, no matter how deeply she slunk into the black.

Her whisper stretched across the scant inches between

them. "I'm helping because I hate that old witch. She'd keep me as her servant for the rest of my days."

"What will happen to her?" Ada asked.

"Trial by fire or water, perhaps. No man will stand as her second, so she'll not be asked to endure trial by combat—not as a lone old woman. But now that *los guardias* have her, I'll need help getting out of the city. No young woman travels beyond its walls alone."

"You want us to be your escorts?" Ada covered her smile with one hand, ignoring the seething male at her side. "Won't that be nice, Gavriel? Another traveling companion for you?"

"I would toss you both in the Tagus, if I could."

"Hardly charitable, novice," she said, her smile refusing to be contained. Realizing she still held his hand, she gave it a squeeze. He dropped her fingers as if they were live embers.

"You strip me of my charity," he said. "Thank you for your assistance, *señorita,* but we can offer you nothing but gold. I cannot assume more burdens in this journey."

"I won't accept gold," Blanca said with a shake of her head. Tears forged silvery paths down her cheeks. "You must understand that gold is useless to one such as me. I'm tainted by my aunt's illegal business. No one will meet my eyes in the marketplace. I've no chance for proper suitors. This town is a prison."

That word may as well have been a streak of lightning flashing between them. Gavriel flinched and averted his gaze. Ada felt something tighten in her chest, a sense of unexpected kinship pinching below her ribs. How often had she thought of Charnwood Forest as just such a prison? The taint of her sister's ailment and her eventual blindness—not to mention Meg's passion for the mysteries of alchemy—had endeared them to none of their superstitious neighbors.

She had since endured the horrors of true prisons, both in Sheriff Finch's dreaded dungeon and in the clutches of her opium thirst, but Blanca's youthful need for an escape brought those years in Charnwood back to life. She remembered believing that any sacrifice would be worthwhile, that anyone offering an escape was a saint.

"We've difficulty enough," said Gavriel. "You must understand. My apologies."

If she had not known better of the taciturn man, Ada would have sworn his words sounded more like a plea. She almost felt sorry for him.

"You can come with us," she said.

A group of men in armor chugged past, the clamor of their metal skins louder than their shouts. Ada wondered at the power of fear. A rabbit hiding from a wolf's jaws could not stay as still as she did. Gripped by that unnatural stillness, she felt Gavriel's body pressed against hers. He hardly breathed. Did his pulse race as hers did? Did he wonder at the heat where their limbs touched?

She had only just experienced the terrible aftermath of her withdrawal. Now the same reckless part of her that still craved the bitter taste of opium was taking stock of the potent male at her side. That she had so little sense heated her cheeks, part from shame, part from a delicious sort of nervousness.

"Shall I signal for them?" Blanca asked, her voice a strangled whisper despite the threat.

"Save your breath," Ada said. "Gavriel is bound to care for me, which means if I won't leave without you, neither will he."

"We could always try those ropes, *inglesa*."

Ada tried to see his face, but Gavriel's dusky skin was made for hiding in shadows. "What does that mean? Do you intend to tie me up and haul me to Uclés?"

"No," he said, the word a low warning that his temper had been stretched to breaking. "It means she's coming with us."

* * *

They entered the bathhouse with a key Blanca pulled from the bag at her belt. She carried nothing else.

Gavriel eyed her with no small measure of suspicion. If she wanted to leave the city, did she truly intend to do so without any possessions? And how did an herbalist come by a spare key to the public bathhouse? Much like darkened buildings on the streets of Toledo, bathhouses after hours only housed the worst sorts of people and the most blatant of temptations.

He followed the women into the pitch-black entryway like a sleepwalker. Lack of rest only accounted for a little of his numbness. Ada, however—Ada had disrupted his judgment and scrambled his life to such an extent that any direction seemed viable.

But his goal remained unchanged, no matter the crooked and thorny path he traveled. Left to Toledo or the countryside of Castile, he would be hunted and killed by the de Silva family's far-flung agents. Left to the dictates of his own soul, he would reverse that scenario, tracking down the exiled Joaquin de Silva in order to run him through. Hunter or hunted, he could be neither. He needed the security of a permanent place with the Order of Santiago. If rescuing Ada Keyworth from herself was the price of that place, so be it.

Perhaps this shifty girl Blanca could be of assistance. The less time Ada spent focusing on her own pain and bitterness, the more willingly she would walk to Uclés. Whether or not she genuinely empathized with the girl's plight did not matter. More likely, she only wanted the girl tagging along to aggravate him.

But a bathhouse?

God had stopped listening to him, surely—if He had ever listened.

"Why do you have a key?" he asked into the black.

"Where else would *una covigera* rather conduct her business? Illicit meetings are best done in secret places."

"I wouldn't know," he muttered. "And you opened the

bathhouse for these couples? Or did you just palm the key tonight?"

"I started coming when La Señora could no longer make the foot journey. I've had custody of the key ever since."

Blanca sounded unbearably weary for one so young, but he crushed that shimmer of understanding.

"Did you call *los guardias?*" Ada asked.

"No," Blanca whispered. "The *alcalde's* wife was caught sneaking to a tryst—not in the act, mind, but with evidence enough to enrage the officials. That was last night."

"And the scandal was the last straw?"

"The people elected him. They were embarrassed on his behalf and could no longer turn away from my aunt's ventures."

Gavriel shuffled through the entryway until he found a wall sconce and a torch. He rummaged through their satchels to find a small leather pouch among his possessions. A few clicks of flint later and the flames jumped to life. "And you knew enough to leave," he said.

Blanca nodded as Ada stepped into the circle of torchlight. "She's clever," Ada said. "Which means she won't be a burden."

"You're clever and a burden, both."

Looking into her eyes was like meeting an entirely different woman. He searched for signs of weakness or pain or mindless desperation but found only Ada—whoever that might be.

"You're staring, novice," she said.

He lifted the torch and took a step closer. Flames cast quick contrasts of dark and light across the fine lines of her face, making her lips appear fuller and her eyes wider. A trick of shadow, nothing more, but desire pushed past his defenses. They had shared much, too much, in that little room.

He cleared his throat. "How do you feel?"

"Better." Like heat lightning across the plateau, a look of contrition covered her face. One he almost believed. Pale pink dyed her cheeks and spread down her throat. She dipped her head and kneaded restless fingers together. "I—I wanted . . . to apologize for the trouble I've been. These last few nights— I have memories of what I did and said. I am . . . I'm ashamed."

He did not move for long moments, watching the burden of this woman's care become more arduous with every tortured word. Witch, addict, harlot—he could cope with any such incarnation. Barely. But like her tears, her humility threatened a deeper part of him, one without ready defenses. He tried to breathe evenly, but no amount of concentration ebbed the twin delights of her appreciation and her mangled apology.

"Quiet now," he said. "There is no shame in fighting free."

Tears gathered at the corners of her eyes. She started to speak but stopped, sniffing back the obvious surge of emotion. She made a marble column of her spine, straight and rigid, and darted her eyes away. Tendons stretched taut beneath the skin of her neck.

Not only did he have to remain vigilant about her addiction, he had to be wary of this new, clear-minded woman. He had chastised himself for thinking of her as his enemy, but the designation was more accurate than ever.

"This way," Blanca said, passing through a wide entryway. "You won't be safe in the open. *Los guardias* might think to look for us here."

Gavriel picked up the bundle of their belongings and hoisted them onto his back, only to find Ada standing before him, hands out. "Let me carry my things," she said. "You have borne too many burdens for me already."

He shook his head. "I think not. I foresee you and your possessions on horseback returning to Toledo."

"Which would leave you stuck with Blanca, poor thing. Can't have that."

"No."

"Then let me carry something of yours," she said, her expression surprisingly bright and open. "I insist."

He had no idea how to interpret this new woman. Not an hour before he had carried her. Now she was volunteering to share the weight. Fair and exotic, this mystery from England—would she taste different from other women?

"Here." He shoved a light leather satchel into her arms and nodded for her to follow their guide. "I'll not have you walking behind me either."

She offered a smile. "All of these rules, Gavriel. Are they by your design or a product of the Order's training?"

"Mine. Now go."

Chapter 10

"La Señora is not the first to use these facilities for secret meetings," Blanca said. "She inherited the knowledge of their existence from the woman who trained her."

Ada smiled and looked around the small enclosure they entered below the main rooms of the bathhouse. While sparsely furnished and a little drafty, it seemed just the place for an illicit meeting. Perhaps with the advent of a fire, or heated by the danger of such a tryst, the otherwise cramped and barren rooms might feel more inviting.

"*Covigeras* have apprenticeships?" she asked.

Blanca shrugged and sat on a low wooden chair. "Convincing a married woman to accept the suit of a man who is not her husband takes skill and patience, as with any trade."

Gavriel snorted and dropped Ada's bundle. "That is no trade."

"She earns a living providing a service," Blanca said. "I know of no other definition."

"She's a criminal," he said. "She makes a living destroying good women and ruining marriages."

Ada shook her head. "Do you adhere to every *fuera* a city invents? Beware your own hypocrisy, Gavriel."

"And you mind your tongue. Remember where you were not a week ago before we talk about good behavior."

His glower pushed at her to step away, but she held firm. "What happened to 'no shame,' novice? Or are you planning to hold these last few days over my head?"

He pinched his brows together, the look of a man in pain. "Forget I said anything. We should sleep through the day and leave for Uclés tomorrow afternoon, before the guards close the town gates."

She exchanged a quick glance with Blanca, as well as an almost identical shrug. Ada shivered, seeing her sister in the young woman's poised movements and calm expression.

Meg rarely had cause to become angry, but when she did, silence was her weapon of choice. Marble and iron held more warmth and showed more emotion than did Meg when she became cross. Except there at the last, during that final, fateful argument before Ada had left for Spain. Meg had laid bare every feeling, from fear and love to disbelief and pain. And why not? After what Ada had demanded—making Meg choose between her sister and her husband—she deserved no less than a tirade the size and fury of a thunderstorm.

Suddenly breathless from the surge of guilt, she looked toward the door. "Are there baths down here, in secret?"

"Yes," Blanca said. "Along this same corridor and to the right. We're closer to the source of the spring, so the water can be quite hot."

Ada rifled through her satchel, past a bundle of scrolls and the chess set, and found her tortoiseshell hair comb and a small cake of lemon and olive oil soap wrapped in waxed linen. Jacob had remembered all she would need, and that shiver of guilt increased.

Gavriel caught her arm. He stood tall and powerful—chest out, head up—his posture unlike any mincing clergyman. "You cannot go by yourself," he said.

She flicked an appreciative look down his body and smiled. The rich brown color of his closely shorn hair, very dark, complimented the deep tan of his skin. "I didn't know you wanted to watch, or I would've extended you an invitation."

He tugged hard on her upper arm until they stood together, hips almost touching. That same look of outrage darkened his sharp features, but something more primal lurked behind his eyes. "I merely want to guarantee you'll stay here."

She looked at her gown. Fine embroidered linen of a dark red hue had been stained with all manner of questionable refuse, reminding her of the terrible ordeal of her withdrawal.

"I want a bath," she said, hitching the satchel over her shoulder. "Nothing more. Let me wash away the filth of these last few days."

He did not look at her shabby clothing, only at her eyes. "But I will be outside the corridor the entire time. You'll not try to leave."

"And why would I try to leave when I have such charming company?"

Gavriel paced the scant length of the secret underground corridor. Every time he passed the closed door that shielded his eyes from Ada and her bath, he glared at the solid oak. The very idea of her naked body stretched beneath the warm and enveloping waters of the bath threatened to send him to his knees. He could hack it open. He could bust it down. Or he could keep glaring until the wood caught fire.

But no. He continued pacing. The litany of reasons why he had to remain in the dank and cramped corridor pounded against his brain like the strike of a hammer. It would be wrong and dangerous, a knife to cut down the last of his vows.

Physical torture—he had known those terrible pains. But the torture of having guided Ada through the worst of her sickness, tending her every need and walking the narrow path between caring and distance, gnawed on his control. He deserved something. He was no saint. This test, this terrible test was more than he could endure. Any deity that claimed otherwise would never understand the failings of mortal man.

He trudged to a stop in front of the door.

How long had she been in there? Blanca had warned her about the high temperature of the spring water. But had Ada taken heed? The picture of her naked, water-bound body had been an erotic vision moments before; now he imagined only danger. She was still fatigued and out of sorts—boiled alive and none the wiser.

"*Inglesa? Inglesa,* answer me!" He pressed his ear to the door and held his breath, to no avail. After a few thundering whacks, he listened again. Nothing. "Ada, you're worrying me. Answer!"

Indecision briefly paralyzed his limbs. He found himself staring at a knot of wood in the door, still waiting for the answering call that refused to come.

Then vows and pride and modesty be damned, he yanked on the wrought iron latch and rattled it. Locked.

"Ada! Open this door!"

He sped back to the private room. Blanca lay asleep on the floor, curled into herself like a human wheel. He grabbed her key and drew Ada's jeweled dagger from its sheath at his waist, determined to make do when a battle ax would have better served his purposes.

But Blanca's key opened the door to the bathing chamber. He prayed for a gasp or a scream of outrage. He hoped that a cake of soap would smack him between the eyes, hurled by a woman who valued her privacy.

No such reaction greeted him.

She had washed her deep red gown and kirtle. The wet garments decorated the stone floor between the door and a shallow well filled with steaming spring water. A softened cake of soap lay at the well's rim, clouded by popping bubbles.

And Ada reclined there—entirely nude, hair wet, eyes closed, head back.

Gavriel was by her side and on his knees before his next intake of breath. He cradled her brightly flushed face in his hands and patted her cheeks. "*Inglesa,* wake up. Do you hear me?"

She moaned, lolling her head toward his thighs. "Wha—? Where am—oh!"

She sat up in the shallow bath, arms crisscrossed over her bare chest. Water splashed the stones around the basin and dotted his hands. *Scalding* water.

"You need out of this bath right now," he said. "How could you be so careless as to fall asleep? Do you want to be cooked like a chicken?"

Dazed at first, her eyes regained focus. "Hand me that cloth for drying."

He lowered his eyes and tried to keep them averted, no matter the tantalizing pull of her bared flesh. But gone was the milky white luster of her skin, replaced by an unnatural redness. He retrieved the length of linen cloth and handed it to her. Mostly covered, she used his arm to support her exit from the bath, her breath coming in accelerated bursts.

"Now come," he said, leading her to sit on a stone bench carved from the subterranean walls. "Let me see your legs."

"I've never known you to be so forward."

"Crazy woman! What would have happened had I not come in?"

She flinched and tightened the linen across her chest. "What you want from me?"

"I want gratitude!"

He hung his head. Failure pressed on him from all sides, mashing any idea of the man he thought he was becoming.

"And this is your charity," she said. "Do you understand what this has been like for me? Gramercy for staying with me over these last days. Gramercy for pulling me clear of the bath. But if I have to swallow my pride and thank you one more time, my head will melt."

"Better your head than your skin."

He watched as his hands reached toward the supple muscle of her calf where it poked from beneath the cloth. That vicious pink looked all the more unnatural against the pale, sun-bleached linen. His dark skin offered yet another contrast. And then he was touching her.

For the first time he found a reason to be genuinely grateful for his monastic life. Had he still been a warrior, his hands would have been covered with calluses born of swordplay and horsemanship. Instead, his hands were smooth and able to appreciate the fine texture and resilience of her leg with such clarity as to steal his breath.

He looked up and found Ada watching him, her blue eyes darkened in the shadowed half-light. Her lips parted. She did not flinch or pull away, and neither did she appear to breathe with the strained effort he did. He wanted her to feel the same mindless pull toward temptation.

He wanted *her*.

"Is it badly burned?" she asked.

"I—shall I?"

The smallest grin tilted her lips. She glanced meaningfully at where his hands cradled the curve of her calf. "If you insist."

Breathing deeply through his nose, he looked down at her leg. To his relief, he found no evidence of severe burns. The skin was puffed, and that unnatural shade of pink glowed in the mild torchlight, but Gavriel could find no blisters. He nudged the cloth aside and found the other calf and both knees in sound condition.

"No serious damage," he said. "You are lucky."

"And you? Can you say the same?"

Gavriel's eyes turned impossibly dark. Arched black brows pulled together, concentrating like a man trying to see through brick, and Ada steeled herself against the need to look away.

She had been with this man in close quarters and under deeply personal circumstances, but she had not been of any mind to see him. Really *see* him. And the man who knelt at her feet—her captor, her unlikely savior—was breathtaking to behold. Not even a master sculptor could recreate the sharp, strong bones of his face, the cut of his jaw and the straight length of his nose. But for a face hewn of so many harsh angles, she also found surprising softness in his full lower lip.

Unexpected heat collected in her veins, turning her muscles to sticky dough and bathing her mind in a sensuous wash of pleasure. But unlike the lethargy of an opium high, these sensations built and bunched and intensified. For the first time in months, she did not crave the bitter taste of her tincture, which would only blunt the bright shock of her desire. Instead she craved the taste of him.

She rubbed her upper arm but nothing dispelled that gathering need. Beneath her nervous fingertips, her skin felt especially soft.

"I must dress," she said, surprised by the husky timbre of her voice. Her smile softened, melting along with her bones. "You can leave. Or you can stay."

Panic blew across his features, making him seem younger and more vulnerable. The stern frown he had worn while scrutinizing her face altered slightly, the brows drawing up above the bridge of his nose. A look of pleading.

Yes. His vows. Heat, flesh, and closeness had banished his vows from her mind. And now he silently pleaded with her to make a decision—not that he would have admitted such a thing.

Her own decision made, Ada stood and looked down to where he still knelt, his fingers interlaced around the back of her calf. She had seen him kneel before, but now he submitted to her. Dizziness from her long, hot bath melded with desire.

"Either way," she said. "You'll have to release my leg."

"And if I don't?"

She grinned, in part because of his question—a threat that sounded more like teasing—and in part because his voice had roughened to sand. The smooth veneer of his confidence had eroded completely.

"If you don't, I'll likely fall into the bath." He released her leg as if she were the fire now. A pent up breath pushed free of her lungs, just as a damp heat licked her inner thighs. "No matter," she said. "I believe you would have caught me anyway."

She turned her back, inhaled, and dropped the cloth.

Gavriel arose, his legs trembling like those of a newborn colt. She stood motionless in front of him with the graceful length of her bare back, buttocks, and legs his to see. She had not eaten regularly in days, and the bones of her spine and her ribs stood out. That should have been enough to temper his crippling lust, to send him away. But after closing the door, he drew closer.

When one step separated his body from hers, Gavriel breathed the scent of lemon and skin warmed by the mineral-rich spring water. The more he breathed, the more lightheaded he became. He felt every heartbeat in triplicate: beneath his ribs, in his skull, at his groin.

He brushed his mouth along the curve of her shoulder. She shuddered but did not pull away. The moist heat of his breath raised goose bumps on her skin and reflected back against his face. He waited, glorying in that intimate caress, knowing he would take her if he tasted her.

She breathed with more urgency now. The sharp bones at the tops of her shoulders raised and lowered. He imagined her nipples would stand tight atop her firm breasts. What color would they be? Dusky or pink? In his panic at finding her asleep in the hot spring, he had not indulged in the luxury of studying her. Now he needed only to turn her around. It would be as easy as taking her arm and tugging.

"Order me to go," he rasped.

Ada looked over her shoulder. He let his eyes fall down the line of her brow and her cheeks and her chin. "I won't do that," she said.

"Why not?" The need to touch her again burned like hell's fires. "No respectable woman behaves as you do."

"We both know I left respectable behind some time ago."

"Then you do this as a game or as punishment."

"You're mistaken if you believe this involves you alone." She spoke with less deliberation and more speed. "Perhaps I do this simply to see what *I'll* do next. I hardly know who I am anymore. It makes me wonder."

He reached out to trace the line of her shoulder blade but pulled back. "Wonder what?"

"Am I the kind of woman to seduce you outright, or will I wait for you? Either way, you've become a most welcome distraction."

She turned, and Gavriel had his answer. Her nipples were pink.

"Ada, don't—"

"You think you've cured me because I no longer shake or cry," she said. "But in that you're mistaken. The need is still here. Right here." She clenched one hand over the other and pressed it to the hollow between her breasts. "It's like thirst or hunger or lust. A need. Can you understand that?"

He could only nod, a weak one at that. A delicious and wanton angel stood before him, his own parable of temptation. The redness of the hot spring had faded, leaving the smoothest white porcelain skin—a feast for his eyes. But he wanted more. No matter his aims or his vows, he was a man who *needed* more.

"I can understand," he said thickly.

"Then help me, Gavriel. Give me something new to crave."

Chapter 11

With one breath, Ada was standing naked before him, as aroused as she ever had been. Waiting. Wanting him to be the man he tried to hide, a man of danger and strength. But that strength had lowly human limits.

And with one more breath, she was in his arms.

Their lips met. The raw, musky taste of him grabbed her tongue. But more than his taste, he was heat. Fire and flame and the deep growl in his throat. The lengthy soak in the hot spring had muddled her body temperature, leaving her cold and seeking more of the warmth his body promised.

Still kissing, still tasting, she wrapped her arms around his neck and threaded trembling fingers into his short dark hair. He matched her urgency, his hands clenching and kneading her backside. He brought one hand higher to press between her shoulder blades and crush their chests together. The coarse wool of his tunic grazed her sensitized nipples, magnifying the urgency of her need.

Ada wiggled against his confining arms, but not to escape— to be closer, to let him claim her. The aching hollow between her legs made her greedy. Never had she felt such a consuming need to be with and near another human being.

Bending into Gavriel's unyielding body, she closed her eyes and reveled in his foreign textures: the roughness of his tongue, the spiky softness of his hair, the rasp of his beard growth along her cheeks and lips. The hard length of his arousal. He squeezed her backside again, nearly to the point of pain, pulling her hips into the cradle of his. Only his breeches separated their questing bodies.

The thought of that barrier—leaving them so close to what they both wanted, but still divided—drew a tangled groan from deep in her belly. He matched the sound, deepening their kiss with renewed drive. The hard thrust of his tongue and the nipping bite of his teeth tested the depths of her passion, daring her to keep up. The restrained power and tension coiled within his muscles added to her excitement. How much longer could he kiss without taking? How much longer could she kiss without stripping him bare and dragging him to the ground?

No, she could kiss him for an eternity.

A masculine shout from the end of the corridor pushed them apart. They stood looking at each other and listening. Gavriel's lips were swollen. His broad chest heaved. He frowned and canted his head toward the door. And with a single blink, the passion that had clouded his dark eyes dissipated.

"Grab your satchel and hide," he said, turning away from her.

Suddenly aware of her nudity, Ada assessed the oval bathing room for possible places to hide and found none. Light from the torch illuminated every surface. Gavriel seemed to read her thoughts. He grabbed the torch from its wall sconce and pinned Ada with one more heated look before snubbing it against the stone floor.

The room descended into black and revived old fears. The rhythm of her breathing faltered as panic overpowered the receding passion in her blood. She hated the dark. Darkness meant captivity, pain, and helplessness. Her limbs refused to cooperate. The buzzing in her ears grew louder and stole her sense of direction. She needed her clothes.

Then a hand clamped over her mouth. She screamed, but the sound stayed close and low.

"*Inglesa,* calm yourself."

Relief sluiced over her skin and sank into her bones. She sagged against his chest, his arm around her waist.

"Someone is coming," he said in a whisper against her ear. "And you must prepare yourself."

She peeled his fingers down from her mouth. "The dark."

"The dark is no danger. I'm here with you. Now find your clothes and stand ready."

For the second time in as many minutes, Gavriel had to let go. And no matter his aims for the future, he did not want to. Just when he had been ready to throw his vows to the four winds and lay Ada down, someone had discovered them. Clinging to her would do nothing to protect them from that menace.

She dropped to the ground, and he heard her scuffling over the stones. He pulled her dagger free of the sheath at his waist and counted three steps to the door. Fingers along the wood-work, he found the latch, locked the door, and turned his back flat against the wall.

"Come to the other side of me," he whispered.

Ada scrambled nearby, his body between her and the door. She wrestled with something, perhaps her kirtle. The scent of lemon snaked into his nose. The erection that had only just started to subside raged to life. Frustration beset him from all sides and stoked his temper. Blood and breath accelerated. He could not rid himself of how distracting she was; instead, he channeled his grinding desire into violence.

A scream echoed down the corridor, still bright and terrified despite the door's muffling wood.

"Blanca," Ada said softly.

"They'll not hurt her if they're looking for us."

"And if they're common thieves or men intent on rape? You're content to take that chance?"

"I'll not endanger either one of us, if that's what you're suggesting."

Ada dug ragged fingernails into his forearm. "You cannot abandon her. She saved our lives."

"We don't know that," he said with more conviction than he felt. "This could have been a plot to trap us down here."

"Ridiculous. Now give me my dagger, since you refuse to help her."

"No."

"And why not? I've seen how your vows hobble your ability to fight."

Gavriel shook his head in the darkness. Vows or best intentions aside, he would defend Ada. In that moment, in that place of danger, the primal impulse to defend his woman took precedent over every higher ideal—even if she could never be *his* woman. A few more minutes alone together and she would have been, no matter the consequences. He would not be distracted from keeping her safe.

He shrugged free of her talons and pinned her against the wall. She wore a kirtle at least, the gauzy linen beneath his hand made warm by the flesh of her hip. He squeezed until she let out a small yelp.

"Are you paying heed, *inglesa?*"

"Yes."

"You're not going anywhere. And I can fight."

"I've always suspected as much," she said. "Now use what you know to help her."

"Not if that means leaving you here and defenseless."

She laughed, a sound more like a sigh. "It pains me that you still believe me defenseless. I'll have to convince you otherwise."

"I take it back. But I'm not leaving you in the dark to scream your fool head off, not after all the trouble you've been."

"Is that all I am, Gavriel? Trouble?"

"Without question."

Metal-clad fists pummeled the door. Ada flinched but did not make a sound. There in the dark, she gave him room to adjust his stance—legs slightly spread, knees easy and ready. Again he wondered at the source of her training.

Finding her hand, he pressed the hilt of her dagger against her palm and curled her fingers.

"What will you use?" she asked.

"We'll find out."

"Open this door!" shouted a man on the other side.

"Not likely," Gavriel muttered.

The sound of a mace or a small battering ram replaced the metal fists. With the rhythmic strength of at least two men behind it, the ram made short work of the door. Splinters and hunks of wood burst into the bathing room, as did stray flickers of torchlight. Gavriel thrust out his hands and grabbed the shaft of the mace. He pulled it free of the surprised attackers, their grips momentarily slack when the wood gave way. Heavy and crafted of iron, the weapon was clumsier than he was used to. But holding any weapon felt *right*.

Two of the *guardias*, perhaps the same men who had just held the mace, used armored elbows and shoulders to bust through what remained of the door. Gavriel reared to the side and swung the spiked end of the mace across the nearest one's face. The nose guard sank into bone and flesh. The man screamed through a gurgle of blood.

Gavriel yanked the mace free of his first victim and turned

to the second. He hoisted the heavy iron shaft, wielding it like a simple club.

"Surrender," the guard said.

"No."

"You are encircled."

Gavriel freed a cold smile. "You'll be dead before that matters."

He spun and slammed the head of the mace into the other man's forearm. Bone cracked beneath the armor, his sword clattering to the ground. Gavriel kicked it out of play, hearing it splash into the hot spring as he swung the mace in a downward arc. He caught the guard across his right kneecap. The other man crumpled in a whimpering heap beside his fallen colleague.

Another two shouting guards pushed through the ruined door, their swords catching the scant torchlight from the hallway. Ada rolled in front of the rear man and curled into a ball at his feet, tripping him and stabbing him in the neck, while Gavriel dispatched his half of the duo.

Ada stayed low and peeked into the hallway. She snatched up one of the fallen torches, then scrambled away as more guards pushed into the bathing room.

Although the thrilling violence of battle infused him with energy, Gavriel resented his lack of coordination. His muscles had lost their reflexive training. The instinct he relied upon for most of his life had dulled, leaving him to consider each attack. He felt sluggish and ineffective despite the gathering pile of bodies at his feet.

"Where's Blanca?" Ada asked from behind him.

He nodded and pushed forward, stepping over the fallen. When he reached the doorway, he looked to the left and stopped short. Blanca was there, motionless and terrified. One of the same shepherds who had attacked them on the road stood behind her, his arm wrapped around her neck and a knife pressed to her windpipe. Another six guards loomed to their rear.

Had they followed all the way from Toledo? Because of Ada and her debts?

"I want the scrolls," the supposed shepherd said.

His rough, salty appearance may have frightened some, but his cultured voice sent chills down Gavriel's spine. The accent was unmistakable.

He tightened his grip on the shaft of the mace. Only stunned curiosity kept him from attacking. "What scrolls?"

The man pushed Blanca forward. A trickle of blood seeped from the skin at her neck. She whimpered, but her captor paid no notice. "I want the scrolls that Jew stole."

"Then perhaps you should find the Jew."

The man hurled Blanca to the floor and leapt forward. Gavriel lost his balance trying to avoid the fallen woman and stumbled over pieces of the ruined door. The mace proved useless for attack; on his back, he could not swing it with much force. Instead, he used it to defend against a downward cut from his opponent's blade. And if the accent had not been convincing enough, the red ruby eagle on the man's signet ring confirmed it.

He was no common brute sent to collect a debt. He was a member of the de Silva family.

Blanca had found her feet and jammed a ragged piece of timber into the back of their attacker's neck. He howled and reared back, flailing to retrieve the barb. Gavriel grabbed Blanca's hand and pulled her into the bathing room.

The other six guards were quick behind them.

Ada watched, amazed, as Gavriel continued to defend them. He had retrieved a sword from one of the fallen. In the other hand, he hiked his grip on the handle of the mace, using it defensively. His natural grace and eye for the weaknesses of his opponents, the grim, unflinching way he confronted each new challenge—just who was he?

Blanca stumbled to her side, clutching her throat. Gavriel's satchel tangled about her shoulders. "We have to get free of here," she said.

"Not until Gavriel clears the guards, I'm afraid."

"No, this way."

Before Ada could even ask a question, the other woman had dropped to her knees on the far side of the hot spring. She searched the walls until she found a slim crevice. A chunk of rock gave way to reveal a shaft just wide enough to accommodate a person.

Ada joined her and pushed the tip of the lit torch inside. "Where does it lead?"

"Up."

"Oh, truly?"

Blanca grinned. "I've never had to use it. The guards shouldn't know of its existence."

"No, but they could follow us. We need . . ." She searched the bathing room. "We need a diversion."

Although plenty of weaponry littered the floor, in and around the fallen bodies, Ada could think of no way to escape through the shaft without being pursued—unless Gavriel killed every man who made his way downstairs. But even he could not remain stalwart and flawless forever. Soon he would tire. He would make a mistake, possibly a fatal one.

She rubbed her arms, up and down and again, remembering how soft her skin had felt upon emerging from the bath, how it smelled slightly of rotten eggs. *Sulfane.*

She skittered away from the secret passage and knelt at the lip of the hot spring pool. She dipped her hand and brought a few drops to her mouth. The water was slippery and tasted brackish. Some sort of oil. The perfect diversion.

Gramercy, Meg.

"Gavriel! Here!"

He shook his head and continued to fight. "Keep down and out of sight," he bellowed over the sound of clashing metal.

Ada ran to Blanca. She thrust the torch and her satchel into the girl's hands. "When I say, count to five and touch the flame to the surface of the hot spring. Don't let the fire go out because we'll need it, but don't let it singe your brows either."

"I don't understand."

"Don't you question me as well! Please, do as I ask. Take our things when you make the climb. I have to ensure Gavriel will follow us." She caught the girl's panicked gaze. *"Comprendes?"*

"Sí."

Ada had to trust as well. She had to trust that Blanca's wide-eyed stare was not a sign of her mental collapse. And she had to trust that Gavriel wanted to live to see the morning, because he fought like a man who held no expectation of surviving an endless onslaught. He held nothing in reserve.

"Ready, Blanca? Go!"

Counting to five in her mind, Ada ran forward and into the fray. Gavriel's opponent, a skinny man with a dark red tunic, swung his sword in a truncated arc. The blade wedged in the nearby wall of moist stone. Gavriel raised the mace to strike the man down, but Ada caught his forearm. She pulled with all her might, yanking him in an awkward circle.

"Down!"

Blanca's timing was perfect. Just as Gavriel opened his mouth to protest, the hot springs went up in flames. A fat cloud of fire burst upward as the water ignited. Ada dropped to the ground in a tight ball and covered her neck with her hands. When the initial burst subsided, she found Gavriel on the ground beside her.

He was staring at the flaming pool. "How?"

"No time."

Chapter 12

"No! Ada, wait!"

But Gavriel's shout did not change her course. He followed Ada as she scrambled on hands and knees around the pool. With floor-to-ceiling flames between them and the dazzled guards, he grabbed her ankle.

She twisted at the waist. "We have to go!"

Where she intended to go he had no notion. Instead he concentrated on smacking her on the backside and along her spine. "Be still."

"What are you doing?"

"You're on fire, *bruja*," he said.

"I'm no witch—ah!"

Flames raced up her kirtle and jumped into her hair. She yelped again but her expression changed from brief panic to determination. She wiggled on her back, crushing the burning cloth into the stone floor worn smooth by countless sandals and bare feet.

Gavriel straddled her and extinguished the fires in her hair with his fingertips. The pain was nothing, and the smell of singed hair and linen hardly registered beneath the overwhelming stink of the flaming spring. He simply worked. Working was easier than thinking about what he had just done. No matter how out of practice, his talent for killing never failed him, unlike thought and patience and best intentions.

Fires out, Ada wasted no time heaving him off her lithe body. That he had been the one to linger irked him.

"Blanca's already gone," she hissed. "Quickly, before they see."

"Out? Out where?"

She disappeared into the smoke at the rear of the bathing room. The stirrings of a violent cough tickled deep in his lungs, but he refused to give in to the sensation. Not now. Not when they were still in danger. He caught up to Ada and crouched with her. She pointed to the back wall, tears running free from her reddened eyes. He turned to see smoke climbing up a narrow rock passageway, funneled to places unknown by the upward draft.

"Blanca?"

Ada only nodded and made to enter the passageway.

"Wait," he said, a hand on her ankle again. The image of her bare legs in his hands, there amidst the smoke and fire and armed guards, reminded him of her bath. But at least some part of his mind was working properly as he asked, "Dagger?"

She wore a dubious expression but did not hesitate. Dagger in hand, Gavriel sliced two lengths from the hem of her kirtle and handed back the graceful weapon. She still frowned but knew enough to keep her mouth closed against the billowing smoke. The only advantage to their location was that, guarded by flames and a poisonous cloud, none of the guards had advanced.

He only hoped that Blanca's familiarity with the bathhouse's secrets was unique.

Taking in as little air as possible, still fighting that unspent cough, he looped the strip of Ada's kirtle around her mouth and nose, tying it at the back of her head. She snatched the second piece from his hands and repeated the process for him. The filtered air nourished his brain.

A popping flame pulled his attention to the right, just in time to defend against the downward arc of a sword. He swung the mace up to protect his face. The jolt of impact sent shocks of pain down his forearms. Metal grated on metal and whined over the low roar of the fire. The guard reared back and hacked again, the force of it opening one of Gavriel's hands. The heavier end of the mace dropped to the stone floor with a hard clang. He spun away from the passage but not as far as he would have liked, trapped at the lip of the pool.

A sliver of white flickered behind the swordsman.

Ada.

She had been his burden for days now, insensate and helpless. This new, resourceful woman took some getting used to. For a brief and shining moment, he hoped she would behave sensibly. Up the passageway. Out of danger. Instead, she slid Gavriel's sword along the smooth stone floor, right between the guard's legs. Hilt in hand and muttering his appreciation for her resourcefulness, Gavriel flared to the offensive.

One jump found him on his feet and chest-to-chest with his opponent, their swords crossed and squealing. He stared down through the guard's visor and into his watering eyes. Muscles along Gavriel's back and arms—muscles for fighting and killing, long quelled—burned in protest, but he did not relent. The first to give way would find a sword in his gullet.

While Gavriel's roughened leather sandals found purchase, the man's mail-covered feet slid. They edged toward the fire in a slow and gruesome dance. With every step, the other man lost ground and weakened. Did that same violent cough lodge in his lungs, aching to burst free?

Enough of this.

With a last burst of strength, Gavriel shoved his blade. Mail scraped on stone. The guard landed hard and screamed, his ankle jutting at an odd angle from beneath his body. Of all the blood he had seen in those brief and brutal moments, Gavriel's stomach pitched at the sight of that ruined limb.

Ada had already abandoned the bathing room, the last flash of her pale calves disappearing as she shimmied up the inclined passageway. He twirled the sword to readjust his grip, leaving the maimed man alive, and cast one last glance around the engulfed room. None of the other swordsmen remained. The man wearing the de Silva signet ring was nowhere to be seen, if he yet lived after Blanca's nasty assault.

Too many questions remained unanswered, making the necessity of that violence even more revolting. He had fought for their survival, but against what enemies? Why?

Dizziness returned, leaving him lightheaded after the close-quarters duel. He shook away the questions and focused on escape. Weapons in hand, he clambered after Ada.

The incline of the passageway became steeper and more difficult to climb as she neared the light at its end. Ada lifted her knees and hiked the kirtle up to her thighs to keep it from tangling as she crawled. Darkness swallowed her courage. She tried not to anticipate what awaited her upon emerging from those tight, dark confines, hoping to find only Blanca at the top of the narrow shaft. Blanca, and a little light.

Behind the strip of linen Gavriel had tied in place, her nose burned and her throat scratched with every breath. She smelled nothing but smoke, that reeking scent of charred sulfur. No matter how she tried, she could not clear the thick taste from her mouth.

Wracking coughs overcame her. She stopped crawling and doubled over, burying her face in her skirts to muffle the sound. Pain gripped inside her ribs as spasm after spasm stole her breath. Tears dripped from her eyes. The sudden violence of that cough reminded her of the sickness she had endured for the past week. She had nearly forgotten its horrors. Those recent pains and humiliations already seemed distant, like someone else's struggle. She did not want to go back to being that pathetic creature.

Catching her breath, she heard the rustling and panting of a man climbing behind her. The bulk of his body blocked most of the light from the fire at the tunnel's base, and the light from a distant exit was not bright enough to illuminate his features. His shuffling advance was accompanied by a scraping echo from whatever weapons he dragged. Was it Gavriel? One of the swordsmen? In that dim half-light, she could not see.

She pulled the dagger from its sheath and struggled to turn around in the tight passageway, preparing to face that menacing male shadow. A full-length sword would be useless in there. If she could get one clean strike, she might have the advantage.

"Put that thing away, *inglesa,* and keep moving."

She crumpled. Days spent bedridden had left her fatigued and weak. But his rich voice reached out in the near-darkness and kept her from losing all fight. The ordeal of their time together made her eager to prove herself to him. But why? They owed each other nothing.

Yet she wanted to show him that the pathetic creature he had rescued was not her. Not truly. *She* was more. And she had not believed such a thing of herself in a very long time.

The dagger back in its sheath, she wiggled around to face the distant exit and continued to crawl. They shared the darkness, she and Gavriel, and the darkness did not seem so threatening. His even breathing followed close behind. The scraping metal that had been such a menace now offered comfort. He was armed. No matter what awaited them at the end of the passage, he would endeavor to protect her.

What a strange novice. And what a strange thing, to think of trusting him.

Ten feet from the exit, he tapped her on her calf. She gulped down a startled noise. He held a finger to his lips to indicate silence, then crooked that finger to beckon her closer. Slowly, quietly, she angled her ear nearer to his mouth. He smelled of sulfur and blood.

"Fast as you can," he whispered. "Get clear of the opening and find cover. I'll be right behind you with my sword."

She silently agreed. The anticipation of danger melded with his warm breath, speeding through her veins.

"But *inglesa,* do not try to help me. I need to know you'll be out of the way."

She pulled away just enough to see him. A man of shadows. But the intensity of his eyes burned bright and hot. Something had let loose inside Gavriel, something bleak and far more threatening than she could have imagined.

Ada nodded before pressing a quick, chaste kiss to his roughened cheek. He blinked. His intensity did not dim, but she felt released from its spell. She smiled, uncertain how much of her face he could see. "I'll only obey because I feel sorry for you."

"Oh?"

"No chance for a bath. You would've enjoyed the hot spring."

"Too hot now," he said. "Ready?"

He jumped free of the opening and landed in a defensive stance, his sword at the ready. But the room was empty, entirely empty save Ada and Blanca huddled low to the ground, just to his left. No soldiers, no furnishings. Only a single window and a waist-high door. Moonlight illuminated the steady stream of smoke flying free of the window casing, lending a dreamlike quality to their newest place of refuge.

"Where are we?" he asked.

"Another hiding place for people who don't want to be found," Blanca said.

He moved to the window and looked outside. "On the top story?"

Blanca nodded. "Yes, at the rear of the building. The door leads down to the main baths. This used to be a place to store belongings for wealthy patrons, but they must have found more benefit in this secret arrangement."

He stood and watched the dark smoke funneling out of the secret room and into the night. Anyone who yet wished to find them, no matter the reason, would only have to follow that dark, billowing line. "We must leave this place," he said. "Gather your things."

Sword in hand, he slid the blade between a strap hinge and the wall. Two quick jerks later and his sword sliced through the leather. He repeated it with the lower strap, opening the door. He grabbed the torch and glanced back. The women stood at the ready—a most unlikely complement of warriors. Ada held her dagger and satchel. Smoke and the filth inside that narrow passageway had stained her kirtle. Blanca used both hands to lift the bloody mace.

"You cannot use that," he said.

"No, but I can carry it until you need it."

He nodded and ducked through the small doorway. The corridor extended to his left, empty and lit only by the torch he carried. Dense curtains of cobwebs shuddered as the flames moved stagnant air laden with dust. Low, bare cross-beams jutted from the ceiling to either wall like ribs, making the narrow space feel even more confined. His instincts demanded freedom and hasty movements, but he fought those impulses. They would need calm in order to escape.

The women soon followed him into the corridor. Ada pushed her back against the half-sized door, which blended almost entirely with the surrounding wood. Despite what Blanca had said about the room's original purpose, he suspected it had always been used for subterfuge.

They encountered no one as they descended two flights of stairs, silent save the rustling burn of the torch. Gavriel focused on his breathing lest he become complacent. His senses sharp, he listened for any noise, any threat. But even as they reached the rear exit on the ground floor, they remained alone.

The focus and intensity he had summoned to confront even more combatants found no release. Hours of overwhelming impulses and sickening violence festered in his gut. He should have been thankful that the necessity for killing had passed. Instead, he wanted to hurl the sword and beat the bricks.

The image of that last man and his twisted, ruined leg pricked his mind's eye like a thorn. Then, layering atop the fresh carnage came the long-buried memory of another killing, that of his half-brother. He remembered a severed head and the screams of horses. So long ago. Sancho. Dead by Gavriel's hand.

Without preface or ceremony, he doubled over and retched. His tolerance for any more temptation or murderous excitement spilled across the hallway floor. Legs trembling and lungs straining for air, he dropped to his knees. The sword clattered and the torch fizzled against the flagstones.

Ada was at his side before he could tell her to keep way. "Are you injured?"

He wiped his mouth. "Leave me be. This I ask of you."

Her indecision became a tangible thing, the shimmering tension of a body locked between staying and going. "I will not," she said. "I must know if you've been wounded."

Gavriel exhaled, his head bowed low. She refused even his one small request. He needed a moment of solitude to better contend with his fresh failures. But still she did not obey. Violence he had thought exhausted rekindled beneath his skin— violence toward this woman and his hateful fate as her guardian. Those dark urges were easier to understand than lust, tenderness, admiration.

Tentative fingers rested on his shoulder. "Gavriel?"

"I'm not injured."

"Thank you," she whispered, almost too softly to hear. "You saved our lives."

He should have shied from her touch, but he wanted to lean deeper into her offer of comfort. He held still, compromising between desire and his best intentions. "You said thank you, *inglesa,* and your head did not melt."

Chapter 13

"I should have pushed you in the fire," she said, pulling away.

"Perhaps." Gavriel stood, his legs aching. "Instead you charged upon two warriors in the midst of a swordfight, distracting me and putting yourself in danger."

"Warriors? And here I thought you were a humble novice from the Order of Santiago."

Madre de Dios.

He had not thought of himself as a warrior in a twelve-month. To no avail, he wiped sticky hands along his hips. Blood had fused to his skin like metal to metal.

"*Inglesa,* any of *los guardias* could have taken the opportunity to gut me. You behaved rashly."

"Forgive me. I hadn't time to inform you of my plan. I took a chance, one that worked out for the best. And unlike my offer of thanks, I've heard nothing of the sort from you. Only mockery."

"How can I thank you if I don't even know what happened?" The thunder of his voice in that small corridor made Blanca gasp. He had completely forgotten about the young woman's presence. "You set the pool on fire? Intentionally?"

She nodded toward their wide-eyed companion. "I told

Blanca to do it. My task was to see if you might want to join us in a fortuitous escape."

"But what happened down there? How does water catch fire?"

Ada crossed her arms. "Are you asking because you want to know or because you want another chance to mock me?"

"Because I want to know."

This time she wore an unexpected smile. She could be laughing at him and he would not care. That smile was simply too beautiful. "My sister would've noticed the oil in that pool long before I did. With enough of it, even water can burn— just like an oil wick."

"How did you know?"

Ada lifted her forearm and pushed back the sleeve. "Smell," she said, raising bare skin to within inches of his nose. "That smell like rotten eggs?"

Gavriel looked not at her arm but into her eyes. With one inhale, he detected the earthy stench of sulfur beneath the pungent residue of smoke. "Yes."

"And do you see how my arm glistens? That's what burned, not the water."

Only then did he drop his gaze. Indeed her skin shimmered in the weak moonlight.

"You do this on purpose," he said, cursing the rough thickness of his voice. "Why? To taunt me?"

"To see what you'll do next. Unpredictable men are entertaining men."

"We're vulnerable here," he said. "Out now, toward the eastern gate."

Ada peered over his shoulder toward the abandoned courtyard. Although free of guards, the city's nighttime defenses would stand between them and the freedom of La Mancha.

They may as well have been walking through a market at midday for what cover could be found.

Blanca nodded to the north. "If we want horses, we should try the archbishop's stables. A line of shrubs decorating the perimeter should provide cover beyond the courtyard, and a low stone wall beyond that."

Ada and Gavriel turned to look at her, then at each other. She had been so unobtrusive; hearing her speak was like a statue coming to life or a cat showing an aptitude for language.

Ada smiled at the girl's resourcefulness, but Gavriel shook his head. "Skulking amongst bushes just before dawn," he said. "I don't like it."

"Which part of you objects—warrior or novice?" Ada asked.

"If it means escaping Yepes without further bloodshed, I don't object at all. But we should leave the horses. We can walk to Uclés if need be."

"Wait." Ada dropped her satchel and rummaged through it until she found the long, dark cloak. She wrapped it around her shoulders and said, "I do not make a habit of wearing solely my kirtle, especially when the white cloth will shine like a beacon."

"Good," he said, his gaze burning through the thick garment as if she wore nothing at all. Her kirtle had been all that separated her flesh from his eyes, his hands.

Yes, the cloak was a very good idea.

"But what about you?" She scowled, taking in the sight of his bloodied tunic. "If guards stop us, they'll want to know what happened."

"Then we cannot let them stop us. Blanca, can you lead us?"

The girl stepped out from the shadows and passed her gaze between Ada's face and his. A tiny smile tugged the corners of her mouth. "Can either of you be led? Truly?"

Ada grinned. "I told you she was clever."

"I need fewer clever females and more peace," he said. "Blanca, go now."

The trio skirted the edge of the courtyard, moving silently as they had down the bathhouse stairwell. Ada fixed her eyes on Blanca's dark headdress, but her thoughts hardly strayed from the man who took up the rear. Heightened senses tracked the rhythmic touch of his sandals on the soft ground and the heat of his body, a contrast to the cool night air. She wanted to shake her head, pull her hair—anything to regain her footing with regard to Gavriel. But nothing changed. Her fascination had blossomed.

Blanca held up her hand. They stopped where the line of courtyard shrubs ended. The flat expanse of the darkened street, lined with a low stone wall, stretched between them and the eastern edge of the village. That distance seemed impossibly far, and trouble awaited them. Eight men wearing the uniform of the town's *guardias* stood careful watch. They carried crossbows, wore scabbards, and flanked each side of the closed doors. Behind one gate made of crisscrossing iron bars awaited another hewn of wood.

"We would've been naive to hope for an easy exit," Ada whispered.

"But eight men is more than I expected," Gavriel said. "The uproar at the bath has them on alert."

He leveled his dark eyes, his face a grim mask. Ada had seen that lack of expression before, during that handful of moments before they had been attacked in the bathing room. The air fairly sparkled around him, energy and purpose and power, as he made the transformation from novice to warrior. But why did he insist on denying this, the most potent and natural part of him?

"The gate itself is straightforward," he said. "Two doors, both on pulleys. No embrasures in the wall. No tower or moat. Another few minutes without fighting and the men will relax."

Ada made herself assess that scene, to see what he saw. But she only found eight armed men standing between them and a way clear of the village. "Simple, then?"

"Not simple. Merely possible."

"Look," Blanca said. She nodded toward an alcove in the defensive walls where two horses waited. A lone squire stood holding their reins, swaying on his feet, eyes closed. "That boy lives on a farm outside the town gate."

"They must have brought more men in from the country-side," Ada said.

"No," Gavriel said. He wore the stains of battle from top to toe and carried two deadly weapons. So different now. "The boy may be from nearby, but those guards are from Toledo. Look at their weaponry—made of steel."

Blanca nodded. "He's right. I don't recognize any of them."

"Blanca and I can get those horses," Ada said. "Gavriel, you subdue the guards."

"Absolutely not."

"We can," Blanca said, thrusting the mace into Gavriel's hands. "I know the young squire. If I can speak to him, I can convince him to let the horses go in exchange for gold."

Gavriel scowled, but he clenched the mace without hesitation. "And he won't think of the punishment he'll receive once horses have gone missing?"

A smile rounded Blanca's cheeks all the more. "He's not the sort of boy to think much of the future. Can you ride, Ada?"

She matched Blanca's grin. "You really want out of this village."

"More than you know."

"Yes, I can ride."

Ada made ready to cross the road, but Gavriel caught her arm. "I don't trust you. Last time you sat a horse, you challenged bandits for the right to make for Toledo."

"That's before I knew better of your charming personality."

His grip on her arm tightened through the heavy cloak. "You'll ride off on your own and find the nearest apothecary."

She wrenched free of his hand, but not from his eyes. "Push a woman toward her vice too often and she'll succumb."

Blanca cleared her throat. "I appreciate your concern, *señor*, but she'll stay with me."

"How do you know? You have no notion of what she's capable."

"No, but she'll not leave her *hombre*."

Ada found no words. The thought of Gavriel being hers numbed her tongue. But his face had hardened. Neither warrior nor novice, at that moment he seemed another man altogether, one surrounded by stone and steel.

She forced herself to look at Blanca, tearing away from Gavriel's sharp profile and hard expression. "Gavriel is my captor, although he might claim otherwise."

"You both argue with great passion." Blanca shook her head softly. "Forgive me."

Gavriel exhaled sharply. "We waste time. Blanca, you get the horses. Ada, be ready at the gate. Be prepared to move quickly."

Ada tried for an easy grin but failed. "Does that mean you trust me now?"

"No," he said. "But none of us will be free of Yepes if we don't work together. Do you want act rashly and risk capture?"

She met Blanca's hopeful, eager eyes. "I'll do nothing rash," Ada said softly. "We leave Yepes tonight. All of us."

Gavriel crouched low, behind the shrubs, as the two women crept farther from the gate and across the street. He strained to see through the deep night, as if watching their retreating backs could ensure safe passage. Ada blended almost entirely, her cloak transforming her into as much shadow as substance.

Only their pale faces escaped the gloom, two bobbing white ovals pushing deeper into the dark.

He shifted from one foot to the other where he squatted, easing the tension out of each leg. They would have horses. And they would be safe.

With the women out of sight, he shuffled along the line of shrubs bordering the courtyard. One step beyond that protective cover and he would stand within full view of the men guarding the gate.

His heart beat at a moderate pace and his breathing was neither labored nor accelerated. So different now, compared to the bandit raid or the attack in the bathhouse. Aside from the blisters lining each finger, rubbed raw by the weapons he had not held in so long, his body had acclimated to battle. He heard every noise. He saw every line and angle of pale light. Nothing escaped his attention, especially not the vows he had broken or the odds against his success. Eight to one.

She'll not leave her hombre.

Blanca's simple statement rang through his head until it threatened to drown out the crickets, the soft, lonely wind, and the low murmurs from the guards. He had only ever belonged to one person: his father and master, Joaquin de Silva. The idea of belonging to a woman, to Ada, was more than he could comprehend. He might try contemplating the divine or the stars scattered against the sky with more certainty. Although he carried a mace and a sword, he could not feel the metal in his hands. He was too numb, stunned, turned upside-down.

Faint moonlight glinted off the deadly metal he held, dulled by dried blood. If he stopped too long to consider his deeds—those in his past, those yet awaiting him—he would never survive. Madness would claim him. God would forsake him, if He had not already. And the eight guards at the gate would sever his head from his rebellious body.

What had Ada said? *But then I might have an end to all this.*

He had not been the sort of man to wish for death, not for years. But the closer he came to the warrior he had been, the more comforting oblivion sounded.

He snarled at himself, out of patience but no closer to relief. Do the deed. Seek forgiveness come morning. If ever.

Chapter 14

Blanca crept among the shadows. Overhead and all around, the night was just beginning to give way to dawn. Stars no longer sparkled with the same brilliance, their brightness tamed by a faint but gathering glow. She imagined that when they breached the wall, the far eastern horizon would reveal the first streaks of blue before sunrise. Moisture gathered along her hem, the dew serving as another reminder that dawn approached like a swift horse.

She briefly wondered *if* they would escape the village. But with a quick glance to her left, to the pale woman with the strange accent, Blanca suppressed her doubts. She had fallen in with a dangerous and amusing pair, a welcome relief from crushing years spent as La Señora's only companion. When—not if—they escaped Yepes, those years would seem small payment for a life of her own.

"Ready?"

"I am," she said, nodding once to the Englishwoman. "And you keep lookout for your warrior."

Ada rubbed her arms. "I told you, he's not mine."

"So says you."

"And he's not a warrior."

"Oh?" Blanca craned her neck to find Gavriel in the shadows but saw nothing. He was more phantom than man. "What is he?"

"A novice to the clergy."

"So says he." She grinned. "Now let me introduce you to Paco."

The young squire stood between the two horses, apparently asleep, keeping himself upright from beyond the realm of dream by gripping the reins of both animals. Slim, wiry, and perfectly harmless, he had asked Blanca for a kiss the previous autumn. She had obliged, unimpressed by the sloppy undertaking and his roving hands, but feeling brave for having defied La Señora's strict rules. No money or ambitions of her own. No suitors.

No longer.

With Ada behind her, the horses standing between them and the guards at the gate, she approached the squire. "Paco? Paco, wake up."

He jolted to wakefulness. The horses neighed and shied, sounding unnaturally loud. Both women crouched deeper behind the cover of those large bodies. Blanca crossed herself and tossed a prayer skyward.

Keep them quiet. Let me free of this place.

When her breathing refused to slow, she pressed on regardless. That evening was not a time to wait for calm.

"Paco, it's me. Blanca. Wake up, *niño*."

"*Niño?*" Indignant and groggy, he pulled free of sleep and peeked around one horse's neck. "Is that all I am to you?"

"Yes, but you could be more." She gently rattled a small bag of coins sitting heavy in her sweat-dampened palm. Crooking a finger, she beckoned him into the alcove.

Paco followed, his head covered by the hood of his short cape and his ambling gait that of a roused sleepwalker. He flung back the hood in the alcove, eyes wide when he found

Blanca and Ada crouched there. "What is this, Blanca? Who is she?"

"All we want are the horses." Smiling, she held out the bag of coins.

Ada added spice to the deal by brandishing her jeweled dagger. "And in exchange, you can have either gold or trouble."

Gaining vigor, old reflexes assumed control of his limbs. Gavriel jumped from his lowly cover and charged the guards, wielding the mace against his nearest opponent. The man slumped to the earth with nothing more than a gurgle, his skull collapsed. In the corner where the shaft of the mace met its round, spiked head, he caught the second guard's blade and twisted. The sword flew free. Metal met bone. Felled, the man's unearthly scream split the still air, bringing all eyes to him, then to Gavriel.

Fatigue vanished in an explosion of energy. He dropped the mace and concentrated on his swordplay. Numbness gave way to the sharp clarity of battle. Mind and body quit their tiresome struggles and worked as one, turning and flexing against every blow. The sound of blood—rushing, flowing—filled his ears with the heady gust of violence.

Another guard slashed forward, the blade whistling near enough to Gavriel that air swished across his cheek. His hands ached with each successive parry. The clang of metal on metal reverberated through his bones and settled in his back teeth. A second man joined their clash.

Gritting hard against the strain, Gavriel fought the paired guards and a surprising flood of panic. He was losing ground. He had blithely broken his vows, a man convinced he would not meet his maker, not that night. But victory was never a certainty. Kill or be killed.

And he would not be the one to die.

Galloping horses and the hair-raising cries of two females briefly distracted the guards. One man ran into the night, disappearing. But Gavriel did not turn to see what he hoped was bearing down. He imagined Ada and Blanca riding with frantic speed, their garments fluttering behind them.

His body never stopped moving, thrusting, fighting. He connected the toe of his sandal with the soft muscle of a guard's inner thigh, setting the man off balance. A set of keys jangled at his waist.

"Inglesa!" With his sword, he absorbed yet another crunching blow. He did not look for her as the horses sped past, only trusted she would be there. Sidestepping, deflecting his opponent, he kicked the felled man. "This one has the keys!"

Shouts threatened his concentration, but the fever of one-on-one conflict narrowed his vision. Watching and waiting, he defended himself in a bid for time, only a little more time to find the guard's weakness. Parry. Retreat. And then what he sought: the other man dipped his left shoulder, turning slightly, tilting. Gavriel leapt forward and thrust with his sword, piercing leather armor and sliding between ribs.

He yanked his sword free and turned. Ada wrestled the keys from the fallen man, the point of her dagger poised over his left eye and her knee pressing against his windpipe. Even in the moonlight, Gavriel could see his face turning unnatural shades, first red, then blue. Ada's expression never changed, grim and fierce.

A shaky hand—his own—rubbed his eyes, his lips and jaw. Had he held a looking glass, his expression would match hers, battle hardened and indifferent.

What are we?

"Behind you!"

He swiveled on his heel, her warning saving him from a sword plunging downward. Iron clanged over stone as the guard lost his grip, his balance. Gavriel kicked him once before sprinting to the gate.

Ada was fast on his heels, keys in hand. She unlocked the winch casing that kept the crisscrossed bars of the portcullis lowered, then turned to guard him. Gavriel hauled on the winch handle, cranking the chains around its spool until the portcullis began to rise. His arms ached.

As he secured the chain to keep the gate lifted, he heard Ada shout. "Blanca, this way!"

Blanca looped back toward the gate, skirting past two men, and dismounted. "I hate horses."

Ada handed her the keys. "You didn't say!"

"No time." She slithered under the bars and ran ahead to open the lock securing the massive wooden door.

The remaining guards began to close ranks, cornering them against the second barrier. Gavriel hoisted his sword, gripping with damp palms, but he did not know how much longer he could hold off another four men.

"None of you move!" Ada shouted.

Ice formed in his veins. He turned to find Ada pressing her dagger to the young squire's throat.

"I'll kill him," Ada said, her voice dangerous like cut glass.

Blanca returned from the wooden door. She squeaked Ada's name. "Don't hurt him, please!"

Ada adjusted her grip on the dagger. "If the guards back away, there will be no need."

"Blanca, get through the gate with your horse," Gavriel said. "We'll meet you outside."

He watched Ada, seeing what any trained warrior would see. Her stance was wide and solid, but she had a weakness. Anyone who moved on her from the left would have the advantage. Gavriel would have to go around, over, or through her to defend on that side.

"Whose boy is this?" he asked the men. "Someone's son? Someone's ward?"

None of the guards responded, their eyes dark and hostile, their expressions unmoved. His suspicions about their coming from Toledo seemed correct. The steel weapons, the martial training—and none of them showed a flicker of sympathy for a local boy held prisoner. If he rifled through one of the dead men's possessions, would he find another de Silva signet ring?

"I suppose if no one values the boy, he's of no value to us. Ada, let him go."

"No, through the portcullis first."

He saw her meaning at once and grabbed the horse's reins. They shuffled backward, the whole world holding its breath. One of the guards moved to follow them, but Ada tightened her grip on the squire's forearm where she twisted it behind his back. The boy cried out.

Gavriel kicked the winch handle to drop the portcullis and ducked beneath it, safely behind its bars when it fell to the ground. He was atop the horse in an instant and circled it to the east, toward the open wooden doors. Ada threw her captive to the ground, sheathed the dagger, and raced on foot to meet him. His horse gained speed. He leaned over and extended his arm. She latched on. His muscles and joints screamed in protest as she held fast, momentum and the sheer strength of two desperate bodies propelling her onto the saddle.

Only when she pressed against his back, hands clasped around him, did Gavriel dig his heels into the horse's flanks and ride.

The horse flew over great lengths of grass, its pounding hooves hurtling them eastward. Ada intertwined her fingers just below Gavriel's sternum. He guided their mount with practiced ease, making her skills atop a horse seem childish.

She could only wrap herself around his tense, muscled body and bury her face between his shoulder blades, trusting him once again with her physical safety.

Trust was something she dearly needed, knowing with greater and more disturbing clarity that she could no longer trust herself—if she ever could. The opium had been bad enough. The kiss she slid past Gavriel's defenses had seemed daring yet harmless, although a deeper corner of her soul knew better. And now she had threatened the life of an innocent boy. She squeezed her hands together, ever tighter, to end the trembling.

He shouted Blanca's name. Ada brought her head upright. The midnight blue sky had lightened along the eastern horizon. Spring grass shone black in all directions, streaked with slivers of white as that faint, distant sunrise graced every blade. The desolate mesa absorbed their three bodies, insignificant on that flat expanse. No trees, no houses. So removed from the village, the landscape was no more inviting than a forest ravaged by fire.

Far in the distance, Blanca's silhouette clung to that of her mount. She rode little better than Meg, without blindness as her excuse. Gavriel caught up to her and took her horse's reins. The girl sagged in the saddle with a tired sigh, apparently happy to give over control.

"Has anyone followed us?" she asked.

"Not that I can see," Gavriel said, his voice scratching like a man felled by an ague. He breathed almost as heavily as did the horse. "We'll circle north until we find the Tagus. Trees along the banks might provide cover."

They reached Castile's most prominent river, its bubbling current made full by the spring run-off from the Albarracín Mountains in Aragon. Nourished by plentiful water, scrubby trees lined its banks, two and three deep. Leafy buds added splashes of pale green to the branches. Just seeing those trees—a place of refuge amidst the hard plateau—allowed Ada to breathe easier. Wash, rest, recover. She might begin to regain a year's worth of lost footing.

Gavriel pulled both animals to a stop. He angled his right arm back and extended it. The corded muscles of his forearms brushed the top of her thigh. She tensed. But at least she did not shiver.

"You first," he said.

Her bones like pottage, she clamped hold of his forearm and dismounted. She looked down, seeing boots planted firmly in the loam and grass, but she could not feel her feet. She was still too numb. Too startled by the night's events.

Gavriel dismounted and gave her an assessing look. But he shook his head and said nothing before helping Blanca down. "You did well," he said to the girl.

If Gavriel's look was fierce, Blanca's was murderous. "I need you to be honest, Ada," she said, bridging the distance between them. "Would you have killed him? Paco?"

Ada sought Gavriel's face, but he remained stubbornly detached and somber. Unable to do anything but meet Blanca's fiery eyes—so striking when set within the placid frame of her soft oval face—Ada exhaled slowly. But she found no answer. No genuine one.

"I've killed men," she said carefully. "Men who intended me harm. I like to think I'm not the sort of person who could take the life of an innocent, no matter the threat to me."

"But you cannot be certain," Blanca said. "Even now you hesitate."

Sickness welled in her mouth. Her conscience dared her to deny what she had become, someone cruel and ruthless, but she could not.

"Blanca, I . . . I don't know what to say."

"His name was Juan Paco de Yepes. He was a friend to me, a young man as eager to be done with our small village as I was." She ran both hands along her cheeks and into her hair, beneath the banded headdress she wore. Tossing the dirty cloth aside, she pinned Ada with another hard look. "I want to know what manner of people you are. Running and hiding, maybe even killing to defend yourself—I can accept that. But Paco did not deserve what you might have done."

Blanca left her horse and walked up river. Ada watched her go, gagging on unspoken words of apology—in part because the girl's changed manner so surprised her and, in part, because she did not wish to add lies to her uncertainty.

She wanted to slump into the ground and sleep for a month. If she had to wake up to being such an unpredictable person, maybe sleep was best for everyone. Safer. Easier. But her legs kept her stubbornly aloft, and Gavriel's bloodied tunic, becoming more gruesome as the daylight crept over the land, caught her attention. "You should wash before someone sees you."

A grimace pinched his face when he looked down, then away.

"You would have killed him, *inglesa*." The rumble of his quiet accusation, one without emotion or judgment, raised the hair on her arms. "I saw your face."

"And it wouldn't have made a difference, would it? None of the guards even blinked at my threat, and neither did they respond to your questions."

"You distracted them long enough to make our escape." Both reins in hand, he motioned her to follow him along the path of Blanca's retreat. "But killing him would have given us no advantage."

"I didn't think. I—how could I?"

He rubbed the back of his neck, appearing wearier than she had yet seen of him. "I ask myself the same, even against men such as those," he said.

Ada stopped short. "What do you mean, 'men such as those'? Who were they?"

"Never mind." Gavriel looped the reins around a low,

gnarled evergreen bough. He removed one saddle, then the other, and rubbed the exhausted animals' coats with firm sweeps of his broad hands. "Your protection is not your concern; it's mine."

"Protection?" Her laugh was sharp. "This from a man who swore off violence."

"We'll be safe in Uclés," he said, eyes distant. "*Los caballeros* will not allow anything to happen to us."

"Have you no intention of telling me?" She closed the distance between them and stopped the restless stroking. He pulled away as would a stranger, quickly, firmly—their kiss like a dream. "If you know something about who they were, I deserve to know."

"And what do you deserve? I've done everything to ruin my future with the Order, breaking my vows. And for what?"

Sword in hand, he left the horses and stalked eastward. She caught up with him a few long strides later, falling in step beside him along the craggy riverbank. He kept talking as if he expected her to follow. "I've fought every man who stood against us, keeping both of you safe, all the while damning myself. How is that just?"

"It's not."

"And you," he said, whirling. "Can you be thankful for the sacrifices I've made? Is it even in you? No. You try at every turn to make my task an impossible one."

"You forget, I never asked to be your mission."

"No, you simply wallowed in a pit without the sense to grab a rope."

Bursts of his breath warmed the tip of her nose. The pulse in his neck beat a haggard rhythm, one to match the pushing, pulling energy between them. Her heart echoed that fluttering as she leaned nearer, anticipating his kiss, needing it.

She licked her lips. Tasting the salt of her sweat and the pungent sting of smoke, she watched his mouth and wondered if he would taste the same. "Are you my rope, then? Shall I grab onto you?"

Ada did not look down, would not break the spell of their locked eyes. Questing fingers found his upper arms by instinct. She tightened her grip and reveled in that thick strength, thinking him invincible—infuriating and difficult, but invincible. And for that span of breath, she saw more than the features of his face. Through anger and frustration, she found a deep and hungry passion in his eyes. Want. Pain and want and a fear she could not comprehend.

What could such a man fear?

Seeking answers, seeking his kiss, she reached an unsteady hand to cup the roughened line of his jaw. He tilted his head into her palm, only slightly, giving her the faintest impression of surrender. She flexed her fingers. The heady rush of victory twined with desire.

"Kiss me," she whispered.

"Do my vows mean nothing?"

"They meant nothing in the bathhouse, or when we fought those men."

His expression soured. The heat in his dark gaze cooled until only two nuggets of coal remained. Calmly, with neither haste nor hesitation, he pulled her hand from his face. The scant distance between them became a wide sea. The flesh and blood man hardened, a cold statue taking his place.

"I do not want you," he said.

She could only stare, defeated and confused, as he walked away to follow Blanca.

Chapter 15

Gavriel secured the horses as the group settled near the river to wash and recuperate. He handed Ada a bundle of dried dates, but she kept her eyes lowered, an unusual silence wrapped around her. Blanca also kept her own counsel. The strained mood in their tiny camp—only two horses, a rim of scraggly trees, and the meager contents of their satchels—stood at odds with the stark, serene beauty of sunrise over the plateau.

He walked to the river, sheltered by thick trees tinged green with spring growth. Only here could trees survive the desert conditions of the Meseta, and they harbored wildlife of all kinds. Thrushes and sparrows paused in building their nests to greet the daylight, while common cranes milled on the opposite bank.

The fat waters of the Tagus rushed past with numbing monotony, loud, fast, and clear. He stood at the bank and edged the toes of his sandals over the moist loam, watching the water. Remembering and sorting. But not a single idea made sense.

How had he become so lost? Two weeks previous, he had been one task away from entering the Order, on the path to becoming a clergyman. He would have been safe then—safe from the men who hunted him, safe from becoming the hunter.

Now his vows lay in tatters. He had killed and wounded too many men to number.

And Ada. His obligation to her safety and wellbeing had burgeoned to an all-consuming need. Every sense, every thought conspired to render him vulnerable. A fire flared in his blood when he recalled her husky voice, when she had stood before him naked and waiting, bathed in the scent of her lemony soap. He groaned at the memory of her deep blue eyes and the stream of dark hair trailing over her shoulders, down to curl around her breasts.

Diós, he had lied to her. He wanted her—wanted her more than any woman he had known. What would it be like to possess her? She had such a powerful sprit and hectic mind. Beneath her unyielding craving waited strength and passion. He had seen it, felt it. He had tasted it. The idea of taking such a woman ignited his body. The idea of holding such a woman, holding her through the night . . .

He scrubbed his hands over his face. Wishing he could vanquish thoughts with swords and brute strength, he stripped out of the ruined, splattered tunic. Dawn air helped cool his ardor. He hesitated briefly, thinking of the Order's strictures against nudity, before removing his sandals and breeches, too. At the retreat, brothers were expected to take sponge baths and sleep in their robes. But he wanted his body clean, wholly clean, even if everything else about him had been corroded and spoiled.

He jumped in.

Breath exploded from his chest as the frigid water enveloped his wayward body. Thought fled. Pure sensation overwhelmed him. He kicked once, twice, and found the surface, swimming against the current to the bank. There he reclaimed his footing on the sandy riverbed, standing in the chest-high water. The cranes squawked and took flight, winged silhouettes against the early dawn sky.

He lifted a handful of sand and scoured his skin and his

hair, every pore stinging from the abuse. The blisters on his palms screamed in protest. Caked blood on his neck and arms dissolved and scraped away, just as new blood flowed from blisters. But he grabbed more sand and kept cleansing. Finally satisfied, he laced his hands at the back of his neck and squeezed, kneading the tendons and taut muscles. A headache pressed back from where it lodged at the base of his skull.

After a quick dunk to rinse, he propelled himself onto the bank and lay flat on his back. He closed his eyes and tried to overpower the shivers of cold, concentrating on stillness. But his body refused. Goosebumps covered him from scalp to sole, and he could no more stop his shivering than he could stop wanting Ada.

He swore softly. Cold water, cold air—none of it mattered. He responded to the mere thought of her name. Blood sped through his veins and gathered in his shaft. Lying there by the river's edge, he wanted to take his hard length in hand and find a moment of release. But he did not. He would not.

Shooting to his feet, he rummaged through the contents of his satchel until he found a change of clothes, all that he owned. He kicked his legs into breeches and punched his arms into a fresh tunic, working, working to regain control.

But what he would tell Pacheco about the past few days, what he would do if Ada approached him again—all mysteries. Baffling and impossible. He could only get them safely to Uclés and stand ready to accept the consequences.

Picking up his ruined, bloody clothes, he briefly considered stuffing them back in his satchel. Perhaps they could be cleaned. But no, he wanted no more reminders. His sharp and malicious memory already served that purpose. He balled the stiff, sickly tunic and breeches and tossed them in the river. Watching them float toward Toledo, he admitted the consequences of his deeds might be more than he could bear.

* * *

Ada pulled the damp red gown from her satchel and laid it across a branch to dry. She knelt next to Blanca where she slept, curled at the base of the tree, and laid her cloak over the girl like a blanket. At home in Charnwood Forest, she had done the same for Meg, a restless sleeper who often kicked their mantle to the floor. Ada always thought her sister would awaken in the middle of a cold night, unable to find it in the perpetual black.

But of course she could. Meg had been capable of anything. What Ada had never thought to accept was that Meg could take care of herself, and that the quiet, reclusive woman could feel so very much. For the first time, she allowed herself to wonder what a trial it must have been for Meg to fall in love, the terror and joy of it. And for the first time, she admitted she was envious of her sister's happiness. Perhaps she would not have been jealous had she stayed in England to repair the rift between them. Then, at least, she would have kept her sister—even gained a brother-in-law.

The vitriol that normally accompanied thoughts of Will Scarlet flared to her hands. She made hard fists, but the reflex was old and drained of its bitterness. He had made mistakes, like Ada. Like anyone. And he must have been quite a man to keep up with Meg, to understand her and find the secret reserve of her love. Ada never had.

Studying the smooth curve of Blanca's cheek, she wondered again why this girl elicited such thoughts of Meg. Perhaps because they shared the same quiet core, one forged of steel. Meg had listened. Blanca watched. But both of them thrived on stillness and observation. On being underestimated.

The women had one other thing in common: Ada had hurt them both.

Her voice was a whisper as she asked, "That boy I threatened, was he dear to you?"

She had not expected her to awaken, but Blanca's eyes fluttered open. "Is someone coming?"

Ada shook her head. "All's quiet."

"Good. I've had enough of running today, and it's not even full daylight." She squinted against the strengthening sun and pulled the cloak tighter around her shoulders. "And Paco was a friend. He defended me when the townspeople would talk, said he wanted to marry me one day. But . . . no, I couldn't have. I wanted only to leave."

Tears pricked the backs of Ada's eyes, some combination of fatigue and swirling emotions. Meg, Jacob—they brought back the worst memories because she had done her best to alienate them both.

"I know a young man like that," Ada said. "And I would be very upset if someone threatened his life."

Blanca frowned and rubbed her button nose. Even now, emerging from the shadows of night, Ada could not determine the girl's age. "We all faced terrible dangers last night," Blanca said. "You and *el hombre* risked a great deal to help me leave. But you . . . you don't behave that way generally." She lifted dark eyes, eyes that were unbearably hopeful. "Do you?"

Ada exhaled. "No," she said, finding strength in that one word. "Can you forgive me?"

"Of course." She offered a shy smile. "Life's too short for ill will."

"You are a strange one, Blanca. *Gracias.*"

She found the sun where it had lifted above the horizon. "*El hombre* has been gone some time. Is all well?"

"I'll find out. Here are dates to break your fast, if you like. But try to sleep. When Gavriel decides to leave, he'll probably give us little notice."

"And a great deal of ire."

Ada smiled. "Yes, most likely."

"He's the strangest monk I've ever met." Her eyes drifted shut with those last, fuzzy words, returning to sleep.

Standing and stretching the ache out of her knees, Ada pressed a hand to her chest. Deep inside, somewhere she could not name or describe, grew an anxious burning. These thoughts of poor choices, missed chances, and long-lost friends and family scratched her pride into shreds. She wanted relief from the shame of it, the loneliness and rejection, and relief meant opium.

Her mouth watered. Breath came in quick gulps while sweat on her forehead caught the early morning breeze. The unending reality of her condition bore down on her, that she would have to make this choice every time, every hour and every day. Strength of body and mind did not seem adequate to combat such a tireless temptation.

She walked closer to the river and lost her cares in the numbing sound of the water. Her eyes closed, urging sleep.

Gavriel entered the tiny clearing, sending a panicky jolt through her body. She clutched the base of her throat with one hand and held her dagger with the other. Had she really drawn it so quickly?

"You frightened me," she said.

He flicked his eyes to the blade. "Who taught you how to fight?"

He was clean and dressed in a fresh set of clothes. The rising sun burnished his skin to the color of polished wood. His dark, short hair still glittered with river water.

She tore her eyes away.

"Jacob," she said at last, gripping the dagger's jeweled handle. "Ever since we arrived in Castile, we've depended on one another. I wanted that knowledge, and he obliged me. I needed to feel that I could protect myself . . . better this time."

"This time? Do you mean your feet?"

"Yes."

Inside her boots, she flexed her toes and told herself that she imagined the pain blazing along her soles. A ghostly burning. But she felt the cut of Sheriff Finch's dagger—the dagger she held—as clearly as she had on that distant day in his dungeon.

She needed opium. Nothing else banished that phantom pain. Gavriel thought he was making her well, and she had to admit that her clear mind and invigorated health were both precious possessions restored to her. But she was terribly thirsty.

"Jacob taught you well," Gavriel said. "But he is young and fights with two blades."

He lunged without warning. Although Ada raised her dagger against the attack, he angled around the arc of her blade. His elbow jammed between two ribs and his hand circled her wrist, taking the dagger out of play.

"He's made you vulnerable, your left side unprotected." Elbow withdrawn, he smoothed his hand over her ribs and let her go. "Right here."

Embarrassment heated her face and the skin at the back of her neck, hot as a sunburn. "I never said I was a warrior."

"Then don't posture as one."

"Fair advice from a clergyman."

"You were close, you and Jacob?"

She searched his expression for clues. But his face, like his voice, revealed nothing. Discussing her relationship with Jacob may as well have been discussing trees or clouds. No judgment or hopefulness. No emotion at all.

"You're not my confessor," she said, toying with one sleeve. Her filthy kirtle reeked of smoke. "I shall say nothing. More intriguing to discover what you're willing to assume."

"Yet the more I know about you, *inglesa,* the less likely I am to judge you."

"Your place is not to judge at all, novice." She looked at his empty hands and his satchel slung over one shoulder. "Because I wonder what happened to the clothes you wore last night. Will you ever be able to remove the stains?"

"This has naught to do with me," he said. "Why did you turn to opium if you had learned to fight?"

"No matter how hard I practiced, no matter what I learned, the nightmares returned. Even after my feet had healed, opium . . . it became everything." She wanted to whirl and pace, but she held perfectly still and drew nourishment from that gathering rage. "I would sleep and face terrible things, bringing none of my new skills into my dreams. Only pain and fear. Opium erased all of that."

His face twisted into a sneer. "And it was far easier than training and working, I suppose. And now? You're not cured, you must know."

"Don't you think I know that?" Tears stung behind gritty lids. "It's here with me, no matter that my sickness has ebbed. A lack. An absence, like a missing limb."

He stood motionless, staring at her. His face softened—only a little, briefly—leaving her to wonder if she had imaged it. "Ada, would you drink the tincture right now if I offered it?"

"Yes."

She shut her eyes and slapped one hand across her mouth. But the blunt, ugly truth had already been spoken.

Reaching up, he tugged her hand away from her mouth and held it in both of his. "You would go back to that life?"

"And why not? Because this place offers such charms? You insulting me—no, kissing me first and then insulting me." Ada wrenched free of his gentleness and pity, at last giving way to the frenetic need to spin and pace and shout. "My head is clearer and my eyes are open wide, but that only means I can see how *awful* this is. I once had family and friends and a purpose. I threw away what wasn't taken from me. Is that what you want to hear? Because I threw it away!"

She slammed her fist into the craggy bark of a cork oak. Pain flamed from her knuckles to her shoulder.

"Ada!"

Gavriel took up the ball of her hands, the right wrapped tightly over the injured left, and pried her fingers back. Skin atop the hill of each knuckle had split. The tears that had threatened all evening, all morning, burst free, but she did not sob. Cheeks wet, she simply stared at the damage she had wrought, all blood and ruined skin.

The fight boiling in her veins cooled and slowed. "Don't touch," she said. "You've just had a wash."

A frown sat on Gavriel's brow but he did not let go. "I've had blood on my hands before."

They walked to the river where Ada rinsed her knuckles in the cold water. She kept her hand submerged long after the wound was clean, welcoming the soothing numbness. Minutes passed as Gavriel used the ripped remains of his white robe to bind her hand. She kept her mind focused on his agitated breathing and that constant frown, a statue no longer.

"Do you see that nothing will keep me from going back?" she asked. "What do I have?"

"Pride. Respect for yourself. A future."

"You speak of futures." She shook her head, eyes closed around the memory of her last floating high. "You have no notion of how beautiful it is."

"No, I won't let you."

Chapter 16

"You'll not let me?"

"No." Gavriel finished binding her hand, grateful to put an end to touching her. Yes, grateful. Tension pressed inside his lungs and threatened to burst. "Not after all I've done to drag you to health."

"What am I, a ewe?" She pulled her hand back, cradling it against her abdomen. Salty lines streaked her cheeks, but at least she had stopped crying. "Would you be my shepherd, leading me back to the flock?"

"What I say is intended to help."

"You care nothing for me," she said. "And your only value to me is as a distraction."

"A distraction?"

"Oh, let's not forget your skill with a sword." She pinned him with a taunting look, one he wanted to kiss off her face. "You think you can offer help, but you are quite possibly the most confused individual I've ever known—without exception for even my sister."

"Confused, am I? I'm not the one who just ruined my hand."

Her blue eyes narrowed. "No, you're a warrior who thinks he has the patience and restraint to become a clergyman. But

I wonder what your masters would think if they knew all that has occurred. Will they accept you, welcome you home?"

The same defeat and despair he had battled moments before, alone by the river, needled him again. But this time he had no illusions. They stripped away as violently as Ada had flayed the skin from her knuckles.

"No, they won't," he said.

"Then I have an offer, if you're willing to hear it."

Insides cold, he nodded.

"A generous boon," she said, smiling slightly. He had learned to be wary of that smile, like heeding the growl of a starving dog. "I'll listen to whatever pearls of wisdom you have for me. And I'll present your story of these last days however you want. The masters need be none the wiser. You don't believe me, but I will. I'll listen and protect you."

"You'll obey?"

Her smile widened. "Of course."

He searched her face, every soft slope and bend. Caution and her devilish smile warned against using rational thought. Nothing they did bore resemblance to logic. Their days and nights were determined by instinct and urges alone—fight, survive, need.

"Nothing comes easily, especially not with you," he said. "What do you want?"

"Tell me who you are."

"Inglesa."

Not even his warning tone diminished her teasing. She rose up on her knees and leaned near enough to tempt him with the dark drape of her hair tumbling over one shoulder. "You have the power, Gavriel," she whispered. "Me—cooperative, sweet natured, genial. Completely docile and willing to listen to you. All I want is something true. From you."

"I am Gavriel de Marqueda."

She traced his earlobe with her fingertip, down to his jaw,

down to his chin. At the slightest pressure, urging him to lift his face, he met her gaze of heat and promise and the sweetest sin. She touched the pad of her thumb against his lower lip. Breath scorched his lungs.

"An imbecile can change his name, and you're no imbecile," she said. "Tell me."

He swallowed. Certainty swirled away, a victim of the desire ebbing between them. All he knew, all he could claim in the world, was that this Englishwoman had become his responsibility. He had sacrificed his future, his security, perhaps his very soul. Her welfare had eclipsed all other obligations.

He grasped her upper arms. Their faces came together, only his hesitation separating them. He tightened his grip but she did not flinch. Her lips merely parted, a silent invitation.

"I am your guardian," he rasped.

"And you *do* want me."

"*Sí.*"

Touching his lips to hers, he felt the urge to punish her for the confusion and useless desire she had thrust into his life. Breeching the boundary of lips and teeth, he plunged his tongue into her mouth, tasting the lingering sweetness of dates. He circled his arms around her back and dragged her flush against him. She did not resist. She accepted him and dueled with him, her pliant body folding into his. Soft, full breasts melded to the firmness of his chest, ripping away the last of his doubt, reason, breath.

He wanted to punish her, yes, but Ada did not relent to the forceful assault of his kiss. She accepted every thrust of his tongue, meeting him with the same urgency. She pushed eager fingers through his hair and rubbed down to the scalp. Her injured hand looped around his neck, her forearm pulling him closer to deepen their kiss. She moaned, the seductive sound weaving into his blood and urging more. She nipped at his lower lip. Tiny sparks of pain merged with mindless pleasure, pleasure he had denied himself for too long.

Every touch, every taste merged with wild thoughts he strove to repress. She was a fantasy made real, a devilish goddess sent to drive him mad. And mad he was, kissing her and cupping the weight of her breasts. He kneaded that tender flesh and found her hardened nipple through the taut cloth of her kirtle. With thumb and forefinger he tugged and pinched, damning the clothes that separated them. She moaned again and pushed into his hand, another invitation that savaged his weak grasp for control.

He pushed her back, back into the rough grass at the river's edge. With his lips he found the crook of her neck and kissed, suckled. She grasped the base of his skull as she arched, tantalizing him with softness and strength. Pent up need burned in his lungs like inhaling fire and smoke. No number of breaths assuaged the ardor. Only Ada, more of her kisses and more of her willing, wanton body.

Unruly fingers made a jest of his attempt to untie the strings at her throat. A knot confounded him.

She pushed against his chest and looked at him directly, teasing him even now. Blue eyes had darkened, her pupils wide. "Slow down, for I cannot help you." She glanced to the hand he had bandaged. "Inconsiderate of me, I know."

"Where's Blanca?"

"Asleep beyond those trees, over by the horses."

He nodded once and reclaimed her mouth, but a surprising gentleness overtook him. The desire to linger over the slick texture of her lips, the roughness of her tongue, and the sharp nip of her teeth infused him with delicious languor. They moved together, hands and mouths working toward a common purpose so unlike their combative history. Gavriel threaded his hand into her dark tangles until he cupped the back of her neck. She shivered. He groaned and kissed her, nothing remaining but his mouth over hers, her body under his.

With more haste than patience, he returned to the kirtle's ties. With more hope than success, he tried to ignore the brown traces of dried blood remaining beneath his fingernails. The dismal reminder of his violence should have stilled his hands and left him ashamed. But what did it matter? What vow of chastity should confine him now that he had ruined his every other promise? He had wanted Ada, and she was his for the taking.

The laces finally parted. He released a shuddering breath, one she matched. Mere moments passed as she shed her kirtle. Rigid and breathless, Gavriel stared at her, absorbing a sight he never thought he would experience, let alone twice. But memories of the bathhouse, that dank and dark place, could not compare. She knelt beside a spring river bathed in early morning sunlight, pale skin made golden perfection. His hands needed the inward curve of her waist and the gentle flare of her hips. His mouth needed the pert pink tips of her breasts.

And her face . . . she looked at him with an open and humbling hunger. Once he had thought to replace the blissful expression she wore during her opium high with one of desire for him. But the opium had created for her a cloudy place of contentment. Her desire proved more devastating and greedy, her eyes clear and direct.

"You're magnificent," he whispered.

She blushed, the first hint of any embarrassment. But it was gone with a blink. Only hunger remained. "Your turn."

If he had taken her breath away—clean, but fully clothed— he threatened her life when he shed his tunic and breeches. Firm muscles flexed beneath burnished skin. Dark hair swirled intriguing patterns across his chest and tapered to the thatch surrounding his large, swollen shaft. A lighter dusting of dark hair colored his forearms, thighs, and calves.

Yes, this is what she wanted. Needed. She knew how he tasted and she knew the hard resilience of his muscles, but the thought of touching that skin, so different from her own, made her edgy and eager. Pain had not made her regret the damage done to her knuckles; knowing she would only be able to touch him with one hand did.

She had not expected him to linger. She had imagined their coupling a quick and furtive thing—Ada pushing and tempting, Gavriel of two minds until the needs of his body dominated his conscience. But standing nude and shameless, he showed no sign of hesitation. Any doubts he harbored had been laid aside with his clothing, even if his expression was clouded by some grim purpose, not joy or affection or even lust.

"Will you change your mind?" she asked.

"I've no mind left to change."

He walked slowly toward her, and she could only stare, mesmerized. The only other man she had seen naked and aroused was Hugo, the duplicitous thief she had taken as a lover to spite her sister, and even that had been fleeting. Ada's affair with Hugo had been a secretive one, conducted behind Meg's back. He had never . . . *displayed* himself with such brazen delight. And he never had so much to display.

"You do this on purpose," she said, echoing his choked words from before dawn. "To taunt me, I suppose."

"No, to see what you'll do next."

He stood before her, his thick member level with her mouth. A dare. She liked it, for daring required a little imagination and maybe even a touch of humor. She licked parched lips and heard him groan softly. She shifted slightly where she knelt, the hot wetness between her thighs allowing skin to slide over skin with no resistance. Deep muscles clenched without thought, wanting him. Needing him to fill her.

But first that dare. She had never imagined such an erotic and unfamiliar act. Sex with Hugo had been terse, unsatisfying, leaving her nauseous and regretful. Now her stomach tensed in anticipation. Gavriel waited, his eyes filled with a need akin to begging, and her imagination lit with pictures of everything she wanted, everything she wanted to do.

Kissing him there, taking him into her mouth—the ideas would not be ignored, thrilling her with heady power. After too long being the weak one, that power was as tempting as the pleasure of touch.

With deliberate slowness, she lifted one of Gavriel's hands, then the other, and placed them on the back of her head. As soon as his palms met her hair, he squeezed to gather thick handfuls. He pulled, bringing her face even closer and forcing her to break eye contact. She could count the quickness of his pulse along the turgid veins of his phallus.

He tasted mildly of salt, her tongue touching his most sensitive skin. He hissed and clenched his hands tighter. Tension radiated from his arms, a fine trembling. Primal and arousing, cleaner than sweat, the spicy masculine scent of him filled her nose. Teasing him with tiny licks became a rushing thrill unlike like any drug. More potent. Less predictable. It had life—tensing and anticipating, in awe of his control and wondering at her own.

She allowed the head to glide between her lips, taking him gently into her mouth. Her eyes rolled shut and she focused on nothing but the foreign texture of him. Smooth, silky smooth, but hard and ridged. She traced circles with her tongue. He groaned and began pumping a slow rhythm with his hips.

Tentatively, accepting that languid rhythm, she slid her good hand up his leg. Yes, that scratchy hair. Yes, those long ropes of muscles. Touching him was just as strange and arousing as she had imagined. She cupped his buttock as he tensed, relaxed, tensed again. Her tentative touching gave way to rougher caresses, digging fingernails into that taut flesh.

Gavriel released her hair and framed her face with his broad hands. He would be able to feel his own hardness distending her cheeks. Wetness rushed between her legs at the thought, that sensuous ache blossoming into hot desire. She moaned. He responded by pulling free of her mouth and kneeling, chest-to-chest before her.

The sudden change dizzied her. His eyes held no clues as to the sudden end of their game. "Something the matter?"

He shook his head, unflinching. "You don't want me to finish alone, I assume."

"Finish alone?"

"To have my release now, instead of between your legs."

She rubbed two fingers along her lips. They felt slightly numb. "Oh."

He bent at the waist and kissed her shoulder. Chaste. Soft. With such tenderness. "I'd not be so selfish," he said, his voice dancing shivers across her skin. "Not without your permission."

"I want . . ."

He kissed her right shoulder. Instead of pulling away, he nuzzled closer and found her neck. Sensation budded her skin, goose bumps everywhere. He smelled of water and sunshine. His hair tickled her cheek. Dipping lower, he took one nipple into his mouth. She gasped and arched. One of his arms supported her lower back as he leaned over her, arching her deeper. He licked that sensitive peak, just patient strokes of his tongue, unhurried and maddening.

Ada wiggled inside her own skin. Just when had he assumed control of this seduction?

"You want what?" he asked.

"I—*oh*."

He caught her nipple between his teeth and sucked. Her eyes closed again, lost in his caress. She found herself lying on her back, once again stretched against the warm earth, but this time her back was bare. The grass tickled and scratched, layering sensation across her heated skin. Gavriel followed her down and took the other nipple in his mouth, repeating that thorough, precious torture.

Kissing again, their mouths dancing in a sweet rhythm, he slowed and stilled. The low sun haloed his head and lightened the sharp ends of his hair, his face deeply shadowed.

"Gavriel? What is it?"

"Some moments are only for now, although we pay for them forever."

She fought the sudden assault of tears. So very tired. Her body craved, but her mind was beyond the capacity to manage that craving. She understood what it meant to *want,* only for the moment. Consequences be damned. She grieved at finding herself in that terrible, inevitable place once again.

"Then make these moments dear," she said. "That is what I want."

He reclaimed her mouth with a groan, the languorous mood between them turning frantic. Hard hands gripped her hips, kneading and pulling. Every sensation banked by their solemnity flared to life, hotter and more desperate. He raised her arms over her head and held her wrists in one hand. The imprisoning position should have frightened her, unable to move beneath his solid weight and unyielding hold, but she thrilled in his raw power. Her body wanted his. And held in the grip of those shocking desires, she found only pleasure in submitting.

His free hand found the nub at the apex of her thighs. She parted her legs without thought, only sensation guiding her. A cry built in the back of her throat as he circled his thumb gently, then rougher and quicker. She raised her hips as much as his weight would permit, rubbing against the hard, hot length of his shaft. But no matter how his thumb rocked her ever closer to release, she refused to let go, not without their bodies joined.

"Are you a virgin, Ada?" The husky tone of his voice pulled her eyes open. The unaffected statue was gone; in its place was a man losing control. *"Tell me."*

In the eye of her own storm, she calmed. "You would be gentle with me, wouldn't you?"

"Yes," he ground out.

She sighed and reached between their bodies, grasping his heavy length. "No need."

Groaning, he filled her with one firm stroke. She cried out. He released her wrists and clamped a hand over her mouth, burying his own mouth in the crook of her neck. His powerful hips propelled their paired rhythm, fast and candid. Every thrust stretched her body and threw her higher into the sky.

She wrapped her feet around his lower back and locked one ankle over the other, absorbing his sweet violence. The sheer rightness of his body over hers, in hers, left her dazed and trembling, her climax crashing down like a warm, pelting rain. From beneath Gavriel's muffling hand, she cried out again.

Rapid breaths fanned over her neck, his hips jerking until he too was overcome by that pleasure. His body stiffened. And buried in her one last time, he did not groan or shout— merely whispered her name.

Chapter 17

Ada rested with her head against his chest, hair draped around her shoulders like a blanket. Gavriel concentrated on the steady cadence of her breathing, lest his mind, body, and soul begin another torturous contest. Lust had dissipated, a cloud blown into strands across the high, blue sky. In its place was exactly what he sought. A place of peace, no matter how brief.

He would have lain by the banks of the Tagus and held her for eternity, nude beneath the tentative shade of spring leaves. Yet the time spent in each other's arms felt more like a blink. Brief, yes, but not without consequence. Not in the least.

Upon arriving in Uclés, he would find either forgiveness or banishment. He would either become a clergyman or return to the life that set him on course to collide with his father. Violently. Ada had no place in either future, no matter their attraction.

He felt the need to protect her even still, especially from herself, and knowing they would be separated upon Jacob's return sat like a thorn between his ribs. His own future was a shambles, but he would not let her slink back into a life of misery and mindlessness.

When she raised her head, Ada wore no more contentment

on her face than he felt. She scrutinized him even as she idly stroked his chest hair, down to the skin, petting. Silently she asked the same question that battered inside his mind: What now?

"You and Jacob were lovers," he said quietly.

"Never."

When he had stood before her, naked and aroused, offering his shaft, she had not shown surprise or fear. And he remembered where they first met, there in the brothel. She had been desperate then, desperate and in debt. What other means of procuring her precious drug had she employed?

The very idea of Ada's mouth on another man burned him from the inside out. He could not breathe, so surprised at the violence of his reaction. His throat ached as if he had swallowed bright red coals.

He pushed her away and sat up, untangling their limbs. "Then you were a prostitute," he said as plainly as pounding blood would permit.

"I never was."

"Then what—?"

Ada gasped. He looked to the side, expecting any manner of villains to intrude on their private idyll—or Blanca, at the very least. Although the girl helped arrange clandestine affairs for her aunt, Gavriel did not intend to share this particular affair with anyone.

But no one approached. Ada had followed him to a sitting position. Eyes rounded, she stared at his back.

Not this. Not now. I am not strong enough.

"Who did that to you?" she asked, her voice ragged.

He had kept her hands above her head purposefully, to save her injured knuckles from further damage and to keep her from touching his back. But she reached for him now, fluttering the softest touch over ridges of scarred flesh. Although he knew her fingertips were cool—knew it in his mind—he only felt the burning slice of a whip. But he did not flinch or pull away. He had learned to hide his weakness, knowing the punishment was worse for those who showed cowardice.

So he sat naked and perfectly still, his back straight, as Ada scuttled closer. "Gavriel?"

"Leave it, Ada."

"Absurd, foolish man."

She stood and found her red gown, shaking out the kirtle that still smelled of smoke. Smoke and Ada. He kept his eyes pinned on the rushing water, deep shame conquering the desire to catch one last glimpse of her naked body. He grabbed his tunic and breeches and struggled into them, his hands numb and clumsy, hands that had only just held her.

"Jacob was not my lover and I was never a harlot," she said, fully dressed, her face surprisingly composed. "The man before you was my sister's intended. I was a wretched, self-ish creature—still am, truth be told. I'd believed no fate could be worse than caring for my blind sister for the rest of our lives, alone together in the woods, and I used Hugo as a means of hurting her."

From the first, he had been able to feel when she lied, a bone-deep knowledge he found so unnerving. His hard stare failed to find a lie in her posture or expression. He heard no deceit.

But, truth at hand—which was worse? That she could sell herself, or that she could be deliberately cruel to her own kin. At least he understood the latter.

"Is that why you left England?"

"No," she said, face turning pink. She had hardly blushed during the course of their sultry morning, but now she did. "The swordsman who detained me for the sheriff, his name was Will Scarlet. He was also the man who mounted an army to come to my rescue. He and Meg had formed an attachment and were married. Because Jacob had always longed for ad-venture, we departed for London, then Toledo." She knelt with him, their faces level, hers a picture of abject grief. "I could not forgive her for what I thought of as her betrayal."

Fear gripped him around the middle. "And this man, Scarlet—he could not be redeemed to you?"

"She abandoned me. For *him*. No matter what I'd done, and no matter what he did to atone, he was the man who had locked me in a dungeon where the Devil played." Wiping at her eyes, she shook her head. "Do you know what it is to need someone to blame?"

Images of Sancho's lifeless body ruined their riverside retreat. The sword that severed his brother's head had been Gavriel's, but the blame for their confrontation was Joaquin de Silva's to bear. His alone. At least, that was what Gavriel had long worked to convince himself.

"Yes," he said. "That I understand."

"That's what I needed. I blamed Will Scarlet for taking my sister from me, when I'd already done my level best." In her eyes he read nothing but concern, more unnerving, even, than if he had seen scorn. She touched his face. "Who hurt you?"

"I will not, Ada."

Her hand stiffened against his cheek. "I've answered your every question."

"You offered."

She sunk her fingers into the cropped hair at the back of his skull, tugging their faces together. Close enough to kiss. Close enough to tempt a saint.

"Your back looks streaked with cart paths." Her hushed voice trembled. "What unearthly animal would do such a thing to you? Who?"

"I did."

"You?" Concern dissolved into disbelief, then something darker. He saw revulsion. "You scarred yourself? I don't believe it."

Her hand dropped to her side, and Gavriel steeled himself

against that loss. Standing, his legs stiff and aching, he clenched his fingers. Blisters rubbed together and split skin throbbed. That pain—yes, he needed that pain.

"Now that you are recovered, we'll be traveling to Uclés," he said. Ada still knelt in the grasses and sandy loam, her face to the horizon. They regarded each other as strangers again, and Gavriel pushed back a strange welling of grief. "Considering what happened in Yepes, you would do best to wait at the monastery until Jacob returns for you. Do you intend to accompany me willingly?"

"Yes."

"And how will you be traveling there?" he asked.

She rose. Tendons tensed in her neck. If she forced his hand, he would make her walk once again—regardless of her scarred feet. He had nothing left but his will over hers, however useless and damaged that was.

She lifted her head. "May I have a horse to ride?"

"Yes. But I hold the reins."

Ada wanted to collapse across the horse's neck. The strain of their long, strange night heightened her fatigue. The stark sunlight, so beautiful and gentle at dawn, had turned fierce come midday. Sweat lined her forehead, and her eyelids did nothing to bank the brightness. She missed wearing a veil, as her skin sizzled beneath those intense rays.

And her hand ached, a lingering reminder of the morning's many follies.

Blanca sat behind her on the horse, the girl's plump arms circling Ada's waist in what could only be described as death's own grip. The quick, steady gait of their mount terrified her. And, true to his word, Gavriel rode just ahead of them, the reins of her horse in hand. Straight and tall in his saddle, he inspected every shallow and rise with unblinking eyes. The sword looked right in his hand, perfectly fitting his warrior's physique.

But seeing him carry it without reservation sent a shiver of regret through her. He had made vows. For her, because of her, he had broken those vows. The rigid determination in his posture meant he was still on the lookout for men who would endanger their lives, but he wore the responsibility like a noose. He would return to Uclés, yes, but to what life?

She stared at the expanse of his shoulders, his back, and tried without success to understand him, unable to banish memories of the vicious scars crisscrossing his supple skin. He claimed to have committed that villainy himself, but she could not imagine why or how. Gavriel was a hard man, almost entirely opaque to her, and the need to touch him again raged through her body with the force of another familiar craving.

No.

She had hurt Jacob and her sister, her own flesh and blood, and had learned to expect as much heartache in return. If Gavriel spoke the truth, if he had truly caused himself those dreadful injuries, then he was entirely too damaged, beyond reach of even the steadiest and most accepting of touches—certainly beyond what she could ever hope to accomplish.

Instead, she would put this miserable mistake behind her. He expected her to stay at the monastery through the month. So be it. She would practice translating Daniel's scrolls until Jacob arrived to retrieve her. Upon returning to Toledo, she would resume her work for Doña Valdedrona. And if the nightmares returned, well, she would be better equipped to handle her craving. She could take comfort in opium's floating release without succumbing to it entirely.

Just as you've handled your need for him?

Gavriel rode alongside them, his hair illuminated by the sun, a great ball of gold in the sky, as it tipped toward afternoon. *"Inglesa."*

"*Sí?*"

"We'll be at Uclés by this evening." He pointed to the eastern horizon, a cathedral and two towers emerging from the endless Meseta. The structures must be massive to appear so large at that distance.

"Is Uclés an exciting place, *señor?*"

His expression did not soften even for Blanca's eager question. "Not particularly. 'Tis the same, I should think, as the town you wanted to escape. Only, come evening, it sits in the shadow of the monastery."

Blanca relaxed her bruising grip only a little. "I never considered where I would go, only that it should be somewhere else."

Ada smiled, memories of her childhood as thick as mud. "I understand you entirely," she said softly.

"How is England, Ada? Is it as terribly dreary as they say?"

She glanced at Gavriel, her eyes and thoughts drawn to him, inevitably. Wiping the back of his neck, he had taken shelter in silence. But she knew he was listening.

"England is lush and covered in forests," she said. "In the spring, green covers the countryside. Winters can be a misery, indeed, but summer is a time for celebration. Crops grow, the sun shines, and everyone comes out of doors." Indicating the rough sun at their backs, she said, "But even at its hottest, our summers are never quite this powerful."

"And what of you, *señor?* How is Marqueda?"

Although his watchful expression never changed, he favored Blanca with an answer. "Midway between the two, perhaps. Hot, yes, but also green and fertile. This—" He waved a hand toward the empty plateau. "This is too . . . *open.*"

"Then why come here?" Blanca asked.

"The Order is here."

Blanca stiffened against Ada's back, quiet now. Smart girl. Far smarter than Ada, for she knew when to retreat.

"My apologies," Blanca said quietly. "I know I sit a horse rather poorly."

She patted the girl's hands where they clasped around her middle. "No matter. We'll be there soon."

The landscape changed from the rugged, barren expanse of the flat Meseta to shallow hills spiked with tall conifers. They stopped briefly to rest their horses before pressing on, the cathedral and castle coming clearer into view. Their shadows stretched long and reached the defenses well in advance. Guards along the saw-toothed stone wall wore identical white robes adorned with the red Cross of Santiago. They nodded a silent greeting but kept the gates locked, lances at the ready.

One stepped forward. "Your name and business, *señor?*"

"My name is Gavriel de Marqueda," he said, easily handling his skittish mount. "I am a novice under the direction of Gonzalo Pacheco. These women are under my care and in need of admittance."

"Of course," the guard said. "Brother Pacheco told us we should expect you. Proceed."

The guards cranked opened the narrow iron gates. Though they passed through one stretch of defenses, another wall and a second compliment of guards awaited them on the other side of a cultivated field. They permitted entry as simply as had the first, leaving Ada to wonder at the ease of their arrival, such a contrast to their most difficult exit from Yepes.

After having traveled alone across La Mancha for the entire day—and before that, isolated in various rooms for her recovery—Ada noticed nothing but people, people everywhere. Women and men tended the monastery's lush gardens. Younger boys used pails of water to wash horses in the waning sunlight. Tall conifers rimmed the inside of the wall, a forest contained, while the Order's *caballeros* practiced jousting and swordplay in a tilting yard along the southern fortifications. And above everything, the cathedral spire and matched square towers of the fortress waited high on the hill like a benevolent parent.

"The fortress retains its Moorish appearance," she said. "When was it reclaimed?"

"Numerous times," Gavriel said. "A century ago, a generation ago, and again two years ago. It's a fortress for a reason, *inglesa*. All of La Mancha is a battleground."

Tension accumulated in tiny wrinkles at the corners of his eyes as he watched, still watching. Their safe arrival had apparently done nothing to alleviate his vigilance. Or perhaps he simply dreaded the judgment he yet faced from Pacheco.

With their horses at a slow walk across the fields, Ada craned her neck. Brick filigree patterned the ramparts atop the two west-facing towers, but the fortress's other features seemed designed to intimidate, all hulky, block construction, rectangular windows and steep stairs. No softness and no weakness.

They skirted the lower rim of the earthworks, around to its southern side where a squat, square building sprawled— a simple companion to the magnificent fortress. This one had two towers as well, but they were blunt and unadorned, one taller than the other.

Gavriel pulled to a stop and eyed the austere building. "The monastery," he said.

Blanca let out a quiet sigh. "And where is the town from here?"

He pointed. "On the eastern side of the monastery and fortress, below the sheer face of the defensive wall. Walking there takes but a few minutes."

A young squire approached and helped Blanca dismount. Ada followed, her knees shaking because of more than simple fatigue. This place . . . this place was intensely important to Gavriel and his future, but she could not diminish her sense of unease. Why had he come here, to this place of contrasts— piety and warfare, charity and opulence?

One of the doors opened. In the archway stood Fernán, a grin splitting his amiable face. "Welcome home, Gavriel. Leave it to you to gather two women when I have none."

Gavriel dismounted. "Fernán, I've not missed you."

"With such company, I should hope not." He smiled wider, his eyes blue and sparkling. Not even those pious robes lent authority or decorum to his teasing expression.

After handing reins to the squire, Gavriel edged past Fernán and into the cloister surrounding the central courtyard. Ada and Blanca followed where they made introductions.

Fernán kissed Blanca's hand. "No need to forego courtly manners, even in such a wretched place of exile."

Blanca laughed, her gaiety finally pulling a scowl from where it had been lurking within Gavriel. "Show the women to appropriate rooms, Fernán, if you would."

With a mock bow to Gavriel, Fernán offered one arm each to Ada and Blanca. "My pleasure, you can rest assured. And come morning, Gavriel, Pacheco wishes to speak with you."

Chapter 18

Gavriel left the women with Fernán, desperately wishing he would never see them again. He made fists so tight that he lost all feeling in his fingers. The lambskin riding gloves he wore engraved deep grooves between his knuckles—he could see the second skin wrapping around his—but he felt nothing, nothing but the choking desire to pull Ada close and taste her again.

So he left without a backward glance. To look back and contemplate anything about their time together would cripple whatever pride or resolve he yet retained.

He strode through the narrow halls of the monastery and to his quarters, its four unadorned walls as austere as a dungeon. He stripped bare. His skin smelled of Ada, of their shared musk. After a quick, brutal wash, he dressed and pulled a second set of robes over his fresh clothes.

White enveloped him. The red cross glared from the left side of his chest.

A sham, all of it.

Rosary in hand, he knelt and began to pray. But somewhere between his mind, his mouth, and his soul—a divide. He prayed to God for guidance, not forgiveness. But he could not concentrate. Soft whispers of Ada overlaid with images of blood to become a black curtain, barring him from the certainty he craved. Or perhaps God refused to hear him.

He set aside the rosary and took a deep breath. Although he had likely decided on his course some hours ago, he finally admitted it to himself. He would lie to Pacheco. He would say whatever he must in order to remain at the monastery. And he would spend the rest of his life atoning for his sins.

He returned the rosary to the small chest at the foot of his sleeping cot. Inside, beneath a piece of wool, laid a long strip of leather. Seven braided cords dangled from a sturdy leather handle, the ends of those cords tipped with tiny iron barbs. He removed the wool and touched the handle. He trailed two fingers down to the shining metal. Memories of pain burned along his back, but so did the echo of Ada's touch.

He dropped wearily onto his cot and faded toward sleep, caught between those contrasting sensations.

Come morning, with the resignation of a prisoner awaiting execution, he departed for Pacheco's common room. Walking through the stone halls held none of its previous familiarity and reassurance. The monastery did not welcome; it confined. Men followed his progress with their eyes as he passed, despite strict rules in the Order's edicts against gossip. A group of canonesses skittered aside. One crossed herself. The robes he had missed for those first few days after the bandit raid twirled conspicuously about his feet as he strode past, head high, but he was the worst sort of deceiver.

A knock on Pacheco's door and the novice master permitted him entry. Gavriel stood at the threshold, then stepped inside the dark, tastefully appointed room. Tapestries from Morocco to the Holy Land lined the cool walls. Plush horsehair cushions circled a woven Sicilian rug, its colors still bright despite the dim illumination of a torch in its sconce. To the left, an onion top archway connected the sitting room to Pacheco's sleeping chamber.

His novice master sat behind a writing desk on a squat three-legged stool at the center of the room. Silver hair and robes of spotless white accentuated his tanned skin, still handsome although touched with wrinkles.

"Gavriel," he said, setting aside a quill. "I am glad to see you safely returned. Did you find success with the girl?"

He remembered Ada's cries of pleasure beneath his hand, her softness clenched around his need. The skin between his shoulder blades itched, burned. "I did, Master. She is well and clear of her sickness, awaiting the opportunity to demonstrate as much."

Black eyes scrutinized his face, but Pacheco did not move. "I heard tell you arrived with another woman. A girl?"

The gossips' tales had moved quickly. "She was the niece of the *covigera* you recommended us for quarter. Blanca is her name. When the old woman ran afoul of the law, Blanca came with us. I saw no harm in bringing her to the canonesses, especially because the Englishwoman and I were left without a chaperone."

"Of course," Pacheco said, his eyes fixed on Gavriel's face. "You sought to do everything properly . . . didn't you?"

Inhaling slowly, Gavriel did not lower his gaze. He could do this. He would save his place with the Order and await the day when Ada left. For good.

"Master," he said quietly. "Are you asking if I have sinned?"

Pacheco relaxed as well as he could on his uncomfortable stool. He missed the creature comforts of his appointments in Toledo, those he had enjoyed while working on behalf of the exiled de Silvas. Forgoing those comforts for the sake of appearances at the monastery had long ago lost its appeal.

Soon, however. Soon he would return to the city. Lord de

Silva would honor Pacheco's success in returning this wayward bastard for the punishment Gavriel deserved.

Tall and proud and thoroughly confused, Gavriel needed to be turned from his chosen path of redemption, back toward the life for which he was destined. The de Silvas needed his strength, but they also needed him beaten. Soulless. And Pacheco, a man of the cloth, had been given the task of stripping away that soul.

He smiled at the irony.

And if Gavriel refused to take up arms for his family, he would be killed. Lord de Silva would have his slave, one of muscle and depravity, or he would have his revenge for young Sancho's death. The choice would be Gavriel's to make. His days of hiding were nearing an end.

"This is not confession, Gavriel," he said at last. He arose from the stool and resisted the urge to massage stiff muscles in his lower back, never at ease with showing his age in front of his subordinates. "These wild rumors aside, we both know I gave you authority over that young woman's condition and care. Just as with your vows, your progression toward becoming a clergyman is the business of no one else."

"Gramercy, Master."

Pacheco walked around his desk to stand toe to toe with the taller man. Gavriel's height was irrelevant. Sometimes power was a matter of internal perspective, and at that moment, Gavriel had lost his entirely. Pacheco would have put gold toward a wager that not one of Gavriel's vows remained unbroken—if anyone in this hole of a monastery would accommodate such a bet.

Fernán would, poor fellow. But his trial would come soon enough.

"I hope your journey from Yepes fared well," he said. "Did you face any trouble?"

"Yes," Gavriel said, eyes fixed and unblinking.

Pressing a fist to his lips to keep from smiling, he knew
very well that the men who tangled with Gavriel were hired
pedones. Gavriel would know it, too. That he was willing to
lie showed how far he had fallen, how near Pacheco was to
completing his objective.

"But you survived, and with two women in tow?"

No reply, at least with no words. Gavriel dropped his eyes
and closed them.

Pacheco raised an eyebrow and glanced down to Gavriel's
hands, but he kept them clasped behind his back and out of
view. "Does she intend to stay, or will she return to Toledo?"

"That boy Jacob will come for her at the end of the month."

He returned to his desk. "Then by all means," Pacheco
said, "you should be the one to acquaint her with our rules."

Those dark brown eyes remained fixed on an unknown
point in the middle distance. "Master, I'd hoped my responsibility to her has been discharged."

"Is there a reason why you wish to relinquish this obligation?"

Life returned to Gavriel's eyes, aggression to his posture.
Then the quietest sigh. "No, Master."

"Good. You are free to leave. Inform me should you require
anything."

Gavriel turned to leave. At the sight of his pupil's hands
still clasped behind his back, Pacheco said, "Gramercy,
please take these documents to Brother Ualard."

He offered a bundle of scrolls. Gavriel returned to the desk
and held out his hands, palms mangled and blistered. The cor-
rosion of combat. Red-faced, jaw tight, Gavriel only stood
there and awaited his verdict. Pacheco handed him the documents and affixed a weighty stare. "You've broken one vow,
at least. But we both know how you can make this right. "

"Yes, Master." That uncomfortable wooden stool held more
life than did Gavriel's voice.

Good.

As the door closed, Pacheco wondered if pride and vanity should prevent him from celebrating this latest success. Not everyday did a slave return voluntarily to captivity, so well trained as to conduct his own flogging. And if Gavriel had actually succumbed to the Englishwoman's charms, the punishment he inflicted on himself would probably be far worse than even Pacheco imagined.

And that made him smile.

Ada untwined her arm from Fernán's for the fourth time and passed him another useless warning look. The strange clown of a man knew no bounds of propriety. He was amiable enough, however, and kept her distracted from the persistent turn of her thoughts. He had also proved perfectly willing to assist her and Blanca in acclimating to their new surroundings, the entire time handing out smiles like alms for the poor.

But that did not mean she wanted to take his arm.

"And this is the entryway to the cathedral," he said with flippant disregard. "I don't know why some of the holier brothers ever bother to leave. They spend so much of their day here."

"You ridicule the faithful," Blanca said. "Why?"

"Because they ridicule me."

"Then why join a monastery at all?"

He grinned at Ada. "Your new friend is brazen. I like her."

Ada exchanged a bemused glance with Blanca, finding curiosity in the young girl's face but no censure. She seemed to have the patience for all manner of people, no matter their faults. "I like her, too, but likely for differing reasons."

Fernán shrugged, his face turned up to the elaborately carved archway leading to the cathedral. "I came to this place as you do, forced by circumstances and without a pleasing alternative. Fourth sons in noble houses cause their parents endless dilemmas. After all, we are not needed at home but have no titles or professions to sustain us." An uncharacteristic harsh-ness tainted his voice. "And as for siblings, they hold us in no regard. Our entrance into the world merely divides an estate from thirds into quarters."

"So you came to the church even though you don't be-lieve?" Blanca asked.

Fernán laughed and tried to retake their arms. Both women slipped carefully out of reach. "I never said I don't believe. I simply have a different idea of how to spend my waking and, well, my *sleeping* hours. A body cannot live by study and prayer alone."

As they walked back through the cloister, Ada considered the differences between Fernán and Gavriel. That they both occupied the same space, maintained the same profession, and struggled with the same duties seemed almost absurd. The dis-tance between them was too great for her mind to bridge.

"*Señor,* do you find it a challenge to keep your vows, espe-cially since this is not your chosen calling?" she asked.

He laughed again. "In that, at least, my father was kind to me. He could've assigned me to the Order of Alcántara or some other Benedictine nightmare. At least here my vows are easy to keep."

Ada stopped in a courtyard full of spring blossoms and herbs. "Your vows are easy?"

"Obedience, the first, is the one I find most taxing. As for the vow of poverty," he said, opening his arms to the lush greenery. "I live nearly as well here as I did on my father's estate. The vow only applies to personal property, which the monastery keeps in trust for the first year. Upon confirma-tion, the property is returned to us, but we are expected to behave judiciously."

Even Blanca frowned. "What a strange order," she said.

"Singular, in fact, but not merely for these reasons."

Whether he realized it or not, Fernán sounded almost proud. "All of the orders have leeway in determining such matters, but Santiago takes pious autonomy to its extreme." He leaned in close like a conspirator. Ada and Blanca eyed each other only once before joining him in the loose huddle. He certainly had a gift for the dramatic. "Knights of Santiago only take a vow of *conjugal* chastity."

Ada's jaw dropped. "Conjugal? They can get married?"

"Can and do, my dear," Fernán said, wearing a leering grin. "Which is why I'm constantly on the lookout for a woman to become Señora Fernán Garza. Unmarried men are confined to abstinence, I'm afraid, but since we share the monastery with an equal number of women—the canonesses who tend to the pilgrims—my chances are good."

His expression turned mock serious. "Well come to think of it, I suppose chastity is the hardest vow to maintain. But the sooner I find a wife, the sooner I can devote all of my energies to flouting authority."

Finding a nearby bench in the courtyard, Ada sat down. She looked to Fernán for answers in the hopes he would be serious, if only for a moment. "The brothers can marry, is that right? And there is no vow to abstain from violence? Not even for the clergy?"

"We are a religious order, the sole purpose of which is defending the kingdoms of Castile and León from the Moorish threat. No one, not even the clergy, shuns violence. It is our purpose." He smiled without mirth. Pale blue eyes fixed on hers. "I wonder, Ada, who's been telling you such tales?"

Chapter 19

For the evening meal, Gavriel sat with a dozen other men in the monastery's smaller dining hall. Pacheco and Fernán ate quietly and kept their heads bowed, as all brothers of the Order did at mealtime. His eyes itched from infrequent sleep, but he did not miss their suspicion.

Ever since he used war spoils to secure a place at Uclés, he had shunned excess attention. Wearing white robes, his hair shorn, he blended in as just another aspirant. Out in the world—and with a screaming devil woman as his companion—those attentions had returned to him. Their safe arrival in Uclés did nothing to erase that old, nagging sensation of being watched.

He kept his eyes on the bowl of talbina before him, seeing the warped image of his fatigued face reflected in the barley broth, and reminded himself of the truth: they were interested in Ada, nothing more.

Pacheco observed him with the same expression he had worn during their meeting, at once evaluating and suspicious. Ever more suspicion. That the novice master had covertly issued instructions for his punishment did not allay a terrible feeling that even more sacrifice would be required of him.

"Good evening."

The soft female voice at his back sent a shiver through his veins. A morning voice, honey and anise. Sweet, spicy, and forbidden. But his reaction was not mirrored on the faces of the other men. Some scowled. Others tugged clerical hoods lower over skittish expressions. Only Fernán grinned openly, his glib mouth asking for the crack of Gavriel's knuckles.

"She cannot be in here," Pacheco said quietly.

Gavriel harvested a fresh supply of indignation. What did Ada know of laws and obeying the restrictions everyone else embraced? Nothing. She knew only her own demands.

He stood and turned, looking Ada in the face. His heart pumped hard, once, then galloped. She wore a plain green gown and stood before him clean, neatly coiffed, and inexplicably angry. Only dark smudges beneath her eyes and a slight waxen sheen to her skin hinted at the hardships of her recent withdrawal.

She blinked once and cleared her throat. "Don't you believe in common civilities?"

Her acidic tone, so different from that honey sweet greeting, made him aware of dozens of eyes on them both.

As if I didn't feel conspicuous enough.

"You cannot be here," he said, guiding her to the wide, arched entryway. A thick tapestry wobbled stiffly as they passed. Blanca, who had been standing unobtrusively behind Ada, stepped out of the way and followed them into the nearby courtyard.

Ada settled her expression into one of boredom, making a mockery of his attempt to maintain an even temper. He caught a hint of lemon. His mouth watered.

"And why not? Blanca and I are hungry."

"Eating in the presence of a woman is not permitted, not even with the canonesses. You're to dine with the women. Didn't Fernán tell you that?"

"Perhaps it slipped his mind." She pinned him with those

clear, sharp eyes, making him long for moments of incoherent rambling and pleas. "Do they fear being unable to resist our charms? Perhaps the thought of fornicating over the dining table hinders digestion?"

"It may have crossed their minds."

"Did it cross yours?"

Thrusting aside the bowls and pitchers, the plates and cups. Pushing her down on the scarred wooden table and yanking up that gown. Burying himself in her willing flesh. He was almost ready this time, letting those images invade his senses, like steeling himself against the snap of leather and the bite of iron. Relax. Accept. And then the shock of it was gone.

The temptation was not.

"Of course it did," she said. "You're a hypocrite. I said as much—then proved it."

"No more than any man."

"Too much to be borne, then." She turned to leave with Blanca. "I'll endure my stay within these walls. You'll see. I have friends here, even if you refuse to be civil."

"Friends?"

She tipped her head. "Blanca and Fernán."

"Fernán is no friend to you, *inglesa*."

The smile she offered was far more suggestive than the friendly amusement she had shared with Fernán. "Blanca, you should find out where the canonesses eat," she said. "I shall speak with Gavriel and join you shortly."

Blanca's smile was also sly, but with a charming innocence—none of the threat and certainty none of the damage to Gavriel's self-control. He had believed arriving in Uclés would remind him of the life he intended to lead, and that the vastness of the monastic grounds would be able to keep his contact with Ada to a minimum.

Such a fool.

He took her upper arm and led her away from the courtyard,

toward an indoor training hall. A quick check revealed the cavernous space empty. They each took a torch from the corridor and entered the hall, pushing them into sconces inside. Swords of all types lined the walls, as did armor, shields, maces, and crossbows. Four archery targets sat against the far wall, just below four corresponding window slits. No light shone inside, the black of nightfall nearly absolute, but flames made the lines of each surface quiver among the shadows.

In that golden light, Ada appeared as a goddess—an irritated goddess, all pale skin and flashing eyes. He should be pleased her hair was up and coiffed properly, but he could not help but remember it down, unbound, glorious.

His palms prickled. The healing blisters, surely.

"And why shouldn't I count Fernán among my paltry number of friends?"

"He spends far too much time in the village. His dalliances with local girls are notorious." Gavriel shrugged. "I only thought to save you or Blanca the difficulty of discovering his character firsthand."

"*His* character? Interesting."

How had he looked into the face of his enemies without blanching, when this woman's unnerving stare transformed him into a chastened boy? But after his tense and nightmarish meeting with Pacheco, he had lost the nerve for such frank confrontations.

"Yes," he said. "I wouldn't want him to take advantage."

"Because you reserve that right for yourself?"

"Ada, I did nothing you didn't want as well."

"And have you considered what will happen if I'm with child?"

The floor dropped from below his feet. Dizziness washed over him like burning tar, viscous and hot. A child. With Ada. So intent had he been on her safety and the consequences of

their tryst with regard to his novitiate that the idea of a child
had escaped him completely.

He closed his eyes but could not banish the image of Ada
cradling his son or a beautiful daughter, a daughter with hair
the same deep brown of her mother. Longing unlike any physical desire stabbed at him. The regret that followed left him
breathless, aching, and hollow.

"I suppose that means the answer is no," she said quietly.

"Ada—"

"Fernán is acting more a friend to me than you. You've decided to treat me like a contagion. *You* brought me here." She
stepped closer, her eyes like the center of a flame, mesmeriz-
ing and fiery. Gavriel breathed deeply, dragging in her scent—
the only bit of her he could have without penalty. "I wonder
what other selfish purposes you have in mind."

"Stop."

"I don't think I will," she whispered. "You wanted me here,
Gavriel. You've taken great pains to make me well, but I think
you've lived to regret that."

The sweetness of her breath washed over his face. *Diós*, how
he wanted to kiss her again. How many hours had passed?
Only a day? And his body felt as starved for hers as if they had
never touched, as if he had never been joined with her.

But never again.

"You're not my only regret," he said.

Ada laughed quietly, melodious and sinful. "But what is
the use of passing your novitiate when you've broken all of
your vows in the process?"

He gnawed the inside of his cheek until he tasted blood.
"Master Pacheco determines the bounds of my novitiate. I've
discussed these previous weeks with him, and he offered me
leave to stay."

Ada nodded slowly and turned to face the wall of armaments. He slowly expelled the hot breath in his lungs, relieved

that she gave him space. She walked along the wall. Slivered glimpses of her face reflected in the surface of every blade. Shards of silvery light dotted her hair and the bodice of her gown. She stopped beneath the fleury Cross of Santiago, eyes lifted to its stark red against a field of white.

"I never realized how different Santiago is from the other orders."

"Yes." He frowned, wondering at the darkness in her voice. "'Tis unique."

"Is that why you chose it?"

"I will not discuss that, Ada."

She turned, her eyes narrowed. "For example, you keep your own property. Isn't that true? There is no vow of poverty."

Gavriel bit his teeth together. *Fernán.*

"What a brother brings into the Order, he keeps," he said. "When he dies, the Order is like his widow and receives the inheritance."

"Interesting, too, that you mention widows—the implication of marriage. Because there is no ban against marriage, and neither is there a ban against violence." She closed the distance between them. One moment, she was standing below the Order's cross. The next, she was within an arm's length. That curiously blank expression had given way to anger. White-hot anger. "Am I mistaken, Gavriel?"

They sparred with their eyes as surely as if they each held one of the deadly weapons lining the hall's chilled stone walls. Gavriel remained as dominating as ever, tall and solid and dark, but she had shaken him with the mention of a child.

A queer sort of betrayal burned at her temples. He had lied to her about his vows and he had not considered the consequences of their lovemaking. She had considered it, and as with every other time she pursued pleasure at the expense of reason, she had chosen pleasure. At least she had made the choice—as much as she could have claim over that function of her brain.

No, I chose to be with him.

But his lies had betrayed every noble intention he claimed.

His jaw tightened. If he knew that the tic gave away his discomfort, he would probably strive to do away with it. Jacob had said as much, that warriors spend their lives ferreting out weaknesses and eliminating them.

"You're not mistaken," he said, his impassive voice like a learned man at lecture—or like Meg reciting scientific facts that the entire world should know as thoroughly as she did. "*Los caballeros* can marry freely, having been given dispensation from Pope Alexander. Once married, the knights can live with their wives either within the bounds of the monastery or on their own estates."

So detached. And so deeply at odds with the struggles he had presented. He had lied. He had talked about his vows as a means of tricking her, not only with regard to her use of opium, but as a seduction. The possibility seemed too despicable, yet she could not soothe the anger burning at her temples.

"And even facing the temptation of lying with a woman, chastity is not strict," she said, working to match his cold tone. "A man can live with his mistress without censure or strife. Isn't that right?"

"Obviously Fernán told you all of this, *las barraganas* included?" His lips curled, not a smile and not a sneer. "I would've thought a noblewoman's translator too detached to care about our quaint local customs."

"I've not lived in a cave."

"Oh?" He arched his brows, a penetrating look in his eyes. "The opium seemed quite good at keeping you apart from the world."

Her tongue burned. The thought of opium coupled with the

distress over Gavriel's behavior only heightened her thirst. It was always there, waiting, tempting. But then, so was the thought of touching him again.

"In England, *barraganas* would simply be another class of harlot, not sanctioned companions," she said. "I hadn't paid them any regard while in Toledo. And I certainly hadn't thought their relationships with *los caballeros* might be condoned by the Church."

"We are all that stand between the Christian kings and the southern tribes. Rules have been . . . altered for us. Even if a man cannot bring himself to marry, knowledge that he has a mistress to protect and provide for might temper his baser impulses."

"And what of the women? Are they ruined?"

"No," he said. "There aren't enough women on the frontier to be so strict."

"But you've vowed chastity?" she asked, her breathless disbelief growing. "You've vowed to abstain from violence? This place stands against all who would threaten Castile. These knights would die to the man to defend Uclés. Yet you want me to believe you've sworn the opposite."

"I never lied to you."

"Then what does this mean?"

"My vows are personal." He stalked the two paces between them and grabbed her arms. He gave a little shake, eyes fierce and wild. "My reasons are personal."

"They must be because they're also abnormal."

She tried to twist her arms free, but his grip intensified. Their faces close, she stared into his eyes and licked her lips. She allowed her body to flag, just a bit, and wilted against him. As soon as her breasts pushed against the hard wall of his chest, he flung her away.

"Bruja."

"You call me names?" She spit at the ground between his

feet, his stance wide and arrogant. "You're the one who's chosen to do what none of the other brothers have. Why? Would you stand by and let this retreat be overrun? Would you leave a sword lying on the ground and allow the people here to be killed?"

"No, and my actions these past few days have proven that."

"Then why make a vow? You must have known it would be impossible for a man like you to uphold."

He tipped his head to the side. "A man like me?"

"A warrior. You're not a clergyman, no matter your delusions."

"I *was*, do you understand? No longer." His staccato shout bounced around the hall. Even the torches seemed to flinch, the flames spiking ghastly streaks of color over his grim face.

"And warriors do not marry? You would deny yourself the comfort and security of a wife, for all your years—when no one else denies you these things?"

He walked to the wall lined with swords of all kinds, from simple broadswords to strange serrated blades from distant lands. Hands behind his back, he looked on them with an unreadable expression. Regret? Sadness? Resolve? He had looked at her naked body with similar confusion.

"All knights under *reconquista* have purpose," he said. "Every garrison must be turned into a town. The easiest way to do that is to turn unmarried men into respectable citizens with obligations, wives and children to protect. That's why they inhabit these outpost towns and why *barraganas* are tolerated. 'Tis not marriage, but a small step toward stability."

"But you stand apart from all of it?"

"I must."

Ada walked to his side. They stood shoulder to shoulder, much as they had in the bathhouse, ready to defend each other against any enemy, no matter their quibbles and frustrations. What would it be like to depend on such a man, really depend on him as a partner and a friend? The idea was as foreign to her as was holding a child, but both resonated in her soul with more power than she dared admit.

That power. He held it.

Kindling her sense of outrage, she stepped in front of him, her body between his and the serrated blade hanging on the wall. Tension bunched his strong shoulders, adding an uncharacteristic slope to his tall, splendid physique.

"Most men only take vows when they feel strongly," she said. "They *believe*. They feel connected to a higher idea. They feel compelled—obliged, even—to make a promise to God. They do not use them as a prison or a punishment. You've hidden from the world and put a cage around yourself."

"You don't know me."

"You're right." Even in the midst of her anger, her pride like a tattered sail, she could only stare at his beautiful face. "I wonder what you would be like free, unfettered by this place."

"Free of my responsibilities?"

"Free of these lies. I know I've told my fair share." She stepped into his space, breathed his air, felt his heat. "You walk apart from this place. Everyone sees how different you are. You don't belong here."

"I . . ." His voice scraped raw. "I belong here. You won't take that from me, no matter your body and your words."

"And what would you be without the Order?"

Dark eyes closed, a man defeated. "A slave and a murderer. That's why I thought to bind myself with these vows."

She shook her head. "I don't believe—"

"It matters naught what you believe, Ada."

"No. No! Only what *you* believe. You fabricate restrictions that cause you pain. You cut yourself off from life. For all I know, you're lying to me about this!" Tears pressed for freedom. He was no monk—that much had been clear from the start. But she had imagined him a warrior, someone powerful and strong. Someone stronger than herself. "Will you tell me the truth? Will you trust me?"

But he did not answer. His eyes warned her like the hiss of a fire. The man she had touched and loved was gone. And she would do well to forget he had ever existed.

Chapter 20

The torches had burned low, shimmering softly at his back. Gavriel stayed in the weapons hall for half of the night, unable to shake free of his confusion. If he returned to his room, he would be alone with his thoughts, his mistakes, and his flogging whip. Never had he considered himself a cowardly man, but he could not face his punishment that evening. The wounds Ada had inflicted on him were vicious enough. Although blood did not leak from his skin, he felt exhausted, shredded, and hopeless.

Tell her, a voice whispered in his mind. *She would understand.*

No. Ada might come to understand why he had chosen the monastic life, but she would never fathom what he had been before Santiago. He had committed terrible deeds, all in the name of the de Silvas and his own warped interests. No motivation justified what he had nearly succeeded in doing.

An attempt on the king's life—how could she forgive that?

Had the tide of battle at Alarcos moved a little faster, a little slower, any number of events altered but slightly, King Alfonso would have been at the mercy of Gavriel's blade. But mercy was an emotion for weaklings, men raised by soft hands. Six years ago, at Alarcos, he had not known the meaning of the word.

He opened his eyes, standing before the wall of swords. Choosing one from the wall, he hefted the perfectly balanced weapon. The weight of the pommel offset the blade and gave it grace and power. Simplicity. Only metal and man. The intentions behind the warrior who held it, the culpability of the victim who received it—unimportant. In the heat of battle, none of it mattered.

He missed that anonymity. He missed the ease. The man who owned him and the man who sired him had been the same. Gavriel had not been permitted a say in where he turned his blade, like a horse who cannot contradict the knight on its back. A mere messenger, he had delivered his father's deadly intent without thought or remorse.

And no matter the anonymity and the ease he missed, those simple paths, he would not return to such an existence. Mindless and soulless. Time away from Lord de Silva had taught him to account for his misdeeds. Master Pacheco had instructed him on the steps he must take to become whole and pure. Painful steps. And when Gavriel had failed, Pacheco saw fit to offer him another chance. He would not fall again. Ada had to realize that.

He gripped the hilt of the sword, the cool metal warmed by his hand. Raw blisters burned between his thumb and forefinger. He would never again use a sword. He would never again kiss Ada, touch her, lay with her. She had to understand that, as did he—really and truly, until hearing her voice or smelling her soft skin no longer held sway.

And all he could use to convince her was the truth.

Two days later, Blanca stared through a window slit to the beautiful view of Uclés far below. The rising sun cast squat white buildings in gold. Much the same in every respect to Yepes, houses stretched across the shallow valley floor, filling every crevice. Although she could not see individual people or animals, she imagined the quick vitality of a morning in the Saturday market. She imagined it and she wanted it.

But from that high outlook, she may as well have been living among the clouds. No such vitality thrived in the monastery, only quietness and stillness and routines enough to make her skin itch. The need to be down in the center of the market and find its secrets thudded beneath her breast.

"This place is not what you expected, is it?"

She glanced at Ada where she sat on her cot. Dressed in that deep green gown—the one that made her skin appear even more fair, her hair even darker—Ada watched with a tiny, teasing smile. Her company, however moody and baffling, had been Blanca's only relief from the tedium of their monastic shelter.

"Difficult to say," Blanca said, forcing thoughtfulness into her words. "I've seen but one building, and I've yet to see the town. To cast judgment now would be unfair."

Ada's smile widened. "But you have already."

"Yes, I'm afraid." She turned from the narrow window and its sunny, tempting view to settle onto her own cot, stretched opposite Ada in their small quarters. "I worry my expectations of life outside of Yepes will prove unreasonable. Perhaps any town is essentially the same as another." She shrugged, trying to slough her misgivings as easily. "Has that been your experience since leaving England?"

Ada tipped her head to one side and began plaiting her long, silken hair. Blanca touched her own hair—curly, coarse, wound tightly atop her head—and suppressed a glimmer of envy.

"You're right in that many towns share much in common," Ada said. "But variations of culture and thinking do exist. The interest is in searching for the differences."

"And what of our escape from Yepes?" Blanca sat on her

cot, memories of their dashing escape hastening her breath. "Can an ordinary life compete with such excitement? And would I even want it to?"

Ada's nimble fingers slowed. Her face darkened, the sun hidden by a cloud. "I've seen enough of such excitements to want peace, nothing more. A peaceful mind."

Blanca studied her new companion, this strange woman with the curious accent and flawless grasp of the Castilian dialect. The circles beneath her eyes should have faded, and her body should have shown the pleasant effects of regular meals and freedom from the opium. But Ada had been suffering horrendous nightmares, fits of screaming and tears that awakened Blanca several times before dawn. She had done her best to offer comfort, yet nothing held the terror away for long.

That morning Ada appeared as beautiful, as fragile, as lost as ever—in body and in mind—but with a strength Blanca admired. She never spoke of the nightmares, only composed herself each morning as if the evening had been restful and secure. She spent her time in their shared room hunched over unfurled scrolls, mumbling in her rough language.

"A peaceful mind." Blanca smiled softly. "After your craving I should find that easy to believe."

"You knew?"

"Of course," she said, suddenly wondering if her words caused offense. "La Señora . . ."

"Ah, she told you."

Blanca stood and motioned for Ada to turn. She lifted the woman's heavy plait and began to arrange it atop her head, pinning and talking and enjoying the novel texture. "You should be proud of yourself," she said. "Some people never escape. The withdrawal is too difficult and they succumb, or so I've heard." She paused, peeking over Ada's shoulder to get a better look at her expression. "He helped you, did he not?"

"Yes," Ada whispered.

"He must care for you."

"No, I'm an obligation. Nothing more."

Blanca stuck a hairpin between her teeth and waved a dismissive hand. "Obligations are dispatched like reluctant parishioners giving alms. I cannot believe what he did for you is mere obligation, can you?"

"I've been told it doesn't matter what I believe."

"Have patience," Blanca said. "These days are a trial, and you are capable of much."

"Good and ill, both."

"As all of us are." Having finished Ada's hair, a crown as elaborate and beautiful as any intended for a monarch, Blanca returned to the window. "Fernán has offered to take me into town, should I wish."

"Oh?"

"A number of the unmarried *freyles* and canonesses travel together, acting as chaperones—or not, I suppose."

"Do you enjoy his company?"

She laughed, shaking her head. "Not particularly. But it will be a way to see the town."

Ada arose from the cot and smoothed her skirts before joining her at the window. "Be careful, Blanca. Fernán's smile hides a great many things."

"It does." She rubbed her hands along her forearms. "La Señora offered endless observations about the kinds of men in the world. She said that one is the kind you trust immediately, while another is the sort who should never be trusted. Fernán may be the latter."

Forcing a smile, she tried to keep from needing to justify herself to this confused Englishwoman. But Blanca felt like a simpleton, a mere girl from the country. To have traveled so far from home . . . one had to be strong for such an adventure. Or very, very scared.

"I've lived my entire life in a small town," she said. "But in

working with La Señora, I learned a great deal—especially
with regard to men."

Ada offered a skittish laugh. "You comprehend more than
I do, I fear. I used to know how to talk to men, to gauge their
moods and personalities . . ."

Her exotic voice trailed off, eyes distant and fogged.

Blanca touched her arm. "When you've lost yourself, it's
difficult to know how to find others."

Ada's face opened into a wide smile. "You are far too wise.
Well if not Fernán, then who?"

"Someone kind, funny, handsome, I suppose. Someone
who could respect me. After how I was treated in Yepes, I fear
being able to find anyone who will look beyond that." Blanca
tipped her head closer, knowing she treaded a path too near
to prying. "And you? You and Gavriel?"

A quick look of panic crossed Ada's face, but then her
shoulders hunched a little. Blanca had heard the two of them
together by the river—quiet words followed by quiet sounds
she knew to be private and intimate. Sleep had not found her
again. She had lain awake, her heart sick with wanting a companion of her own.

Believing Ada had found such a love, her envy of the beautiful woman nearly eclipsed her strange admiration. But since
their arrival to the monastery, the two lovers had worked tire-
lessly to avoid one another.

No, Blanca had rid herself of envy days before. On top of
the endless nightmares, the cost of Ada's fascinations seemed
far too high.

"My apologies," Blanca said. "He is a difficult one, another
kind of man altogether. Whether to love him or to hate him—
who can tell? But he's certainly not for me because he has no
sense of humor."

Ada laughed quietly. "At times I wonder if his face will
break if he smiles."

"You'll do fine, then. If you can laugh at a man, he does not dictate your thoughts."

"I'm glad you're here, Blanca. You remind me of my sister, and I'm reminded of how much I miss her. Without you, I should not know what to do with myself, given the choice between solitude and Gavriel."

"That would depend on his mood."

With a heavy knock at the chamber door, Ada gasped and put her bandaged hand to her throat.

"*Inglesa?* May I speak with you?"

Ada's face drained of its scant color, and then her cheeks burned a dark pink. "Shall I open the door and discover his mood?" she asked.

"Only if I can hide beneath my cot," Blanca said.

"Coward."

"The battle is not mine."

Gavriel pounded again, the heavy door shivering. "Ada? Are you in there?"

"As to his mood, he sounds glowering," Blanca said.

"Inhospitable, at the least."

No, Blanca thought. His voice exactly matched Ada's face—resigned, wary, and unbearably sad.

Gavriel did not merely stand in the doorway; he dominated that space. She had not seen him up close since the night in the weapons hall, and her greedy eyes absorbed the sight. White robes covered him from neck to ankle, but her body responded to the powerful man beneath. She had gripped his taut backside, her mouth on his sex. She had kneaded the muscled caps of his broad shoulders and felt the firm weight of him move sinuously, then more urgently above her.

How could he hide among men half his stature and authority? How did he expect to belong in such a place, following orders and ignoring the most elemental facets of himself? And how could he stand there as if their tryst by the river had never occurred?

For that matter, how could she?

She looked again, searching deeper. Restlessness overlaid his strength and distance. His face was a grim picture of fatigue, his cheeks hollow. His lips were chapped. Did statues grow weary? No, only human men—men like Gavriel beset by demons as vicious and unrelenting as her own.

The waking memory of her nightmares slid across her vision. A dungeon cell and fiery pain. Loneliness. Terror. And over the slivers of her past, these new dreams layered regret and desire— regret for having abandoned her sister and treating Jacob so badly, and desire for a little peace. Be that opium or Gavriel, she no longer cared. They both brought her as much misery as pleasure. Doing without either was slowly driving her mad.

"Gavriel," she said, erasing wariness from her voice. "I'd not expected to see you today, as you've been doing your best to avoid me."

She wanted to slap him, make him hurt and cry out. At the very least, she wanted proof that her words reached him. His potent impact on her life had proven humbling; her every thought turning to him. And so quickly.

"May I speak with you, Ada?"

"We've said quite enough."

Gavriel eased into the sleeping chamber, his broad shoulders making the space feel cramped and overly warm. "I want to tell you," he said quietly. "Everything."

Her mind and her body froze. He was offering . . . what exactly? And was she brave enough to hear it?

She flexed the fingers of her good hand. "You expect my curiosity to get the better of me?"

"Please, *inglesa.*"

Ada had mustered little patience for her sister's experiments.

She had assisted out of obligation but also because, on occasion,
Meg revealed marvelous things—unexpected beauty and wrath,
all pulled from the natural world, manipulated and made ex-
traordinary. The subtle shift of Gavriel's expression reminded
her of those moments of wonder.

As much as she steeled herself against his plea, she remembered the moment she had begged of him, cornered by the
archbishop's physician and his tools made for bleeding. What
weighed so heavily on Gavriel that he, too, felt the need to beg?

She nodded once and moved to accompany him into the corridor.

"No, please stay," Blanca said. After retrieving her cloak, she
flipped the hood over her knotted black hair and made for the
door. "I believe I shall make that trip into town this morning."

Ada stared into the girl's impenetrable black eyes, finding
only caring, sympathy, and a pinch of curiosity—the senti-
ments of a friend. An unlikely friend in that unlikely place. She
breathed a little more calmly when she squeezed Blanca's hand.

"Be careful."

Blanca tossed a cautioning look toward Gavriel. "And
yourself."

With Blanca gone, the stillness between them was like mud
drying on skin, prickly and irritating. Ada retrieved a headdress she had borrowed from a canoness and affixed it over
her hair. His eyes followed her every move. Yes, the statue was
gone, but the man who took its place could harm her a hundred times over.

She swept her gaze over the room. "Where can we talk? I
assume the Order does not allow unmarried men and women
to have conversations in private chambers."

"No," he said on an exhale. "The weapons hall remains
empty. Sunshine lures everyone out of doors."

"Well good. We'll hold swords and talk. If you aren't
honest with me, I reserve the right to be your executioner."

He blinked and turned on his heel. Ada made a face at his retreating back, cursing his severity. One smile. Not so much to ask.

She followed him through the endless corridors of stone and slivers of light, the Castilian spring sunshine weaving its way into every corner. Men in robes passed them in silence, heads bowed, while a group of women in the courtyard knelt among the foliage to tend the new growth. Their quiet chatter offered a semblance of normalcy to the endless quiet. Ada had grown up thinking the forest a lonely and isolated place, but the solemnity of the monastery—for her, an outsider—seemed even worse. How would it feel to be among so many people, all of whom worked toward common goals and held common beliefs?

As soon as Gavriel closed the door to the weapons hall, Ada stepped clear of his heat and his scent. She pinned him with her eyes, merely waiting. No sense in making this easier for him, whatever he felt compelled to say.

"I wish to tell you about my past," he said. "I should, for no other reason than you must understand how important this is—that I stay here."

"Why must I understand?"

He flicked his dark gaze over her body. Heat rippled beneath her skin, deep in her bones and in soft, aching places. "I want you," he said. "But I cannot have you. This is why, and why you must understand. You . . . you can help me."

"You're asking that I help deny you? Deny us both?" She laughed, a ragged sound. "Do you remember who I am? I have a mean history of damaging myself."

He pressed a fist to his mouth, eyes never leaving hers. "You must. *I* must."

Ada threw up her hands and sought solace in the ceiling. Only cold stones. "Say what you will, Gavriel. I'll not interrupt, nor will I tempt you unreasonably. Have done with it, just as we both want done with this confinement of mine."

Chapter 21

"I was born to a Berber woman," he said simply. "My father is Lord Joaquin de Silva, a nobleman from León. He brought her from Mora, here in Castile."

Ada nodded. Wide blue eyes traced the lines of his face. Yes, she would see the Berber influence on every plane, in the tint of his skin.

"I know Mora," she said quietly. "Southwest of here. Another Castilian outpost town."

"The town had been newly taken from the Moors when I was born. According to local *fueras*, a father has a great deal of power over a child's future when there is no marriage."

Marriage. His brain spat the word again and again. There had been no marriage. Only slavery. And after what Gavriel had witnessed of his father's behavior, she had been forced. Repeatedly. For the pure pleasure of controlling another person, utterly and completely.

Past and present fighting a pitched battle behind his sternum, he opened his eyes to escape the visions he had conjured. He focused on Ada—Ada, who was beautiful and who was listening. How he wished she had not bound her hair beneath that plain headdress, but it was best she had. Taking her head between his hands, threading fingers into those thick tresses, kissing her. So natural and easy.

He cleared his throat. "A father can have his illegitimate son baptized to become his heir. As long as there was no adultery, the child is natural. That is, unless the mother was a slave."

"And then the child is a slave as well," she said, her eyes widening. She reached for him like a mother reaching out to steady a babe's first steps—quick, protective, without thought. But she jerked her fingers back and tucked them within the folds of her gown. "What did they do?"

Gavriel wanted none of her forgiveness, for such a luxury would weaken his tenuous resolve. He turned away and traced the blade of a sword with his gaze, over and around the honed edges. "He raised me without an education. I knew nothing but weapons, horses, and fighting rings. I breathed and ate warfare, a feral child with no language beyond violence.

"A year later, de Silva married and had a son named Sancho. He was groomed to be the rightful heir, but our father pitted us against each other, to make him strong and to remind me of my place. Then when I was fourteen, I killed Sancho."

"Your brother?"

"My opponent."

Ada recoiled, eyes wide and wary. He forced his body to relax even though his mind was awash in vile memories. She did not deserve the anger he reserved for only his father and himself.

"We were practicing the joust," he said, more calmly now. "He was my opponent. That was all. My father ensured that I knew nothing else, all the better to make me a killer."

She nodded, looking lost. But how could she understand that life and death struggle? Every morning, every night, he was the enemy of Sancho de Silva. The weakling heir of a no-bleman against the illegitimate half-Berber slave who had neither the wits nor words to defend himself. Sancho's taunts and humiliating jests had defined their childhood. When Gavriel had known naught but violence and the thrill of success in the training arena, Sancho taught him shame. Only when they took to the practice ring did Gavriel find victory over his nemesis.

That Sancho would retaliate all the more at the next opportunity never stayed Gavriel's hand. Perhaps such knowledge had pushed him to fight all the harder that day. He had charged at full speed, sword drawn. Nothing held in reserve. No mercy for his own kin.

Ada stood at his side. She had crossed the floor without his noticing, the fresh warmth of her scent pulling him back from blood and death. Sunshine from the window slits above the archery targets slanted across her face, shadow and light.

"I became my father's greatest enemy and his strongest ally," he said. "He did not prosecute me or do me harm, nor did he turn me from his house, as was within his right. Instead he bound me to his family even more surely than my indenture."

"And you agreed?" She shook her head. "Of course you agreed. What choice did you have? You had no other perspective, growing up as you did and harnessed with the responsibility of your own brother's death."

"It makes me ill how quickly you defend me."

"Would you prefer that I condemn you?"

Yes. Condemn me and hate me. Go back to Toledo and leave me be.

But he found only open curiosity in her expression. He had not succeeded in driving her away. He would have to dig deeper and bear more of the memories.

"Six years ago at the Battle of Alarcos, the de Silvas sided with the Almohads to the south—all the better to conclude an old blood feud with King Alfonso. I rode with them, blending in with my dark skin and barbarism. Our victory . . . our victory was unparalleled."

Images of that day would not disperse. Every angle of sunlight and every scream had been engraved on the surface of his brain. Although those memories were supposed to repulse him, he could not suppress how proud and triumphant he had been. The height of that battle had been the highpoint of his life. No restraints. No scruples. No mercy. Only a warrior in his element, unfettered and victorious.

His stomach crumpled. Now he paid dearly for that freedom.

"How many I killed that day I cannot know—Castilians, even members of this Order who defended their kingdom. Afterward, I rode with Moorish raiders for a number of years, until the death of their chieftain meant the end of my protection."

He held onto shreds of the truth, those secrets he could not reveal. De Silva hunted him, wanting him dead—not because of young Sancho, but because Gavriel had failed to kill King Alfonso. Fear of his father and fear of the reckoning that awaited him kept the truth buried.

"And you came here," she said. "Why? Why this place?"

"Simply another place of refuge. But from what I've learned here, I'd have been better served staying ignorant and barbaric, hiding in exile as a raider."

"Without thought or soul, yes. But you didn't. You came here, to this place of learning and spirituality. It must have opened your eyes to the world you missed."

"Yes." Customary anger shot through his limbs. "I learned, for example, that I was kept a slave illegally. For my entire youth I was told that my mother's fate was my own. Servitude. But I was *baptized,* Ada. I was not instructed in the ways of the Church, but I am Christian."

Ada gasped as understanding dawned. "But slaves are freed if they convert. Isn't that true?"

He masked his anger well, just as he masked his loneliness

and lust—every human thing about himself—but his forearm had turned to rock beneath her hands, muscles rigid and taut.

He might refuse to voice his outrage, but she could not keep silent. "You should have been raised a free man!"

"Yes, but I was not." His grim resolution scarred her nerves. "Now I fear being free of this place. I would rejoin their ranks as a warrior, or I would kill the father who bound me."

Her head jerked as if slapped. These dark secrets and the need for revenge had burned within him, but he used the Order as a shield between his lethal hands and his enemies. And she threatened his acceptance into that sanctuary, not only her stubborn resistance to the aid he offered, but by putting them in situations that required violence.

And she had lain with him. She wanted to still.

She tightened her fingers on his forearm, the only physical contact he had permitted in days. "But if you want to stay, why do you make it so difficult on yourself? Don't these vows pinch and bind? Don't they make you all the more eager to run free?"

"Yes!" Gavriel flung his hands. "Have you listened? Do you know what I've done?"

"You did so at the behest of despicable men. You punish yourself for their wickedness."

One step, then another, he allowed her approach. She reached out to stroke his face. The rough grain of his cheek, freshly shorn but still masculine and course, intriguing, scraped the delicate skin of her palm. "You punish us both," she whispered. "There is such a thing as forgiveness, Gavriel. You've been here long enough to see that, I should hope—to read it, to understand for yourself."

He closed his eyes. "I cannot read."

"No?" Their bodies whispered to each other, so near now. "You've been here for more than a year."

"We say our prayers, keep our vigils and routines."

"As a substitute for thought?"

Dark eyes open, he watched with such care and thoroughness that he might be touching her, yet his arms hung like lances at his side, hard, deadly, and unmoving. "Pacheco thought me more apt to respond to lessons of the flesh. To purge myself."

His voice caught on the word 'purge,' and the image of his scarred back blazed in her brain. A quiver warped her chin, near to tears. "He told you . . . to hurt yourself? Is that—?"

"Yes. My back."

She could see it happening again, Gavriel transforming to stone. In his face and in the hollow deadness of his voice, he was withdrawing. Even his body felt colder. Is that how he dealt with the hardship and abuse of being raised a slave? He banked his body and mind like a fire, saving only enough to survive. Never enough to feel.

"Aren't you curious?" she asked. "Isn't there a void inside you needing to be filled with information? Questions that need answers? You may not be a man of letters, but you could read if you studied."

"No one has ever . . ." His eyebrows pulled together, a quizzical expression, nearly hopeful, but his body remained tense. "You believe me capable?"

She smiled. "Think how easily you bested me at chess. You have a quick mind and the stubbornness that cannot be matched."

"You are my match," he said roughly.

His kiss was sudden and unexpected. Warm lips covered hers and his strong arms gathered her near. His tongue thrust into her mouth. Sensation burrowed into her core. Her body had been whispering to his, but now it cried out: *closer, tighter, never let go.*

Relying on his strength to keep her from falling, she met his questing tongue and sparred. The rough stubble along his upper lip abraded hers. His low moan set her alight. She poured every drop of her desire and sympathy and confusion into that kiss. She memorized his cinnamon taste and the spiky softness of his hair, uncertain as to whether she would ever touch him again.

A sigh mingled with frustration as they reached the limit of the kiss. She could have kissed him forever. But stretched between *yes* and *no,* his indecision cooled her desire. She would not lie with him again, not when he permitted so little. Bodily desires had ruled her for too long, and from this man—this mystery and temptation—she wanted more. Or nothing at all.

His hand still held the curve of her backside. Mouths parted, panting, she found his eyes blackened with desire. "Are you content with being miserable?"

He swallowed in that compulsive way he used when trying to regain control. "I deserve this life," he said.

"And yet here you are living, breathing, and with what looks to be a second chance," she whispered. "But you refuse it. I've never met anyone as stubborn as you. If you knew my sister, you'd understand that to be a remarkable statement."

His face darkened. "What are you suggesting? That I laugh? Will that banish my cares?"

"It might . . . but no." With her forefinger, she traced the curves of his upper lip. Even now, so close, touching him, she could not imagine him smiling. "I don't recommend anything of the sort. It would be akin to running when you've not learned to crawl. Perhaps you should start with a tiny grin, work up to a smile. As for laughing, I wouldn't want you to fail right at the start."

He stared at her with those unnerving eyes. "And I suppose you think I should fall in love with you."

She ignored the sudden leap of her heart. He was a man at sea, looking for any piece of flotsam to cling to, and she was steadily replacing one craving with another. Her anger returned in force, knowing she could no longer trust her own judgment.

"You can if you want," she said, pushing free of his embrace. The cool air of the training room sliced between their bodies. Later, alone, she would have time to mourn the loss of his heat. "I have no intention of reciprocating."

"No?"

"No. There are so many good men in the world. Why would I want you?"

He flinched.

"Did my words hurt?" she asked. "Did they make you wish circumstances were different?"

Gavriel stood straight, arms at his side once again. "I wish you would listen to me. Enough of this, Ada. It ends now."

Chapter 22

"Ada, you are distressed."

Fernán smiled down to where the Englishwoman sat alone on a stone bench outside the monastery. From the slope of her shoulders to the wrinkles pinching the skin around her eyes, she appeared deep in thought. Sunset illuminated her fair skin, her hair concealed by a white linen veil similar to those worn by the canonesses. That Ada would begin to take on the dour and stern-faced behavior of Jacobean women seemed an affront. She was a far more frank and worldly sort. Life in the Order would only see her dissolve away.

But perhaps, considering the task Pacheco had assigned, Fernán only tried to convince himself of as much.

Ada offered a cursory smile. "I wish to be left alone, please."

"Come, come—none of that," he said, sitting despite her lack of an invitation. He turned his eyes to the sun where it dipped behind the defensive wall at the western edge of the grounds. "Your dear Blanca is quite a girl."

She shot him a look midway between assessing and warning. "Did she enjoy herself in town today? I haven't seen her since the morn."

"Of course," he said. "She's quite the inquisitive type, all smiles and conversation with the locals."

When Ada smiled too, he breathed a silent sigh of relief. In truth, he had spent no more than a few moments with the girl from Yepes. She seemed quite at home among the doting canonesses and their quiet hierarchy, merely content to be included.

Fernán, however, had abandoned the group upon reaching the outer walls, as was his wont. He had found Abez, held her, stood with her as they watched young Najih sleep. And as always, he had said goodbye, leaving the woman he loved with little more than a lingering kiss and the last of his morabetins.

Let the gossips believe him a philanderer and a spineless buffoon. A hateful man with a bawdy tongue. Any such assumption kept them from the truth.

But Pacheco knew, curse him. He collected tasty morsels about nearly everyone in the monastery, the better to bend his subordinates and blackmail his rivals. That Fernán had been careless enough to fall into the man's trap still rankled. If his father discovered the truth . . .

He fiddled with the alms bag at his waist. His father would *not* find out. No one would.

"And how is our mutual friend?" he asked.

Ada released a breath, her eyes never leaving the far wall. Beyond its boundary, two days to the west, Toledo awaited sunset. "He's no one's friend," she said softly.

"Alas, I believe you may be right. What a difficult character, him. Been here a year and no one knows who he is."

"A year. Ten years. No difference." She sat straighter on the bench. "I've given up trying to know who he is."

"Probably for the best, wouldn't you think? Considering his vows and his commitment to this place, that is." He nodded toward the west. "You'll be leaving come the end of the month?"

"*Sí.*"

"Take care, Ada," he said with a laugh. "Don't let his foul temper rub off on you. Quite unbecoming anybody, let alone a body as fine as yours."

"I'm in no mood for your humor, Fernán."

He placed a hand over his heart and affected his most earnest expression. "I see I've offended you. My apologies."

"No matter," she said. "I should go inside."

He had to do this. For the safety of his fledgling little family, he had to do as Pacheco asked.

And then Gavriel would kill him. Fernán had kissed Abez goodbye knowing he would never see her again.

"Wait." He touched her hand, roughly taking her fingers and ignoring the trembling in his own. She frowned at him, but at least she stayed. From the alms bag he removed the packet Pacheco had given him: two poppy seedpods wrapped in a strip of linen.

"A gift," he said. "For you."

Her eyes widened. Her bow-shaped lips parted. Ah, but her mouth was lovely. No matter his love for Abez, he prided himself on being a man who appreciated the fairer sex. And only the thought of that love steadied his conscience and kept his hand from snatching back the unholy offer.

She had not lifted her gaze from his gift. "What is it?"

He raised the packet to his nose and inhaled the cloying sweet scent. "I think we both know."

"How?" Her breath was coming fast now. So very close.

"Don't ask, my dear," he whispered, pushing the pods into her hands. "It's yours."

She sat on the second pew in the cathedral for hours. Brothers came and went, praying, lighting candles, exchanging quiet instructions. Two young novices swept the central aisle, silent in their work. No one bothered Ada. She only noticed them as a buzz of insects behind her thoughts. The poppy pods pressed as heavy as lead in her hands. She had not even opened the linen wrap, but their scent—more pungent than smoke, dust, and the smell of cathedral's sun-baked stones— wove into her nose, tapping deeper memories.

Freedom.

She had spent the better part of a week contemplating her future, one that involved selling Daniel's scrolls and indulging once again, but now the moment was at hand. And she did not know what to do. She should fling temptation away like so much refuse and clutch her temperance with both hands. But the poppies waited. They called to her.

She stood and quickly left the cathedral. Gavriel would help. They had parted on poor terms that morning in the weapons hall, but he would not turn away her pleas on this score. None of their hard work—his hard work and her suffering—would be sacrificed. She only had to ask for his aid, her pride an easy victim to the fear of falling again.

Breath burned hot in her throat, and her pulse pumped as quickly as her legs. Running. Through the maze of the monastery, the corridors repeated the sound of her boots slapping the flagstones. Two canonesses wearing matched habits and censorious looks pushed against a wall to avoid her. And with every step, Ada could have flung away the poppies.

She would, just as soon as Gavriel told her to.

Outside his chambers, she pressed her forehead against the wood and breathed. The erratic beat of her body would not be stilled. He would see her as a crazy woman at his threshold, hair whipped free of her headdress and eyes wild with need and fear. He would *see* her, this humiliating vulnerability, and he would not fail her. He could not.

She knocked with her good hand and cradled the pods with the other. Waiting, panting, she heard a smack. Then another, like the slap of reins against a horse's neck. A third sent shivers up her back.

His back.

"Gavriel?"

She pounded the door this time, both hands, not caring about the pain shooting between her raw knuckles. A few kicks later and she shouted his name again, her face aflame. Frustration pinched at her temples. She placed the poppies on the ground and tried the handle, flying two steps forward when the door opened.

Gavriel knelt wearing only breeches, his back to the door. Illuminated by a single tallow candle, he bowed his head low. Long streaks of flayed flesh angled from his right shoulder to his left hip. Rivulets of blood trickled down, nearly black in that pale light. Slightly older wounds, covered in scabs, crossed the opposite direction, the remnants of another recent torture session.

He raised his arm and flogged himself again, apparently oblivious to her presence. The metal-tipped leather bit his skin once more, opening another furrow of flesh. His whole body convulsed around that pain but he made no sound. The arm may as well have been that of another man for how little mercy he showed. Every strike was more shattering, more powerful than the one before.

The lash pulled a chain of whimpers from her throat. She covered her mouth. Tears rained over her fingers until she could stand no more.

"Stop!"

She rushed to him and grabbed the handle of the flogger. Even taking him by surprise, she was no match for his speed and strength. Gavriel shot to his feet and flung her away. She landed with a grunt against the wall.

He stood over her, his handsome face contorted into a grotesque mask. "Why are you here?"

She recoiled from his thunderous voice and smacked her head against the stone wall. Her every reason for coming to him had vanished into vapors of fear and shock. "I—I . . ."

"Come to stare, *inglesa?*" He sneered and hefted the grim leather flogger, displaying it for her. "Come to see what punishment I endure for having kissed you?"

Her heart twisted. "This is because of our kiss?"

Blood dripped from the steel tips to the ground, dotting the floor. "Because I must make my body obey. My body—or you."

He bared his teeth and lifted the flogger again, ready to strike. She screamed.

Gavriel flinched, blinked. "Ada?"

"I've never been afraid of you, not until this moment," she whispered, fingers clenched around the hilt of her dagger.

A flicker of Gavriel—the man she knew—returned to his eyes, as if trapped behind the mask he wore, fighting to break free. But for Ada, it was too late. She used his momentary confusion to find her feet and flee.

Half a dozen paces down the corridor, she ran back and grabbed the poppies.

Hours later, Gavriel finished washing the cuts on his back, content to have stopped the bleeding. A fresh tunic covered his skin. He rubbed the back of his neck, his hair still wet from washing, and he stared at the flogger where it lay on the floor. Having simply dropped it when Ada fled, the venomous tool lay in the blood—his blood—dried black on the stones.

She had been afraid of him, truly afraid, just as he had been terrified of himself. Not at all the man he had hoped to become. And now, no matter the consequences, he would apologize. She deserved that much from him, if not abject begging for her forgiveness.

Shame rolled through his body like a thunderstorm over the land. If he had hurt her . . .

His gaze caught on the metal barbs at the ends of the flogger. They glittered with sinister purpose. The skin on his back twitched, but his body and mind remained unbowed. He could deliver as many lashes as there were stars and Ada would remain a part of him. Nothing he had done or could ever do would sever the connection strengthening between them, but he had nearly taken his anger and fear out on her.

Grizzly images of Ada wearing scars to match his burned behind his eyes. He crossed the scant distance to the sword he had wrested from one of the guards in Yepes. Why had he kept it, when he thought never to use a sword again? Now he knew. He kept it because he might need it. Picking up the flogger, a lifeless opponent that threatened his body and his mind, he wrapped the leather strips around the blade and sliced them from the handle. Tiny, excruciating metal barbs tinkled against the flagstones, harmless now except to bare feet.

It was done. Never again.

He quietly closed the door to his chamber and walked through the corridors to Ada's room. No one stirred at that late hour. Torches burned low, if at all, and shadows worked to get the better of his imagination. But what could the shadows—or his imagination, for that matter—conjure that he had not seen or done or thought?

"Ada?" He knocked gently on the door. "Ada, I've come to apologize. Please, *inglesa*. Ada?"

The latch sounded on the other side of the door and opened to reveal Blanca, her eyes two full moons. She would not open the door any wider. "*Señor,* she's not well."

"I understand," he said, quelling his frustrations. "I'm responsible."

Blanca frowned. "I should hope not."

He pushed his hands together, the heels of his palms

grinding bone on bone. "Yes, I am. I—I frightened her, and I should like the chance to apologize."

"Oh, *señor,* no."

She opened the door wide. Ada lay slumped on the floor at the foot of her cot. Her hair fell over her shoulders, half-concealing her face, strands plastered to her forehead. The gown she had worn lay in a heap beside an empty mortar and pestle.

Air punched free of his lungs. Dizzy, hot, defeated, he slumped against the doorway.

No!

"Hello, Gavriel," she said, her voice as bleary as her addled eyes. He had seen that expression on her lovely face once before. "You're not supposed to be here."

"Saints be, Blanca." He cornered the smaller woman, barely reigning in his temper. "How long has she been this way?"

She passed a nervous glance between him and Ada. "I returned from midnight Mass and found her."

"Did she ask for me?"

"No, *señor.* She said I was not to bother you." Blanca hesitated, her cheeks heating with a pink blush.

"There's more, *sí?* What did she say?"

"She said you were in a foul humor and she wanted to enjoy herself in peace."

Gavriel nodded, slowly, as if the bones in his neck had rusted. She had come to see him, but why?

Ada laughed behind him, the sound of madness. A shiver rolled down his arms. Blanca crossed herself and moved to join Ada.

Gavriel put a hand to her shoulder. "Blanca, do you trust me?"

She did not hesitate now, not like when she was protecting him from the truth of Ada's condition. She simply nodded.

"I need to stay with her tonight," he said quietly. "Do you understand? No one can know."

"Of course, *señor*." Her dark eyes held trust and fear in equal measure. "And you can make her well again?"

"I can," he said.

But the conviction in his voice belied the quivering apprehension in his gut. He had driven her to this, after all those days and horrid nights dragging her free. Why would anyone entrust him with her care after how he had behaved?

Because she needs me.

Blanca gathered her cloak and tied it around her neck. "I will sleep in the chapel. Find me there if you need anything."

"Are you certain?"

"*Sí.* Take care of her tonight."

With that she was gone. The latch clicked, shutting him in with Ada.

"Where is it, what's left of it?"

"Nothing left," she said, her face smooth and serene. "Just the mortar. So innocent now. Harmless. And now you can't hurt me, either."

Gavriel knelt and pushed the hair from her brow, smoothing. "Who did this? Who gave this to you?"

Eyes filled with stars met his. Nothing of Ada remained in that elated gaze. They had defeated this demon need once, but it had returned to steal her again.

"A friend," she said. "One who likes me much more than you do."

"Fernán."

She smiled like sharing a secret. "Possibly."

After a deep breath for patience, he gathered her in his arms and lifted her from the floor. A keen sense of helplessness stole the strength from his arms. He clutched tighter, suddenly afraid of dropping her. She snuggled against his chest, that secret smile still gracing her lips. Her face was sallow and waxen.

Working to banish his doubts, or at least to lock them away for a few hours, he steeled himself for the task of sitting with her, vigilant, for her euphoria would not last forever. He settled with her on the cot, sitting propped against the wall despite the flames of pain across his back. She curled into his body at once, head on his chest and softly humming to herself.

"I never wanted this for you." He kissed the top of her head. Her sweat smelled sticky sweet, not like her at all. "I am trapped, but I wanted you to be free."

He had not expected a reply. The distance between their minds was too great—his writhing in regret, hers floating high above. Yet she sighed and whispered, "But you didn't want me for yourself."

Gavriel pulled her closer and shut his eyes, but he did not sleep. The throbbing along his back was too insistent, and the storm in his mind would not quiet. He needed to decide what to do about her lapse.

And come dawn, he would kill Fernán.

Chapter 23

She returned to him just before sunrise, slowly and cloaked in anguish. The tears began ever before she opened her eyes, dampening the linen of his tunic and setting fire to every decision—even the ones he had been certain of. Her tears held that power. As he lay cradling her limp body, he felt stripped and defenseless when once he had been powerful, confident, unyielding.

Ada sobbed against his chest. "What have I done?"

"Quiet now, *inglesa,*" he said. "You made a mistake, nothing more."

Her face crumpled and she rubbed fists over her red-rimmed eyes. "You must be furious with me. I am with myself."

"Ada, be calm. We knew this journey would be a difficult one, filled with obstacles."

Gavriel urged her to sit up and away from him. Relieved to come away from the wall and shift positions, he shook feeling back into his right arm. But the room was colder without her body pressed close. She shivered too, and he fetched her cloak to loop around her shoulders.

"May I have water?" she asked.

He handed her a mug filled from the clean water basin and

resumed his place on the cot. Ada drank with greedy swallows. Even that small task left her winded and slumped against the wall. Her face shone with unnatural paleness, shrouded by the black wool cloak and streams of her dark hair. Her chapped lips were puffy, the deep pink of raw meat.

But her eyes. The snap of vitality and intelligence peeked out from behind those tired, tired eyes. Despite the fatigue, she was herself. She was Ada. And he wanted to keep her locked in that room until she swore never to leave him again.

He froze. What right did he have to expect any such promises? He had behaved like a madman. Since arriving in Uclés, he had done everything possible to distance himself from her, from the temptation she represented.

"Ada, why did you come to see me last night? Do you remember?"

Her cloudy blue eyes opened wide and flicked around the room. "Where's Blanca?"

"She went to the cathedral when I offered to see you through till dawn." He gently cupped her chin. "Please, Ada. I am as you see me now, not . . . not how I was last night. Why did you come to my chamber?"

She scrutinized him, looking deep—just as he had looked for her, someone dear hiding deep beneath the terror. "You frightened me," she said. "Do you know that?"

He closed his eyes but his temper stayed calm. She deserved his humility, not some false display of arrogance to conceal shame and injured pride. She had returned from that dark place, as he had. Simply seeing the life in her expression, not that numb and vacant pleasure, stripped him of pretense.

"Yes, I frightened you," he said. "I know, and I apologize. I could have harmed you. Not because I was angry, but because I didn't want you to see me. Not like that."

She bowed her head. "I didn't want you to see me either. Did Blanca tell you?"

"She did."

They sat facing each other on the cot. They were not strong enough for teasing and laughter, not when hurt and disappointment were easier to expect, easier to deliver. Her expression as lost as he felt, Gavriel pinched the bridge of his nose.

"Why did you do it?" she asked.

"Penance."

"Surely, God has decreed nothing of the sort. He asks for prayer and pleas for forgiveness, good works—not mutilating your body. Did Pacheco command you to do this?"

"Yes." His voice sounded as if he spoke from another room, distant and hollowed. "When we returned from Yepes, he instructed me to make amends for the violence I had done. He knew of my broken vows, perhaps even of you and I."

"But Gavriel, you're no longer a slave."

Raising his face to the ceiling, he released a shuddering breath. "Why did you come to me last night?"

"I brought the poppy pods," she said, her words breathy. "I'd hoped you would help me discard them."

Failure struck him in the chest. She had set aside her pride, seeking his help. He turned on the cot and knelt, taking her hands in his. The oil wick had burned low and cast deep shadows over her grief-stricken face.

"Instead you found a monster, not an ally. *Inglesa,* forgive me. I don't—" His voice went hoarse. He shook his head. "I don't know how to make this right, for you or me."

"Neither do I."

She had asked if he would be gone long.

No, *inglesa.* Not long.

Gavriel strode through the corridors as sunlight frightened away the dreariness of the previous night. Never had darkness stretched across so many hours, but now the day fairly glowed with the vitality of spring.

Ada had come to see him because she needed his help. The blunt truth of his failure knocked behind his eyes. He stepped out of the monastery and squinted against the sun. Nothing had changed, but as he strode around the training grounds to the distant fields, Gavriel could find no part of himself left untouched by previous weeks' events. Untouched by Ada. He had breathed her in, there by the riverside, and now she invaded his thoughts and permeated his pores, intoxicating him like the drug she craved.

The drug she would always crave.

When she only had herself to harm, she would never find a reason to stop. He had learned as much about himself last night, clutching his flogger and standing over Ada's hunched body. He had nearly struck her, the shame and pain of his ritual taking control of his brain and his limbs. Only some deeper feeling had stayed his hand, one more frightening to consider.

He found Fernán at the edge of the field, chatting with one of the young canonesses, a pretty girl of Blanca's age. She blushed and ducked her head. Her soft laughter eased across the newly planted fields like a breeze.

"Fernán, I must speak with you."

The canoness fled before another word was spoken. Fernán watched her go, his wistful face in profile and his shoulders tight. "I know why you're here," he said.

Gavriel admired that much, at least; Fernán refused to take the coward's way.

"Why did you give her that poison?"

"I cannot say," Fernán said, facing him with the poise of a nobleman, one of authority and bearing. Every hint of his customary humor had disappeared.

Gavriel narrowed his eyes, seeing the ridiculous buffoon as he never had. "What can you say?"

"You'll never be permitted to join the Order, and if she remains here, Ada will not be permitted to recover. Her life is in danger."

"From whom? I must know."

Fernán assessed him with a calm, aloof gaze. A trace of his ironic smile twitched his lips. "You care for her."

Gavriel hesitated but could not lie. "Yes."

"Then get her free of this place."

"And you? Shouldn't you leave as well?"

"I have reasons to stay, the same reasons that prohibit me from revealing all." He looked into the morning sun and sighed, appearing suddenly older than his twenty years. "You came here to punish me, yes?"

"Yes."

"The penalty for beating a fellow Jacobean is harsh, and yet you would do this for her. I wish . . . well, if I had been—no matter now." Despite his strange calm, the younger, smaller man glanced at Gavriel's fists and blanched. "And now?"

Hesitation made lead of his muscles, numb and heavy. "You deserve all I can mete."

"Yes, I do. And for both of our sakes, it needs to be done."

Understanding blossomed in his mind. Whoever had induced Fernán to give Ada the poppies likely expected Gavriel to retaliate. To do otherwise could offer proof that Fernán had confided.

They expect me to behave like an animal.

But he had been ready to. For Ada. And because that animal lurked inside him, awaiting any excuse.

"Whoever does this to us—they know us well," Gavriel said quietly.

"And why not?" He seemed to force a shrug. "We're the imbeciles who offer him confession. Might as well dictate a list of our faults and the means of best manipulating us."

Pacheco.

The taste of copper tainted his tongue.

Fernán nodded only once. His blue gaze, a pale pretender to Ada's deeper blue, followed Gavriel with unnerving clarity. "Now, are you the sort of man who can convincingly beat another without provocation?"

Images of Ada sprawled on the floor of her chambers jumped to the fore. Looking into her eyes had been like staring into a thick fog, obscuring all she was. She had cried against his chest, the defenses they painstakingly rebuilt—destroyed.

"No, Fernán. The question is, are you the sort of man who can endure such a beating?"

The tapping of Ada's boot heels on the flagstones matched the spiky anxiety of her heartbeat. She paced along the corridor in front of Gavriel's room. Evening shadows penetrated the dry quiet of the western wing. After enduring a sleepless day in her room, body aching, bruised from the inside out, she fought to regain control of her life, herself, for just a single moment.

A persistent itch lodged just under her skin and at the back of her throat. That one taste . . .

She had slipped. Now, finding another taste dominated her attention, except for thoughts of Gavriel and what he had done to Fernán. Blanca had come to her, furious and confused. Ada's own confusion had done little to provide them with answers.

Pieces fell into place like rain. His solitude, his need for discipline and answers, and his uncanny understanding of her suffering. Gavriel hurt himself as deeply and as terribly as she did with opium, only his release was physical pain. No wonder he flinched whenever she touched him and why gentleness set him on edge.

She collapsed against the wall, the tiny, isolated world of

the monastery spinning around her. This was a realm of Hell, surely, a place in which she was trapped, perhaps forever. If she managed to leave when Jacob returned, she would never escape the strangling blackness of her own mind. To cure the nightmares, she had found opium. To cure the opium, she had relied on Gavriel. But the three tortures converged until every wisp of herself had gone missing.

Forehead pressed against the cool stones of the wall, she breathed through her mouth to stem the rising bile. Excuses that sounded perfectly logical sided with an infant's wailing cry for satisfaction, working in tandem against her better judgment. This was her life. This was her future, until her mind collapsed and she succumbed again.

But first she lost the fight against her nausea. She retched, thankful at least she had not yet taken her evening meal.

"Ada?"

The door to Gavriel's room was open and he stood at the threshold. She breathed his name. He came to her and knelt in the corridor, his arm around her, protective. She remembered their morning by the river, lying safely in his embrace.

Never again. He had made that clear in words, yet he insisted on behaving as her champion. No matter his initial motives, his attention and care held the rich flavor of caring. Genuine caring. And she was a fool for thinking as much.

"*Inglesa,* what happened?"

She caught the censorious look on his face and thought better of trying to lie. "I'm unwell. The tincture, I'm afraid."

"Ada, have you taken anything more?"

The heat and wood smoke scent of him could soften the hardest souls, and she had no such strength. Only anger. "I've taken nothing, which is the difficulty. I—I want more. You knew I would. *I* knew."

His eyes, filled as always with the hunger he would rather

deny than indulge, lingered on her mouth. "You struggle with this," he said. "In your mind, you know what is right."

She spat against the wall, another wave of nausea boiling in her stomach. "Do not lecture me, novice."

"But your struggle is a welcome one. At least you know the right way, even if you don't want to follow it."

"Is that what you tell yourself?"

"Come inside," he said, pulling her none-too-gently to her feet. "You'll upset everyone."

She tried to glare at him, but her attention caught on the smooth, corded length of his neck. "My first consideration, of course."

He closed the heavy oaken door behind them, the air in his room cool and still. All evidence of the scene she had encountered the night before—the dim candlelight, Gavriel bared and bleeding—was gone. The sun dipped low beyond the narrow window. Pure, clean breezes from the spring evening blew in with the shadows.

And the flogger lay cut into pieces at the foot of his cot.

She rinsed her mouth with clean water from his washstand and sat heavily, watching that flogger as she would a snake. Gavriel remained by the door, his arms crossed and his body swathed in white.

"I'm glad you came to me."

She laughed sharply. "I do not seek your counsel, not after last night. I came to find out why you beat Fernán."

He blinked. Nothing more. She sat on her hands, sat on the desire to beat him until he felt something, anything. But the image of his scarred, ruined back changed her mind. She only wanted him to admit to the pain and fear she knew lurked inside.

"His face," she said clearly. "I saw him at the noontide meal. Someone thrashed him. I can only imagine what the rest of him looks like."

He lifted an eyebrow. "I know nothing about it."

"God hears you when you lie."

"Yes." He stepped away from the door and sat on the floor in front of the cot. Head bowed slightly, he seemed to be watching the toes of her boots. "And He saw me when I beat a man this morning."

"He didn't deserve it, Gavriel."

His head jerked up and his dark eyes snapped, that veneer of serenity stripped away. "We came here to retreat from the temptations of the world. He brought that poison and gave it to you purposefully. For that, he deserved the punishment I meted. And more."

Chapter 24

Ada's shock and confusion were palpable, and Gavriel could not hide from her scrutiny. His gut still churned at the memory of bloodying Fernán's face, beating a man who had submitted to his blows even before they began. Yet a more ancient instinct had found satisfaction—a satisfaction that extended even beyond protecting Ada. That beast had been freed, the one he found within himself in times of battle, the one that had been dragged into existence at the hands of his father.

Two *caballeros* had been needed to pull him clear of Fernán's limp body.

"Does the *Trecenezago* know what you've done?" she asked.

"No, but Pacheco does." His head throbbed, unsure whether he was more disgusted with himself for relishing his violence against Fernán or for handing their novice master control over his life, his very soul. And now representatives from the *Trecenezago*—the Council of Thirteen that governed Jacobean life—would punish him. "Grand Master Rodriquez is absent, touring the Order's territorial holdings. My sentence will be decided when he returns."

Blue eyes opened wide. "What will happen to you?"

"Beating another member of the Order, even for novices, is

an appalling crime. Punishment will last for six months, during which I'll have my cross taken," he said, glancing at the glare of red on the left side of his chest. "I'll take my meals on the floor, and endure floggings and solitude if I do not comply."

The soft lines of her mouth tightened. She shook her head, dark curls shaking loose from a hasty arrangement of plaits. "You'll be mad at its end."

Slavery had been the mark of his childhood, but he would no longer submit. Pacheco did not work alone; that much seemed obvious. His plots involved Gavriel but likely at the behest of a higher hand. Bleak forces worked against him, and he would not meekly bow his head and leave Ada alone.

He would be forced to choose between protecting Ada and obeying the tenets of the Order. Again. Only now that the Order suddenly seemed an unholy place filled with untrustworthy masters and spying eyes, his choice would be a simple one.

But he refused to decide until he knew where her addiction would take them.

She picked at the hem of one sleeve, the fine embroidery beginning to fray beneath her ragged fingernails. "Why did you do it?"

"He hurt you."

Her eyes glistened. "I brought this on myself."

"Fernán set back all our progress," he said, his voice barely more than a growl. "I showed him that such actions are not without penalty."

"I've made no progress, Gavriel."

"I'm afraid I have to agree with you."

Ada's head jerked up, her expression wounded. "You agree?"

"I do."

He stood from the floor and massaged the small of his back. The sharp snap of pain beneath his fingers, his lacerations throbbing, made him stop. Over the past year, that echo of pain as the cuts healed assured him of his spiritual improvement. He was conquering the beasts and expunging the blackness from his soul. Now that he doubted Pacheco's cruel advice, the reminder only amplified his anger and strengthened his resolve to unravel the man's motives.

He removed a small leather pouch from beneath his pillow, its contents surprisingly light for all the damage they wrought. "And because we've made no progress, I brought something for you."

Gavriel sat on the cot, his bent knee barely brushing the softness of Ada's upper thigh. They both glanced at that spot, a small moment of connection, and then at one another. What would she read in his eyes? Did she see the shift that had taken place in him? Or just the anger—no longer directed at her, the source of his temptation, but at the wickedness and the vice that worked to keep them apart. His own included.

Without explanation or ceremony, he dumped the contents of the small leather sack on the bed. Four poppy pods tumbled onto his coarse woolen blanket.

Ada's gasp filled the room. Eyes wide, she scrambled away as if burned by fire. "What are you doing?"

He shrugged and lifted one of the poppies, the location of which Fernán had disclosed. Pacheco had given him six, enough to have stolen Ada for days rather than hours. That Fernán had only offered a third of his supply had kept Gavriel from doing him permanent harm.

Just.

"Can't you see? I've decided you are a hopeless case, Ada. Denying you is even harder than keeping my own vows, and we both know how wretched I've been at that."

He drew the washing stand near to the cot and retrieved a flask and the mortar he had taken from her room. Layers of resin coated the head of the hardened clay pestle, making it sticky. Using the washing stand as a table, he mashed the green pod to release its milky juices and added a splash of wine. He strained the liquid to another bowl and repeated the process until all four poppies had released their devilish essence.

"That's how to do it, *sí?*" He waved a hand over his offering where it waited on the stand. "I must apologize for the wine. It's new and bitter, and I'm at a loss as to what spices you prefer."

Ada had backed against the wall, as far from the opium as she could manage without leaving the bed. Face pale, eyes wild, she looked just as he had found her in the hallway— alight with struggle and fear and the knowledge that what she wanted would be the end of her.

"This isn't fair," she whispered, licking her lips once, again, until they began to redden. "You know I . . . you know I can't . . ."

"Face this? Look temptation in the face and say no?" He leaned across the space between them and touched her cheek. "Because you will not be well until you can do that on your own."

She slapped his hand, a stinging crack like the whip across his back. "Is that what you're doing with me? Keeping temptation within reach for weeks so you can practice and say no and say no again? It's not fair to me. This game of yours— I don't want anything to do with it."

"I've never played games," he said, throat raw. "But let me assure you, the rules I live by are changing."

Her eyes burned hot and angry. Anything but the numbness. Anything but the vacancy he had once mistaken for peace. "How opportune for you," she said. "Now you think to have me join you in falling?"

He nodded to the bowl. "Take it, *inglesa.*"

"What do you want for it?"

"I said it was a gift."

Doubt spread over her face. Doubt and desperation. "Fernán said the same to me, and you made his face a plate of meat as thanks. You've fought me like a cat in a bag, trying to keep me from it. Why this change?"

"I don't require anything of you," he said. "But I do have a condition."

She exhaled. Her shoulders sagged. "I knew it."

"For every swallow you take, I shall take three."

Trembling fingers covered her open mouth. She seemed incapable of stopping the rocking rhythm of her body, her eyes never leaving his. That crazed stare clung to him. "Are you mad? You must be! Haven't you seen? Haven't you seen what I've been through? And you would bring that on yourself?"

"I've seen what you've endured, yes." He edged nearer. One of her plaits had fallen loose, and he stroked the ragged ends of her dark chestnut hair. "But I've also seen your joy. Why shouldn't I have a taste?"

"You're scheming."

He wished he could deny her accusation, but in truth, the tincture called to him. How easy would it be to succumb, as she did, to the release that drug offered? No more pain and bitter memories. No more conscience to war with his impulses. No more obstacles in his search for peace.

Gavriel lifted the bowl and inhaled its sickly sweetness. "Take a sip. Let's find out."

"No!"

She jumped off the cot. The skirts of her gown caught beneath her boots. With a curse, she fought free of the entangling fabric. Standing with her back pressed against the door, she pushed frantic breaths in and out of her open mouth. Her hysterical eyes never touched the bowl in his hands.

"Do what you will, but I'll not be party to it."

He brought the burgundy tincture to his lips and smiled. "More for me."

* * *

"Gavriel, no!"

Ada bridged the span between them with one leap. She swatted the bowl from his hands and watched with grim satisfaction as the tincture spilled over the washstand, dripping to the floor. The earthenware bowl cracked into half a dozen chunks against the wall.

She stood silent before him, breathing fast, neither of them moving. No matter how her body yearned for the debilitating bliss of that sweet poison, she could not allow him to become like her. Yes, she had known moments of sweetness, but so too had she known mindless craving and the deepest despair. In her mind, she knew the release was not worth the pain. She knew she would endure any deprivation to keep Gavriel from suffering what she did.

So the tincture gathered in sticky burgundy pools around the wooden feet of the washing stand. It coated the floor, not her tongue. But for all her craving, she felt no regret. Only a profound sense of triumph.

Her gaze covered Gavriel's angular, unreadable face in search of his mood. Had he been bluffing? Had he really intended to drink the poison? Would he be angered or relieved at her actions?

He arose from the bed and stepped over the sticky mess. She smelled what remained of the concoction and her mouth watered, but then he stood near, very near. The spicy male scent of him mingled with the opium, overtaking her completely. She wanted him—whole and safe and hers. Whether she was simply replacing one craving for another hardly mattered when he loomed near enough to touch, to kiss.

"Say something," she whispered.

The warm tingle of his fingers along the side of her neck covered her in shivers. His eyes darkened to the purest black, his pupils and irises bottomless. "I'm proud of you, *mi inglesa*."

She inhaled and closed her eyes, hoarding the sound of

his deep voice, his praise, and that familiar endearment—
possessive now. Every fiber of her body yearned for satisfaction. With the opium tincture spilled across the floor, he
remained as her pleasure of choice.

"What do I do?" she asked, feeling hollow and limp.

He slid her into an embrace. Their bodies touched, thigh to
chest. "I've been telling you what to do since we met."

His voluntary closeness and droll teasing set her off balance. All she knew was that he held her. He had saved her yet
again. "Yes, you have."

"Now it's your turn to give the orders."

An unexpected smile lifted one corner of her mouth.
Warm, wet heat pooled in her stomach. What would it be to
have this man at her command?

"Is that an order?"

The darkness in his eyes turned to pleading. "A request,"
he said. "For I'm as lost as you. No matter what I've insisted
or denied, I am lost."

Expecting him to retreat with every passing breath, she
gingerly slid a hand around his ribs, to his spine, down the
length of his muscled back. Where smooth flesh should be,
he had only scars and pain.

But he did not retreat. His eyes slid closed and his head
angled back, just a little, as if savoring the feel of her hands
on him, her body pressed to his. Impossible. Even when they
had lain together by the river, he had never succumbed, never
enjoyed her touch—not entirely. The barrier of his vows had
stood between them. Even with the deed done and his promise of chastity a broken one, he had resisted.

Her limbs stiffened, limbs that wanted to fall into him, made
molten by him. "What has changed?" He began to shake his
head, denying her yet again. "This is my command," she said.
"Tell me."

Gavriel watched her for a long, lingering moment, his lips

parted as if the words waited just inside, sitting atop his tongue. She would dive in after them if she could, enjoying his taste along the way.

"I cannot," he said at last. He stepped out of their embrace and placed the softest kiss on the back of her hand. "But believe me, I'll know. Soon. And then we will . . ."

"What?"

"We will talk. I'm through making vows I cannot keep, vows that are not my own."

A pounding knock rattled the door on its hinges. Ada jumped from her skin. Gavriel tossed a quick look around the room, finding what she did: a shambles coated in drying wine.

He pulled the door ajar, just enough to let Blanca enter. Her eyes widened at the sight of his chamber in such a disarray, but he breathed easier with the moment's distraction from Ada, her body, and the embrace they had shared—one that had nearly felt easy. Right.

Although knowledge of Pacheco's manipulations might excuse him from his vows, he had not decided where that left him. The Order was no longer the safe haven he had imagined, which meant his future gaped like a wound. He would not permit Ada to accompany him down a dark path when he had no notion of its destination.

But the expression on Blanca's face set the issues aside.

Ada stepped clear of the mess on the floor and took the younger woman's hands. "What is it, Blanca?"

"Someone has pillaged our room," she said, her voice tremulous.

"Our room? I only left it but an hour ago."

"I returned from the gardens and found it a disaster." Her dark eyes roamed over the disorder in Gavriel's chamber. "Did the same happen to yours?"

"No, this was our fault," Gavriel said. "Have you told anyone?"

Blanca eyed them both and took note of the shattered bowl but said nothing. Gavriel appreciated her reserve. "Fernán was with me when I discovered the crime. He advised me say nothing, merely to find you both."

Icy stiffness wrapped around his arms, his legs. "Does he have an explanation as to where he was?"

"When the room would have been raided?" She lifted her chin and met his gaze directly, wrapping a light woolen shawl more tightly around her shoulders. "You suspect him, perhaps?"

Gavriel pushed a fist into his palm, squeezing until two knuckles popped. "I have no reason to exonerate him."

"You do if you believe me. He was with me in the gardens. Forgive me for saying, but he seemed a man in need of a considerate ear."

Ada touched Blanca on the forearm. "You said yourself he is not a man to be trusted. He was the one who gave me opium last night."

"That he did," Blanca said quietly. "But if you knew his reasons, you might . . . understand. You might even forgive him." She sniffed, loud and exaggerated. "Seems someone else has made a similar offer since."

"This was different," Ada began.

With a wave of his hand, Gavriel interrupted whatever Ada's explanation would have been. "Let us see your quarters."

Chapter 25

Ada studied the damage, having yet to recover from the terrors of her morning. Only standing within the warm circle of Gavriel's arms had calmed the dread, but then her heart had pounded for an altogether different reason.

Now she stared at the upended ruin of the chamber she shared with Blanca. Nothing remained untouched. Their cots had been overturned. Straw poked out from the woolen ticking. Their washing stand lay tipped on its side. Her tortoise-shell comb lay among the ruins of straw, as did her scattered chess set.

Blanca searched but found her possessions as well. "But why would anyone want to merely . . . rummage?"

Ada looked to Gavriel for answers, as if belonging to the Order, to that strange and confining place, qualified him to set her confusion to rights.

"And everything you had is here?" he asked. "Intact?"

"Yes, except for the scrolls."

"How do you mean?"

"They're safe, just not here. I hid them."

"Why?"

She rubbed her face and exhaled, feeling a hot blush beneath her fingers.

"Ada?"

"The scrolls are vellum parchment," she said. "I'd stolen them from my mentor, Daniel of Morley, with the intention of selling them. They can be stripped of their ink and used again, making them valuable."

His expression darkened. "You were keeping them to sell."

"For when I returned to Toledo, yes."

Her cheeks heated, looking across the distance between the respectable scholar she had been and the struggling woman she had become. Day and night. Only now she had sense enough to recognize the vast difference. Until Gavriel's intervention, the creeping sadness of who she had been and what she lost had never touched her. She had merely drowned in it.

"But that decision seems a long time ago," she said.

He held her gaze for another moment, assessing, looking deeper. "I'm glad to hear that, *inglesa.*"

She gestured to their wreck of a room. "But what do you know of this?"

"Only that Fernán was right in suggesting Blanca keep this a secret. The rest is simple speculation. For now." He looked around as if expecting to find someone watching. And perhaps he was right. The walls seemed to listen and wait for their next move, the most patient of opponents. "Where is Fernán?"

Blanca pressed her lips together. "I cannot say. My guess is that he would want to return to town."

"But why? You said something about his motives for offering Ada the poppies. Do you know what information Pacheco used to earn his cooperation?"

"I am not at liberty, *señor.* Understand that, please."

Ada lifted the tortoiseshell comb and squeezed its teeth into her palm. The tugging pain kept her mind from spinning too far afield. "What has Pacheco to do with this?"

"We may not have time enough to explain fully," Gavriel said. "You wanted me to tell you what to do. Now try."

A single nod and he stood up, away from her. Arms crossed, he stared out the window as he spoke. "Pacheco vouched for me when I came to the Order. He knew some of my past and played on my eagerness to start afresh. In exchange for his support, I was to follow his instructions."

Ada frowned and broached the scant distance between them. "Instructions?"

"For cleansing myself. For becoming pure and worthy of the Order." A shuddering breath escaped his body, revealing his distress more plainly than the monotone of his voice. "He was the one who insisted on my three vows, the ones in excess of the Order's requirements. If I failed to keep them or revealed his requisites to other members of the Council, I would be expelled. He insisted everyone had secret vows, sworn tests between them and God. I believed him."

The expression on Blanca's face matched the feelings coursing through Ada's body. Confusion, yes, but also indignation. The unfairness of it all.

Ada touched his back. Beneath the robes and the tunic he wore was the skin he had so abraded and abused. "Did he do this as well?" she asked in a whisper. "He asked you to hurt yourself?"

Gavriel's head jerked down, humiliation rippling through his warrior's muscles. "I felt I had to . . . to start again. To be rid of what I'd done."

She wanted to close her arms around him and touch a flaming torch to his past, their past—and to anyone who caused him pain.

"And he held Fernán to unusual expectations as well? Some knowledge of his past?" She looked to Blanca for confirmation.

"He gave you poppies under Pacheco's orders. That was all

he revealed." Blanca picked up the bit of straw and pulled it in two, lengthwise. "I suspect it has to do with a woman he knows in town. I saw him with a dark-skinned woman last week when I went to market."

Ada narrowed her eyes. "He protects her?"

"Or their connection, perhaps. Their bodies together . . . they were on intimate terms."

"But Gavriel, why would Pacheco want to punish you like this?"

Standing taller, he seemed to pull himself out of a well and shake free of his confession. "I know not. I never assumed he did so for his own benefit, but to aid my penance. Only this morning did Fernán reveal Pacheco's hand in providing you with opium. Ada, these scrolls—may I see them?"

"Of course. What do you suspect?"

"Blanca, do you remember the guard at the bathhouse? The one you stabbed?"

She nodded.

"Yes," he said, his eyes harder and more like himself. More in control. "He said he wanted scrolls. I had no notion of what he meant."

"Mine?" Ada asked.

"He said he wanted 'the scrolls the Jew stole.'"

"Jacob?"

He nodded, the grim set of his mouth never changing.

Jacob had worked for Doña Valdedrona in the realm of espionage, never confiding his missions or discoveries to Ada. She had been hurt by his reticence, but only when his visits coincided with her temperance. Other times . . . well, she never would have confided in herself either.

What had he discovered? She searched her memory for reminders, clues, anything to solve the mystery of Jacob's mission before he had relinquished her to Gavriel. But all she remembered was the bitter pain of his betrayal. So enveloped by her own suffering, she had been blind to the dangers and deaf to the secrets he bore without fanfare.

Gavriel returned to Ada's room with her satchel, retrieved from a weapons cache where she had hidden it among anti-quated shields the knights no longer used. He had no time to ponder the events he had shared with Ada in his chambers: her refusal of the opium, his powerful, last-minute desire to try the foul stuff, and her rescue of sorts. Until they discov-ered what motives and trickery lurked in the shadows of the monastery, they were in danger. But the victory she had won over her need gave him hope. If nothing else came of their ac-quaintance, she might yet crawl to the freedom of a new life.

Where that would leave him, standing on the edge of exile from the Order, he did not know.

Every minute they spent within the walls of the monastery scratched at his nerves. Every moment that passed without Ada at his side left him a useless wreck. And now that he knew enemies were gathering, the fact he wore no weapon had never seemed more senseless.

The women had righted their chamber; he could see no ev-idence of a raid. Ada had changed clothes splattered by the spilled tincture, now wearing a borrowed brown gown. The deep color warmed her complexion. She had gained weight at the monastery, barely rounding the sharp angles of her hollow cheeks, and if she continued to win her fight against the opium, that push toward health would only gain momentum.

He nodded a greeting and closed the door before handing the satchel to Ada. She rummaged through the well-worn Cordovan leather, then tipped its contents onto her cot. Rolls of parchment, some sealed and some unraveling, spilled over the simple woolen mantel. Blanca sat on her cot just opposite, elbows on her knees, her expression one of a child expecting a treat.

Gavriel felt nothing so childish or innocent about his anticipation. If Ada possessed scrolls from the de Silva family, he would hear the words of ghosts. The monastery had been his refuge from sacrifice and evil deeds, from those men who had warped his life. But now they invaded what he had hoped would be his home and refuge.

Violence simmered in his body, coiled, awaiting a release.

"These are cheaper parchment filled with samples of various local dialects. Portuguese. Mozarabic," Ada said, indicating the papers that had unrolled, unsealed. She rubbed a thumb over one crest, a frown marring the smooth line of her brow. "These are the ones I took from Daniel, these with the eagle crest seal."

"That's the seal of the de Silva family." Gavriel took the scroll from her. He wanted to ruin that hated symbol. Bend it. Break it. Burn it.

She loosened the seal and unrolled the stiff, thick parchment. Gavriel and Blanca moved around the bed to secure the edges while Ada leaned close. Indecipherable scribbles of ink lined the entire sheet, close enough to make Gavriel's eyes cross. Individual marks blurred. But she read it with apparent ease. One slender finger traced from right to left.

While Gavriel's ignorance kept him silent, watching, waiting, Blanca found no shame in asking questions. "I've never seen so many symbols on a single sheet," she said. "Most times a merchant will write mere bits on scraps. What language is that?"

"Maghreb Arabic, from the Moorish territories." She leaned nearer and scratched at an ink smudge before beginning to translate. "It's addressed to Muhammad an-Nâsir."

"The young Almohad caliph," said Gavriel. "His father was

their leader at Alarcos but died two years ago. Control fell to an-Nâsir, his son."

"Seems Lord de Silva is none too pleased with how he has led his people. 'The time to strike is at hand, with summer and the end of the truce.'" She sat away from the scroll and rubbed her eyes. "What truce?"

Gavriel sat heavily on the floor, his back to the parchment containing his father's words. "After the bloody year following Alarcos, a truce was declared between the Christian kings and the Almohads. This summer marks the end of that five-year peace. Without it, the Almohads will be free to resume their invasion."

"But the motivation is not theirs. It comes from de Silva. This says, 'Matters in Africa have diverted your attention away from the Peninsula.'"

Blanca shook her head. "A Leonese nobleman conspires with the Moors? Is this how politics work?"

"It shouldn't be," Gavriel said. "A long-standing feud between my father and King Alfonso meant he sided with the Moors at Alarcos."

Ada had opened the second scroll. Silent, her eyes danced over the text until a single gasp echoed across the tiny chamber. Gavriel rose from the floor and knelt beside her, seeing nothing more from this parchment than from the last. He resented the language he could not understand, even as he admired her singular knowledge.

"What is it?" he asked.

"What if Lord de Silva wasn't the only one who sided with the Moors?"

"Who?"

"King Ferdinand of León."

His mouth went dry. "It's possible. More than possible."

Blanca shook her head. "The kings of León and Castile are cousins. First cousins. And they are both Christian, charged by the Pope to defend the Peninsula against the Moors. Everyone on the frontier knows that."

"But the blood between the two halves of the royal family, Leonese and Castilian, is very bad," he said.

"Here." Ada pointed at the line of address. "This one is also written by de Silva, but to Ferdinand. It reads, 'Next time, when the moment comes to crush the Castilian opposition, you will do more than drag your feet.' What does that mean?"

Gavriel sat back on his heels, eyeing that parchment as if it flashed venomous fangs. "Ferdinand was to reinforce his cousin's troops on the battlefield at Alarcos, but he strayed in León. His delay helped the Almohad armies gather momentum. We had the battle in hand, entirely and decisively, before the Leonese arrived."

"Then he was purposefully late?"

"Impossible to know for certain," Gavriel said. "But it seems Lord de Silva wants Ferdinand to take a more active role against the Castilians this time, not leaving the dirty work to the Almohads. A show of faith in their conspiracy."

Blanca touched the dried ink. "Can he write such things to a king?"

"Perhaps that explains the trouble we've had," Ada said. "Not La Señora or my debts, but men sent by de Silva to retrieve these missives."

She continued to read, her eyes dashing along every line.

"Anything else?" he asked.

She shook her head and rolled the parchment, shoving the scrolls back into her satchel. "Jacob or his men must have intercepted them. You said he was returning to Segovia, yes?"

Gavriel stared at her, suddenly certain that she hid something from him. The idea of her deception—more lies from Ada—stuck in his gut. "He was to speak with Doña Valdedrona, and possibly to Alfonso."

"He works for Her Excellency to collect information.

Maybe he left them to Daniel for safe-keeping while she was away at Alarcos."

Blanca smiled wide. "He's a spy? Is he truly?"

"It's been quite some time since I held such enthusiasm for his profession. Mostly it meant long absences and secrets." A blush tinted her cheeks and she ducked her gaze. "I could abide neither."

"He would have been in great danger carrying these scrolls with him," Gavriel said. "As we learned for ourselves."

"Unwittingly. He'll be very disappointed in me."

Her overcast face had him wondering again, with more intensity, as to the nature of her relationship with Jacob. Young, English, educated, devoted—Gavriel could not begin to duplicate their connection. But he touched her shoulder nonetheless, as if touch could banish the doubts and barriers.

"You're not the same woman he left in my care."

Her lips turned up in a wobbling smile. "Is that good or bad?"

"Depends on what he wants from you," he said, recalling Ada's description of how Jacob provided her with opium, how he doted on her. "As for the scrolls, we'll keep them safe and let King Alfonso decide what to do with my despicable family. And his treacherous Leonese cousin."

"What are you suggesting?"

"Dress for travel, both of you," he said, standing. "We should not stay here to be discovered."

Ada began to collect possessions for her satchel. Blanca nodded, seemingly childlike, but the expression on her face was one of resolve. "Since you've beaten Fernán, they'll watch you. All of us."

Fernán. The man was a boil, a terrible wretch of a human being. After what he had done to poison Ada, he deserved better acquaintance with Gavriel's fists. But those cryptic comments about Pacheco had splintered under Gavriel's skin, prickling into every decision he tried to make. None of his former certainty and purpose remained. Fernán seemed the only person who might be able to answer his questions. Whether Gavriel could believe the replies remained a mystery.

"Find Fernán," he said to Blanca. "Please. For once in his miserable career as a novice, he'll attend Mass. Tonight."

Chapter 26

That Brother Telles stood ready to conduct Mass in the fortress cathedral meant Grand Master Rodriguez was still absent. The *Trecenezago* had yet to meet. *Los caballeros* would wait until given the command to seize him by force, ready to stand accused for Fernán's beating.

As villagers streamed into the cathedral for midnight Mass, Gavriel looked for Ada. If all went smoothly, they would be clear of the village, clear of the threat by dawn. Beyond that . . .

He closed his eyes to the assembling congregation and saw only blackness behind his lids. No clear path. No certain future. Terrifying as that was, he breathed easier than he had in a year. Perhaps the time had come to imagine and fill that black void with a new future.

He opened his eyes, disoriented by the sight of several hundred parishioners gathered from the village below. The vast cathedral ceiling arched high above, adding strength to the echo of voices. His loneliness among all those people crushed into his chest, but Ada was there. From the pews where the canonesses sat, she had turned to look across the aisle. She smiled when she found him, tentatively, as if asking permission for the liberty.

Where had she gone, the woman who had stripped bare before him in the bathhouse? He knew little of people, less of women, and barely a thing about Ada. The closer they drew together, the more hesitant she became. Shedding the unnatural freedom of her drug had made her a different woman. Or was it his constant rejection?

Blanca tugged Ada's sleeve, and he caught sight of where she subtly pointed: Fernán sat four rows up from Gavriel, his white robes and shaven head nearly anonymous. Only when he turned his head did Fernán display the array of purple and blue bruises on his face.

Gavriel did not like or trust the thin clown of a man, and he did not find any shred of forgiveness within him for what Fernán had done to Ada. But the sight of those bruises made him ill, even as his knuckles ached from the beating he had dispensed.

The Mass began with a sermon aimed squarely at Gavriel, extolling the necessity of love and gentleness toward one's brethren. Countless eyes touched his face and flickered away, likely bouncing between him and Fernán. Smoke from torches and candles stung his nostrils, and the shuffle of hundreds of bodies murmured in his ears.

As the congregants moved toward the altar to receive communion, one pew at a time, he saw Blanca slip away from the canonesses. Ada kept her eyes forward, her face serene. Row by row, the ceremony dragged deeper into the night—until a shout and a scream whipped heads to the back of the cathedral.

Gavriel and Ada took Blanca's cue and shuffled in opposite directions away from the scattering throng. Another scream, not Blanca this time. The sudden confusion intensified the villagers' frightened rush for the exits. Gavriel elbowed past wide-eyed congregants and caught up with Fernán. He pushed him into a confessional.

With a hand over the man's mouth, Gavriel stared into startled, fearful eyes. "Why did you do it?"

Fernán glanced down at the hand muffling his reply. Gavriel crooked his knee and wedged it between his captive's legs. "Words only, understand? If you cry out or call for help, you'll be less of a man for it."

Fernán's eyes widened slightly, then he nodded. Gavriel loosened his hand but pinned his forearm over his windpipe. "Talk."

"*Now* you demand details," Fernán said. "You wanted nothing but the bare facts before turning me into a walking bruise. Do you know how hard it will be to find a decent harlot now?"

"You'll heal, unless you continue these jests." He pressed deeper. Fernán grasped at the unyielding forearm at his throat. "Why did you do it? What does Pacheco know about you?"

Fernán inhaled through his nose, a wheezing draw of breath. "I have a son."

"What?"

"A son," he said, gasping. "I fell in love with a Moorish girl last spring, just after I arrived here."

"And you bedded her? Relations between a Christian and a Moor—that's not legal."

"You should have been a scholar, Gavriel. Such a wit. And so quick."

Gavriel shifted, pressing more of his body weight against Fernán's groin. "And you confessed to Pacheco?"

Sweat beaded across Fernán's scalp. "I did. He threatened to tell my father if I did not do as he asks. I stand to inherit one quarter of my family's estate, just as my brothers will, and my father would never permit me to name a half-Moorish heir to those lands." He grunted, the bones in his throat pushing against Gavriel's skin. "I did it to protect them."

"Where are they now?"

"On my last trip to market, I gave her money enough to

flee to Toledo with her family. I'd hoped to meet them there
when . . . when—"

"When?"

"When you had gone. That's why Pacheco wanted me to
hurt Ada, so that you would leave the Order."

Gavriel restrained the need to use his fists. He relinquished
his grip and stepped away.

Blood flooded back to Fernán's face and he gasped, massaging his throat. "I speak the truth," he said.

"Why? What does Pacheco want?"

"I have no notion."

Gavriel watched his wide eyes, reading both fear and resolution. The man who had defied the law to fall in love with
a Moorish woman pressed against the back wall of a confessional in the midst of a mob scene, but he did not cower.

"Come away with us," Gavriel said at last. "Ada and
Blanca are securing horses. We can get you to safety outside
of Uclés."

"As long as you keep various body parts to yourself. Even
if I don't see Abez again, I'd rather do without your knee between my legs."

"Abez?"

Fernán inhaled, standing straighter. "Yes. I'll make her my
wife if I can."

Knocked aback by the unexpected strength in Fernán's posture, in his voice, Gavriel merely nodded. From bawdy buffoon to sacrificing family man—the change was too much to
be borne.

"Strip your robes then, brother. Our tenure at the Order of
Santiago is at an end."

Fernán crossed himself and ducked free of the white linen.
"At last."

* * *

Like a boat riding a wild, cresting wave toward shore, Ada moved with the maddened crowd toward the arched double doors on the cathedral's eastern side. Blanca's single scream had been enough to excite the entire congregation to senseless action and reaction. Bodies crushed and pressed against hers. She breathed through her nose, deliberately, slowly, to help stem the rising panic.

Nearer the exit, she found space enough between the villagers to breathe easier. She pushed into the clear, crisp night, the cool darkness whipping her frayed senses. Men led their wives and children down the steep path toward Uclés, moving hastily but without the same mindless fright of escaping the cathedral. Torches held aloft lighted the way for the river of people returning home.

Ada abandoned those flickering beacons and stole into the black, edging around the stone foundation toward the stables. There she waited until the two men standing guard drifted away from their posts to investigate the ruckus at the cathedral. Her dark cloak blending her body with the night, she kept a ready hand near the hilt of her dagger, just in case, and slipped inside.

Memories of darkness, old fears, old pains, threatened to steal the air from her lungs. She stopped and pressed flat against the nearest wall, closing her eyes as dizziness soaked her senses. Fingers behind her back, she pressed her palms into stones that held the faintest heat of daylight.

Even more fearful of the guards' return, she forced her body off that wall. A search of the stalls revealed a pair of accessible horses. The heavy saddles would not budge from their hooks, not without risking a noisy collapse should she drop one. Instead, she threaded the bits and reins, convinced that bareback would suit them.

Except, perhaps, for Fernán. And Blanca.

Saints be.

She draped an armful of blankets over one animal. Mounting

the other, she clutched the reins and tossed a quick prayer into the darkness overhead. With a sharp click of her tongue, she urged both horses to a canter and fled the stables. If the guards noticed her flight, they did not pursue, for soon she had circled around the cathedral. Ada spun her horse in a circle and passed her gaze over the crowd. Gavriel, Blanca, even Fernán— nowhere to be seen.

A tickling idea at the back of her mind urged flight. She would ride away to safety, abandoning the people who asked her to make good choices and selfless sacrifices.

No. That was too much to ask, and the rewards would not be nearly as easy as they had once been. She had smacked the opium away from Gavriel's mouth because she cared for him. Denying their elemental bond was an impossible task. And more than Gavriel, she cared for her own future for the first time in more than a year. By force and by pure stubbornness, he had returned that awareness to her. To relinquish it now, on the cusp of escaping altogether, would be an act of hopeless cowardice.

Tucking her heels into the horse's flank, she edged into line with the villagers descending to Uclés. A glimpse of movement caught her eye. A man on horseback turned, a curving blade glinting in the wan moonlight. The metal of a crossbow jutted from behind his back.

She hissed his name. "Jacob!"

Jacob blinked once, believing first in a trick of the night. But a second blink and the sound of his name from her mouth made her real. Ada.

Only when they were clear of people—down a slight rise and out of sight of the monastery's defensive wall—did they dismount. Jacob shrugged out of his weapons and opened his arms to Ada's embrace, the feel of her body like a long draft of ale on a blistering day. He squeezed tight and relished the soft, strong woman he held. The hair pressed against his nose smelled of plain lye soap and candle smoke.

"Jacob, I cannot believe it," she said in English. "You've returned at last."

"I have, though sooner than we planned. Why are you out here at night, and with the whole village in a lather? What happened?"

Ada stepped back, only enough to see his face. "Much, I'm afraid."

Jacob inhaled deeply. The previous year had seen her slip from steadfast companion to a woman ruled by unshakable desires. Her eyes, although clear, were still ringed by circles of fatigue. "How are you, Ada?"

"I'm well," she said, her words a mere breath. "I have much to say to you. An apology first, I think. And then my thanks."

He smiled. Her keen expression and the natural set of her limbs revealed no addiction. None of the despairing agitation between doses. None of the incoherent bliss of a high.

Relief washed through him. "We'll save that for a safer hour, I think."

"Yes." She untangled their arms and began to pace, restless, her gaze constantly flickering to the top of the rise. "We're in danger from one of the masters here at the Order."

"Pacheco?"

"You knew?"

"I've learned much in these weeks."

"The scrolls," she said. "You hid scrolls with Daniel, didn't you?"

He frowned. "I did."

"I have them." She waved a quieting hand. "Don't bother asking how. I'll explain later when the thought of what I did doesn't turn my stomach. Just know that I've read them."

"Pacheco's a bad seed," he said, eyeing her, wondering how far he could trust her. "When I was in Segovia, I learned Doña Valdedrona's spies had discovered his connection to the exiled Lord de Silva. He works for him in secret—has done for years, hiding here, awaiting their return to prominence."

"At the end of the truce."

"Yes. He and Gavriel, both."

"What do you believe Gavriel had to do with this?"

"He's not safe," Jacob said. "Believe me on this score. He's not to be trusted."

"Don't tell me that. I read the scrolls."

"He's dangerous. That's why I came back."

"I won't believe it. I'll believe it of Pacheco, but not Gavriel." Her pacing grew more agitated. "And Pacheco had control of him the entire time. The bastard. I'll see him dead for what he did."

"I mislike when I cannot understand your English words," said a voice out of the darkness.

"Gavriel!"

She propelled herself into the arms of the tall, angular man. Behind him, the buffoon Fernán and a petite young woman walked over the rise.

His eyes prickling, Jacob watched the embrace between Ada and Gavriel. Stripped of his robes, the novice appeared nothing short of a hardened warrior, just as Jacob had suspected and feared. Gavriel, like Pacheco, had been in waiting. And now that the de Silvas set their sights on military action at the conclusion of the truce, they would want their most esteemed assassin returned to them.

And that assassin had been ordered to kill the King of Castile.

At that moment, Jacob did not care about plots, intrigues, and broken truces. He hardly cared that the woman he loved had been freed of the drug that warped her personality and claimed her soul. He only cared that she held onto Gavriel de Marqueda as if her life depended on it. And that he held her in return.

Chapter 27

They traveled a wide path around Yepes, with Fernán and Blanca on foot. Sunshine toasted the grasses and released a scent midway between hay and fresh bread. A flock of birds took to the brilliant blue sky as the horses pushed on, moving them father away from the monastery. Gavriel traced the arc of their flight and squinted as they flew in front of the sun.

Obligations and doubt tightened the muscles that bound his chest, constricting, while the wild landscape and the exuberance of those fleeing birds called to him, offering the promise of negligent freedom. What would it take to simply cast off the reins he held? Nothing. A flick of his wrist. But he wrapped his hands all the tighter and glanced back.

Ada sat astride her saddle with accomplished grace. She rode alongside him, at times even ahead of him, but never challenged him for control of their progress. Her back straight yet relaxed, her body flowed and her legs absorbed the horse's every movement. She rode well, she fought well, and she was argumentative to a fault. With every accumulated detail, he tried to balance what he knew against the relentless memories of the sick woman he had shielded and nursed through grueling nights—and the naked woman he had touched, kissed.

When Ada caught his eye and offered the tiniest smile, he sat taller on the saddle.

But he also had Jacob to consider. With his crossbow and his curved knives, the young man watched them with a sharp, narrow-eyed look. If he knew about Pacheco's connection to the de Silva family, he would know about Gavriel's past as well.

More than the knowledge Jacob must be privy to, the possessiveness in his eyes stoked an uncomfortable jealousy in Gavriel's chest. Ada was cured, or as cured as she might ever be. The need for opium would scratch under her skin and in her blood for the rest of her life, like a cough that would never quite clear. Jacob had not been strong enough to complete her treatment. Now he had returned, his expression one of hope and happy reunions—except when he looked at Gavriel. Daggers were none so sharp.

They stopped to rest along the Tagus. The horses needed water, but Gavriel would have given one of his hands to keep from returning to that place. Ada would not meet his eyes, not even when he found the mettle to seek hers. Memories of her body, her kiss, her sweet passion grated against his defenses, leaving him exposed to base desires.

"What plan have you, Jacob?"

Ada's voice sent a shiver up his backbone, no matter that she addressed another man and spoke of strategy. Only when he had reined in his need did he take a seat apart from the others. He was lying to himself. He wanted her more now than he ever had. Impossible, ridiculous—he did not care.

"We need to take the scrolls to King Alfonso," Jacob said. "They can implicate the guilty parties, not only for current plans but for the conspiracy at Alarcos."

Ada flashed her eyes to Gavriel. She seemed skittish, as she had when bent low over those scrolls.

"We should camp here for the night," he said quietly, wondering just what Ada had read.

* * *

At dawn they followed the lowlands along the Tagus, through the eastern mountains, and arrived in Toledo as the sun dipped low to the west. Gavriel followed Jacob across the river on a wide stone bridge, the others trailing behind as they approached the city gates. As much as his pride rankled, he recognized that Jacob held the most authority of any in their small group. Gavriel had no intention of challenging him now, weary and short-tempered as they all were. No one had slept well. Blanca could have been walking with her eyes closed for how alert she appeared.

Far below the bridge, moss covered the craggy rocks that stepped down to the rushing waters, while prickly junipers, crude mud shelters, and fleet-footed goats clung to the jagged cliff face. The city, by contrast, brimmed with art and splendid architecture, that uneasy mix of cultures.

But no sooner had they dismounted, just inside the defensive wall, did a dozen armed *pedones* circle their tired little band.

"Halt!"

The guards surrounded them in a quick clatter of metal. The horses shied. Fernán and Blanca huddled close. Before Jacob could draw his knives, one of the men sighted him with a loaded crossbow. Jacob raised empty hands above his shoulders.

Gavriel angled his body between Ada and danger. She clung to his left bicep with tense fingers, an unspoken pledge of faith in his strength and skill. But any move to draw his sword would put everyone at risk. He could buy them only an instant of chaos, hardly worth the danger of unleashing the belligerence painted across the guards' faces.

"The girl comes with us," said one, a thick-set man.

Blanca gasped and drained of color. Fernán and Jacob supported her body as it dripped toward the street.

"Not that peasant." The guard never took his hawk's eyes from Ada. *"La inglesa."*

Jacob snarled at the guards, his temper bared and blunt. Gavriel admired the young man's protective reflexes, but his mind cautioned calm. They would be dead in the street if Jacob pushed too quickly. Armed hordes obeying orders did not respond well to reason, and even less so to aggression.

Amidst the tense silence, Ada inhaled and spoke in her strange language. The frowning guards puzzled over the foreign words, but Jacob shook his head. They argued briefly in English before the lead guard raised his sword. "Enough! You will speak the language of His Majesty, the King of Castile," he said. "You must be the woman we seek."

"I am," Ada said, smiling. "May I have the pleasance of knowing why you wish to detain me?"

Gavriel recognized her playful tone. He would have chewed wood to break his fast before wishing to have that infuriating cadence directed at him again. But he also felt the slender fingers clutching his arm tremble.

"By Castilian law, you must reveal the nature of her detention," Jacob said, looking up from where Blanca sat heavily on the dew-damp cobblestones. "She is a member of Doña Valdedrona's court and lives in Toledo under her protection."

The lead guard exchanged an uncertain glance with his second but did not lower his sword. "No matter her patron, the woman has been charged with defaulting on numerous debts, breaking a contract of sale, and inciting a riot. She will stand trial for her crimes and be punished accordingly."

Ada's eyes darted to Gavriel's with the speed of a rabbit. The opium. The debts. The slaver who had lost his lovely stock. Her past had caught up to her, and her pale, stretched expression admitted to every fault and flaw. No matter her command of languages, she could not have spoken about shame as eloquently as did her face.

"Comprendo," she whispered. "I'll go with you. But please, do not hurt these people."

Her fingers loosened and she stepped away from Gavriel. "Ada, don't," he said.

"I can do this. I'll see this right, and then we can start again."

He wanted to drag her back to his side and envelop her, tightly, as a shield against her fate. But the lead guard nodded and lowered his weapon, taking her into his custody. There was no resignation in her posture, only the stiff, proud acceptance of her responsibility.

"Where are you taking her?" he asked.

The lead guard ignored him. "Are you wearing any weapons, *señorita?*"

Ada silently knelt and retrieved the sheathed dagger from her boot, tossing it behind her. The metal skittered to a stop at Blanca's feet. "That is all."

Circling ropes around Ada's wrists, the lead guard tossed a negligent look over the small band. "She'll be tried on the morrow at the Court of Justice."

Gavriel's voice died in his throat. Words sat there, unsaid, as he watched the cadre disperse into the city, Ada with them. She never looked back. He watched until nothing of her remained—no hint of brown cloth from her gown, no shimmer of her unbound hair. His heart marred by bruises, he fought every impulse urging him to pursue and strip those guards of their precious prisoner. But influence, not violence, would be the tool to free Ada.

Gavriel had none.

He had to come to an accord with the only of their number who did. Not that the task would be an easy one.

Jacob stood toe to toe with Gavriel. "Is this how you keep her safe?"

"Safe?" Worry gathered in his chest like floodwater as he snatched the crossbow off Jacob's shoulder. He flung it across the mossy cobblestones. "*Safe?*" With another quick motion, fingers steady, he stripped him the curving blades. Jacob stumbled backward, dazed, his eyes wide. Gavriel towered over him, wanting to release every drop of frustration on the young Jew. "As I recall, you left her in my care."

Jacob rubbed one wrist, his eyes never far from the crossbow. "I did, before I inquired among Doña Valdedrona's informants and learned who you are, hiding like a coward in a religious order. Such is why I traveled Uclés earlier than I planned."

Gavriel loosened his stance. The fresh promise of combat raised the hairs on his forearms. "She would be with you—*safe*, as you say—had you been stronger in the face of her craving."

"I did what I thought best!"

Blanca pushed between them. "Please, stop this! We're tired, all of us. Have you any notion of how few allies we have? And you want to pound on each other like barbarians?" She nodded to Gavriel's fists before turning her pleas to Jacob. "He would kill you."

"He can try," Jacob said harshly.

She knelt and retrieved Gavriel's sword and one of Jacob's knives before returning to the square of neutral ground between them. "He would kill you, Jacob, and Ada would be sorry for it. Don't make me be the one to tell her you've each done murder."

She raised her arms, offering both the weapons and a caustic look.

Gavriel eyed the hilt of his sword, then Jacob, seeing the young man do the same. "I cannot harm you," he said. "Ada would never forgive me. She thinks well of you."

"Do you agree with her?"

"When you behave beyond your years." Gavriel put his sword away and crossed his arms. "Now what can we do?"

Jacob took his weapon. He glanced once more between

Gavriel and the blade, its metal made dull gray by the evening light, and sheathed it.

"Doña Valdedrona has returned to Toledo," he said. "We shall speak with her."

Wide awake, Ada stared at the walls of her cell as the sun changed the night from black to deep blue, then lighter still. The stench of rats and excrement had long since muddled her senses, until even the meager ale tasted foul. Or perhaps it was foul, having spoiled in that hellish place. Somewhere beyond her confines, a steady drip, drip wore away her patience, just as that water must wear away the stone. Although a tick stuffed with relatively fresh straw lay along one wall, she had not slept. Sleep would mean dreams—dreams even more terrifying than her wakeful nightmare.

Gavriel. He would be there at sunrise. Of course he would be.

But the darkness played tricks with all she believed. What if he was not? She considered the possibility that Jacob's warning held merit. Or perhaps Gavriel would decide that their erratic history together was not worth his trouble. He would finally be rid of her.

She stood and stretched muscles weary from worry and a lack of sleep, shaking free of those ominous thoughts. No matter whether he appeared at the Court of Justice, she would stand for herself.

But how she wanted him to be there.

She yearned for it because, for the first time in a year, she had discovered a reason to keep opium at bay. Gavriel, the man who had wanted her with unexpected fire and tenderness. Gavriel, the man who broke impossible vows, scarred himself, and hid everything but his concern for her wellbeing. And despite Jacob's suspicions, Gavriel was no longer the brutal man he once was.

She hoped.

Hunger bit at her insides. Thirst shriveled her tongue. The old need for a false escape only intensified as the sun promised its slow ascent.

She stepped to the sliver of a window and peered through with one eye. Below the fortifications of the Court of Justice, the hangman had prepared nooses for those found guilty of the most heinous crimes. Two ropes dangled, the harsh angle of the sun casting shadows like snakes across the courtyard. Already, merchants and peasants who had started their day— the merchants with carts full of goods bound for market, and the peasants with empty baskets and sacks—began to gather around the platform.

Ada shuddered. Morning had not yet banished the chill of night, and contemplating her fate in that courtyard did nothing to assuage her shivers.

I brought this on myself.

She shook free of that old accusation. Yes, she had. But she would get herself out as well.

The lock rattled at her back. She turned to face the guard who entered her cell. Anonymous behind his helmet and uniform, the man held out a rope just as Ada offered her wrists. She would not struggle, not now. She would not cower. The decision to face the ordeal with as much dignity as she possessed helped outweigh her humiliation. She had cried and begged long enough.

She followed the guard through the darkened halls. The metal adornments on his uniform caught bright chinks of sun as they passed regular intervals of narrow windows. He walked with precision, the metal of his armor clanking an even cadence. Ada swallowed her hunger and buried it alongside her fear, but her knees did not stop shaking.

As they traversed the long corridor, other guards brought prisoners out of their cells and tied them to Ada like links in a chain. Soon they numbered seven, and she wondered which two faced hanging. For her crimes, she would likely face trial by fire. She would be forced to walk nine paces while holding a red-hot rod of iron. Her skin would peel away, as skin tended to do, and her guilt would be decided three days later when the wound festered. Only divine intervention—a pair of palms miraculously healed—would proclaim her innocence.

But she was not innocent. She glanced down and flexed her fingers. The verdict would not matter when the burning rod warped and ruined her hands.

She tripped. The guard roughly yanked her up, barking a command. She puzzled at the unfamiliar words, her understanding of Castilian suddenly as exhausted as her courage.

Chapter 28

Gavriel paced the small, stark room they had let for the night. Sunlight slowly spread across the tattered rushes beneath his feet. He felt caged. Helpless. Blanca sat on a mattress jammed along the outer wall. She could have been furniture for all the attention Gavriel paid her. And Fernán—he had simply disappeared.

Had Ada been able to sleep? No, not confined once again, probably surrounded by darkness and her old fears. His arms shook. Reassuring her and pulling her through each moment of weakness had become his only reprieve, slowly working to make him a better man. The thought of losing her ripped a hole in his plans for the future. That he kept those plans so near to his heart only proved what a fool he had become. For her.

When Jacob returned at daybreak, Gavriel finally stopped his restless pacing. "Did you speak with Doña Valdedrona?" he asked.

Jacob nodded. "Last night, she wrote a missive that clears Ada's debts. Ada will work as her translator for a year, but she will be free of the charges."

Blanca clapped her hands. Relief flooded Gavriel. The air smelled sweeter, not the stench of that rotting room. Sunlight shone brighter. Jacob's successful return assuaged the helplessness Gavriel had felt, himself unable to offer a plea on her behalf.

"What will you do now?" Gavriel asked.

"These must be delivered to His Majesty," Jacob said, pulling the scrolls from Ada's satchel. "King Alfonso moved court to Doña Valdedrona's palace, and he brings members of the Leonese delegation. I must warn him that he dines with traitors."

Blanca offered Jacob a plain canvas sack to carry the documents. "Do you think that's wise?" she asked. "They may think to kill the messenger, so to speak."

"I trust discussing the matter with Her Excellency," Jacob said. "She will proceed with King Alfonso as she sees fit."

Gavriel frowned. "You're leaving Ada?"

Jacob yanked his crossbow over his shoulder. The quick, keen sparkle in his eyes had dimmed entirely. Grim lines pinched the skin around his mouth. Where once had been a young fighter eager to risk his life for the woman he loved, a much older man stood. "She needs you there, not me," he said.

Panic mingled with a sensation akin to victory, thrilling and hot. Jacob loved Ada. That much he had known from the first. But Ada's feelings toward her young guardian had always seemed ambivalent. She never displayed toward Jacob the same fiery range of emotions Gavriel had experienced. Her anger. Her teasing. Her passion.

Although Blanca stood near at hand, watching the exchange in silence, she may have missed the deadly promise in Jacob's eyes.

But Gavriel saw it.

If you hurt her, I will kill you.

Gavriel merely collected his weapons and nodded in answer. *If I hurt her, I'll have no reason left to live.*

* * *

Judge Hermán Natalez looked up as a distinguished Jacobean entered his chambers. Wrapped in white robes that matched his silver hair, the older man paid no heed to Natalez's frown. No one entered his chambers before the morning's trials, not even his mincing little clerk. No one dared. Except this stranger.

"You mislike my being here, I can see," the man said.

Without preamble or introduction. The gall.

Natalez set his grooming comb aside and stared with all the weight inherent in his position as judge. "An imbecile could see that. Who are you and how dare you behave with such disrespect?"

"I am Gonzalo Pacheco, brother of the Order of Santiago and servant of His Excellency, Lord Joaquin de Silva." His black eyes glittered like those of a crow at feast. "You are detaining a prisoner of interest to Lord de Silva, a prisoner whose sentence he would like to, shall we say, influence."

Natalez snorted. "Influence. Dictate, you mean. But that is out of the questions. My verdicts are not for sale."

"And I respect that." Pacheco smiled, deadly as any beast but with none of the wild impulse. Every movement spoke of control, intelligence, and the firm expectation that he would be obeyed. With the notorious exile de Silva as his employer, that might be the case. But not that morning.

Natalez stood from his writing table and turned his back, deliberately dismissing the wiry old Jacobean. He stretched his robes across his bulky body, but Pacheco did not leave.

The patience Natalez had held to like a greased rope slipped away. He turned, his voice a boom of thunder. "Why are you still here?"

Pacheco did not flinch. His smile had evaporated. In each

hand he held an item: a lumpy leather pouch in his left and short sword in his right.

"How did you get that sword past my guards?"

The glitter in Pacheco's eyes turned to fire, a man who had abandoned civility. "My men outnumber yours, especially now that two of yours lie dead."

Natalez felt his authority drip through his feet and into floor. "This is an outrage!"

"You are a judge, *señor*," said Pacheco. "Weighing the relative merits of the evidence is your responsibility. So let me present the evidence to you as I see it—and the way I see it is the only option. Do you understand?"

He dropped the leather pouch laden with coins. It landed on the writing table with a metallic thump, settling crookedly like a decaying orange. That left the intruder free to wield his short sword within those tight confines, unfettered by his other, more attractive offering.

Natalez glanced at the shadow behind the door Pacheco had left ajar. His own sword waited there, but it was sheathed. And the silver-haired man stood in the way.

Pacheco did not look behind him, but his smile returned. "When was the last you took up arms, *señor*? Many years I should think, judging by your girth. Now let us cease these games and come to an accord."

Instead of returning to the weapon that may as well have been in Rome for all its usefulness, Natalez let his eyes travel between Pacheco's bright black stare, the short sword, and the fat bag of coins. He slumped into his chair. "What accord?"

"There is a woman who will be tried this morning, an Englishwoman named Ada."

"*Sí,*" he said, rifling through a scant trio of documents he had been examining. "I have word that she is under the protection of Doña Valdedrona."

"That Sicilian whore?"

"The Englishwoman's debts have been paid, her contracts settled. She will be released."

Pacheco stepped forward once, twice, and pressed the tip of the sword into the roll of fat beneath Natalez's chin. "Unfortunately for you, my dear judge, that is not the verdict I seek."

Sunlight burned her eyes, eyes accustomed to the darkness of her confinement. Voices swirled like an unearthly wind. Sound and scent melded together. Ada used to love the moment when the world fell away, washed clean by opium. But stumbling again, tripping into the square as the gathering crowd jeered, that riot of sensation—overlapping, freeing her from language and thought—only heightened her terror.

She could not afford to lose her wits. But she barely managed to keep her feet, focusing on the metal-clad heels of the guard holding the rope.

She was first in line; the wait to know her verdict would not be long. As the judge settled his hulking body onto his stool, the bailiff read a proclamation of the court's authority according to the charter of the Prelate of Toledo, sanctioned by the King of Castile, Alfonso XIII. His deep voice blended the legal terminology of the edict into an indistinct drone. Fatigue threatened to pull Ada's eyelids closed no matter the rushing pulse of her blood.

"Bring the first prisoner forward!"

She jerked upright and caught sight of the bailiff motioning her toward the judge. The foremost guard untied the ropes that bound her to the other prisoners and pushed her up three steps, his sword at her back. Knees like clouds and her thighs trembling, she climbed.

Her mind flashed to the slave auction. She had ascended those few steps without feeling her feet, high above the dingy brothel, insensate to the bargain she had made for a single bottle. She had not thought to want a rescue, but Jacob and Gavriel had saved her nonetheless. The urge to look across the hostile crowd and find them nearly got the better of her, although she needed every drop of concentration to keep her wayward, nauseated body moving.

Judge Natalez was a grotesque man, full of face and body, his nose a map of red veins. Open at the neck, his robes revealed an expensive, ornate tunic woven through with gold and embroidered with seed pearls. Greased black hair clung to his forehead in an ornate pattern of stringy strands designed to cover his bald spot. His coarse beard needed a trim.

A strange cross between vanity and careless indulgence, he sat on the stool one step higher than Ada, looking down at her. All around their central platform, the citizens of Toledo watched the open-air court, awaiting each bloody verdict.

"State your name," Natalez said, his voice loud and theatrical for the awaiting crowd.

She cleared her throat and raised her chin, meeting his small, deeply set eyes. "Ada of Keyworth."

"And where is Keyworth?"

"Inglaterra."

The crowd murmured its interest in her answer, seeming to press closer to the judgment platform.

Natalez only raised an eyebrow, sweat gathering at his temples. He glanced over a piece of parchment and said, "This woman, Ada of Keyworth, stands accused of the following crimes: failure to pay debts to Señor Alvarez in the amount of eight morabetins, failure to pay debts to Señor Calavaras in the amount of nine morabetins, both Christians of Toledo. She is also accused of breaking a contract of sale with Salamo Fayat, a Jew residing in Toledo, originally from Córdoba, and inciting a riot in his place of business."

Each additional charge brought back unpleasant memories,

the desperation she had felt while trapped in those moments. Her tongue went dry.

"Will anyone stand for this woman against her accusers?" Natalez asked with that theatrical voice.

"I will."

Hundreds of eyes bounced from face to face, searching for the man who had volunteered. Ada only closed hers, savoring the blissful sound of Gavriel's voice. And then he was beside her, holding her hand.

He came.

His body, warm and solid beside hers, offered strength when she had wondered if all of hers was gone. Fresh-washed, with sunlight sparkling on the tips of his damp hair, he smelled of soap and warm wool. His hair had grown, she noticed. No longer cropped short as a member of the Order, it curled slightly around his ears, a little wild at the nape of his neck.

He looked down at her. Although he did not smile, he offered an unfamiliar expression. One of . . . expectation? Hope? His sharp, hard features had softened. For her. She gripped his blunt, rough fingers and stood straighter.

"And who are you?" Natalez asked. Sweat gathered in earnest at his temples and dotted the thick cluster of hair along his upper lip.

"Gavriel de Marqueda. With the Order of Santiago, I was responsible for this woman's wellbeing. Her craving for opium has been cured, and she stands ready to make good all of her debts with the help of her patron, Cilia, Condesa de Valdedrona."

Her name charged the assembly with excited whispers, but the judge paid them no heed. He stared at Gavriel, his glassy eyes direct.

"No matter that you stand for her, *señor*, or that you claim she is cured," Natalez said. "I have read the testimony and heard the applicable witnesses. This woman will face trial by combat to determine her guilt or innocence."

Combat?

Ada's ears filled with the murmuring delight of the crowd. She thought her knees would have weakened. Or maybe she would vomit. But she remained upright, receiving the judge's sentence as if he had condemned some other prisoner. Only the sharp cut of Gavriel's voice penetrated the protective numbness.

"I demand an explanation, *señor,*" he said. "Doña Valdedrona herself paid the debts this morning."

Natalez curled the edge of one document between his thumb and forefinger. "I received no such notification from Her Excellency, and I resent the implication that I would thwart a noble decree."

"I resent that you call yourself a judge," Gavriel said. "This is a mockery!"

Natalez pointed at him. "You will stand down!"

"¡Vaya al diablo!"

Gavriel surged, but Ada caught him around both shoulders. She held him with all her strength, wanting him safe from the guards who stood ready to pierce her unarmed protector.

Natalez edged backward until the stool tottered, then tipped. Hundreds of voices lifted in laughter as he landed hard on the wooden platform. His fat face purpled. "Restrain that man!"

Long minutes passed as the guards restored order. They pinned Gavriel and Ada from all sides, circling with drawn swords. One helped return the rotund judge to his place on the stool. She clung to Gavriel's arm, finding the entire scene bizarre and comical, like the performance of a minstrel troupe.

She hiccupped, a sound suspiciously close to laughter—mad, helpless laughter.

Gavriel raised an eyebrow. "Are you well?"

"Of course not," she said for him alone. "Everything has become decidedly absurd. I used to enjoy it."

He covered her hand with his. "Ada, Her Excellency promised your release. Jacob saw her personally last night. And he would have no reason to lie to us, would he?"

"No, not Jacob. But this judge?"

"Are you suggesting that men in positions of power may be manipulating us again?"

"Are you on the verge of smiling?"

"The only alternative to madness with a *bruja* like you."

He did smile then, his face breaking into a wide, boyish grin. The hard angles of his face softened around full, curving lips stretched wide. Beautiful white teeth shone from the dusky hue of his skin. Lines bending around his mouth revealed the slightest of dimples, and delicate feathers crinkled at the corners of his dark eyes. Those lips, dimples, eyes— they conspired to start a wicked fluttering behind her breastbone, one that had naught to do with the danger they faced.

"Enough!" All eyes returned to Natalez, his face still colored like lavender in bloom. His thick, unkempt beard shook. "I have decided on the correct course," he said. "My word as a judge of Toledo makes it so. You!" He pointed to Ada with a pudgy finger. Jewels from a pair of rings glinted in the morning sun. "Stand before me!"

Although reluctant to leave Gavriel's side, Ada unknotted their hands and wove between the swords to stand before the judge.

"Hear this," he said. "You will face trial by combat tomorrow at midday."

"Judge Natalez," Gavriel said, his temper threatening to burst through his skin. "She is a woman. Trial by combat is no just gauge of guilt. The measure is too harsh."

"I deem it appropriate. Be thankful that, considering the evidence against her, I do not declare her guilty this moment."

Gavriel stared at the judge, looking past the fat, officious face and the tiny eyes. First Pacheco, then Fernán—he had learned that public faces rarely matched the souls beneath. Ada, too, had taught him that lesson. He had first seen a woman dragged through life by her own weakness. At that moment, as she stood in quiet defiance of the judge and her own past, she demonstrated the strength he had come to expect of her.

But this judge.

He was as corrupt as his ruling. Women did not stand trial by combat. It was unseemly and unjust.

He inhaled. "Then I claim the right to take her place."

Natalez frowned. "Right? What right?"

"She is my wife."

Chapter 29

Ada inhaled sharply.

Natalez glanced at his bailiff, the purple rage fading to a sickly paleness. He seemed to maintain his bearing by force of will alone. "What proof do you have?"

Threatened as they were by unknown forces, Gavriel set aside caution. She eased hurts that had been so much a part of him, like bones and blood and breath. That she caused a deeper sort of pain at the thought of her suffering loosened the worry in his chest.

"What proof is needed?" he asked. "We're both Christian, having lived on the edge of the *reconquista* frontier where neither banns nor priest are required." Gavriel found Ada's blue eyes and did not look away. Swords and men in armor separated them, but he spoke to her in a voice barely louder than a whisper. "You need only my word. And hers."

She looked at him as if the crowd, the judge, the verdict—none of it mattered. Only him. Only the words he had said in an effort to save her life.

He knew better. And by the way a smile began to change her face—first the light in her eyes, then the gentle curve of her lip—she did, too. He had made the claim of their marriage because he wanted it.

Tell them. Tell them we are married.

The words pounded against the inside of his forehead. Noise from the throng of onlookers faded, or else he had ceased to hear them. He only waited for Ada's reply to his most unconventional proposal.

Natalez's rumbling voice cut between them. "What say you?"

Ada turned to the hundreds of people in the courtyard. Considering the unjust nature of the judge's ruling, appealing to him seemed of little consequence. "Yes," she said. "He is my husband."

Applause and laughter jumped from the crowd. Dressed in green, her hair whipping free in the morning breeze, Ada tossed Gavriel a carefree smile. He drank in her vigor, her beauty. Tingling warmth flooded his veins when she blushed. He would not take his eyes off her, but he knew if he closed them now, images of his future would be filled with her. Them. Together. If he proved strong enough.

This is Ada. And this is me in love with her.

"Silence!" Natalez jumped from this stool. Soldiers began to string along the perimeter of the courtyard, subduing those who heckled the proceedings. "You've made a mockery of this court. Ada of Keyworth will stand trial by combat, and if you disagree with me again, *señor,* you will be imprisoned too."

Gavriel lunged, breaking through the distracted circle of guards to attack Natalez. His knuckles met jowls, then ribs, then kidneys. He whirled the battered judge. With fingers pinching around Natalez's windpipe, his other arm ready to break the man's neck, Gavriel used him as a shield against guards who had quickly gathered their wits.

"Who bought your ruling?" he asked near the judge's ear.

"You're mad."

"Do you fear their reprisal?" He pinched his fingers deeper, grinding the bones together. Natalez gagged. "Because at present, you should fear only me."

"Then kill me. I'll admit no disgrace."

"Your behavior has been disgrace enough."

Natalez's hulking body began to sway, his face resuming its sickly purple shade—this time from lack of air rather than rage. "You'll die for this," he sputtered.

"Without her, I'm already dead."

"Guards," Natalez gasped. "If he kills me, run the girl through. And turn the soldiers on the crowd."

The bailiff frowned, the sword he held ready dipping slightly. "*Señor?*"

"I will be obeyed!"

When Gavriel hesitated, the lead guard grabbed Ada. She screamed and struggled until he raised his sword to her throat, one arm looped around beneath her ribcage. A glitter of red rubies shone on his forefinger. The de Silva eagle.

That same shepherd.

"You are beaten," he said. "Surrender now or there will be no second chance. For either of you."

Even Natalez seemed nonplussed by the man's words. Ada's eyes were wide and terrified, her face an ill shade of gray. Bright sunshine reflecting off the sword made the contrast between steel and skin appear all the more deadly. The man wearing the de Silva signet stood ready to end her life.

Gavriel pushed the judge away like flinging refuse to the ground, the stink of hair grease clinging inside his nose. The remaining guards surrounded him. Ropes burned his skin from wrist to elbow, bound behind his back. Rough hands pulled him from the platform.

Through the confusion and the powerlessness that followed, yanked as he was across the courtyard toward the justice building, he tried to find Ada. A glimpse. One more look at her face. Some assurance she would be safe.

He found none. But the idea of being his wife had made her smile.

An hour later, Gavriel lay flat on his back in his cell. No window. No light. Only the sound of the crowd below as each new verdict made them shout or applaud. Perhaps they thrilled to the sight of two men stretching from paired nooses, just as they had when Gavriel defied the judge and Ada had affirmed their marriage—nothing more than a moment of entertainment before the people of Toledo went about their day.

The darkness and the close space did not affect him. He appreciated the solitude if only to find his own mind. Instances of confinement were scattered through memories of his youth, but physical punishment had been far more common. Starvation. Exposure to the elements. The lash. Pacheco had known exactly how to reach into Gavriel's deepest fears and exploit them. The clarity of his motives and techniques aligned like eyes finally working together to focus.

The darkness would have tortured Ada, though. His stomach tensed against the knowledge that he had failed her. He should have fought to his last breath, chancing that the hundreds of people in the square would rally to their cause. He had seen it happen before, when mobs determined the verdict and brought powerful men low.

But that glint of ruby had stayed his hand. If Lord de Silva had orchestrated Ada's charade of a hearing, he would not let a little mob justice stand in the way.

Surrender now or there will be no second chance.

The words of the false shepherd wormed into his brain. Was it a promise or a taunt? He could only wait and hope that Ada was safe, at least until the following midday. But what would he do then? He could not think of her pain without suffering himself.

A key turned in the rusty lock. Gavriel jerked upright and scrambled to the back wall. The feeling like a cornered beast needled his pride. Torchlight illuminated the corridor, behind a man silhouetted in the doorway. Tall and silent, no aggression stiffened his posture. But Gavriel's skin prickled.

"Who are you?"

The man accepted a torch from a guard, then turned to face Gavriel. Flickering, golden light sprinkled over his face. Too many summers spent beneath the powerful Moroccan sun had cured his skin to a color of a roasted nut, stretched taut over pointed cheekbones. Hair a shade lighter had been cropped close around his head and shaped into a neat beard. A *qamis* draped over his spare body, shapeless and billowing, but an ornate *wishah* circled his waist, the jewels of that double belt seeming to move in the shifting torchlight.

"Do you recognize me, Gavriel?"

The voice was rougher, as if scrapped by busted stones. Different. Foreign in both accent and cadence. But Gavriel still shivered.

"You're Joaquin de Silva."

"I am," he said, stepping into the cell. "And it is time you finally kill King Alfonso."

Ada sat with her knees drawn to her chest and watched the slow, steady journey of a splinter of moonlight across the cell floor. Shivers of cold and fear passed over her skin like shadows, hardly felt, blending into a monotony of waiting. Sleep was as impossible as it had been the night before, a distant dream, like breathing without fear or looking with gladness to what the next day held.

On the previous morn, she had waited for sunrise with a sense of expectation. Faith had buoyed her hopes. Faith in

Gavriel. In herself. For all of their misguided weeks together, he had jeopardized her heart but never her life.

She is my wife.

But no one waited to rescue her come morning. Her debts and Gavriel's past had come together, like strong hands to tear them apart. She would do combat and she would die. Of that she had no doubt.

Ada had needed to be free of the opium because it threatened to take her life, slowly, certainly, with every taste. She had done so reluctantly, fighting first Jacob, then Gavriel, and always fighting herself. Her freedom had been a second birth. She knew she was better for the struggle. Better for being free.

But there was no good to be found in losing Gavriel. He had pulled her from the darkness, held her, kissed her. She loved him with a stubborn possessiveness that had terrified her until that moment in the dark, caged and alone, when he was gone. Her life would end at midday, and she would die regretting the time they had spent fighting and resisting.

He is my husband.

And I love him.

The sound of his voice came as no surprise, her thoughts bathed in him. Memories and regrets. But the cold air rushing over her tears was real. The door had opened, and Gavriel found her in the darkness before she could find her voice.

Powerful arms gathered her close, his voice a murmur against her neck. She had sat huddled and alone, but now she held fast to Gavriel. His strength. His scent and heat.

Real. All real.

"What are you doing here?"

"I asked to see you," he said.

"And they consented? How?"

"Don't ask questions, Ada."

"All I have are questions," she said, tugging at his hair,

stripping his tunic. She could not get close enough. Only the
need to kiss him remained.

Trembling fingers found his mouth in the near-darkness,
her lips quickly taking their place. Wide hands threaded into
her unbound hair and angled her head, bringing their mouths
together fully. She parted her lips and moaned as his tongue
pushed inside. He tasted of copper—blood or thirst, maybe.
She kissed deeper, his primal taste more ambrosial than any
wine or spice. Just him. Only him. Blood swirled through her
ears, burned at her cheeks, and gathered low and heavy in her
belly, a deep rhythm she had only found with Gavriel.

She hugged his powerful body. Nothing felt as strong and
steadfast as he did, his long bones and wiry, dense cords of
muscle. Beneath her fingertips, she felt the ridges of flesh
crisscrossing his shoulder blades. Her wounded warrior, the
man who was as much his own enemy as she was to herself.
Only together had they found a measure of quiet and sanity,
of peace and forgiveness.

He tugged at the hair he held and tipped her head back, ex-
posing her throat and scattering the tormenting thoughts. He
tapped tiny kisses along her jaw, across, down. She missed his
mouth on hers, but she gasped at the fiery touch of his tongue
against the pulsing place where her neck met her shoulder. He
did not nip or play but sucked deeply, marring her skin with
his impatience.

"You don't believe we have much time," she whispered.

Motionless now, his lips still touched her skin. "No. Not
much time at all."

"You said no questions, but there's something I must ask."

He loosened his grip on her hair and dropped his head to
her shoulder. Tension made stiff branches of his limbs, his
back bowed at an exhausted angle. "Very well. Ask it."

Chapter 30

At first she could not form the words. She said them in English in her mind, once and again, playing with the absurdity of that moment. Their bodies wanted each other. That much was plain. But it took another try before she could voice what she desperately needed to know.

"Why did you say that I am your wife?"

"I thought it might change the judge's ruling," he said. "I thought I could protect you."

"Is that all?" She pushed his chest until he sat back. A quiet hysteria filled her lungs. She forced more words into the air. "Is that all, Gavriel? Truly? I'm apt to die tomorrow and would like to hear the truth from you." She reached out to cup the side of his face, two days' worth of stubble scratching her palm. "Please, the truth shouldn't be so difficult."

"I wish circumstances were . . . no, this is useless." He shook his head, but the fatigue she felt arching through his body stole his vigor. "This wishing for change. Useless. A waste. I won't burden us both. Let me hold you, *inglesa*. That I can do for you, at least."

"Try. You were willing to do battle for me. Try now. For me."

"I don't know how!" His hoarse frustration bounced

around the cell. She flinched and jerked her hand away. "I don't know how to wish for what I cannot have."

"Because dreams make demands of you." So many sleepless nights had worn holes in her emotions, but she banked the tears that threatened. "If you want something, you must take risks or hope or sacrifice. You take the chance of being disappointed."

The sliver of moonlight angled across his shoulders, the resilient, smooth curves of his chest. "Have you no notion of my life? I would have gone mad years ago, wishing for freedom."

"And what of me? I didn't want to dream because all I found were nightmares. It was easier to lose myself." She rose on her knees and looked down at his troubled face. "Do you have a dream, Gavriel? I should very much like to hear it."

His breath came as a slow, shuddering exhale. "I said you were my wife because I wish it were true. I wish I could be your husband and that we . . ."

"What?"

"That we could be in love."

Gently, afraid he would flinch or push her away, she took his hands and flattened them on her hips. His fingers tightened ever so gently. She toyed briefly with a whorl of hair behind his ear before pulling him close, cradling him at her breast. When she kissed the top of his head, he shuddered and sighed.

"The *fueras* here in Toledo," she whispered. "Do they permit marriages without posting the banns? Without witnesses?"

"I know not."

"I believe the answer is yes." She framed his face with her hands and found his eyes, two sparkling black jewels. "Don't you agree?"

"Yes," he said softly. "Will you be my wife, Ada?"

"Yes."

"Here? Tonight?"

She laughed, relishing the bubble of happiness wrapped around her heart. "Right at this moment. But only if you kiss me again."

He did—a quick, fierce kiss that stole her balance. Her knees trembled. Gavriel took the weight of her body against her own and lowered her onto the mattress beneath the window.

"Ada, *mi inglesa. Mi ama.*"

My love.

She shifted against the long length of him, feeling sheltered and cherished. Their touches made the darkness intimate and close, not a fearful place at all. But she had always felt that way with him. The nightmares would not come. The worst would not happen. Not with him.

"You were right," she said, petting his face. "I had nothing to live for. I think you knew what that was like, to face each day as a burden. I only wondered how and when I would find my next taste. Without that, I had nothing. No future or dreams. I didn't know what it was to live. This has been living, you and me these few weeks. Fighting. Risking and trying."

A quick, sharp memory of that morning, standing before the judge, cut through her happiness. The bubble burst, leaving only fear. "And now," she whispered. "Dear God, I don't want to die."

"Then you should not." His voice was hard, stripped of tenderness. His hands squeezed at her hips. "You can do this, Ada."

"Do what?"

"The trial tomorrow. You can survive it."

"I'm not a warrior!"

"No, but you're a fighter. What have you learned from Jacob?"

"Not enough!"

His face shrouded, Gavriel yanked her hands above her head. Moments before, she would have thought the move one of sexual teasing. He had held her in that same position by the river, claiming her, but now he would not relent.

Anger replaced thoughts of love and tenderness. They had so little time together, and he was determined to ruin it. She wanted comfort, not more instruction. Thrashing, she tried to kick free of the skirts that kept her legs tangled, free of his imprisoning weight. Gavriel pushed a knee between her thighs and leaned into his hip. She was pinned.

Old instincts pushed forth, giving her strength. She twisted her wrists until one slipped free. Her elbow smacked him in the face. Reflex made him snap away from her, clutching his nose. She scrambled out of reach. When she found the empty clay chamber pot, she busted it against the wall and took two shards in hand.

"Bruja," he said, wearing that teasing half-grin.

"Matón."

"Bully? *Mi ama*, I'm only proving the point." He gestured to the shards of hardened clay she still clenched in her fists. "Now set those aside."

Ada sat cross-legged but she did not release her weapons. "Explain yourself."

"You've learned your strengths and how to find weaknesses. You cannot lift a sword against a trained man, but you learned how to wield your dagger—the very dagger once used to cause you pain. You know how to run. You're stubborn. And you can be cruel."

"You're mocking me."

"Not at all." He urged her back to the squashed mattress, divesting her of the impromptu weapon. "You will fight. Tomorrow. With no tears or resignation."

"For you."

"No, not for me. For us."

A moment of darkness crossed his face. He touched her cheek with an aching tenderness. Ada kept from blinking or moving lest she find herself in the midst of a beautiful dream, so rare and fleeting.

"You won't tell me why you've come here or why it was allowed," she said. "Will you?"

"No."

"Is your life in danger because of it?"

"No."

"Do you love me?"

"More than I thought possible," he said harshly.

"Then we have tonight, and I am thankful for it."

His hesitant, teasing smile appeared. The untried attempt at cheer looked almost comical on her stern warrior, this man she would have as her husband. But she wanted to throw her arms around him and celebrate the effort, Gavriel's strange and unexpected victory.

So she did.

With her arms wrapped tightly around him, she pulled him down to the mattress. The heavy, solid weight of masculine muscle settled over her as his mouth found hers. They tangled together, all limbs and tongues and impatient sighs. Ada closed her eyes and gave herself over to the experience, her strange wedding night. She pushed fear and regret aside to make room for the delicious heat building between their bodies.

Gavriel kissed her deeply. He seemed to touch her everywhere, all at once—closing a rough hand over her breast and kneading the sensitive flesh, cupping the back of her neck to draw their kiss into a long, breathless discovery. No furtive touches and shame this time. No feeling of manipulation or struggle. Just a sweetness that imbedded in her bones and turned her body to flame.

He clenched his fingers in her hair and yanked backward. She expected to feel his lips on her throat once again, anticipating his journey lower, lower to nuzzle between her breasts.

But he stopped.

* * *

"What is it?"

Gavriel winced at the crack in her voice. She was still so quick to doubt. Even now, she expected him to hesitate and withdraw. Not that he blamed her. Skin burned too often expects pain from a fire, not warmth and comfort. He had to ease past her worry and help her forget the morrow. She possessed strength enough to survive the coming trial, but he could not leave her until he knew she planned to use it.

He studied her delicate features and tightened his fingers down to her scalp. She winced again. "You hair," he said. "'Tis a liability."

"What do you—?" He yanked again, harder. Her head snapped back. "Ow!"

"A beautiful liability," he whispered, kissing behind her ear in apology. The soft, tempting skin urged him to linger. He licked the salt, tracing a path down to the notch at the base of her throat. He dipped his tongue inside and gloried in her gasp.

"Cut it for me."

He raised his face to see her, wishing for a stronger light. Silk tangled around his fingers. He pulled a handful of those deep, glossy strands to his nose and inhaled. "*Inglesa,* do not ask that of me."

"Cut it for me," she said with more determination. Blue eyes shone wide and black in the dim moonlight. "Use the shards I was ready to use on you."

Dread gave way to relief. If she was willing to wrestle free of him in that little cell and ask him to lop off her hair with a shard of pottery, her instincts were thriving. She would fight. The compact he had forged with his traitorous father, permitting a single night alone with her, would be the end of Gavriel. He no longer cared, for she might be strong enough to survive.

If she did not, he would dedicate the rest of his short life to ending his father's.

"Not yet." He did not recognize his own voice, a breathless plea choked with grief. "Let me see your neck. Let me kiss you there."

She peered through the darkness like the witch she was, able to read languages and speak in tongues and see into his very soul. Never had he felt more vulnerable; she threatened much more than his life. His heart beat in her hands.

She stood before him without embarrassment or pretense. Only Ada. With infinite slowness, as if they had a lifetime, not mere hours, she raised her arms and gathered that thick, shimmering mane of hair in one hand. She swept it forward, every strand, until it draped like a cloak over one shoulder. The sight of her pale, arched neck stole the moisture from his mouth.

It had taken weeks for them to reach this point again, poised on the verge of pleasure, but the act of disrobing took only moments. The laces at her bodice slid free beneath her nimble fingers. She pushed free of the fine linen garments that had once been beautiful, expensive creations, now worn to frailty because of their exploits. Entirely bare, her skin glowed in the moonlight, a pale vision he would never trust as real—and certainly not as belonging to him.

But there she stood, gazing at him with heavy-lidded eyes and a teasing smile that had once threatened to drive him insane. The insanity building in him now had more to do with lust and want, the insatiable need that tempted him to untold wildness. He took her hand and grazed a kiss across her knuckles. She shivered.

"You're cold," he said.

"Then warm me."

Ada slid to the floor, all grace and curves, until she knelt with him. He took one hard, bare nipple in his mouth, the only place where he touched her. She arched slightly, offering all he cared to take, but neither did she reach for him. Her soft moans charged the air as blood gathered thick and pulsing at his groin.

Why did he resist, using only his mouth? Why did he merely tease first one nipple, then the other? His body ached with the effort to keep from grabbing her, turning her, entering her. But he feared the devastating pull of their desire. He feared missing some detail that, in the days and weeks of madness to come, he would regret overlooking in the mad rush to have her. So he kissed, licked, and nibbled with infinite care, learning her body.

A sob mingled with her moans. Gavriel raised his head to find her face bathed in tears. He kissed one, then another, hot and salty on his tongue.

"Don't cry, *mi inglesa*. Please."

"How can I help it? I—this is breathtaking."

Succumbing to his need, he filled his hands with her flesh. The soft weight of her breast fit his palm, the perfect temptation. "Yes, you are."

The soft slope of each breast, the hollow of her belly—still too thin after her illness—and he could resist no longer. He had sold his soul for the promise of her safety. His woman. His wife. The need to possess crashed over him. He held her close and arched her more fully, claiming a nipple once again. He sucked deeply and ran his tongue in faster circles. Her hoarse cry split the night air and banished her tears.

He roamed over her torso using only his mouth, worshipping the gift of her body. Now calloused and rough, his hands were not sensitive enough for him to appreciate the smooth softness of her skin.

Another shiver ripped through her body. Another breathless gasp. She writhed in his arms, twisting her hips until her pelvis pressed close to his. Gavriel groaned.

"Let me kiss your neck," he whispered. "Before we cut your hair."

Before Ada could reply, he turned her around and pushed her down to her hands and knees. He swept the long curtain of her hair aside and gathered her close. His body curving over and around hers, he kissed the nape of her neck. She arched and pressed her backside more fully against his rigid shaft.

Gavriel shucked his tunic and breeches and returned to her, flesh over flesh. He reached around and found her wet folds. The feel of her slick skin, so ready for him, stole the last of his tattered control. Sliding into her was sweet bliss, air burning in his lungs as she opened for his slow penetration. She whispered his name on a long exhale.

"Mi inglesa," he rasped against her neck. *"Mi esposa."*

Their dance ebbed, a gratifying pattern of slow to frantic to slow again. Unhurried, Gavriel withdrew until they nearly parted, then pressed inside. He reveled in the aching, exquisite feel of her body accepting his, each time, every time, until his measured pace became a torture. Fire flooded his veins. Breathless, he pulled her torso flush to his and barely withdrew before driving into her again.

He bowed his back and rested his forehead in the valley between her shoulder blades. Somewhere in his mind, he knew he should slow. He should savor. He should tend to her aching body and give her the release she sought. Yet every muscle quivered and throbbed as he committed himself to the mania of his need. Tenderness fled. Months and years of restraint gave way to the sheer, brutal violence of his passion.

But Ada did not retreat. She matched his need for more, pushing back to meet his quickened thrusts. Her cries gained such strength that Gavriel released her breast and covered her mouth. He clenched her body, poised with her on the edge of satisfaction.

"Hush, *mi ama,*" he ground out. "Keep the storm inside you."

With his hand clamped over her mouth, and with her teeth nestled against the fleshy pad where his thumb met his palm, he began to thrust again. He nuzzled his mouth in the tangle of hair just behind her ear, pressed his lips there, tasted her. Urgent breaths matched the fierce rhythm of their bodies. At the sudden, sharp spasm of her release, she bit hard and shuddered. Her every muscle tensed and trembled.

Gavriel plunged into her once more. Hot light blazed behind his eyes as the pleasure crashed over him, dark and right and beautiful.

Chapter 31

Collapsed on her side, Ada lay with Gavriel on the floor of the cell. He curled around her, sated, still nude, their pose a soft imitation of their coupling. Having shifted his hand from her mouth, he gently stroked her stomach. The lazy rhythm of his touch lulled her to a place of utter contentment, her body, mind, and soul joined.

Forever. Yes, she could stay in that place forever. And she would have, no matter the cost.

As the euphoria of their passion receded, cooling, she shivered in the fading night. Not even Gavriel's warm, lean body and the shielding strength of his arms could protect her from the morning. Grief scratched the inside of her eyelids. It settled across her naked body like a shroud, one that knives could never cut or tear.

But if she had hours, mere minutes left with him, she would not waste them on useless grief. The future was not fixed. If Gavriel believed she was fierce enough to fight her way to freedom, she would do it. She would survive, eager to wake in his arms for the remainder of their days.

She rolled over and warmed the front of her body along his. He smiled against her cheek, a beautiful smile that still

surprised her. Humbled her. But she felt the ridges along his
back. He flinched and his smile died.

"Let me see," she said.

He did not move. His breathing accelerated. An echo of that
familiar distance hardened his face, so near to refusing her.

She petted up and down his back, like easing a terrified
child. "Please, Gavriel. Share this with me."

With a shuddering exhale, he rolled onto his front and
rested his head on crisscrossed forearms. In the slanting
moonlight, the scars on his back stood in exaggerated relief.
Roads and valleys of old, old injuries stretched beneath newly
healing wounds. Sitting back on her heels, she traced one diagonally from the cap of his shoulder to his hip. Layers of
pain. Years of hatred, from others and toward himself. The
physical proof of his past added scars to her own heart.

Can you forget this?

She continued to pet the furrowed skin. His muscles bunched
beneath her fingers—a man at war, not a man who had just
found satisfaction. But she kept touching, not knowing how else
to reach her wounded warrior. The smooth rhythm of her hands
across his body soothed her own nerves, and Gavriel's breathing evened, softened. She moved to his shoulders, arms, and the
back of his neck. Her fingers pressed deeper, more massaging
than touching. Then she skittered a touch up, along his sides, the
lightest feather's caress.

He laughed.

Ada held perfectly still. "Are you well?"

She moved her hands again, along his ribs. His shoulders
quivered. Laughter shook free as he flinched, protecting himself from her touch. "Ada, stop!"

The startling sound, one she never thought she would hear,
echoed with the strength of a shout.

"Let me see your face," she said.

She leaned low over his body and turned his face to the side, meeting his eyes. His tentative smile eased into deep, masculine laughter. As she had wanted to that morning, when he had first offered his smile there at court, she touched his face—his lower lip, then his dimples and the rounded tops of his cheeks. Fire tingled against her fingertips. His gaze never left hers, as dark and intimidating as ever, but made more potent by the emotion swirling in his eyes.

"You aren't supposed to be laughing," she whispered.

"Then don't tickle me."

Breath clogged her throat. Breath and wanting. "Remember what I told you about small steps."

"I remember."

The temptation to continue beyond the boundaries of those scars pulled at her. She slid her palms down his sides to his hips. He groaned. Not from pain. He groaned like when he pushed into her, the sound of a man in need of more.

Bolder now, she touched his firm, rounded buttocks. He tensed and choked on some sound. She grinned and straddled his thighs, clenching hers to keep him still. The rumbling vibrations of his welcoming laugher slid up the insides of her thighs. Although he could flip her, pin her, take her with ease, he lay there and let her explore. The heady strength of him coiled in waiting. She tightened her fingers into muscle, deeper, deeper still. He hissed and exhaled a shaky breath.

Rubbing his backside, his thighs, she felt the pulse of desire accelerating again, beating a familiar pattern of push and retreat. She leaned into each stroke of her hands, putting more force into the sensuous, massaging strokes. He groaned again. The deep and dangerous sound settled low in her belly.

"Lift up," he said.

She raised on her knees, just slightly. He turned beneath her with one fluid movement. Instead of looking at his scarred back and his taut backside, she found herself staring at his face. Then down to the breadth of his chest. Then to the rigid length of his manhood. Her fingers hovered above the feast of his flesh, uncertain which of the bounty to touch first. He smelled of sweat and of her.

His smile flashed, that bright and unexpected lightning. The very wonder of it stole her will to resist. How could she? Why would she?

"Come to me, *inglesa*."

"Did you still want me to cut your hair?"

Ada roused from her near-sleep, snuggled alongside Gavriel's body. Muscles she had never known protested as she stretched.

"Yes," she said groggily.

Then, before she changed her mind, Ada struggled free of his bewitching arms and retrieved the two largest clay shards. The chill air nipped at her skin, but Gavriel stretched across the tattered mattress like the promise of a roaring fire.

He raised his brows. "You won't try to attack me with them again?"

She handed him the shards and knelt, her back to him. "No. I'm trusting them to you."

Gavriel pushed to his knees and leaned close, placing a kiss on her cheek. A tender kiss. The heat and scent of his body enveloped her senses. "You're certain?"

"You said yourself, 'tis a liability I cannot afford."

He used the wall to hone one of the shards. The scrape of each stroke grated against her contentment, a violent sound that brought terrible tidings of the day to follow. He flicked the pad of his thumb against the sharpened edge and nodded.

Ada straightened her back and waited. His hands cupped her face from chin to ear.

"Right there," he said. "Where you catch the moonlight."

He gathered her hair, pulling each wisp away from her

face. Then he smoothed the long strands until she nearly closed her eyes, drifting on the tender cadence of his touch.

"Still now," he said.

She set her shoulders and held her neck firm as he began to cut. The clay blade sawed against her hair, rough and noisy in the near darkness. Gavriel worked at his chore with steady patience. He stopped twice to sharpen the edge, never speaking. Hunks of hair fell around her hips, then shorter, tickling filaments, until nothing remained to be cut.

Gavriel sat back, still naked, his eyes unreadable. She raised a hand to her head, which felt light and awkward. Unencumbered. Long, glossy hair had been chopped to short, uneven locks around her chin. She rubbed the back of her neck, itching. Roughened fingernails scored her scalp as she scratched the short strands into a wild mess.

Although Gavriel offered a proud smile, she ducked her head. "I must look ridiculous."

"Not at all," he said. "Not for a warrior."

She exhaled. "Well, 'tis done. Nothing that can't be undone if I survive the day."

"When. *When* you survive the day."

"You believe I can do this? Truly?"

"Truly," he said. "I would not have marred your beauty for any cause less worthy."

She pulled at a short lock. "Marred my beauty? I knew it must be bad."

"Come." He held out his hand, that smile quirking at his lips. "Let me show you how little it matters to me."

Although Ada slept, Gavriel could not let go of the world. She lay beside him, her leg draped across his middle. His tunic served as their only blanket, and she used his shoulder as a pillow. His greedy body had claimed hers once again, bringing them both to that dizzying point of exhausted completion, but he felt none of the peace he hoped to find.

Only dread.

He kissed the top of her head and smiled there, her short hair tickling his lips. But the twinkle of amusement faded. Although he was glad to have convinced her of the need to fight, now he faced the consequences of the morning.

And if she was with child . . .

They were married, at least. Their child would not be raised a bastard. No matter what she eventually believed of his decision, she would raise their child to be strong and well-loved.

That she might resent him so terribly as to neglect the child pressed against his temples. Perhaps she would return to opium. Perhaps she would find the reminder too painful to keep.

Behind closed lids, he pictured her astride him. She had laughed when she took him inside her once again, shaking her shorn head, enjoying the freedom of it. With every lift of her hips, she had brought him closer to release. Then she had collapsed, trembling like him.

But memories of their coupling paled to the thought of her hands moving over his back. She had explored those terrible scars without fear or revulsion, easing the pain of his past. For a breath or two, he had felt released and revived. Ada helped him lower those defenses, and he had done so when the reward was her love.

Now he would be stripped of the armor forged by long years of pain and discipline. He would return to the masters of his youth with no more resistance than a child could muster, a slave once again. To do their bidding.

And he was terrified.

Eyes wide, he looked up to the narrow window and saw the glimmer of fading moonlight. He found himself desperate enough to ask for assistance. He begged for it, in truth, and approached the idea of prayer with a soul uncluttered by

Pacheco's warped demands. He prayed—not for himself, but for Ada's safety. He prayed she would find the strength to live well and raise a child with all the love she was capable of providing, love that he might have shared.

But with his face upturned to the night, he knew he could not trust his future to Joaquin de Silva. His father had never kept a promise. Promises meant honor. De Silva had none.

He stared into the black as his mind raced across the possibilities. This was a game, nothing more. He sat on one side of the chessboard, his treacherous father on the other. Only when the dawn began to cleanse the sky of darkness did he find the maneuvers that might set them both free.

"Quickly now. Ada, quickly."

She snapped to wakefulness with the rattle of keys down the corridor. Gavriel was already tugging her kirtle over her head. She pushed clumsy male hands aside and finished dressing, gown to boots.

"Wait," he said.

Gavriel knelt before her, taking the clay shard in hand. She thought he was ready to fight back with that crude weapon. But her giddy hope dried to dust. She did not want him to resist because the guards would only kill him. No matter the bargain he had made to stay with her through the night— and she knew he had made one, knew it without a doubt—they would not hesitate to end his life. Even her warrior could not stand before such poor odds.

She was ready to kick the shard from his hands, but he touched the sharpened clay to the hem of her gown. He split the fabric with two rough slashes, then tore away the bottom third of her skirts. From her knees to the tops of her leather boots, her legs were bare.

"What are you doing?"

"You can run faster now." He flashed his grin. "And the sight of your naked legs will distract any man you face in combat."

"Certainly, like my hair."

The door flew opened and hit the wall with a thick wooden thud. Six guards stood ready. Their leader held two sets of manacles. "Ada of Keywood—"

"Keyworth, you dullard," she mumbled in English.

"You are hereby ordered to accompany us to where you will be tried by combat."

She glanced at Gavriel. His face had turned to stone, having shared their goodbyes through the fleeting night of loving. "And what of him?"

"His fate is not your concern. You're coming with us."

"Answer me or I'll die right here."

Gavriel seized her from behind and offered her hands to the guard, who slapped on the manacles. Metal bit into her wrists. Breath burned her throat in sharp gasps.

"My warrior," Gavriel said, his voice deep and close. "Open your eyes."

She watched his expression change. The guards would not have noticed. Perhaps no one else would. But Ada did.

She had come to dislike the shrewd mask he wore when he was ready to finish a game of chess, his victory a certainty. But on that morning, she welcomed it with all her soul.

The room righted itself. She breathed through her nose, confronting each guard with unblinking coldness. The manacles were heavy and sharp around her wrists, but she would not be bound when she fought. As for her husband, she had no notion of what he planned, but she trusted him. No matter his past or Jacob's warnings, she trusted him implicitly.

Her head light and unburdened, her hands bound by steel, she walked from the cell without a look back, her lips curved into a tiny smile.

Yes, Gavriel had been a remarkably quick study at chess.

Chapter 32

Gavriel paced his cell, alone, his mind with Ada. If he stopped, he would break in two. With every movement, he felt the tender ache of the muscles he had used to move with her through the night. He smelled like her. He still tasted her.

His plan was honed by a madman, he knew. But his choices had been whittled until only one remained: he would fight. He was long past submitting to Lord de Silva again, doing his bidding—not that he trusted his father's promise that he would be reinstated among the family's elite.

When the guards returned, he brought his aim into focus. Matters of revenge and right and wrong no longer mattered. His tasks lined up like chairs along a dining table—neat, ordered, one after the other. Accomplish one, move on to the next. At the end, God willing, he would hold Ada again.

Manacles around his wrists, he followed the guards past a dozen locked cells. De Silva waited at the end of the corridor, tall, strong, and dangerous.

"Gavriel," he said, his smile smooth and cunning. "I hope you enjoyed your night."

"I did, Master. She is a serviceable woman." He looked to the pair of men standing behind his father. "I thought you

would greet this morning with a smile, relishing the prospect
of seeing me in chains once again."

De Silva laughed without mirth. "I never tire of that sight,
mi hijo."

"Your son? I'm no more your son than you are my father."

"You cannot deny your lineage, Gavriel. Neither could I,
much as I wanted to." He motioned for the guards to unlock
the manacles. Blood rushed back to Gavriel's hands. De Silva
stepped closer and caught him by the chin, their eyes level.
"Don't forget what I know of you. You hate me, without a
doubt, but tell me your body doesn't thrill at the thought of
the de Silva family—our power and potential."

Gavriel closed his eyes, demons clawing deep in his gut.
He had lived and thrived and rode amidst barbarous men, all
of whom shared his capacity for brutality. The call of that old
life sang a careless, murderous song. His mind swam, breathless, as if he had slipped below the surface of a lake. A shiver
chased over his skin.

When he opened his eyes, he found de Silva smiling again.
"Good, *mi hijo.* Very good."

The sick appreciation Gavriel found on the man's face jerked
him free of his moment of weakness. Ada faced the fight of her
life. The sickening, hypnotic way his father spoke of violence
and freedom seemed like the Devil's own tongue, weaving tales
of disgusting temptations. What was Gavriel doing, his mind
sweeping over La Mancha with old and brutal memories?

He was saving his own life. The only chance he had was in
convincing de Silva that his slave had returned to him, all without truly succumbing. And then he might be able to save Ada.

"I see you've not lost that stony expression," de Silva said.
They strode side by side down the corridor and out of the justice building. Eight guards fell into step around them. "Good
to see you have your defenses about you. I shouldn't like to
think I've missed the chance to break you, once and for all."

"Pacheco tried."

"Yes, but Pacheco is a fool. He believed he could control you with his little games, but I never believed it. He is, however, a very good killer. Not so good as you—or myself, for that matter."

But he'll suit your aim. I know your plan, Father.

"You failed to kill the king," de Silva said. "Tell me, does it still burn in you, Gavriel?"

"My life would be very different, Master, had I succeeded." Sunlight stung Gavriel's eyes. The ease with which he fell into calling him *master* set his confidence off balance. The man brimmed with influence.

De Silva grinned. He slapped Gavriel on the shoulder and pulled him into a rough embrace. "See, my boy? It's as if you never left."

Gavriel looked down. His father pressed a palm-sized dagger against his ribs. A single push and the blade would pierce his shuddering heart.

"Are you listening, Gavriel?"

"I am."

De Silva's eyes burned like blue flames. "I don't trust you and never have."

"You do not truly expect me to kill the king."

"Of course not," de Silva said with a twisted smile. "You agreed last night because you sought pleasure between the legs of that English harlot."

"Then why give me the privilege?"

"So that her death will ruin you. This morning, you will watch her die—a small compensation for the son you took from me."

No!

Gavriel swallowed a quick surge of nausea.

"That is my pleasure," de Silva snarled. He pushed the

dagger deeper, just enough to draw blood. "The king will
die anyway, and then I will end your life myself."

But Gavriel surprised them both by smiling; it was like
practicing a new maneuver. The shock of it registered on de
Silva's narrow, lined face. "The move is yours, Father."

Fernán sat on the top of the wooden barricade surrounding
the tiny arena. A ripe orange in his hand, he sucked the juices
from each segment and looked across the citizens assembled
for the combat trials. Sunshine, always more dratted sunshine,
baked the tops of a few bare heads and pulsed from the
packed clay floor of the arena. Sweat leaked from his temples
and made a wet mess of his cropped hair. He ran his fingers
through it, hoping for a breeze. But hundreds of bodies meant
no relief, even from his elevated vantage.

Two days of searching had revealed Abez's whereabouts,
safe in the southern quarter of the city with his son and her parents. They had escaped that hideous sort of captivity in Uclés,
free of Pacheco's threats. Happy as he was—eating an orange
and mere days from fleeing south with Abez—the poor bas-
tards ready to die in the arena seemed particularly pathetic.

But, strangely enough, he spotted Gavriel in the crowd.
The former novice was hard to miss. There was no mistaking
that stern face. But his stride had been stunted. Gavriel's
shoulders dipped slightly, the muscles stiff around his neck.
Such a change from when Fernán had last seen him on the
day Ada was detained. Another man, equally tall and even
more arrogant, walked alongside. Just what the world needed.

And still another familiar face peeked through the crowd:
Blanca, her eyes like those of an owl. He looked side to side,
as if the peasants gathered around him could explain the co-
incidence. Having worked to blend into the dregs of Toledo,
he did not relish the idea of falling in with such familiar and

dangerous company. Any minute, Ada and Pacheco would reveal themselves and Fernán would be as poorly off as ever.

But at least Abez was safe.

He stood, intent on fleeing the scene and getting back to his family. No blood sport was worth the chance of being seen. But Blanca spotted him. That strange girl—was she, in fact, related to an owl?

He motioned for her to join him and, minutes later, dragged her through the crowd to an empty alleyway. The last thing he needed was for Gavriel to see them again. Fernán's face still throbbed from the healing bruises.

"Why are you here?" he asked.

At their backs, the crowd surged to life as the first trial began. Blanca flinched and went pale. "Ada."

"What do you mean, Ada?"

"Ada was sentenced to trial by combat."

"Surely no." But he chewed on his lower lip as Blanca related the story of Ada's hearing, from the corrupted judge to Gavriel's imprisonment. "But what is he doing here? He's with another man, under guard although he wears no restraints."

"No notion. But Pacheco's here too. I saw him this morning when I arrived, first thing. He's lurking about and wearing all black."

Fernán held up his hands and waved her away. "No, no, no. I cannot be here with that man about."

"But I need your help."

"You don't," he said, smoothing his sleeves. He wore no Jacobean robes and held fast to that happy fact. "You look well and safe and good. Now keep it that way. Go home."

She checked the alley for relative privacy and leaned close. "Very well, *they* need our help."

Fernán rubbed the back of his head, sweating and uncomfortable. "Surely the young Jew and those knives would be better suited to a rescue? Where is he?"

"At Doña Valdedrona's palace. He's to present evidence to King Alfonso against the de Silva family."

He tried to muster a bit of callousness for Jacob but found none. Only envy. The boy was far too heroic, making everyone else look foppish and careless by comparison. Not that Fernán offered much of a challenge on that score.

"With that excess of daring, the boy wants his head to dance separately from his body."

Blanca narrowed her eyes as the crowd chanted for the first combatant. "Ada's turn will come soon."

"Only a madman would come to watch his woman be slaughtered. The only reason I would watch Abcz killed . . . no, that's not possible."

"What?"

Blanca's cheeks had flushed pink, lips parted. He might have considered her a very pretty girl under different circumstances. He shook his head again.

"I'd have to be forced," he said.

"Then perhaps Gavriel is being forced? But he must have a strategy."

Fernán exhaled sharply. "He must. Even if forced, I'd be watching for any opportunity to fight back—and me, I'm a coward."

Her face, already soft and youthful, eased into one of sympathy. "You're not a coward."

"I am," he said. "Gavriel de Marqueda may be out in that crowd right now, awaiting Ada's execution. He may die in some foolhardy attempt to save her life. And Ada—she'll fight. You know her chances are slim, but she'll fight to the end." He slumped against the nearest wall, the air pushing from his lungs. "But I'll go home to Abez."

"You won't."

"I—"

He looked up, curious as to Blanca's certainty. Arms folded

across her youthful breasts, feet planted firmly in the dirt, she stared at him with the serene expression of a woman having just received absolution. Clear. Certain. Strong.

"You hardly know me, and what you know is highly unflattering," he said. "Do you really believe in me so much? How can that be?"

Blanca raised her chin and offered an unexpectedly cold smile. "Because I know where Abez lives. Help me find Gavriel or she won't be in hiding much longer."

On shaking legs, he stood and looked the diminutive rustic in the eye. "You're crueler than you appear."

Chapter 33

Outside Doña Valdedrona's private audience chamber, Jacob twisted and untwisted the tunic laces at his neck. He waited although so little time remained. As the sun neared its zenith, Ada would be facing the trial of her life. If he left for the arena, he would only arrive in time to watch her die. No, his best chance to expose the treachery aligning against Castile was to wait for his patroness. And, as much as it pained him to admit, his duty was to the greater security of the kingdom. Gavriel would take care of Ada.

The anteroom door opened to welcome Cilia, Condesa de Valdedrona. His thoughts slapped to a stop and he interlaced his hands behind his back. Standing before him, the midday sun flowing behind her like the aura of an angel, her brief welcoming smile collapsed.

"Jacob, you're here."

She greeted him in Norman, a language shared by her Sicilian family and the English nobility. Jacob's father had taught him the courtly language, hoping he might grow to become a royal physician or tutor. He found it none so difficult as Castilian. Their shared secret.

"Your Excellency," he said with a bow. "Where are your guards?"

"I sent them away. You have much to say, I know, and I want no curious ears."

She rested against the closed door, her creamy skin drawn tight, eyeing him with a directness he admired. Resplendent in a gown made of pale blue silk and the finest teaseled wool, her shining, honey-colored eyes revealed far more experience than her twenty years. Jacob felt a swell of admiration for the young mother of two, the widow who had given him his first opportunity in Castile.

"I thank you for seeing me," he said softly. "And for keeping my visit a secret from His Majesty and his guests."

"He doesn't need to know all that occurs in my household." Her smile was swift and bittersweet. She walked to a table and poured two mugs of wine. "Now tell me everything."

"I intercepted scrolls on my last assignment before you left for Segovia." He smiled and accepted a mug of wine. He was no longer sweating, and his hands were steady. Always the same. The thought of speaking to her sent him to shivers, but the act itself was simple.

"You didn't bring them to His Majesty today. Why not?"

He exhaled and fingered the hilt to one of his curving blades, noting that she had not asked him to remove his weapons. She should not be so trusting, even in the company of a man who would die defending her.

"The de Silva family has returned from exile under the protection of King Ferdinand," he said. "They conspire with the Leonese and the Almohads, intent on conquering Castile and sharing its spoils."

Her pale honey eyes widened, but she quickly masked her shock. A consummate aristocrat. "These scrolls implicate the Leonese? Do they dare—?"

"Listen to me!" Her flinch would have stopped him, but the

safety of too many lives depended on his being understood. "You were disobeyed. Did you know that? The judge who was to release Ada sentenced her, instead, to trial by combat. He did not allow her a second. She fights for her life in the trial arena. And you—" He drew one of his blades and brandished it in the bright sunlight. "And you did not demand I remove my weapons."

She backed away in haste. Drops of wine sprinkled onto the heavy woolen rug. "You would do me harm?"

Despite her obvious fear, her voice remained steady.

Jacob sheathed his blade and held out his hands, empty, palms up. "Of course not, milady, but you're too trusting."

"Perhaps."

From behind her back, she drew forth a dagger just as long as her hand. Their eyes held for a moment.

He grinned and nodded in approval. "The de Silva family has returned to the Peninsula. They assume hostilities will resume—"

"—at the conclusion of the truce. Just in time for a summer campaign." She tucked the blade into a sheath hidden somewhere in the many pleats of pale blue silk. "What of His Majesty? Do you fear for his life?"

He hesitated, every answer jamming in his throat like water behind a dam.

"No reason to hide your thoughts, Jacob," she said, her words a mixture of steel and softness. Few men would have been able to resist her quiet authority. Jacob had no desire to. "You've had access to the scrolls and all of the intelligence. Please, I ask your opinion."

"Milady, I believe the de Silvas have positioned an assassin here in Toledo."

"Do you know his identity?"

He swallowed. "I do."

"Then I'll ask my personal cadre to accompany you. Secure the traitors, and feel free to dispatch my men to free Ada."

If she yet lives. Please, God.

Ada stared at the latched doors. Outside the chamber where she stood in wait, the crowd bellowed its approval. Wild applause followed. Three men had walked out those doors. Three men had not returned. Each time one fell, the arena erupted into that same gleeful riot of noise.

Her wrists remained bound by manacles, the chains draping heavily to just above her knees. In her right hand she held the short sword she had selected from among the armaments available to the condemned. She was not officially condemned, not like those men who hanged for their crimes. She merely stood on the cusp of providing a fair amount of spectacle to a bloodthirsty crowd, all in the name of justice.

But there was no justice if her debts and broken contracts meant death.

She exhaled, eyes closed. If she intended to survive the next hour, she would need every resource and all of her wits. Clear and focused. Other thoughts would only get her killed.

Flanked by two guards wearing helmets and quilted armor, the bailiff approached. He did not wield an ax or tie nooses, but he would open those doors and send her out to do battle, one on one, with a trained warrior.

"Ada of Keyworth," he said, reading from a scant piece of parchment. "For the crimes of debt and negation of contracts perpetrated against citizens of the Prelate of Toledo, Kingdom of Castile, you have been ordered to endure a trial by combat. Best your opponent and you will be released. Do you acknowledge these charges?"

"I acknowledge I've been judged by a corrupt minister of these courts."

She could not help herself. The truth was simply too gruesome. She felt the absurd need to confront her captor with it, as if her tale might open a mind long closed to the pleas of the guilty. Having read from the parchment, he had at least a little education.

Lord, let him be a thinking man.

But the bailiff merely blinked. "If you are innocent, this trial will prove as much."

She gripped the hilt of the dull sword. Although the metal was relatively light, her forearm already ached. Waiting. "Do you really believe that?" she asked, her eyes direct.

The man glanced behind her and around the cell. "Where's your second?"

"I have none."

He blinked again, but this time his brows drew together in a frown, one that seemed to surprise him too. "You have no second?"

"I was not permitted one," she said. "The judge banned my husband from standing in my stead. Did you think I came here by choice or sheer pigheadedness?"

"But you're a woman."

"I am." Ada smiled, a little saddened by the man's confusion, desperate enough to use it against him. "You're sending a woman into the trial arena. I hope you'll be able to sleep tonight."

Whatever fleeting moment of doubt she saw on his face vanished. He nodded to the guard on his left who used a key to unlock the manacles. The bailiff turned and opened the doors.

Her time had come.

Every morsel of food she had forced herself to eat that morning splattered onto the grimy, blackened floor of the chamber. Half-kneeling, she fought the endless waves as they stole her courage. But she never let go of her sword. It was part of her now.

Looking up to the doors opened wide, she watched how the bailiff negligently turned his back. His posture said she was no threat to him. Her fate had already been decided. Ada drew nourishment from her indignation. She was not done yet. And no captor should ever turn his back to his prisoner, especially when she held a sword.

Once she had thought to kill Hamid al-Balansi. To kill for opium—the plan seemed, in hindsight, too terrible and wretched to contemplate, and that old need flooded her with shame. But could she kill an innocent man to save her own life, as she had threatened Paco?

Before Ada could steal her nerve, the bailiff returned and knelt beside her. He gripped her forearms and pulled her upright, his mouth close to her ear. "Rumor has it he's blind in one eye," he whispered. "I don't know which, or even if it's true."

Soaking up the words, she set aside thoughts of taking the bailiff's life. He had offered the only help he could. Now the responsibility was hers.

Luckily, she knew a thing or two about blind opponents.

Gavriel wondered if it was possible to go mad by bearing witness to the unimaginable. As Ada stepped into the dazzling spring sunshine, he put his palm to his forehead, half expecting to feel his mind give way beneath the bone. His life, the one he wanted to share with Ada, was poised on the verge of destruction, and he would die before allowing that to happen.

Hundreds lined the arena's four sides, armed with quick judgments and insults. De Silva stood silent and tall beside him, his eyes riveted to Ada, just like the other fifty people perched on that high observation platform. A tiny smile curled the corners of his mouth. He snapped his fingers.

Four hands like vices seized Gavriel's upper arms. De Silva family guards, including the false shepherd who had been following them for weeks, held him fast. The man grinned, his ruined eye like a blight across his face. Soon Gavriel was bound by ropes at the wrists and ankles. He struggled, pulling against each new restraint. As his knees hit the wooden platform, he was forced to kneel. De Silva's fingers wrapped around his skull and wrenched his eyes forward. Gavriel could not look away.

"Are you watching, Gavriel? This should be quite a display."

The crowd cheered the arrival of Ada's opponent. Bloodied from his previous three victories, he wore battered armor and a dull steel helmet with a full visor. His curved sword was Arab in origin, possibly brought from the Holy Land.

And Ada, a scholar and a woman, was supposed to defend herself against such a man?

The awaiting warrior caught sight of her by the open doors and strode forth to initiate their duel. She waited, her agile little sword balanced easily in both hands, feet planted.

Even as his mind shouted for her to run, he waited until the men pinning him against the wooden platform relented, just a bit, their attention shifting to the arena. He shoved his shoulder hard to the right, toppling the nearest guard. Ankles and wrists bound, Gavriel could only use the bulk of his body as a weapon. He ground his elbow into the fallen man's sternum, then jumped away from two more guards who mustered against his aggression.

Before he could stand, he kicked both feet up and connected with the hand of a man bearing down on him. The sword flew free and into the crowd, well out of reach. He rolled to his feet, all grace gone, and shoved into the guard's gut, pushing him hard against the platform's railing. Wood cracked. Gavriel's thighs ached with the tension of pushing, pushing against his enemy, fighting to keep his own balance. One slip and he would plummet into the crowd below.

A second sentry attacked, sword raised, but Gavriel shuffled aside. When the sword sliced downward, it found the metal of the shepherd's armor. The clang of iron preceded another splitting crack as the wood gave way. Momentum propelled both men through the barrier and down, landing atop the bloodthirsty spectators below.

Ada would live. She had to. All he could do was fight, hoping she kept running until he could reach her.

Gavriel spun away from the arena and right into his father's fist. His nose exploded in pain. His head snapped back, blood rushing into his throat.

Instinct pushed to the fore. More quickly than he would have thought possible, he recovered from the punch and bowed his body into a crescent to avoid de Silva's sword. He somersaulted forward.

"Gavriel!"

Blanca?

And there she was, shoving closer with Fernán at her side. Armed with more steel than sense, they frightened onlookers with random swings of their weapons.

"I would've liked to finish what I started there in the baths," she said about the fallen shepherd. "But your way will do, Gavriel."

With Fernán's sword momentarily holding de Silva at bay, Blanca used Ada's dagger to slice the binding ropes. Gavriel was free. He snatched the sword from Fernán and jumped past his unlikely aides, catching his father's blade with his own. Fury propelled his movements and infused them with more speed, more strength.

De Silva caught every blow with expert precision. He backed away from Gavriel's assault with measured steps, the crowd fleeing from their duel. Hot red anger on his face admitted no defeat and offered no quarter. His tunic ripped at the armpit as he struck out and sliced Gavriel's left arm.

Gavriel skirted backward, hunched over, his sword lowered

and one hand clutching his wound. Blood oozed through his fingers. His knees shook. An agonizing fire sapped the dexterity from his muscles, but he, too, refused to yield. Death had no power to frighten him, not when he had already seen the worst of all scenarios: Ada fighting for her life.

She needed him.

Slippery fingers interlacing with dry ones, he gripped the hilt and attacked anew. De Silva continued to accept each jolting strike of metal on metal with an expression perched between amusement and fury. Gavriel was a nuisance, a broken slave, a barrier to be stepped over on his way to power. But that barrier still had a weapon and a reason to fight.

Renewed power surged through his body. The sword he held became lighter and more agile. He moved with longer strides, pushing de Silva back, back still. His throbbing wound faded into the back of his mind, like Fernán and Blanca fending off the soldiers or the continued shouts of the crowd. He could only hope they shouted for Ada.

One last furious strike and de Silva lost his balance and fell backward, clinging to the broken handrail. Gavriel twirled his sword for a better grip and raised it for a killing blow. Easy. This was easy, the pain and rage finding a home, like the tip of a sword imbedding in flesh.

But he hesitated. All he vowed had been to keep from exacting revenge on this man. His father. His master. He had learned strange lessons in the monastery, the foremost of which was that he could no longer kill as blithely as he once had.

When forged steel finally met flesh, de Silva's right hand and the sword it held dropped to crowd below. His savage howl sailed over the noise of the crowd. He clasped the ruined limb to his chest as the howls collapsed into sobs.

Another scream climbed Gavriel's scarred back. *Ada!*

Blanca slid across the platform and pressed Ada's dagger to de Silva's neck. "Go!"

Fernán jumped forward, guarding de Silva with his sword—
a sword he held with convincing authority. "She's right! We
have him!"

Gavriel nodded once and, weapon in hand, he flew through
the crowd to the arena floor. His vision narrowed, his limbs
shook, and his heart pounded only for Ada.

Chapter 34

Ada ducked behind haystacks, gasping for air. Onlookers shouted and whistled. They were clearly on the side of her attacker, their jeers forming a wave of disapproval when she ran.

Her arms ached. Her calves throbbed and her lungs burned. The constant taste of rancid fear coated her tongue like black tar. The short sword she held felt as nimble and useful as timber. She gathered her wits and assessed her surroundings. Running had served her well, but her opponent had already battled and bested three men in that space—if not others on previous days. He knew the arena. He was skilled and strong.

He would find her.

She shook her head and inhaled, swallowing the tar taste. Calm. She needed to be calm. She needed to stop mocking the idea of ever being calm again.

The warrior's sword stabbed through the crisscrossed hay, narrowly missing Ada's head. She yelped and jumped clear. He lunged after her, swatting at her head, but his glove slipped off her hair. Long tresses would have been a trap. Even as she ran, she grinned. She had nothing left but small victories.

In an open clearing, her entire world defined by the circling, shouting crowd and a barrage of soldiers, she sought cover. Cover and weapons. Near the eastern edge of the arena, she found a scattering of egg-sized rocks. But what could rocks do against armor and a sword?

Her opponent barreled across the clearing, sword at the ready, charging her like an angered bull. She backed, backed away. When he strode across the loosened rocks, he stumbled just enough to upset his attack. The downward arc of his blade wobbled wide.

Ada skittered to the side and around his back. She turned and, using both hands, swung her sword with every bit of strength. Dull and rusted from lack of proper care, the blade only slapped the warrior's thigh. He spun to the right—always to the right.

She dipped around his left side and, when he pivoted to follow her escape, she stayed in his blind spot. Using the blunted sword as a club, she aimed for the backs of his knees. The man sagged to the ground with a grunt. The force of the blow radiated up her arms. She abandoned the sword and ran behind him, yanked off his helmet, and tossed it into the crowd. They responded with an unexpected cheer in her favor.

From overhead, two soldiers fell off the wooden observation platform, their armor rattling like an empty bucket. Women screamed and men pulled them away from where the fallen soldiers lay immobile. Ada spotted Gavriel on the platform where he fought a sword duel with another man. She cried out in surprise, in giddy joy. Although he did not look down to see her, he was alive and fighting. She only had to survive another few moments.

Her opponent had regained his feet. Face bare, enraged, he carried her sword, too. A jagged scar marred the skin between his forehead and jaw, just missing his left eyeball. The eyelid drooped and the slightest haze covered that iris. He stalked toward her with deliberate slowness, but the crowd no longer supported his deadly intent. They began to jeer and toss items into the arena: first old produce and mud clods, then stones and ever more insults.

Ada noticed his pronounced limp and offered a sweet smile. She raised empty, blistered palms. "I don't suppose we could call this a draw? Maybe these folks would forgive a blind man his foibles."

"You will die for this affront," he said.

"Hardly just." She backed toward the platform and stooped to pick up a fist-sized rock. Its jagged edges gnawed at her palm, sharp and reassuring. "But then, little of this experience has been fair."

His lip curled into a sneer, knotting the scarred skin. "Kneel and die quickly."

"No."

He sheathed his weapon and hefted her short sword. "Then you will die slowly by your own dull blade. You cannot escape this place. I've never been bested."

She smiled again, her stare raking over his face. "Seems someone came right close. And I intend to do him one better."

A bellow from above grabbed her attention. Where Gavriel had been doing battle, his opponent lay on his back, perched halfway over the edge. Two body lengths separated the man's right arm from where his hand and sword landed on the ground. Blood rained down on a dozen upturned faces.

The warrior grabbed her from behind, her windpipe wedged in the crook of his elbow. His armor pinched her skin. The tip of the sword poked into her lower back. "I'll not be humiliated by a woman."

"Too late, seems to me. Or did everyone here know about your eye?"

The sword gouged into her flesh. Hot blood seeped beneath her kirtle and dripped down her spine, buttocks, thighs. Pain like an afterthought slid between her nerves and dove into her brain. A scream shredded her throat.

She slammed her rock up and back. The man's nose exploded in a crack of bone and gore. She wrenched his arm from around her neck, rolling free.

"Ada! Take this!"

She whipped her head up to the wooden platform where Blanca stood. The girl tossed a glittering sheath to the ground. Her jeweled dagger.

Ada snatched up the beautiful, lethal weapon, her lower back a riot of pain and disobedient muscles. She pulled the dagger free of its sheath. Although she shouted up to Blanca, she kept her eyes on the injured warrior who had dropped to the ground, clutching his ruined face. "Where's Gavriel?"

"Here."

She spun and found Gavriel within an arm's distance, the glimmering sword he held streaked over with blood. But reflexes and the persistent blaze of fear dragged her arm up, ready to strike. She stood there, poised, limbs frozen and mouth agape.

"Inglesa," he said, his smile thin. *"Mi inglesa."*

The dagger dipped. She lowered her hand, carefully, slowly, and sheathed the weapon. Then she dove into the safety of his arms. *"Mi amo."*

Hard muscles gathered her close. She flinched.

Gavriel pulled away. "What?"

"My back." He tried to turn her around but she resisted. "Not now."

With the warrior felled, soldiers who had encircled the arena closed in. From all sides they approached, fully armored and armed. The bailiff, the judge—they were nowhere to be seen. She did not know if they were city *pedones* or members of de Silva's personal guard.

"Who calls it off?" She looked around but found no one but

soldiers and anxious citizens. The jeers and applause had faded to tense silence. "Who comes to say I've been pardoned?"

"I know not," he said quietly. "Although my guess is that the ordinary means have been corrupted."

Side by side, she took Gavriel's hand. He gave her fingers a quick squeeze. "What was your plan?" she asked.

"What plan?"

"Your plan! You—your face. In the cell. You were wearing your chess expression, when you're ready to win."

"You're mistaken, *inglesa*," he said with a grin. "That's how I look when I'm ready to bluff."

His smile broadened. Hardened warrior, stoic servant of God—they transformed into a teasing man who stole her breath. She wanted to slap him, but instead she threw her arms around his neck and held on. Tight. She found the soft hollow behind his ear and kissed him.

As Gavriel raised his sword, she tucked her face into the crook of his neck. They might die, but they would die together.

"Halt!"

Up on the wooden scaffold, Jacob and Doña Valdedrona stood over the man whose hand Gavriel had severed. They looked like angels of mercy, ready to offer calm justice. Jacob nodded to them when Ada called his name. Although his face remained impassive, he winked.

"I'd wager *he* has a plan," Gavriel whispered.

"Good that one of you does."

He rubbed a playful hand over her bobbed hair, their bodies still clinging. "I've been imprisoned with you. You're very distracting, *inglesa*."

"I demand that every soldier stands down," said Jacob. "Detain de Silva's men."

"By what authority?" asked one of the soldiers.

King Alfonso, dressed in layers of silk and fur, distinguished by his fine lineage and decades of authority, stepped into view on the platform. "By mine."

Gavriel kept Ada's body close to his, their fingers interlaced, hers growing colder by the minute as men cleared the arena of curious spectators. Soldiers remained at the ready as the king and his attendants descended. They bowed to the monarch, Ada managing awkwardly despite the blood seeping through the back of her dress.

"Your Majesty, you are not safe," Jacob said, rising from his bow.

Alfonso looked Jacob up and down, then passed his keen eyes over the crowd. Those who met his gaze dropped their eyes in deference. "I will not be intimidated by traitors in my realm."

Searching among the prisoners, Gavriel could not find his wounded father. "Jacob, where is de Silva?"

"On the platform with two soldiers and a physic." The young man struggled to hide a grin but failed. "We found Blanca and Fernán sitting on him." He turned to Ada. "Are you well?"

"I'm alive," she said tightly. Gavriel needed to get her to safety and tend whatever wounds she had sustained. "The judge who oversaw my hearing is in de Silva's pocket."

"No, the judge is in a cell." A young noblewoman with dark hair and flawless skin stepped through the line of soldiers and took her place between Jacob and the king. "I do not appreciate being disobeyed," she said.

"That's Her Excellency," Ada whispered.

The noblewoman's displeasure ebbed from her in frosty waves. "This woman, Ada of Keyworth, was to be cleared of charges and remanded to my custody. That she has been made to fight for her life like an animal in a baiting pen is reprehensible." She glided toward Ada and inclined her head. "I am pleased you fared as well as you did. My apologies, *señora*."

The word *señora* lingered in the air. Jacob had been standing tall, imbued with the authority of his connections, but now he studied the toes of his boots. Yes, Ada was a married woman. She had married him, Gavriel de Marqueda, a slave and a bastard and a man struggling to find a better way. That Doña Valdedrona acknowledged it in public made it real.

Ada squeezed his hand. Her face shone with a private smile, so much like the soft smile of peace he had first seen on her face. But this one was natural, unclouded. A smile for him.

But the moment escaped him as two soldiers pulled them apart. Ada stumbled. Jacob kept her from falling, but she swirled free of his reach, eyes ablaze. "What are you doing? Not him! Jacob, tell them!"

The sheepish look of a little boy had gone. Jacob stared only at Gavriel. "I ordered all members of the de Silva family to be detained. That includes Gavriel."

"No!" Another pair of the king's guard held Ada back. She hissed in pain but did not relent. "Let go of me!"

"Please, I won't resist. Just let her be." Gavriel went still, his arms slack beneath the soldiers' restraining hands, but inside he raged. "*Inglesa!* Stop! You'll do your injury worse."

"What injury?" Jacob took charge of her and gently turned her around. At her lower back, blood stained her gown. "Saints be! Where is the physic?"

"Let him go, Jacob," Ada said. "He's not one of them. He was their slave. Even in the scrolls, they doubted whether they could count on him to do their treachery. You read it, just as I did. Do not insist on thinking the worst of him."

Her words thrilled Gavriel, even as he wanted to go to her. She had never distrusted him. She had believed his violence a part of his old life, and so had the men aligning against them. He was not that killer. Even in sparing de Silva's life, he had proven as much.

Ada sagged against Jacob and slid to the ground. Gavriel surged again, but the guards held fast.

"Jacob, you must get her to my palace," the condesa said, kneeling.

Ada's face had gone sickly pale. "No! I won't leave without my husband!"

"Milady! Please, milady," said Gavriel. "Let me talk to her."

Doña Valdedrona looked to the guards and nodded. They kept sword points at his back, but they let him approach his huddled wife. He rolled his shoulders once as he took the condesa's place, with Ada's hand cool and trembling in his.

"Go with them, *mi ama,*" he whispered, petting streaks of saltwater from her face. "I'll be treated fairly now. You know that."

Wide blue eyes fixed at a point over his shoulder.

"Ada? Ada, talk to me."

"Pacheco," she whispered. "Check mate."

He froze. He had known as much. Pacheco had slipped through. Whether or not Ada lived, whether Gavriel died as a final punishment for Sancho's long-ago death—none of it had mattered to de Silva.

He had only wanted the diversion.

Gavriel held Ada's gaze and blinked once. Between their bodies, she pushed her dagger into his hands. He kissed her forehead with all of the strange, beautiful love he possessed.

"Time to end this," he said.

He jumped to his feet and swiveled to face the king. Alfonso and his attendants gasped, their wide eyes pinned to the bared dagger. Gavriel moved faster than their startled thoughts, thrusting past shocked bodies to where Pacheco lurked. Sword at the ready, mere steps from Alfonso, Pacheco wore an expression Gavriel knew well—one of desperation.

"Drop the sword!"

Pacheco laughed, a sound just short of madness. Jacob

pushed onlookers away from the impending duel and caught the condesa around the waist, pivoting his body in front of hers. Armed guards locked into place around the king.

"You are the weakest sort of traitor, Gavriel," said Pacheco with a snarl. "You could not kill your father or the king. Is it possible you still hope to be redeemed? I know the truth you are too ignorant to understand."

Gavriel circled warily. He kept his back to the small entourage, his body between Pacheco and the king. "And what truth is that?"

"God does not want men like us with Him. We were better off making our way down here. A good life of comfort." He jerked his head to the wooden platform where a physician still tended de Silva's grievous wound. "You have ruined that chance for both of us."

"You should've considered that before your plans threatened Ada."

"That drug-addled girl. You were supposed to fail her just as you fail everything!"

"I haven't. And I won't. None of us foresaw that. Now put down your weapon."

Pacheco parried. His sword glanced off Gavriel's dagger and sent it flying. Agile and determined, Pacheco lunged toward King Alfonso but Gavriel spun forward. The condesa screamed. Pain burst to life in his gut where Pacheco's sword imbedded below his ribs.

Ada shrieked his name. "Help him!"

He staggered back, his shoulders supported by unseen hands as he collapsed to the ground. Half a dozen men pounced on Pacheco, the man's enraged shouts suddenly silenced.

Alfonso's voice boomed over the shocked group, demanding the return of his physician. "This man's loyalty is no longer in question. Is that understood? Now offer him aid!"

Gavriel found no strength, no vigor left. He slumped back.

The world swam in mottled colors as if he had opened his eyes under water.

But then Ada's face appeared over him. Tears bathed her face. "Gavriel!"

"Mi inglesa." He wanted to kiss her, but she seemed so far away, her face at the end of a long tunnel. "Is he dead?"

"Yes," she whispered. "Stay with me. The doctor is coming."

He forced his eyes wide, trying to focus. "Last night, I gave you everything I am. I would not kill for them, not even for the promise of your safety. Couldn't trust them. Had to fight."

"Oh, God. Is that what you promised de Silva?"

"Please, Ada." She leaned closer. He could barely hear his own voice. "Please, don't go back. Don't go back to that darkness. Promise me."

"No! You cannot leave me."

He tried to smile and wondered if it worked. His body was floating. "Promise me, because I won't be there to drag you free again."

"I promise, *mi amo*, but don't leave me. Please. Do you hear me, Gavriel? I'm asking please."

Chapter 35

Jacob waited in a sitting room at Doña Valdedrona's palace. The sun angled across the thick tapestries as afternoon began its long, bright fade into evening. Dust motes clung to each slanting ray. Two serving girls talked in hushed voices outside in the corridor, but otherwise Jacob was left with his thoughts.

Three weeks had passed since the day Gavriel de Marqueda saved the king's life. Jacob split his days between answering questions, translating documents with Daniel of Morley's aid, consulting with the authorities, and spending hours by Ada's side. She, in turn, held Gavriel's hands, her lips always moving around some prayer or whisper, stubbornly ignoring Jacob's pleas that she rest or eat.

His body ached from the fatigue of it all. Ada had never been his, and too much time had passed since he had last entertained the thought. She belonged to Gavriel. The only thing Jacob could ask for her sake was that her husband wholly recovered. Other wants and other daydreams no longer had any place.

He turned to find Doña Valdedrona standing in the doorway. Lovely as ever, draped in finery, her elaborately plaited black hair accentuated the pale perfection of her skin. She whisked into the room and proffered her hand. He bowed at the waist and brushed a gentle kiss atop her knuckles.

"Milady," he greeted in Norman. He escorted her to a settee and took the opposite seat. "What news? That is, if you're at liberty."

"For you, I am," she said. "His Majesty has reached an accord of sorts with his cousin. Ferdinand has admitted no wrongdoing, but he agreed to exile the remaining members of the de Silva family. With Lord de Silva dead of his wounds, the clan is quietly preparing to leave for Morocco. For good."

Impotent anger burned beneath his skin. "Then the Leonese get away with their scheme? We broke their alliance with the Almohads, but they may find another renegade family. Any of the *ricos hombres* with funds enough to equip an army can threaten us."

"The kings are meeting in Segovia to negotiate a renewed truce. Another five years of peace." She looked down at her clasped hands and shook her head slowly. Sunlight blazed against her inky hair. "I know it isn't ideal, but at least Alfonso is safe. For now. We have you to thank for that."

His mind jumped to the small room where Ada still sat with Gavriel. She had suffered. They both had. Jacob thought himself young and floundering when compared to their sacrifices. But at least he had seen the truth before it was too late. Ada had been right; the scrolls implicated Pacheco. Jacob had played a ruse of his own on that day of combat, allowing the king to venture into the crowd as he had, allowing everyone to believe Gavriel would be arrested.

Yes, his plan had worked—but the cost had nearly been two innocent lives.

"I . . . I did so little."

"Nonsense," the condesa said, her smile widening. "You did all I could ever ask from one in my employ. And King Alfonso agrees with me."

"Oh?"

"You've been awarded a *juderia* in the north."

His mouth gaped wide. Manners dictated that he should mask his surprise, but he could not find the resources. "You're in earnest, milady? My own estate?"

Her smile eased into a gentle laugh. "Your very own. And you'll have use of my men and materiel until you become established." She hesitated, a blush fanning across her cheeks. "Some resist the idea of awarding parcels to Jewish courtiers, but I cannot think of a reason why you don't deserve this. And my thanks."

He choked back the throb of emotion in his throat. "I am . . . milady, I—"

"I know, Jacob." She reached over and squeezed his hand. But for reasons he could not discern, her smile dimmed.

"What is it?" he asked.

"His Majesty has offered one other reward: a position with his guard. He values your skill and shrewdness and would like you with him at court. The opportunity is a marvelous one."

He frowned. "You're sending me away?"

"The choice was not mine," she said, her voice catching. "In truth, I had hoped you might remain in my employ. My trusted advisors have been killed. Those who remain are more loyal to my late husband than to me." She appeared young and strong, yes, but also tired. Her honeyed eyes never left his face. "And yes, His Majesty has asked it of you, Jacob ben Asher. Would you refuse him?"

Jacob had always wanted to be a warrior, a man to be respected among brave, skilled peers. Now he would have his chance, serving at the court of the most powerful king in Iberia. But he would have to leave the condesa's service . . .

"And what of you?" he asked.

"I'll fare as I always have, except I'll have Blanca to keep me company." She sighed quietly and forced a wan smile.

King Alfonso would never need him. Not this much.

In a rueful humor, he shook his head. Maybe he would never learn. These years with Ada should have taught him hard, irrevocable lessons about wanting what could never be. Yet faced with Doña Valdedrona's faltering bravery, her tense shoulders and nervous fingers, Jacob made his decision— one as reckless and needful as any Ada had ever made.

"I would be honored to serve our king, milady," he said, the words low and intimate. "However, I will obey his summons only if his request becomes a command. My place is with you."

Understanding slowly transformed her expression into one of placid, gentle hopefulness. "You'll stay?"

"For as long as you require, milady."

Doña Valdedrona inhaled deeply. Her demeanor seemed to brighten, as if his pledge had transformed her burdens into nothing more weighty than a spider's silk.

"Now," she said, elegantly lacing her fingers in her lap, "how is Ada and her patient?"

Jacob basked in her shimmering happiness and knew he was lost. *Here I go again.*

"Her father trained her in pharmacology," he said. "Did you know that? Years ago, back in England. Now that Gavriel is recovering at last, I believe she's prescribed bed rest."

She arched a dark brow. Her lips quirked. "Bed rest, Jacob?"

"Yes, milady. Plenty of bed rest."

Ada awoke from a light doze to find Gavriel's eyes open and watching her. After three weeks on the mend, she had not stopped holding her breath. Although his skin retained the taint of illness, and his cheekbones jutted from his gaunt face, his vigor continued to surprise her. The grievous stab wound no longer threatened him. Those dark, dark eyes teemed with life.

Daylight had almost faded. Shadows alternated with deep

orange streaks of sun, playing in a pattern of stripes across the bed. Beneath the woolen mantle that covered his body, Gavriel wore nothing. His long limbs would stretch from his naked torso, hard, lean, covered with dark hair. She had washed, tended, and wept over his inert body, praying as she never had for mercy. The fierce and ragged gash below his ribs had burned red, a defaced altar, and the scars on his back still had the power to bring her to tears.

But now it was different. He was awake, healing. *And he was hers.* A hot, fierce need to touch and adore coiled inside her, the longing for passion and for an assurance of his health.

They had yet to speak of their marriage vows or the future. Assuming they would both awaken in the morning still seemed dangerous. Now she had to suppress her fear once again. Her need for him was as strong and undeniable as it had ever been, all the more powerful because of the danger they had survived and the daring promises they had made. She had to know what he wanted.

Straightening in her chair, she went to push hair from her forehead. Although it was a little longer now, trimmed neatly with proper shears, the reflex to tend her missing hair remained. She glanced to Gavriel and found him smiling.

"You'll start a new custom," he said.

"Hardly. I'm more a cautionary tale."

"Castilians take pride in a good scandal. It sets them apart."

She joined him, sitting on the edge of his bed. Pain brushed up her back.

"You shouldn't be sleeping in that chair," he said. "Not with your own injury on the mend."

"They offered me opium. Did you know that?"

His expression darkened. "Offered?"

"And I refused."

"Ada," he said quietly, his eyes full of triumph, "you did it on your own."

A slow warmth unfurled in her chest as she took a long, deep breath. She *had* done it. She knew temptation would always follow her, but the time for thoughtlessly heeding its call had passed. That knowledge and Gavriel's proud devotion healed the last of her dark wounds, the unseen wounds that had plagued her for so long. A future unlike any she had ever dared imagine opened before her, beckoning them both.

"And then I called in Jacob, just to be safe," she added. "No sense in being arrogant. He about slapped the physic across the back of the head, poor man."

Gavriel nodded, his expression still one of fierce wonder.

Drawn to him, she brushed her fingertips over his forearms, petting the dark hair that dusted his skin. The blemish where she had sliced his arm, a lifetime ago, had faded into a slim pink scar. "How are you feeling?"

"When will you stop asking me that?" He grinned, his teasing tone erasing any harshness. But always, always, the smile faded. No matter how bright and unexpected, he caught himself in the act and tramped it down.

"You still don't trust it, do you?"

He looked to the ceiling beams. "Happiness is new to me."

"Are you happy?"

"I will be when these stitches are gone and I can hold you again."

"You can hold me now. Make room."

The confusion that flashed across his face made her laugh. She pulled back the mantle and slid gingerly alongside him. Her skirts pulled and bunched in a tangle around her knees, but a few wiggles and twists later, they nestled body to body on his luxurious bed. Strong, sure arms hugged her close. Mindful of his wounds and her own, she lay with her head on his chest. Although desire pulsed within her, she simply sighed. The safety and comfort of that moment overshadowed everything else.

"Jacob never doubted you. Did you know that? Not after he read the scrolls. He agreed with my translations and knew a diversion would bring Pacheco into the open."

"I'm glad of that," he said, the words rumbling out of his broad chest. "He's a young man whose respect is worth having."

Thoughts of Jacob would always cause her a regretful sort of pain. He had helped save her life, and she would be forever grateful that he was her friend. She only hoped that one day he would find a worthy woman who loved him in return.

"I know," she said quietly. "He and I . . . we've made our peace."

"I'm glad of it. Truly." Gavriel kissed the top of her head. "But now, what will make you happy?"

"Between Jacob's testimony and your heroism, you've been cleared of all suspicion, and Her Excellency has released me from my obligations. Now I only want you on the mend."

"Is that all?"

She mashed her lips together and made up her mind. If they had the slightest chance of beginning a life together— the dream she had never dared to believe—she had to hang onto her bravery and speak. Speak to her husband.

Propping on one elbow, she looked down at his face. Dark eyes studied her, and the hand at her hip traced distracting circles, fingers tightening and releasing.

"Grand Master Rodriguez arrived two weeks ago to collect Pacheco's body," she said. He tensed. "Doña Valdedrona spoke with him, along with Jacob and me. He said the *Trecenezago* has absolved all grievances against you with regard to Fernán. You're welcome to return to Uclés, if you wish. Or . . ."

"Or?"

She stroked the smooth skin of his upper chest, where the hair tapered to nothing and he smelled like rainwater. "The Order has newly acquired holdings abroad. They are in need of a brother to found a new parish."

"Where?"

Memories clamored for her attention. Green fields and endless forests. Overcast skies that made a body want to stay inside, seeking warmth and friendly company. Cold winter frosts over the endless, rolling countryside.

And Meg. She would to go home to Meg.

"Inglaterra," she said quietly.

"And how do you say it?"

"England."

Gavriel had not been able to breathe since Ada climbed into bed with him. One thigh rested atop his, and her fingers played restless games with his sanity, aimlessly touching his chest. Had it not been for his injuries and the anxious look on her face, he would have hauled her across his body and parted her legs. An image from their unconventional wedding night flashed through his mind: Ada astride him, her face tightened against the building tremors of pleasure.

He inhaled deeply and stemmed a swift flush of need. With day fading into night, they had hours to discover each other anew. First, they would discuss the future. Their future.

"And what of your sister?"

She gnawed on a ragged fingernail. "'Tis time for me to go home, if you're willing to come with me. Fernán has said he and Abez would like to come as well. Too many barriers remain for them here, although I've told them England still resists foreigners."

"How far is the journey?"

"Weeks overland to Santander, as many again by sea, then again overland to the Midlands."

"That's an intimidating amount of time to spend with Fernán."

"You're teasing me."

"Yes," he said, freeing his smile.

She laughed, the sound of magic and promises. Every fleck of darkness he had once seen clouding her eyes had vanished. That she loved him left him humbled and looking for reasons why they could not be together. But none remained.

He searched his own heart, his own soul and felt nothing but breath and life. He thought of his father, dead now, and awaited a return of his old terror and rage. Already it was fading, releasing him a little more each day. He could be free. Dizziness that had nothing to do with wounds or hunger or desire stole over him, leaving him humbled. He took a deep breath before finding her eyes again—two blue pools, hopeful and expectant.

"The journey will be long and uncertain, I admit," she said. "But it will be simple and restful compared to clearing the air with Meg. Meg and Will, both."

"I've never traveled so far."

Ada smiled and fingered a whorl of hair on his chest. "We've done a great deal we've never tried before. Why stop now?"

She slipped a hand beneath the mantle and found the ticklish spot along his ribs. Laughter and pain simmered together. He snatched her hands, ready to beg for mercy if he needed to. She stopped her soft torture to lean nearer and kiss the corner of his mouth, light and possessive at once. Gavriel slumped into the mattress. Giddiness made the room spin.

"England," he said. The spoken word in Ada's native language felt strange on his tongue. Heavy. Thorny. How did she manage?

"Yes, England."

"That damp little island?" At her crestfallen look, he smiled again. "My Ada, we'll have to take this in steps. I know little about smiling, which leaves you ill equipped for my teasing."

Her expression brightened. "You never were a novice. You were a scoundrel in disguise."

"I'm trying." He sobered, cupping her cheek. "But I was also hoping you'd think of me as a good man. One day."

"One day? How about when you rescued a sick woman from herself, or the day you nearly sacrificed your life to save the king?"

"Nearly," he said with a sharp laugh. "You and your potions were worse than the blade's cut. I knew you were *una bruja*."

"I insist, my sister is the witch."

"I'll have to decide for myself."

"Does that mean we can go?"

"Anywhere, Ada. Anywhere with you."

He closed his eyes as she peppered his face with kisses. Catching the back of her head, he pulled her into a deep, slow, lingering kiss. All sweetness and heat, she tasted of oranges. Gavriel drank her in. His body tensed, his shaft rigid. He had wanted her for too many nights. Their moments of indulgence had been few, snatched out of terror and fear.

But this was a kiss of celebration. His soul spun with hers in a potent vow.

The thought of vows stopped him.

"*Mi inglesa,* I haven't been the man I want to be. My failures are many. I don't trust myself and I don't know why you trust me."

"I love you," she said quietly. "Never once have you failed me. No one—not even you, stubborn man—can convince me that you ever will."

"I don't deserve you."

"If you make a saint out of me, you're forgetting how we met and what a trial I was." She outlined his mouth with her forefinger before kissing him, slowly, just lip to lip. "Besides, you already vowed to be my husband. Will you go back on that promise?"

"*Never.*"

The ferocity of his reply startled him. But then, his promises had always been easy where Ada was concerned. Only when he denied their love did he find himself at a loss. Wholly lost.

"We're bound as husband and wife," he whispered. "I love you."

"Do you swear it?"

Although she asked the question, she looked at peace. She knew the answer as well as he did. Gavriel smiled and allowed that same peace claim him, easing his soul.

"I do, Ada. I do."

Author's Note

I hope you enjoyed Ada and Gavriel's love story as much as I enjoyed writing it. To bring their unusual tale to life, I took the following liberties with history.

In 1201, the King of Castile was named Alfonso VIII, while the King of León was his first cousin, Alfonso IX. For the sake of clarity, I changed the King of León to Ferdinand—the name of his father and at least one of his sons. The character of Joaquin de Silva is based on Pedro Fernandez de Castro, a Leonese nobleman who, because of a grudge against his two royal cousins, sided with the Almohads at Alarcos. Exiled, he died in North Africa in 1214.

The town of Uclés was frequently attacked and besieged between 1195–1212. I've chosen to portray that, throughout this story, Uclés was safe from harm and under Castilian rule. During this same period, the Order of Santiago fractured. They twice elected opposing Grand Masters, one loyal to León and one loyal to Castile. I've simplified this power struggle immensely.

And while Germanic countries sanctioned trials by combat, I've taken the liberty of importing the practice to Castile, where trials by fire or water were more common.

Details about the Order of Santiago's unusual practices, the frontier's lenient marriage customs, the availability of opium in Iberia, and the history of treachery between Castile and León are as accurate as I could portray. And for you chess lovers, the early queen could only capture one square diagonally. She was not invested with her current powers until after 1475.

Should you wish to know more about this exciting period in Spanish history, my Web site contains additional facts, links, and resources.

Wishing you all the best,
Carrie
www.carrielofty.com